STEEL CITY

STEEL CITY
A Story of Pittsburgh

A Novel

WILLIAM J. MILLER, JR.

ESSEX, CONNECTICUT

An imprint of Globe Pequot, the trade division of
The Rowman & Littlefield Publishing Group, Inc.
4501 Forbes Blvd., Ste. 200
Lanham, MD 20706
www.rowman.com

Distributed by NATIONAL BOOK NETWORK

British Library Cataloguing in Publication Information available

Library of Congress Cataloging-in-Publication Data

ISBN 978-1-4930-6843-2 (cloth : alk. paper)
ISBN 978-1-4930-6844-9 (electronic)

♾™ The paper used in this publication meets the minimum requirements of American National
Standard for Information Sciences—Permanence of Paper for Printed Library Materials, ANSI/
NISO Z39.48-1992.

Dedication

*To three smart, beautiful women: my wife, Warren, and
my daughters, Sara Miller and Megan Miller Flanagan.
Your early reads and insights made this a better book.*

And to the next generation: Finn Miller Flanagan and Chloe Elle Flanagan.

In Memoriam

To J. Mabon Childs Jr., the best of friends and a true son of Pittsburgh.

"*If any one* [sic] *would enjoy a spectacle as striking as Niagara, he may do so by simply walking up a long hill to Cliff Street in Pittsburg* [sic], *and looking over into—hell with the lid taken off.*"
                    —THE *ATLANTIC* WRITER JAMES PARTON IN 1868

"*Pittsburgh, without exception, is the blackest place I ever saw. . . . I was never more in love with smoke and dirt than when I stood there and watched the darkness of night close in upon the floating soot which hovered over the house tops of the city.*"
                    —ANTHONY TROLLOPE, THE NINETEENTH-
                    CENTURY ENGLISH TRAVELER AND WRITER

Author's Note

1890s dollars today: Based on the Federal Reserve Bank of Minneapolis Consumer Price Index from 1800, one dollar in 1901, the year of the creation of U.S. Steel, would be worth $32.62 in 2021. For simplicity's sake, **take any dollar figure you see in *Steel City*, add a zero, and multiply it by three**. For example, a yearly salary of $10,000 for a steel executive would be roughly the equivalent of $300,000 today. A worker in a steel mill in the 1890s might make $10 a week or 17 cents an hour. That translates to $5 an hour today. The minimum wage in Pennsylvania in 2022 is $7.25 an hour, the lowest rate in the United States except for non-federal employees in Georgia.

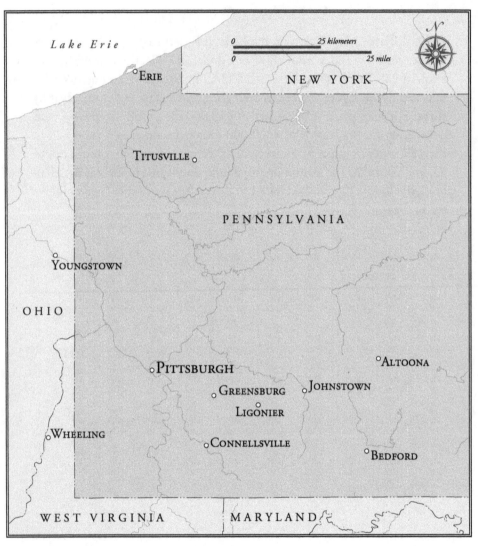

Western Pennsylvania

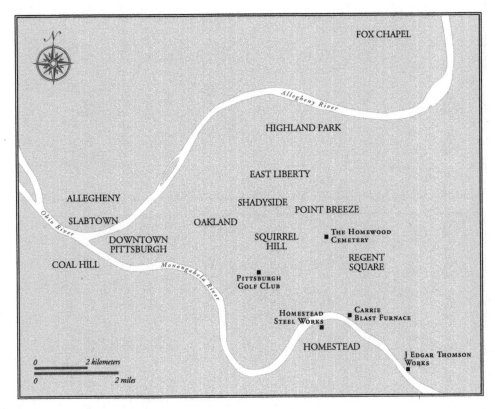

Pittsburgh Neighborhoods

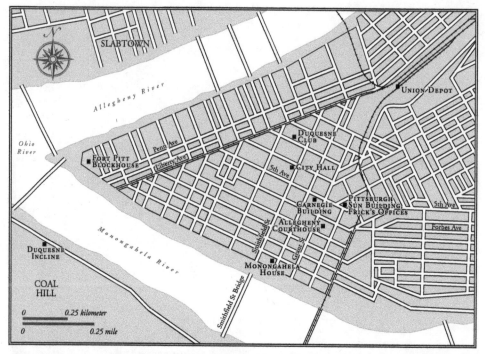

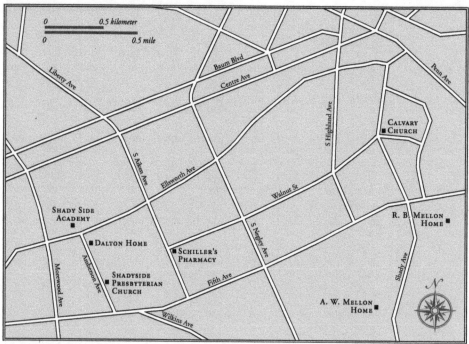

Downtown Pittsburgh (top)
Neighborhood of Shadyside (bottom)

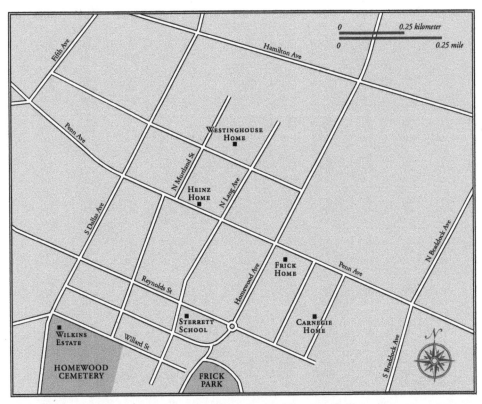

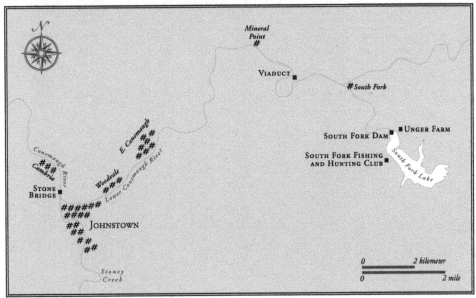

Neighborhood of Point Breeze (top)
The Johnstown Flood (bottom)

CONTENTS

PROLOGUE

The water poured over the top of the dam. Standing with a dozen others on a bluff looking over South Fork Lake, we watched in horror knowing it couldn't hold much longer.

I had come to the South Fork Fishing and Hunting Club in late May 1889 to contemplate my future. The club was a perfect getaway, fourteen miles up a tight river valley from Johnstown, Pennsylvania, which was two hours by train due east from Pittsburgh. After a bitter argument with my father over my intention to become a reporter for the *Pittsburgh Sun*, I needed time to think. Father had been nothing short of apoplectic, shouting that I was wasting my life with such a dead-end profession and insisting that I become a lawyer, like him, or take advantage of the family's many contacts to gain a position with one of the Carnegie steel companies. It was two weeks since I had graduated from Yale.

The disagreement with my father didn't seem important now. I was panting from my efforts to clear the spillway and squinted through the rain at the top of the dam. Then I heard the riprap on the front side of the dam fall with a loud rumble.

There was no dramatic moment, no explosion, no sudden collapse, but a few minutes later the earth of the huge dam, one hundred feet high on its front face, slowly, inexorably, began to slide away. First, the top of the dam collapsed as more and more water rushed over it. The water ate at the sides, and in a minute the whole dam was gone. All that remained were the fifty-foot promontories on either side of where the dam had been. Then we heard the horrifying roar of the water, as the lake emptied fast. We all knew where the water was headed—down the Little Conemaugh Valley and through the small towns on its way into Johnstown.

My future was decided. I had to find a pencil and paper.

1

The Family

For the first eighteen years of my life, my world revolved around our house on Amberson Avenue, and it seemed like a very big house to me and my sister, Katherine, and my brother, Wills, who was named for my grandfather Willis. It was what in Pittsburgh is called a four square, for the four rooms that define the first floor. A brick walk from the street led you up three solid stone steps, across a narrow porch that extended the length of the house, then through a thick, oak door with a sturdy doorknob, brass but tarnished beyond recognition. Two lead-glass windows accented by red and blue stained-glass panels at top and bottom flanked the door. A large key in the middle of the door could be twisted to make a rasping sound that would alert us to visitors.

The first floor of the house was formal and the domain of my parents. On the second floor is where Kat and Wills and I spent most of our time. Upstairs, Mother and Father each had their own bedroom at the corners of the front of the house with a connecting bathroom equipped with a tub, commode, and two sinks, but we never ventured into these rooms without being invited. I was the oldest and had the next-largest bedroom at the back-right corner of the house, and that's where we would play games like sardines and checkers and Parcheesi. The most fun we had was seeing whether Mother would greet the women who would call on her in the late afternoon the way people would in those more formal days. We would peer through the balustrades overlooking the entrance hall and watch them hand their calling cards to our maid, Agnes.

"Who is it this time?" Kat would ask.

"The Frothinghams again," I'd say, then we would both have to keep Wills from giggling too loud about the name we made up for the endless series of callers.

After the guests took seats in the parlor to the right of the entrance hall, Agnes would let Mother know they were there. More often than not, Mother would tell Agnes to say she was indisposed and ask if they could call later in the week. Shunned courtiers would hear us sniggering as they departed.

The only other place where we spent any time was in the kitchen and the little breakfast room off of it. The kitchen was functional, not fancy, with a wood-burning stove, an icebox that extended through the wall for the daily ice deliveries, and a deep zinc sink where the plates and silverware were washed. In the breakfast room each morning, our cook, Eileen, would serve us griddle cakes and scrapple, a western Pennsylvania delicacy made from pork scraps. The walls of the room were lined with cabinets that held Mother's vast collection of china and glass. I was fascinated by the array: dinner and butter plates, dessert and salad plates, tea services with pots and cups and saucers, as well as water tumblers and wine glasses of every shape and size, some clear, many a deep red or blue, all handblown with various accents that would reflect the gas lighting of the dining room with great effect.

Mother would lay out all her finery for the Saturday night dinner parties she and Father gave. The guests were men Father worked with and women Mother knew from her women's clubs and Calvary Church charities. We knew one of these dinners was in the offing when Mother would have Agnes polish the stolid cedar dining room table and its silver candlesticks and fill the silver epergne with seasonal shrubbery. Mother would feather dust the crystal chandelier she loved—it had been a wedding present from her Aunt Cynthia, her mother's sister, who she was closer to than her own mother—and made sure its tiny gas lamps were all in working order.

The children, of course, were not invited to these dinners, but we spied on the guests from our perch on the second-floor landing. Mother always looked so glamourous. She was the center of attention at these parties and seemed to be having so much fun. We'd be surprised the next morning at breakfast when she would say, "What a dreary bunch."

On Sunday we attended services at Calvary Episcopal Church on Shady Avenue, where the oldest and some of the most prosperous families in Pittsburgh worshipped. So the family could go to church together, my father, who was brought up as a Roman Catholic, became an Episcopalian when he married my mother. Other wealthy families attended Shadyside Presbyterian, across Pembroke Place from our house on Amberson.

The Calvary services were very structured. Each family, led by the father, followed by the mother and the children, dressed in their finest "Sunday" clothes, would file into the pew assigned by the church vestry. A family's status was evident from how close their pew was to the altar. We were in the fourth row. Parents tried to keep their children's eyes on the hymnal as the congregation sang hymns such as "A Mighty Fortress Is Our God." Halfway through the service, the pastor would intone a dry sermon, citing obscure texts from the Bible that exhorted the parishioners to heed God so their lives would be fulfilling. Implied was the promise of worldly success. Since we attended the High Mass, after the sermon communion would be served to the adults and any of the children who had received their First Communion.

After the service, depending on the weather, the families greeted each other on the front porch of the church. After no more than five minutes of socializing, the congregation would repair to their carriages, lined up on Shady as far as Fifth Avenue. Then everyone hurried home for the Sunday meal.

Families like ours would have a very similar Sunday dinner, as we called these midday meals. Mother and Father took their seats at the head and foot of the table with the children in between. Mother would tinkle the crystal bell to prompt the servants, and they would deliver the first course, an oyster soup in fall and winter, consommé madrilene in spring and summer. After a palate-cleansing fruit, Mother would ring the bell again and out would come the Sunday staples: roast beef, garnished with boiled potatoes and a vegetable that the children would eat so they could have the last course: vanilla ice cream with cherry syrup that would disappear in minutes.

After dinner would be the obligatory carriage ride. The Daltons and other families in the area would join a procession of carriages, each more elaborate than the last. Phaetons and broughams were pulled by brown bays and gray Arabians, all stately and perfectly groomed. We had a covered rig with a driver, but some of the carriages also had a groom on the front seat and another man posted on a metal stand extending off the back.

It made for a grand parade from Fifth Avenue down Penn and back, past all the impressive homes that lined the route, big stone piles that conveyed the wealth and importance of their inhabitants. The owners were heads of the lucrative metal manufacturers—iron and steel, coal and copper, brass and aluminum—that made Pittsburgh thrive. The men in the carriages tipped their top hats to each other, while the women with their dresses buttoned up to their chins gave brief, delicate waves, when they weren't corralling children who poked their necks out carriage windows in hopes of giving a halloo to a school mate. It all was structured and obligatory, but we loved those Sunday rides.

Our grandparents, my mother's parents, Bertha and George Ricketson, or Father's dad, Willis Dalton, would each come once a month for Sunday dinner. We dreaded the arrival of Grandfather and Grandmother Ricketson but looked forward to Grampa Willis's visits.

Grandmother Ricketson scared my brother and sister and me. Always dressed in voluminous black, she was short and stout and charged into a room like she would knock down anyone standing in the way. Her face was powdered to cover her blotchy skin. Her mouth, a thin slit that she could contort into a variety of displeasures, was rouged bright red. We dreaded being kissed with that cruel mouth. When we couldn't avoid it, we would look away and wipe off the odious stain. We didn't mind hugs from Grandfather Ricketson, a short, dignified man who tried his best to ignore his wife's physical and verbal excesses.

The only time we would use the formal living room at the left of the entrance hall was when the Ricketson grandparents came for lunch. An Oriental rug graced the floor, as it did in all the rooms. There was a coal-fired stove in the corner, and paintings of unknown provenance covered every wall. The draperies were heavy and dark, and even the constant ministrations of our housekeeper, Gert, couldn't keep them fresh, what with the all-pervasive soot that drifted up from the iron and steel mills along the Allegheny River to the north and the Monongahela to the south. The requisite half-hour to sip sherry—the children had ginger ale—seemed to last forever. Grandmother would launch in on all the deficiencies she saw in the Dalton household, and Mother would purse her lips with her hands folded in her lap. Father and Grandfather would talk about the price of iron ingots. Our parents encouraged us to speak at the table, but we didn't dare say a word when Grandmother Ricketson was there.

At the dinner I was often seated between Grandmother and my mother. I remember one Sunday, I think I was ten, when Grandmother finally pierced Mother's protective shell. After the roast beef and boiled potatoes had been served, she turned up her nose and announced, "I will not be eating this overcooked meat. You know I like it blood red."

No one said a word, as Mother looked down at her plate. "Anything else not to your liking?" she asked. Before Grandmother could answer, Mother went on, "Perhaps it's my dress or my children's fingernails or the way Richard carves." Tears were welling in her eyes. "You are always right, and I am always wrong. That has never changed and never will. But I won't listen to this at my own table."

"You ungrateful . . . ," Grandmother snapped back, but Grandfather stopped her.

"That's enough, Bertie. Eleanor, you must make your apologies."

"I will not. I have made them too many times before. Daddy, you know how mean she is and always has been."

Father tried to intervene. "Now, ladies, let's not have any more unpleasantness."

Grandmother turned on him. "Because you pulled yourself up to be a lawyer, you think you can talk to me that way? You, a boy from Slabtown. Eleanor is far from perfect, but she is still a Ricketson. You should be very thankful we allowed her to marry you."

"Richard is a fine man," Mother shot back. "Maybe if you hadn't made us slink around Point Breeze to see each other, you would have known him better. We had to meet on a bench in the Homewood cemetery to get away from you."

"You acted like a tramp! He was only interested in you for your family's position in society. He's a climber, this one."

This was beyond cruel, even for Bertie. I'd never heard anyone speak so disrespectfully to my father, and I recoiled back into my chair so hard that I nearly tipped over. Kat grabbed her fork and looked like she might stab Grandmother. Wills wasn't sure what had happened, but he dove under the table to get away from whatever it was. Father had always seemed invulnerable to me, but he sat frozen in his seat at the head of the table with a blank look on his face.

Then Mother cried, "You'll always take any chance you get to belittle me and Richard. You shall leave this table and not return until you are invited."

Grandmother's fleshy face reddened, her eyes narrowing until they disappeared. Her red mouth twisted as she glared at Mother. Then she raised her piggy nose and said, "Come, George. We are not wanted here." The rest of us didn't say a word as they retrieved their overcoats and dashed out the front door to their waiting carriage.

Mother sat with her shoulders back, staring at the wall behind Father. When she was sure that her parents were gone, she dabbed at her mouth with a napkin, said, "Excuse me," and headed up the front stairs to her bedroom. We didn't see her again until we came home from school the next day. A month or two later my Ricketson grandparents would return. Another uneasy truce between mother and daughter would last a time but was soon broken, and the cycle of anger and conciliation would continue.

Grampa Willis's visits were of a very different sort. We would wait on the porch for his arrival no matter the weather, then rush down the path when we saw the buckboard approaching, pulled by his dappled old dray, Tecumseh. Before he could even alight, we would scramble to be the first one to sit on his lap, then would hang off him as he pulled us along into the house.

Mother would be there to greet him with a smile she reserved for few others. "The children are always so glad to see you," she would say. "As am I, of course." Between father and son it was "Hello, Richard" and "Hello, Father."

The dinners with Grampa Willis were casual. He would ask us whether we were doing well in school, and each of us would say whatever was on our mind. I liked to brag about hitting home runs and scoring touchdowns for my school teams. Kat would tell him what she had been reading and how much she enjoyed science, while Wills would talk about the animals he had trapped in the woods down by the Allegheny.

Grampa loved Pittsburgh history. He delighted in taking carriage rides with Kat and Wills and me to show us our city's historical sights. We rode out Fifth, then south on the Braddock Road to a bluff overlooking a broad field, and Grampa would tell us how the British under the command of General Edward Braddock and Colonel George Washington lost a battle with the French and Indians, not five miles from our house on Amberson. On that same field, the citizens of the western counties of Pennsylvania gathered to secede in protest of a tax on whiskey, the infamous Whiskey Rebellion, which was abandoned with the approach of federal troops. And we could see the smoke from the colossal iron and steel mills along the Monongahela River. The biggest treat of all was when Grampa would take us up the funicular railroad known as the Incline to the top of Coal Hill, where we could look out over Pittsburgh and its three rivers—at least we could on a clear day, which it seldom was.

We loved these excursions and couldn't wait to get home and tell our parents all that we had seen and heard. They were happy that we had enjoyed ourselves and were close with at least one of our grandparents.

Grampa Willis's favorite topic at the dinner table was why Pittsburgh was the mightiest industrial city in the country, the part he had played in its growth, and how he had never received his due.

"Two great rivers, the Monongahela and the Allegheny come together to form the Ohio, which flows all the way to the Mississippi and the sea. Them rivers bring the coal and iron, and Pittsburgh makes the steel the rest of the country needs to grow.

"And right across the Allegheny from the point where the rivers meet is a place called Slabtown."

I smiled at Kat because we had heard about Slabtown so many times.

"That's where the families from Scotland and Ireland lived when we got off the railroad cars from the East. It was just a bunch of shacks, but great men have come out of Slabtown, don't you ever forget! Carnegie, Phipps, Lauder, the Oliver Brothers, the businessmen making Pittsburgh rich, even if they treat some men underhanded. Just ask the Kloman brothers, who first made quantities of steel from iron in a short enough time to show a profit. Andra Carnegie cheated them right out of their business.

"And me! All the new ways of forging iron and steel I developed. Didn't pay me a cent for them, beyond the pittance of my wages."

Father would cough when he heard criticism of the men who were his clients, and he and Grampa would stare at each other for a second or two, but it never came to more than that.

Then one supper the forced civility between him and Father snapped.

"Tell your Da what we saw today, Jamie boy."

At fourteen I sensed the danger signs but paid them no heed. "We saw the burned-out railroad cars from the big strike of 1877."

Father bristled. "And who did he tell you burned those cars?"

"The men seeing that their wages weren't to be cut!" Grampa exploded.

I could see Father grind his teeth. "Their wages were not being cut. In any case, the railroads have the right to pay what they want. It's their property."

With that the two were off. In loud voices they called their foes capitalists or socialists, preceded by words that we knew but would never say unless we wanted our mouths washed out with soap. Mother tried to intercede, but her quiet voice was drowned out. When she'd had enough, she used her butter knife to rap on a water glass until I thought it would break, but that got their attention.

"This bickering will stop! I have heard this argument too many times, and you should know by now that neither of you will give an inch. What an example you both are setting."

Grampa was the first to say anything. "My apologies, El. Now, Dickie, you just keep in mind that all that money your fancy clients are making should be spread around some."

Father hated being called "Dickie," but after a hard glance from Mother, he kept his temper. "I'll try to remember that, Da, when those same men are taking the risks to keep their businesses growing."

"Not another word from either of you," Mother said. She rang the crystal bell, and Gert brought in chocolate cake with whipped cream. No one argued about that.

———

My parents were formal and agreeable with each other, but I rarely glimpsed any affection. This didn't seem at all peculiar since my friends' parents behaved the same way. Their routine was fixed. Father would board the Fifth Avenue trolley, pulled by a team of horses, at eight each morning for the four-mile trip downtown and arrive back at 5:30. One or all of the children would meet him at the head of Amberson for the short walk back to our house. This was the only time we would be alone with him.

We, of course, spent much more time with my mother. I knew that she was a beautiful woman, with her thick, shining hair, aquiline features, and tall, slender frame. To me she was different from the other mothers, and when I saw her with them, she seemed uncomfortable, unwilling to engage with their chatter. She never had the ubiquitous pile of knitting in her lap like the others, and her fingers fidgeted. The only place she seemed at ease was on horseback. Each morning, after walking us to the neighborhood school at Fifth and Morewood, Mother galloped gracefully away toward the woods and hollows of Mrs. Mary Schenley's vast estate.

———

I was twelve when I noticed that Mother would withdraw after the fights with Grandmother Ricketson over the midday Sunday meal. For the next few days, she would seem nervous and only relax after she drank wine at dinner. But after particularly brutal exchanges, she would stay in her room for a day or two, not even appearing for meals. Then Father would bring her downstairs wrapped in a blanket and drive her and Agnes down to the Shadyside train station.

"Your mother is going to the mountains for a few days," was all Father would say. Kat and Wills and I wouldn't think much of it because she would always be back in a week or so and life would go back to normal. Until the next time.

As the years went by, Mother's trips to the mountains became more frequent. When Father returned from yet another trip to the station, I was waiting for him on the front porch. "Why does Mother leave like this?" I asked.

"I've told you. She goes to Cresson Springs for a rest."

"Why can't she rest here? I'll make sure Kat and Wills don't bother her."

He looked at me for a minute, then said, "Let's go into the library."

I followed Father in, and after he closed the door, we sat in the two easy chairs by the fireplace. This was a new experience for me.

"I don't want you to worry about your mother. She is always better when she returns."

"But why does she have to go away?'

"She has these spells. The doctors call it nervous exhaustion. She gets very sad, and being in the mountain air in Cresson Springs calms her until she feels strong enough to return."

"I hope we don't make her sad," I said.

"No, no, she loves you all so much. Nothing makes her happier."

"Then why does she get that way?"

"I wish I knew the answer to that, Jamie. Your mother is still hurt by Bertie's tantrums, but there is more to it than that. I wish I knew what."

Father gazed out the window. "You see what a beautiful woman your mother is. And when she is feeling herself, there is no one more charming. I've loved her since the first time we met, but she has always been up one minute and down the next. She can talk about any subject under the sun, and people are naturally attracted by her grace and wit. From the butcher to the crustiest old steel man, people are drawn to your mother."

Father turned to look at me. "Please don't say anything to her about this conversation. I can't always be here to comfort her. Be as kind as you can without her thinking you are making a fuss. Can you do that, son?"

I assured Father that I could, but I was not sure how. He never said anything about her drinking, and I didn't ask. But I didn't think it was a coincidence that she didn't drink wine at dinner right after she returned from Cresson Springs.

When I was thirteen, a new school opened in the neighborhood: Shady Side Academy. They put me in their ninth-grade class because I was big for my age and good at sports. I knew most of the other kids, and because of my size, no one picked on me. But my relationship with my parents began to change, and I thought only of myself.

At Shady Side my main interest was sports. Since I was the best player on the football and baseball teams, I didn't care that I got lousy grades. But my parents did and every time I brought home a report card with Cs and Ds, my father would call me into the library and give me hell. "Don't think being captain of the football team is going to get you into a good college! I expect these grades to improve on your next report card." I'd give a sullen response and get out of there as fast as I could. Father had gone to Western University in Pittsburgh, and I was sure I could get in there, whatever my grades were. They always wanted athletes.

Mother took a gentler approach but was just as insistent that I could do better. "I know these classes aren't that hard for you because I remember how easy it was for you to get good grades when you were younger. And I see how you pore over the newspapers and how you enjoy talking to your father and me about what you've read. You have so much potential, Jamie."

I knew she was right but wouldn't admit it. "Not you too! Isn't it enough that Father is on my back?" Mother would start to cry; I would say I was sorry, but I would be just as rude the next time she would chide me about my grades. I would tell myself that Mother was fragile and I shouldn't upset her, but at that age I had a hard time controlling myself.

That showed up in other parts of my life. I ran with the other jocks, and our success on the playing fields made us arrogant and entitled. At the beginning of our junior year, our pack would ride our horses into the small, working-class cities around Pittsburgh and find taverns that were more than happy to serve us beer and whiskey. We would even get into harmless fights, more shoving matches, with the locals and laugh about it on our way back to the comfortable confines of the East End.

One Saturday afternoon in the spring of my junior year, I had more to drink than usual at a place called Chief's in Wilkinsburg, just a few miles east of Point Breeze. There were a couple of ruffians I had tangled with before glaring at me, and I wanted to let them know they couldn't intimidate me. After throwing back my third shot of whiskey, I banged my glass on the bar and shouted, "I can take any man in the place." This was too much for even my rowdy friends, and they all backed away from me. Then the biggest guy in the place, at least ten years older than me and with muscled arms covered in grime, stood in front of me. I figured he was a mill worker. Without saying a word, he punched me in the face, and when I collapsed to the floor, he kicked me in the ribs. Then he calmly sat down and threw back a shot.

My friends managed to get me on my horse for the painful ride back to Amberson Avenue and took off as soon as they had deposited me on the porch. I staggered into the front hall and saw in the mirror that my right eye was shut and bruised. I held my side and hoped nothing was broken.

That's when I heard my mother cry, "My God, Jamie, what has happened to you?"

"I was out riding with my friends and fell off my horse."

"I doubt that," she said, then took me into the kitchen and washed my eye. She poked gently at my ribs, and I grimaced but didn't cry out. "Doesn't seem too serious. Now go up to your room. Your father will be home soon." Mother was never this abrupt with me, and I did what she said.

I lay on my bed with a cold washcloth on my face, and an hour later Father threw my door open. "I want to know what you have gotten yourself into, and don't try to tell me you fell off a damn horse."

"It's nothing. Leave me alone." My whole body ached.

Father slapped my feet off the bed. "Stand up when you talk to me!" I struggled to stand as he went on. "You smell like liquor, and this isn't the first time. I can see you have been in a fight, and you are lucky that you aren't hurt worse. Here's what is going to happen. No more baseball, and if your grades don't improve, you will be sent to Culver Military Academy for your senior year."

"But that's in Indiana!"

He turned his back and slammed the door of my room on the way out.

Back at school, my friends all wanted to know what my parents had said. "You won't be seeing me at baseball practice," was all I answered. What I didn't tell them was that my mother had left on Tuesday for Cresson Springs. Before then only Grandmother Bertie could trigger that kind of reaction. Now I had. Mother was back on Amberson by Saturday. She seemed herself, but I resolved never to upset her like that again.

—◦—

With no baseball practice, I came home after classes were over and sulked. Kat and Wills stayed out of my way, and Father wouldn't speak to me other than to tell me to get upstairs and do homework after dinner. After she returned from the mountains, Mother was polite but formal and told me more than once how disappointed she was in me.

I didn't want Father to know I was giving into his demands about schoolwork, but I grew so bored that I did study more. Not a lot, but enough to make the time pass. By June I had Bs in English and Latin and brought algebra up to a C. But they didn't get any better than that for the first two months of my senior year, and that wasn't good enough for my father.

He called me into the library one night in November. "Your grades aren't where they should be, and they won't get you into an Ivy League school."

Between my mediocre marks and recklessness, I was surprised he thought I had any chance at these august eastern colleges. "I always assumed I would be at Western University because you went there."

"That was fine for me, but there are better options today. The three finest schools in the country are Harvard, Yale, and Princeton, and your mother and I have always hoped that you would attend one of them."

The possibility of attending an eastern college sounded glamorous but so removed from my life in Pittsburgh that it seemed a fantasy. "But, Father, I've never been east of Harrisburg. I know what states those colleges are in but not much more. And my grades . . ."

"Several of my partners' sons have gone east to college, many to Yale. As to your grades, you can and will pull them up."

"How are you so sure? And I don't care what your partners' sons have done."

"I've worked damned hard to get where I am, and it wasn't always easy. I'd studied law but didn't know a thing about finance. Now I advise Mr. Carnegie on every acquisition he makes. You need to make something of yourself. Your job is to get higher marks, and I'll see that the right men tell Yale what a fine candidate you are.

"But look into Harvard and Princeton as well. Read all their pamphlets in the school library, and when the college men are home for the holidays, you can ask them about their experiences. I am very sure they will be positive."

We locked eyes, and after a few seconds, I said, "All right, sir. I will do that." He looked back at the papers on his desk, and I went up to my room and tossed a football up and down. Could I bring my grades up enough to get into these storied eastern schools? Could being the captain of the Shady Side football team make a difference? It would be exciting to play in a Harvard-Yale or a Yale-Princeton game. My true reaction wasn't as negative as I had led Father to believe.

The college booklets at Shady Side's tiny library all said pretty much the same thing about the quality of the faculty, the rigor of the academic program, the dedication to Christian principles. I had to laugh. These pamphlets were designed to assure the parents of the sobriety of the colleges, not to attract potential students. Did I want to go east for college? I would have to wait until the Christmas holidays to see what the boys a year ahead of me had to say about their experiences.

My opportunity would come at George and Marguerite Westinghouse's annual Christmas party at their estate in the fashionable Homewood area where so many of Pittsburgh's elite had chosen to live.

I loved the Christmas party at the Westinghouses'. It was ironic that they had named the house "Solitude" because they entertained more than any other couple in Pittsburgh. This was the premier event of the

Christmas season with a crush of more than 250 people. After greeting Mr. and Mrs. Westinghouse in the entry hall, the guests were escorted into an enormous room with laden buffet tables at one end and a full orchestra and dance floor at the other. Listening to the waltzes the orchestra played, I surveyed the assortment of foods: hams, turkeys, and racks of beef; trays of oysters and clams, no doubt delivered overnight from eastern shores; an assortment of breads, next to butter sculptures; an extensive variety of fruits and vegetables, some of which I couldn't identify. Most distinctive of all was the separate dessert table with vanilla, chocolate, and strawberry ice cream; a chocolate fountain; and an untold number of cakes and cookies. Waiters were standing by with champagne for whomever asked for it.

I wanted to gorge myself as I had at past Westinghouse Christmas parties, but this year I had a mission. I needed to learn as much as I could about the vaunted eastern colleges.

I was disappointed by my first two encounters. The Harvard man talked of scholarly pursuits and a professor in the new field of psychology, William James. The fellow from Princeton spoke about the architecture, the social events, and the opportunities for fox hunting in the unblemished New Jersey countryside.

Nothing they said stirred my interest, and I looked for someone who went to Yale. If it sounded as unappealing as the other two, Western it would be, no matter what my father thought. Right then I spied a Yale man at the food table.

"Checking on the competition, Jack?" I asked a fellow I knew, about my height with black hair and an overhanging brow that partially hid his dark-blue eyes. Jack Heinz had a formidable look.

"All our products on display tonight! Try the horseradish; it's made from my grandmother's old recipe," he said.

"I'm sure it's delicious, but what can you tell me about Yale? That's where my father wants me to go next year. I hope it sounds better than what I've heard about Harvard and Princeton. Nothing could make me go to those schools."

As we picked through the delicacies, Jack was delighted to talk about Yale. "New Haven—that's how we always refer to it—is the real deal, Jamie. The best men I've ever met, smart, sporting, and always up for a good time. The singing groups, publications, plays are all first rate, and the athletics are without peer."

When he started in about the club system, I paid little attention and was happy when he told me more about the sports. "I'm sure you will go out for football in the fall, and a strapping lad like you is sure to be recruited for the crew." I had a vague notion of what he meant by "crew," that it had something to do with rowing.

Just then a young lady in a green velvet dress strode up to Jack and took him by the elbow. "Come have a punch with me, brother, then maybe a waltz?" Jack snatched his arm away, but his smile told me the affection he had for the girl.

"This would be my annoying little sister, Henrietta."

"Jack, you know I hate that name!" She turned to Jamie. "Everyone calls me Rita."

Rita had brown, round trusting eyes in a pleasing face with ringlets of brunette hair down to her uncovered shoulders. Her figure was slight, but she held herself in a self-assured manner. I liked her immediately. That made me nervous, and it showed. I towered over her and didn't meet her eyes as I mumbled, "Jamie, Jamie Dalton."

"Dalton is thinking about New Haven," Jack told her.

"Why, you must go to Yale!" Rita piped up, then grabbed our arms and guided us to the punch bowl where she introduced us to Peggy Hillman, a friend of hers from Miss Mitchell's. The three of them chattered while I nodded my head and tried to smile.

When Jack and Peggy wandered off, I knew I had to say something, "Rita, I'm surprised we haven't met before."

"Oh, we have, but you never paid any attention. I'm three years younger than Jack and two grades behind you. The younger girls always know who the older boys are."

"You're just a kid," I laughed.

She didn't think I was funny. "You don't seem all that grown up to me. You certainly don't know how to talk to a young lady. Excuse me, I'm going to find Jack."

She was right. Shady Side was all boys, and the only activity I did that included girls was Mrs. Benedum's dreaded dancing classes. The boys in suits and ties stood on one side of the room, the girls in long dresses on the other. We all had to wear white gloves: the boys' sweaty and filthy, the girls' pristine. When we were forced to dance as couples, always at arm's length, the girls all giggled at how inept the boys were at even the most basic steps. I never said much of anything, and they made fun of that too.

Before Rita could leave, I said, "Wait, I'm sorry. May I have this dance?"

She hesitated. "I suppose."

I held out my arm and escorted her into the ballroom, where we blinked at its brightness. While the rest of the house was lit by dim, flickering gas lights, the ballroom blazed bright. There were hundreds of tiny electric lights mixed into the evergreen boughs, and the chandeliers seemed on fire.

We took our dancers' pose with the requisite twelve inches between us and moved to the center of the dance floor. When I made a few missteps, she said, "Haven't learned much at dancing class, have you?" I blushed. "C'mon, Jamie. I thought you were an athlete. You can master a few simple dance steps."

I managed not to tread on her toes, and we both relaxed. I got her to laugh with comments about some of the older, stodgier dancers who clumped around the floor with big smiles on their faces. When the music stopped, we dropped our hands and arms, but neither of us said anything. We walked back to the punch bowl where Jack stood with Peggy. He took out a silver flask. "Like a nip, Jamie?"

"Very much!" I replied.

I tried to make up for my earlier faux pas and asked Rita whether she had plans for college. Strike two. "Do you think I'm a silly nit that will sit here in Pittsburgh, planning my debut, then waiting for a marriage proposal? I intend to go east for college, maybe to Smith. From there it's an easy train ride to New Haven, and I can see Jack during the college terms."

"Maybe you will see me as well," I said.

"I'll have to think about that. My family is leaving, and I must go."

As she turned and walked away, I admired her rich chestnut hair that covered her bare back down to the top of her dark-green velvet Christmas dress. I didn't want her to leave. I called good-bye, but she didn't look back. Maybe she hadn't heard me over the din of the party.

————

I decided to apply to Yale and filled out the admission form with a few sentences in the essay section about why I thought Yale was the right college for me. I stressed some of the things that Jack had mentioned: my interest in football and perhaps crew and my hope to find a place at the *Yale Daily News*, which I had heard was more selective than the sports teams. I hoped the letter from the headmaster at Shady Side to Yale would be positive since I had brought my grades up. The most important letters came from two senior partners at Knox & Reed. I told Father that I didn't think they were necessary, but he scoffed. "Jamie, you better learn now how crucial these types of connections are. My colleagues are wealthy alumni of Yale, and the college can't afford to ignore men like them if it is to prosper."

Getting into Yale now seemed like a real possibility, and I didn't want to settle for Western. When I did receive the "Mr. Dalton, we are happy to inform you . . ." letter in mid-April, I was pleased and a little surprised. I was glad that three of my schoolmates got the same letter from Yale.

My family had always escaped the summer heat at the Cresson Springs Hotel, but this year that would change. Our father, along with many of his well-off friends, had taken a membership in the South Fork Fishing and Hunting Club on a lake above Johnstown, which was less than seventy miles east of Pittsburgh. There would be fishing and sailing, neither available at Cresson, and a big clubhouse for dining and dancing. Mr. and Mrs. Heinz were members, and I hoped I would see Rita there, but that didn't happen. Mother told me that the Heinzes had taken a house in the Berkshires for the summer.

The first month of the summer I had lots of time to think and read, which I enjoyed when it wasn't an assignment. I discovered Mark Twain, in particular *Adventures of Huckleberry Finn*, and saw how he could bring people, places, and conversations to life on a printed page.

As much as I enjoyed Twain, I didn't like being cooped up in our house on Amberson and was thrilled when we packed up our trunks for the two-hour train trip to Johnstown. From there it was a bumpy carriage ride up the fourteen-mile trail through the Little Conemaugh River valley to South Fork. The final leg to the club was across a narrow path along the top of the dam that held back the South Fork River to create Little Conemaugh Lake. When we arrived, Mother and Father dealt with the drivers and the porters, while Kat, Wills, and I walked down the wood-chip path to the lake. We loved what we saw. There was a float just offshore with a slide and a diving board. Small boats with children our ages in the cockpits had their sails up, ready to catch the stiff afternoon breeze. Along the shore I saw several men my father's age, dressed in lightweight summer tweeds with fishing creels hanging down their backs, casting for the bass that had been stocked in the lake, their lines tracing graceful parabolas until the fly skimmed the water. I didn't see any fish rising, but the men didn't seem to mind. I knew this was where Father would be spending most of his time. I also knew that I did not have the patience for fly-fishing.

Several gazebos stood next to the shore, and that is where the ladies in their long white cotton dresses with sleeves to their wrist and broad feathered hats had congregated. Some crocheted and others played cards, while a few twirled their parasols and looked out over the lake. I knew my mother would feel she should join these women, but I was just as certain she wouldn't enjoy it. At least South Fork didn't have the blue feelings associated with Cresson Springs for her.

During my high school years at Shady Side, I no longer went on the Sunday carriage rides with Grampa Willis. I was busy with school during the week and had baseball and football games on the weekend.

As the years went by, my parents saw how much we loved our crusty, irreverent Grampa, and even Father softened his attitude. Willis was no longer as bitter about the steel men and the failure of the laws to protect the common man from their greed. They could see that under the prickly exterior was a loving and lonely old man that needed his family around him. Father and Grampa still had their occasional blowups, but they were less heated. At Sunday meals Grampa would go on about the perfidy of

Andrew Carnegie and his partners, or Father would lecture about the rule of law and the importance of lawyers, and off they'd go. Mother would smile and let them vent, before saying, "Richard, Willis, that's enough. The children and I have heard this all before. You never can find common ground on these topics so indulge us and talk about something less controversial." There would be some huffing and puffing, but soon both of them would calm down and see the futility of their bickering. These tests of wills became less and less frequent, and by my senior year at Shady Side, we could laugh them out of it.

Their relationship had become so comfortable that Father invited Grampa to South Fork for the last two weeks of August. Grampa grumbled about spending his time in "a rich man's playground," but he was thrilled to be with his grandchildren and away from the numbing heat and dirt of a Pittsburgh summer.

Once there he overcame his misgivings and every day sat by the lake in one of the slatted wooden chairs with a slanted back and wide armrests. Grampa was happy to look out at the lake and smoke his pipe before joining us all for dinner at the clubhouse.

It was the last day of the trip, and I had taken Kat and Wills out for a final sail before heading back to Pittsburgh. As we came up the path from the lake, we saw that Grampa was dozing in the late afternoon sun, his arm fallen to his side and his hand holding his still smoldering pipe. There was something about his posture that bothered me, and I ran ahead, shouting, "Grampa!" as I went. When I got to him, I shook his shoulders. "Wake up, please, wake up," I implored him, but he didn't respond. By then I had attracted the attention of others sitting by the lake, and several of the men had come by to see if they could be of assistance.

One of them said, "I am Dr. Chalfant, son. Let me take a look at him." I moved out of the way and put my arms around Kat and Wills, who were both crying. The doctor put his ear to Grampa's chest for more than a minute, then stood up and said, "Children, we need to find your parents." After asking another man to stay with Grampa, he walked us to the cottage we had rented that was up a slight rise from the clubhouse, Wills, Kat and I holding hands on the way.

Father was standing on the porch gazing out at the lake when he saw us. "Dr. Chalfant, is something wrong?" At the sound of alarm in Father's voice, Mother joined him.

Seeing the look on the doctor's face, Mother steered Kat and Wills into the cottage, but I didn't move. When they were both inside and it was evident that I wasn't about to join them, Dr. Chalfant turned to Father, "Richard, I'm sorry to tell you this, but your father has died. I've left Nick Byers with him down by the lake. I believe his heart gave out. In any case, he went peacefully."

I stood beside Father with my head bowed, as the tears rolled down my cheeks. Father answered mechanically, "Thank you, Robert. I must make arrangements. Do you know a proper funeral establishment in Johnstown? We need to get my father back to Pittsburgh for burial."

Both he and Mother were consumed in comforting Kat and Wills and getting us organized for the train trip back to Pittsburgh. I tried to be whatever help I could, but I was in a daze the whole time. The one indelible memory I have is seeing a plain pine box being loaded onto a baggage car as we boarded the train. Everyone knew Grampa was in that makeshift coffin, but no one said anything. When we arrived back at the Shadyside station, men from the McCabe Brothers Funeral Home were there to take over the arrangements for the burial and furnish a more appropriate casket. The service would take place in two days at St. Mary's Cemetery out the Mount Troy Road. Father knew that Grampa Willis would insist on being buried in consecrated grounds.

It was a clear, cool September Saturday, and Father McCluskey from St. Boniface's was to perform the burial service at Grampa Willis's graveside. Grampa never spoke much about his friends, and I hadn't spent enough time around his house in Allegheny City to know how many people outside the family might attend his funeral. The five of us had all taken our seats next to the grave at least a half an hour earlier than the 11:00 start of the service. At first there were only a few others, and even Father didn't recognize them. But in ones and twos, then in larger groups, people approached the gravesite until there were two hundred people standing among the headstones around Grampa's grave. Out of the crowd a beefy man approached Father and doffed his cap.

"I am Len Doyle, sir, and I represent all these folks who wish to convey our condolences to you and your family. Willis Dalton was respected by iron and steel workers all over Pittsburgh. He was a strong man, who stood up for what he believed, even when it put him at odds with the powers that be. We will all miss him, but none so much as you." With that, Doyle rejoined the others.

After the service a few friends of my parents came back to our house on Amberson for tea and cakes. We were happy when they all left, and we could get out of our stiff, formal clothes and be left to our own devices. I tried to read in my room but soon got restless. I was leaving for New Haven in two days, and maybe some of my mates would be up for a farewell drink or two. I walked over to Bill Ireland's house on Westminster, and we picked up Sidney Maxwell on St. James. It was a short walk to Cappizano's bar, just off Walnut Street on Bellefonte. I'd miss the old neighborhood.

We toasted each other's success at college with glasses of Iron City. Bill was off to Harvard and Sid to Princeton, and after a couple of beers, we switched to shots of whiskey and tried to remember our college fight songs. All I could come up with was Boola-Boola and Sid mumbled something about tigers. Bill didn't have a clue whether Harvard even had a fight song. There was one other patron, a guy dressed in shabby clothes who didn't look up from his half-filled glass. We kept at the shots for another hour or so, then bought a bottle from the barkeep and stumbled out the door. The last thing I remember is passing the bottle back and forth as we staggered home, arm in arm, singing at the top of our lungs.

I woke up the next morning with a raging headache and a very sore nose. I rushed into the bathroom and drank four cups of water, then sprawled back on my bed. It was then that I noticed that I was still in my clothes from the night before. My God, I thought, what had happened? I had never been blackout drunk before, and I was scared.

Father was ashen when he walked into my room. I propped myself up on my elbows, and he glared at me. "Do have any idea what you've done? Your mother and I were asleep when we heard a crash on the front staircase. We both got out of bed, and that's when we saw you sprawled out on the stairs, blood all over your face. Your mother was scared to death.

It took all our strength to get you onto your bed. We cleaned your face as best we could, but when you started thrashing around, we couldn't get you out of your bloody clothes.

"James, this is beyond unacceptable. I have a half a mind to wire Yale and tell them you will no longer be attending. Put you to work in the mills! But it's too late for that. You will have one semester to straighten up, and if you don't, I will pull you out of there and you will owe me for the wasted tuition."

I was sitting on the side of the bed with my head in my hands. I felt humiliated and didn't know what to say. "Father, I am so . . ."

"Save it for your mother. She is horrified. Clean yourself up and apologize to her. I don't want to see you."

I washed off the dirt and the liquor, but I couldn't scrub the shame away. When I looked in the mirror, I saw my nose was swollen but it didn't seem broken. At least there would be no awkward visit from Dr. Chalfant. I put on a button-down shirt and khakis, then knocked gently on Mother's bedroom door. She didn't respond so I walked in. She was sitting up in a bed jacket, her legs under the covers, reading a book.

"Oh, Mother, I am so ashamed."

She looked up, her eyes ablaze. "You should be! I've never seen behavior like this and on the day we buried your grandfather. Your father was upset enough! I wanted to keep you here in Pittsburgh, but your father insists that you have the chance to prove yourself at Yale. If you don't, you will be put to work, manual labor. Don't take a college education for granted."

"I want to make you and Father proud," I said. But she was looking back down at her book.

I ate a sandwich that night in the kitchen, then packed my valise. I still felt lousy and went to bed right after it was dark. By the time I got to breakfast, Father had gone to work. Mother came down in her riding clothes and told me she would drive me in our carriage to the Shadyside station. When we pulled up, she gave me a quick hug, and I felt her tears on my cheek. "You must be careful," she said. "Be a good boy." Then I waited alone for the train.

2

Yale

As I walked down the aisle of the train, I felt groggy from my latest binge. I knew I should be thinking about what I would need to do at Yale to gain the approval of my parents. The train was crowded with older college men, and none of them gave me a welcoming look. I was happy when I saw an empty seat next to a classmate from Shady Side that I knew but not well, Jason Garland.

There had been a natural split at school between the athletes and the academics, and Jason and I were on either side of that divide. Jason was five inches shorter than me, maybe five foot nine, with unruly brown hair, a short stubby nose, and wire-rim glasses. Like me, he was clean shaven. Despite our distance at school, I was happy to see someone I could talk to on the train.

I greeted Jason with a cheery hello and a handshake somewhat firmer than his. "Ready for the long trip to New Haven?"

Jason surprised me with his quick, forceful response. "Why, yes, I am. I've read up on train travel and also spoken to some of the Pittsburgh men who attend Yale about what to expect. If there are no delays, we should arrive in New Haven at 8:30 this evening, and that's even with the ferry over the Hudson River and the transfer to the New Haven line at the Grand Central Depot."

I was impressed by his knowledge and maybe a bit jealous of his mastery of our situation, but I tamped that down so there wouldn't be any tension between us. "I always admired how diligent you were at Shady Side."

"You're a poor liar, Jamie Dalton, but I'll give you credit for the effort." Despite our obvious differences, I liked this guy and could use a friend at Yale.

"Tell me what your interests will be at college," he said. "I'm going out for the literary publications. *The Lit, The Review,* the *Yale Daily News.* I want to take a crack at all of them."

"It's the sports teams for me, but maybe the newspaper as well. I hear it's very competitive," I told him.

"Hasn't sports made you competitive?" he asked with a smile.

We arrived in Jersey City around eight o'clock, then had a short ferry ride into Manhattan. A driver hoisted our luggage onto the back of a hansom, and we jostled through the chaos of 42nd Street, making it to Grand Central in time to board the last train to New Haven.

For the next two hours, we both drifted off until we heard the conductor intone, "New Haven!" The train had barely come to a stop when there was a mad push to drop down the steep steps to the platform and find yet another porter and hansom to deal with our trunks. On the way to the campus, Jason told me what we were seeing.

"This is Elm Street and up ahead is New Haven Green. And those three spires? They are the town's churches and right behind it is Yale," Jason told me. He was looking at a map he had copied in his own hand from one of his books about the college. Behind the churches off to the left, lights flickered in the windows of a four-story colonial brick structure. Since this was the building always seen in any depiction of the college, I knew it to be Connecticut Hall, where we would attend lectures. Looming over the street as we moved up Elm were imposing buildings constructed of the large brown stone that dominated the campus. When we came to the next intersection, our driver stopped and pointed to a building on our left that was at a ninety-degree angle to the rest. We knew from Jason's map it was Durfee, the freshman hall.

We went through a portal, and off to the left I looked over the broad lawn that ended just before Connecticut Hall. About a hundred yards in front of me was another stone building, but this one had a curved façade. I would later learn that it was originally the college chapel but had been converted into Battell Library. To the right of that building was a low fence made up of two separate white-painted slats, each about ten feet long, and fixed into low iron stanchions that repeated up High Street. Lounging on the fence were clusters of men that I presumed were Yale students. I thought I heard faint sounds of singing.

The porter opened the door to my room in Durfee and dropped my trunk into a bleak, cold space that had rough wooden floors and no rugs. A black potbelly stove stood unlit in the corner, and there were four doors along the wall facing the window that looked onto the lawn. I shook the handle on the first door on the right and found it was locked, as were the next two. The last opened, and I peeped inside. The room was tiny, the bed old and rusty, the mattress thin and stained. I shoved my trunk along the floor until it was beside the bed, and there it would remain the rest of the year. There was one rickety dresser and a small closet that wouldn't hold more than two suits and an overcoat. A rocker was in the corner and a gas lamp on the floor. After I unpacked, I put the lamp on top of the trunk. Since there was no desk, I would be doing my reading in bed. For the first time since I boarded the train in Pittsburgh that morning, I was feeling alone and wondering whether Yale had been a wise choice.

Then three fellows burst into the room. The shortest of the three lagged behind while the other two looked me over. "Dalton, isn't it?" the taller of the two asked. "James?"

"Jamie," I answered.

"I'm Sam Lawrence, and this scruffy fellow is Whitney Gillespie. We both are down from Andover. The runt is Simon Peters. He has the misfortune of being an Exeter boy."

Lawrence was about my height with wavy brown hair and broad shoulders. He had a long straight nose, a small mouth, and large brown eyes. Gillespie stood around five foot ten and had red hair and freckles with a broad smile and darting green eyes. They both exuded a sense of superiority that rattled me

Peters had short, curly black hair with a round face spoiled by acne and seemed very nervous and uncomfortable. He shuffled his feet and never looked up as he mumbled something unintelligible by way of a greeting. I assumed I would never be close to him.

"Sam, let's head down to Mory's for a quick lager before curfew," Whitney piped up. I knew that all freshmen had to be back in their rooms by 10:30. "Care to come along, Dalton?"

"What's Mory's?" I asked with some trepidation.

"For your edification, Dalton, Mory's is a Yale institution," Sam said with more than a hint of condescension. "It started as a provision store, apples, salted beef, tobacco, and the like. The Yale men asked the proprietor, Mr. Moreland, to convert his front room to a tavern and serve beer and brandy. Peters?"

"Think I'll stay here. Got some reading to do," he answered, his eyes still fixed on the floor. Since our lectures hadn't even started, what did he need to read? There was a stack of books on the floor next to the one threadbare chair in the common area where he had taken a seat. I saw the authors' names on the spines: Darwin, Marx, Spencer. Heady stuff.

We walked up Elm to Spring where we found Mory's. Shouts, songs, the clinking of tankards, it all sounded very gay. We wedged ourselves in the door and elbowed our way to the bar. Jack and Whit ordered brandy, but it was beer for me. On first blush the joviality seemed forced, but it was contagious, and soon I was singing along to the faintly obscene drinking songs.

Before long, the barmen clanged an old ship's bell and announced, "Ten o'clock, you newbies. Best be getting back to your rooms." I could see the youngest men quaff the last of their drinks and head toward the door, with my roommates and I close behind. Soon we were back in our rooms, and I struggled to sleep in my very uncomfortable bed. It would take most of that first semester to become accustomed to it and get a decent night's sleep.

———

I easily slipped into Yale's normal first-year routine: lectures and study groups, sophomore hazing, fraternity rush, and, most important to me, football. My inclination was not to join a freshman fraternity. When I asked why we needed to sort ourselves into groups when we had just arrived at Yale, Sam replied, "You really are green."

Whit was less superior. "Yale has changed. In years past it was all about academics and sports, but now it's associating with the top men. All these fraternities and societies in the first three years are leading up to the most important distinction of all, getting tapped for a final club. And there are only two that mean a damn: Skull & Bones and Scroll & Key. No one has much idea what goes on in those spooky tombs of theirs, but one thing is clear. They choose only the best men, the football captains, the strokes on the crew, the men from the finest families. No more than fifteen each. Those clubs can decide your future. The men from Bones and Keys secure the top positions in whatever field they choose."

There was a degree of privilege exuded by the eastern prep school men that intimidated me. They all seemed to know the same people, attend the same cotillions in New York and Boston, summer in the same handful of seaside resorts. In Pittsburgh I was always secure in the knowledge that my family was well respected. Here at Yale, I was nothing special. I did join a freshman fraternity, not one of the top ones like Sam and Whit, but I never spent much time with my new brothers. Simon Peters declined a bid, and he would remain a neutral all four years. I gave little thought to the august final clubs. A mere thirty men out of the four hundred in our class would be selected. Would the other 370 be doomed to failure as my roommates seemed to suggest?

I played football in the fall and rowed on the second freshman boat but spent most of my free time with Jason Garland. We worked just hard enough to get the "Gentleman Cs" that the prep school guys touted as an acceptable level of academic achievement. Bored with the fraternity antics, we decided to explore a seamier side of New Haven.

We ventured over to the more disreputable establishments on State Street to get away from the Yale men. Their cave-like darkness and the working-man clientele reminded me of the places my friends from Shady Side and I used to haunt outside Pittsburgh.

We saw women leading men up the stairs and knew these places served more than just liquor. One night at the Oyster, one of the seediest spots on the street, we drank enough to admit to each other a major source of embarrassment. We were both virgins!

"These easterners think they are so worldly. I bet they don't have any more experience than we do. Jason, we need to do something about our . . . situation, and this is the place to do it!"

Jason didn't seem convinced, but after a few more shots, he was all for it. "Let's ask the barman!"

I called him over and said, "How much to go upstairs?"

"You tykes don't look like you're ready for my girls."

"How much?" I insisted.

"A buck each. Fifty cents for a blowjob."

Jason and I gave each other a blank look. "Better keep it at a buck for you rookies. Do you have it?" We scraped together every piece of change we had and slid it across to the barman. Then he whistled and put two fingers in the air.

The two women who approached us wore loose tops and black pleated skirts over their broad hips. Their hair was tied back and the heavy makeup they wore couldn't hide their age. "Treat 'em gentle, girls," the barman said. Without a word, they took our hands and led us upstairs. I was relieved when we went to different rooms.

The act itself couldn't have been more impersonal. She rubbed me until I was ready, then slipped something over it. I wasn't sure what and was too embarrassed to ask. Without a word, she lifted her skirt and guided me inside her. "Now move, honey."

I did as I was told and soon it was over. "Your time's up. Get on out of here while I clean off." I was too shy to even ask her name and did as I was told.

Out on the street, Jason and I gave each other faint smiles and were silent as we started the walk back to campus. After a few minutes, Jason turned to me. "At least that's over!" We both laughed, then related our similar experiences.

"Do you want to go back?" Jason asked.

"Don't you?" I replied.

"Damn straight!" he said.

And that began our forays into the pleasure dens of New Haven. One of us would say, "State Street," and we'd be off. The more we went, the more pleasurable the visits became. We visited four or five different establishments and got to know the girls' names, even experimenting with more than just the basics. We'd drink with the girls down in the bar after our fun and thought we were quite sophisticated.

—◆—

Despite his grumbling, my father didn't pull me out of Yale after the first semester. Because I was on the football and crew teams with them, Sam and Whit began to accept me, and the three of us decided to take rooms together for sophomore year. Jason and I had continued our drinking and whoring, and I wanted him to take the last room in our suite. Since he wasn't on any of our teams, they had only seen him when we returned from one of our binges.

"Kind of a mess, isn't he?" Sam said.

"He's a good man. You'll see." They reluctantly agreed.

Jason had an infectious enthusiasm in those days, often fueled by alcohol, and Whit and Sam soon joined us on our excursions into town. We were a pack, special somehow.

Vacations in Pittsburgh were not as enjoyable. Father and I would bicker about my grades. Mother would say that I looked like I wasn't taking care of myself. Things came to a head the spring of my sophomore year. Wills and Kat both were spending the night at friends' houses, and it was just my parents and me at dinner.

"I have heard accounts from New Haven about you and your friend's dissipated life, and I'm disgusted," Father said.

"You don't know anything about that."

"You think people don't notice such abject behavior, and they love to gossip. Lots of Pittsburgh men at Yale, you know. The drinking is bad enough but the other. I'm shocked at your depravity."

Mother stared at me. "I knew you always look awful when you return on holidays, but if there is more than liquor involved—and I can only imagine what that might be—then I'm disgusted with you." She got up from the table, and we heard her walking up the front stairs.

"Can't you see what you are doing? Your mother cried herself to sleep for a month after you left for college. If you don't straighten up, you could send her back to Cresson. If not for yourself, do it for her."

What Father said about my mother shook me. When I woke up in New Haven on Sunday mornings, I had often said that this was the last time I would go to State Street, but by the next weekend one thing would lead to another and off I'd be. At the very least I should stop seeing the whores. I did want my parents' respect and didn't want Mother to relapse.

"I could get a job here in Pittsburgh for the summer, I guess." I had planned on being in New England that summer staying with my friends in their summer homes, but I knew Father would never agree to that.

Father drummed his fingers on his desk. "I suppose I could find you a clerk's job at the firm, but you have to take it seriously. Be on time in the morning and do what the partners ask, even if it means staying into the evening."

The prospect of shuffling papers and enduring the hot, dirty summer in Pittsburgh was not at all appealing, but I didn't see that I had any choice. "I won't disappoint you, Father," I said. He looked at me skeptically but said he would make the arrangements.

Back in New Haven for the remainder of my sophomore year, I made an effort to curb my excesses. At times, I would spurn Jason's call to head for State Street. He'd be disappointed but would go anyway. Seeing the condition he was in when he returned gave me caution but didn't stop me from going with him a couple of times that spring.

—◦—

That summer, as I had feared, was miserable. The hot dusty trolley rides to and from downtown seemed to get longer each day. The lawyers were curt and demanding, and the work was duller than I had imagined. By August I'd had enough and begged Father for two weeks off before returning to New Haven.

"I can see you have already begun to slack off," he said. "Someday you will have to learn what work is." Nothing more was said about it between me and my father, and in mid-August I told my dour supervisor that I would not be returning the next Monday. He didn't seem to care.

I joined Mother and Kat and Wills at South Fork for the last two weeks of the summer. I spent much of my time with my brother and sister and tried as best I could to be charming at dinner. When I saw Mother sitting alone, I would take the Adirondack chair next to her. Sometimes we would just gaze out at the lake, and other times we would talk about books and what we had read in the newspapers that were delivered to the club each day. She would never ask about Yale, and I never brought it up.

Rita Heinz and I overlapped for a week at the club. We had seen little of each other since the Westinghouses' Christmas party, and I hoped to make a better impression. She seemed glad to see me, and we would take walks or row on the lake. Rita tried to get me to fish with her, but I preferred to sit back and watch her cast. She was excited about going to Smith that fall, and I talked about football and crew and my friends at Yale but was vague about my social life.

On her last night, Rita joined my family for dinner at the club, and afterward I walked her back to the Heinz cottage. As we stood at the bottom of the steps up to her cottage, I reached for her hand and pulled her in for a kiss.

"You are such an oaf, Jamie Dalton. I thought you had grown up." She ran up the stairs, and the screen door of the cottage slammed shut behind her.

Was that strike three? The rest of my time at South Fork was very dull.

———

It was the first football game of junior year when my dreams of sports glory were shattered. I was carrying the ball on a sweep, known as "Student Body Right," when two men from Columbia hit me, one high, one low. I heard a snap from my knee, then the pain hit, and I blacked out.

I woke up an hour later, and the first thing I saw was my leg propped up and a bulky plaster cast around it. I was in the recovery room of two young doctors, Jackson and Lamb, who specialized in repairing the broken bones of college athletes.

"Besides breaking your leg, you also tore some cartilage," Dr. Jackson told me. "You will be on crutches for two months and a cane for another month after that. And I'm sorry to tell you that your injuries will keep you from playing football ever again." Dr. Lamb nodded and gave me a sympathetic look.

I stared at the two of them with tears in my eyes and balled fists. "You can't know that." What would I do without giving my all for the team each day, feeling the pride of my exhaustion, the tantalizing competition? I got up off the table and hobbled toward the door. "You'll see," I spat over my shoulder. I stormed out of their offices, damning my crutches and the bad luck that had landed me on them.

When I limped into our flat, only Jason was there, and he had heard from Sam and Whit what had happened. "Are you in pain?" he asked.

"None now. The doctors gave me a shot and some pills for when that wears off." I stumbled crossing the living room but managed to stay upright on the crutches. "Damn these things. I'm going to be on them until Christmas, the doctors said. And football's over for me."

"Sports aren't the only extracurriculars."

"Don't humor me!" I limped into my room and slammed the door.

The next morning Sam and Whit gave me a "tough luck" and "you'll be back in no time" and hurried out. These were my teammates? My roommates?

Jason asked whether I needed any help. "You won't be able to carry your books."

I slammed one of my crutches against a chair. "Did I ask for help?"

"Don't be stupid. You need a hand, and I'm willing to give it."

I slumped into our one easy chair. "Sorry, Jason. You're a good friend." I was trying not to cry.

"I've always looked up to you since we were at Shady Side. You can handle this," Jason told me. We talked into the night, but I couldn't get to sleep.

Over the next weeks, Sam and Whit were standoffish, but Jason was good to his word and helped me get around a campus that was not built for a man on crutches. In the evenings we would laugh about our escapades, but when I had gone to bed, I would hear him sneak out. He would look god-awful the next morning but would never fail to ask me whether I needed anything.

And he continued to encourage me to try out for the Yale publications. "Maybe you should go out for the *News* or the *Lit*? The college needs to de-emphasize Latin and Greek and add courses in French and German, modern history, literature, civics, science. Then there is the elitist club system. The college needs a more democratic alternative."

"Not ready," was all I would answer.

———

A month later I insisted the cast come off. Using a cane, I limped onto the train for the Christmas holiday trip back to Pittsburgh, then sipped from a flask the whole way there. The whole family was assembled in the front hall to greet me, and I could see the concern in all their eyes as I struggled across the threshold. "Oh, Jamie," Mother cried.

With my eyes downcast, I mumbled, "I'm very tired from the train. Please excuse me." With that I hobbled up the stairs and slammed the door of my room behind me. For the next ten days of my three-week Christmas vacation, I only came out of my room to eat. My responses to questions at meals were perfunctory, while the trivial holiday talk swirled around me. I refused to attend the many balls and family get-togethers, not wanting to see the sympathy in people's eyes. When Rita Heinz delivered her family's Christmas presents, I refused to come downstairs.

After she left, I heard the rustle of Mother's skirts on the stairs, then she threw open my bedroom door. "I won't have you hiding for the entire holiday. You act like God has personally singled you out for his wrath. I know your leg hurts, but it has to be something more than that."

My head snapped up from the book that I was pretending to read. "I can't play football anymore. I'm a cripple!"

"With the kind of life you have led in New Haven, you are lucky that nothing worse has happened to you. And now you come home smelling of whiskey. It has been terrible seeing you throw your life away, but I won't stand for it a minute longer. It's time for you to grow up!

"And the first step is for you to stop feeling sorry for yourself. Tomorrow we are going to the food kitchen the church runs during the holidays, and you will see what crippled really looks like." I was about to object when she held up a hand. "No arguments. If you are going to act like

35

a spoiled child, I am going to treat you like one." There was no sense in infuriating her any further, and I bowed my head. "We will be leaving tomorrow morning at eight," she added.

I came down for an early breakfast, and Mother was wearing a plain dark dress, no bustle, no frills. She had me drive our carriage down Fifth to Penn, then straight south on Braddock to the little mill town of the same name. We stopped in front of a church that was identified by some strange writing that I couldn't read. "This is the Slavic Orthodox Church of St. Barnabas," she told me.

Mother led me down a set of stairs, where a crooked door on rusty hinges led us into a dark room that stretched the length of the church. Along one side were tables heavy with food: steaming soups, turkeys, hams, piles of bread, baked potatoes, and a mash-up of vegetables that looked none too appetizing. Behind the tables were ladies I recognized as friends of my mother. They were wearing forced smiles and dresses as drab as hers.

Shuffling in front of the tables were long lines of men, women, and children. Their clothes were worn and their faces dirty. Some of the men were on crutches because they were missing a leg, and others had sleeves pinned to their side because they had lost an arm. The women had kerchiefs on their heads with pockmarked faces and dark bitter eyes. Children as young as ten had burn marks on their hands and arms, but with the smell of the Christmas meal in the air, I could see some smiles as well.

I grabbed my mother's arm. "I had no idea."

"Your grandfather has taken you to a steel mill. You must have seen how dangerous it is."

Mother and I took our places serving the endless line of people. Each father, whether or not he had all his limbs, would shepherd his brood past the tables, then mumble something unintelligible by way of thanks. We served for more than three hours before we left. On the way home, Mother said, "I hope you have seen another side of our booming city today, Jamie. We live a cloistered life that is built on the backs of these people.

"They came to Pittsburgh from countries where they were serfs, little better than slaves, for the promise of a new life and look what we have given them. They work harder in more dangerous conditions than they ever did before. They live in dilapidated company shacks and can barely feed their families. On holidays they come to this church basement where the wives of the steel men try to atone for their capitalist husbands. I hope you see why I brought you here today."

I had no idea how to respond. If Mother wanted me to stop feeling sorry for myself, she had succeeded. After seeing all the burns and missing limbs, my anxiety over the end of my football career at Yale seemed callous. I could see the suffering in their dark, starving faces, but I couldn't fathom how Mother or I could change the equation between the thousands of immigrant workers and the select group of men that ran the steel industry, men like my father.

I'd heard Father expound at the dinner table enough to know where his sympathies lay. He wasn't a cruel man, but he couldn't afford to see the transgressions of his clients. He believed that without the diligence and foresight of men like Carnegie and Frick, the workers and their families would have no jobs at all. It was their "duty" to make steel as cheaply as possible for the good of the nation. If that made them became rich beyond imagination, their talents and industry justified it. Didn't their ministers tell them they were doing God's work?

———

The night before I was to leave for New Haven, I lingered after dinner to speak with Mother. With Father in the library and Kat and Wills in their rooms, Mother and I enjoyed coffee and ginger cookies. The gas light in the dining room had a warm glow.

We made small talk about how Kat and Wills were doing in school—good and not so good—then I took her hand. "Mother, I know I have disappointed you in the past, but I want to thank you for snapping me out of my funk. And I'm not drinking as . . . ," my voice trailed off.

"Oh Jamie, you never need to thank me for being your mother."

I hesitated before I continued. "You seem very well."

"You sound surprised," she laughed. "But you are right. I am well."

"Father told me you haven't been to Cresson Springs in over a year."

She blushed. "No need! There are the Cavalry charities, and I have a new passion."

I took another cookie off the plate. "And that is?"

"Suffrage! The woman's right to vote. What could be more important than allowing woman to be the equal of men at the ballot box? Nothing!"

"How did you get involved?"

"I heard Miss Susan B. Anthony and Miss Elizabeth Cady Stanton speak at the clubhouse of the Colonial Dames one afternoon. Jamie, these two women are a revelation. Miss Cady, in particular. She is a tiny little thing with a soft voice, but when she started to speak, everyone in the hall leaned forward. She explained why women should have the vote. Think of all the wars and panics men have gotten us into, she said. The audience laughed when she asked what would happen to our households and children's educations if left to the ministrations of men. But above all, it is about fairness. Why should women be deprived of such a fundamental right in a democratic society?

"After the talk, I told Mrs. Cady how she inspired me. She asked my name, and when I said Mrs. Richard Dalton, she answered, 'Your name, my dear, not your husband's.' I stood up straight and said, 'Eleanor Ricketson Dalton.' Jamie, I felt like she could see into my soul. The meeting sponsors have asked me to hand out leaflets all over the city and organize letter-writing campaigns to the state legislators."

"Mother, I am so happy for you." I kissed her on the cheek and went upstairs to bed. As I packed for New Haven, I thought about how I wanted her to be proud of me. My cane stayed in Pittsburgh.

———

I returned in a much finer fettle than when I went home three weeks before. With a year and a half left at Yale, I was determined to make the most of it. *The Yale Daily News* was where I set my sights, and Jason arranged for me to meet the *News'* faculty advisor, Mr. Harlan Simmons.

Simmons was in his mid-thirties, of medium height and a body that had grown soft. His brown hair was thin on top, and he wore glasses with elliptical frames that narrowed his gaze. I visited his rooms in Farnum

Hall soon after returning to campus. "Yes, Mr. Dalton. Garland mentioned you," he said. "How is Garland? Haven't seen him around much."

"He's tip-top," I lied. Fact was I hadn't seen much of Jason either. Mr. Simmons furrowed his brow and looked out the window of his office. Then he turned back to me.

"Why the sudden interest in the *News*?" he asked.

"I injured my knee and can't play football. I'm looking for a new challenge, and I figured the *News* could use a fresh voice like mine. I excel in my language classes, I'm well read in the latest fiction, and I will work just as hard for the *News* as I did for my sports teams."

"Seems like sports should be your beat. I'll put in a word with Addison Phelps, the managing editor. He'll contact you."

The next day I received a note from Phelps asking me to meet him at Mory's that afternoon at 4:30. Right from the start Phelps proved himself direct, with a dollop of arrogance. "For some reason our esteemed faculty advisor has asked me to speak with you, though I'm not sure why. Seems you're the athletic type. Since we must cover these silly games, do you think you can write about them?"

We were off to a bad start, but I wanted to prove to him I was up to the challenge and couldn't be cowed either. "Not the beat I had hoped for but writing about games or races will be easy for me. Then you can move me on to something weightier." My feigned insolence caught his attention.

"Cocky fellow, ain't ya?" he retorted but with a smile. "You and me will get along fine. It's January so there's not much to be covered. The crew can't row on the frozen rivers, and football tryouts won't begin until spring. Guess that leaves wrestling and indoor track."

I groaned. The gym was rancid this time of year with the sweat pouring and the windows closed. He saw my reluctance. "Easy enough to find someone that is more eager to rush the paper. This is a trial, ya know?"

"OK, OK. I accept the challenge. I'll write you the best damn wrestling stories the *News* has ever seen."

As promised, I immersed myself in the exploits of the sweaty gladiators and made each meet seem like a struggle of the gods. The pieces were overwritten, but I was able to sound like I was serious with a wink to how absurd the sport truly was. I hoped that my pieces had caught Phelps's eye.

One afternoon I found Phelps lounging on the Fence with some other *News* editors. "Dalton, over here," he called.

I didn't know what might be coming. He looked grave, but then his face went from a frown to a smile, and he stuck out his hand. "The other men and I just voted. You passed muster with that nasty wrestling beat. Congratulations! You are on the staff of the *Yale Daily News*." The other men then circled around me and with huzzahs clapped me on the back and tousled my hair. This was the happiest that I had been since I heard that ligament snap in my knee six months back.

"What will you have me cover now?" I asked.

"We want you to tackle the curriculum fight. This is the end of the nineteenth century, not the middle of the eighteenth. We aren't to be ministers anymore, and we shouldn't have to memorize dead languages. The older faculty is opposed to any sort of change, but some of the younger ones and all the students want a modern curriculum.

"Of course, we need to report the facts, but the *News* has an opinion on the matter, and your articles will need to support our editorial position." That gave me pause. Don't the facts inform the opinions? For good or ill, I would never lose that naïveté.

———

I was spending less and less time at our boardinghouse with my sporting friends, Sam Lawrence and Whitney Gillespie, and more with my literary friends, Jason Garland and Simon Peters, who encouraged me to dig into my first substantive *News* assignment. I tried to report both sides of the argument, even though Phelps thought I was being too fair. By May Timothy Dwight V, the Yale president, announced Greek and Latin would no longer be required and that the trustees had agreed to provide funds for a social studies faculty, as well as a new laboratory dedicated to science and experimentation. I hoped my reporting had contributed to his decision to make those changes.

A week after Dwight's announcement, Professor Simmons left me a note telling me to come to his office. "What are you doing this summer?" he asked as I walked in the door.

I was taken off guard. "I hadn't thought about it. In the past I have tended to my sister and brother in July, then the family vacations at a lake in the Allegheny Mountains in August."

"Ah yes, the privileges of the wealthy." Before I could argue with that assumption, Simmons said, "Shouldn't you be more productive?" I didn't answer, and he went on. "I've been impressed by how you've handled the curriculum controversy. You have a good eye for detail and an evenhanded approach. I know a man in Pittsburgh who might be willing to take you on for a month to show you what big-city newspapering is all about."

I was flabbergasted and could think of nothing intelligent to say so I kept quiet, and Simmons continued. "The man's name is Cleveland Brooks, and he and I were in the same class at Harvard. He grew up on Beacon Hill in Boston, and after attending Nobles and Harvard, he wanted to be out of that stodgy old town. Pittsburgh was the most obvious choice since it's the most dynamic city in the country. Cleve is the managing editor of the *Pittsburgh Sun*, and he has often asked me whether there are any Yale men who would be interested in working at a newspaper. Care for me to contact him on your behalf?"

Now I couldn't avoid responding. "Sir, I'm very gratified that you would think I'm worthy of your recommendation, but other than sports pieces and the articles on the curriculum, I have very little experience. Why would someone like Mr. Brooks have an interest in me?" At the same time, I was also thinking what my father might say.

"False modesty doesn't become you, Dalton. This is a significant opportunity. Tell me now or I'll look for someone else."

"Yes, sir. Please arrange it," I said, squaring my shoulders and trying to look and sound as sure of myself as possible.

Two days later Simmons sent me another note. "Brooks will speak with you on June 7 at 11 in the morning. He's a busy man so please be prompt." My final class was June 5, and I would be taking the train back to Pittsburgh the next day. I had a lot to think about before then. Did I want a career in journalism? Was I ready for the fight with my father that was sure to come? Nobody my family knew ever worked for a newspaper, but this was one month in the summer. How could he object to that?

— ⌢ —

One rite of spring that I approached with ambivalence was Tap Day, when selections were made for the senior societies, believed to guarantee entrée into whatever business or social elite you aspired to after New Haven. To make it worse, the ceremony was played out in public with the whole junior class lined up on the Lawn waiting for their elevation or humiliation. Even my friends at the *News*, who had disdained the underclass fraternities, were not immune to the potential of the societies' imprimatur, and they were out on the Lawn with the rest of us.

I was cocky enough to believe that I didn't need to join one of the societies to succeed and had convinced myself that I didn't care whether I was tapped or not. I had my own goals and didn't want to give up my resolve for the trivial rituals of the senior societies. And I had matured. The brawling of my days at Shady Side was in the past, and though Jason was still making trips down to State Street, I hadn't joined him in months.

Besides, it wasn't certain I would be tapped. I had excelled in athletics, but because of the injury, I wouldn't be on a team for my last year and had just started at the *News*. The students at Yale were aware of my family's place in Pittsburgh society, but how important could that be? Maybe the diversity of my experiences would make a difference, but did I care?

On Tap Day I stood on the Lawn shoulder to shoulder with the other fellows, who to a man were shuffling their feet and twisting their sweaty hands in anticipation. Then I saw a line of men dressed in robes with cowls over their heads emerge from the York Street entrance to the campus and spread out over the lawn. I could see from the insignia on their robes that they were Bones men. In the moment I feared the indignity of being passed over, but at the same time I pondered how I would react if I was chosen.

Moments later, Keys entered from Elm. Heightening the suspense, men from both groups broke up and began circling their victims. I saw Sam Lawrence approached by Bones, not surprising given that he was captain of the football team. We all knew that each society would select only fifteen, and along with all the others, I counted down how many more men would be tapped. Keys was selecting men from the *News*, while the athletes and society types were marching off with Bones. As much as I had thought about it, I still didn't know if I wanted to join either.

My heart raced when a Bones man that I had rowed with approached me. "Mr. Dalton, will you come with me?"

I didn't say anything.

"Step forward," he shouted.

I peered beneath the cowl but didn't move. He waited a few more seconds, then spat at my feet and walked on to the next candidate who happily accepted the honor.

The assemblage buzzed at my blasphemy. I was glad the ordeal was over but couldn't rid myself of the thought that I had made a life-changing mistake. As the clubmen strode off the Lawn, I looked back to see who was left standing without a bid. Jason Garland tried to look indifferent, but there were tears welling in his eyes. This culling of my classmates was as brutal as it was exhilarating.

I didn't see Jason for the rest of that day, and he hadn't come home when I went to sleep that night. The next morning, I found him on the couch in our living room, dead to the world. I shook him and yelled his name for more than a minute until he sat up and blinked his eyes. He peered around the room seeming not to know where he was. Then he collapsed back on the cushions with a groan. I noticed his left shirtsleeve was rolled up and there were red welts on his arm.

When he saw me looking, he rolled his sleeve back down and tried to act casual. "Another great night on the town! You should come with me again, Dalton. The ladies miss you."

"I'm worried about you, Jason. I know you were disappointed you weren't tapped, but it's not ..."

"You worry about yourself, Dalton. I have a hangover. So what? I've had them before, and I'll have them again." And with that, he went into his room, and I didn't see him again until the next evening when he rushed out without saying a word. I decided not to follow him.

I arrived home late on the night of the sixth of June. After greeting Mother and Father, I said I was exhausted from the trip and repaired to my bedroom. I needed to think about what I would say to Mr. Brooks and decided there was not much more I could do but tell him about my experiences at the *News* and hope for the best.

At five till eleven, I walked into the *Sun* building on Fifth Avenue between Wood and Smithfield and took the stairs two at a time up to the fourth floor. I looked out over the open room and saw twenty desks, all littered with newspapers, copy paper, pens and ink, and mugs of coffee. I even saw a few typewriters. The room was filled with the pounding of the presses on the floor above and the rattle of the Associated Press teletypes in the corner of the room. The men in their white shirts covered from wrist to elbow in protective black sleeves were bent over their desks, either scribbling or typing on sheets of unbleached paper. Many of them wore green eye shades, and none of them looked up as I walked into their space. At the first desk I came to, I asked for Mr. Brooks. Without looking up, the man flung out his arm, pointing to a desk in the corner that was enclosed by a short wooden railing. Avoiding the wastepaper baskets and spittoons dotting the floor, I made my way over there.

Cleveland Brooks leaned back in his leather chair with his feet propped up on an overturned ink crate. He was moving pieces of copy between his hands, alternately reading and untangling himself and bending over his desk to make corrections with a thick black pencil. He seemed to be enjoying himself. Catching a glimpse of me inching toward the railing, he called out, "You must be Dalton. Come in, come in."

Brooks was about my height and lanky. He had thick brown hair with wide eyes and a bushy chevron beard. I opened the creaky gate, and he extended his hand, which I pumped with nervous enthusiasm. "Very nice to meet you, Mr. Brooks. Professor Simmons speaks highly of you."

"Simmons is a good sort. We both were happy to escape Boston. Give me an uproarious town like Pittsburgh. Such vitality, such growth. And the wealth of news! Now, tell me why you are interested in newspapering."

I knew this would be the first question he would ask, but I hurried through my answer, worried he would think I came to journalism by default. "My academic strength has always been writing, but when I first got to New Haven, my sole extracurricular was athletics. Then I was injured, and the doctors told me I couldn't play football or even row. A couple of friends that are editors on the *Yale Daily News* encouraged me to heel for that paper. I'm glad I did. Did you receive the clips of the pieces I wrote this spring on the controversy over the curriculum?"

"I did. They are rough, but I can see you have a spark of talent," Mr. Brooks said. We talked about the sources I had used and the interviews I conducted for the curriculum story, then he asked, "Do you intend to pursue journalism after college?"

"Yes, sir. No question about it!" I knew that was the answer he wanted to hear.

He stared at me for a moment, then said, "I'll take a chance on you for a month or so. Be here at eleven next Monday."

Brooks took up his pencil and resumed editing. I thanked him and hoped he would tell me more about the job. When he didn't, I stood, then hurried back across the newsroom. No one paid me the slightest heed. On the trolley home I was excited but wary about telling my father about my summer job at the *Pittsburgh Sun*.

⌁

"I hope you are more serious about this job than the one I gave you," Father said in his study after dinner that night. "And why work for a newspaper? What's the future in that?"

"I thought you'd be proud that I did this on my own," I answered with more hope than conviction.

"I'll be proud of you when you stop your juvenile carousing, when you stop squandering the opportunities that Yale affords you. The Yale men in Pittsburgh are outraged about your performance on Tap Day. You were a fool for turning down Skull & Bones! When will you grow up?"

"Don't you see that's what I'm doing, Father?"

"Do you think a summer job will give you a career? They won't have you do much more than set type. You'll go back to New Haven, and your dissipations will continue."

My face was red. "You haven't been paying attention. I'm going to work hard at this job, you'll see."

Father dismissed me with a wave of his hand. I slammed the door to his study behind me and saw Mother in the hallway. "I hope you have more faith in me than Father does," I said, hurrying past her on the way to my room.

— ◆ —

When I arrived at the *Sun* for my first day, I was surprised that Mr. Brooks was not there. A man approached me and introduced himself as Ike Stebbins, city editor. I noticed the traces of an Irish accent. "Brooks is at City Hall covering Boss Magee's explanation of the new street lighting contract. He thinks there is something shady going on, but Magee will never admit to it. He assigned you to me today. I can see you're all bright-eyed and bushy-tailed, but the boys and I are betting a toff like you won't last the month."

And there it was, just as I had feared. Anyone from the moneyed side of Pittsburgh was anathema to the second-generation Irish that manned the newspapers as well as City Hall. Brooks they had to accept since he was the editor, hired by the owner, but there would be no breaks for me. "And if you think you will be reporting or writing, you are mistaken. I intend to make this a very long summer for you."

That began a hazing that made any I had experienced at Yale seem tame. Most of the time I shuffled papers up and down the stairs. The reporters would yell, "Copy!" with pages extended above their heads, their eyes still focused on their desktop. I would spring forward, grab what they'd written, and bolt up the stairs. The pressmen would snatch the pages with their black-stained hands as if I was no more than an automaton, created for their convenience. Stebbins even assigned me the dirtiest, sloppiest job possible: cleaning and repairing the presses.

The one blessing was that all these tasks and the breakneck pace made the days go by in an instant. I would drag myself home in the evenings and try to scrub the dirt and ink off my hands and face before falling into bed. Mother showed concern but didn't baby me. Father didn't say much of anything.

In late July I was waiting at Stebbins's desk when Mr. Brooks stopped and asked, "How you gettin' along, Dalton?"

With as much enthusiasm as I could muster, I replied, "Tip-top, sir," while giving a wary glance at Stebbins, who was standing nearby. "In fact, I would like to continue up until the last week in August." I didn't dare explain that was the longest I could work without making at least a short appearance at South Fork with my family.

"Damned if I'll have you underfoot for a day longer than necessary," Stebbins cursed.

"Assign him the police blotter," Brooks said in a tone that foreclosed any argument.

That night I told my parents that I would not be coming to South Fork until late August. Father looked surprised, Mother smiled, and nothing more was said. And that began my three-week immersion in some real reporting. All I had to guide me was the confidence Brooks had shown in me and a prominent sign on the newsroom wall that said, "Who, What, Where, When, How, Why." It was my job to get the essential facts on robberies, street brawls, even murders. It thrilled me to see my short write-ups under the "Police News" headline on page seven of the eight-page paper. The next three weeks at the *Sun* flew by, and after a relaxing week in South Fork, it was back to New Haven for my senior year.

Wanting to assert my newly won independence, I decided not to live with anyone from Bones that fall and took rooms with Simon Peters and Jason Garland. Peters and I were so wrapped up in our work on the paper that we didn't spend a lot of time at the rooming house. Jason never seemed to have much to do, and I noticed that at night he would skulk off, not to return until well after I was asleep. During the days he would say he was going to class or to study in the library, but I would often see him drifting down Elm Street, heading away from the campus, toward downtown New Haven.

At the *News* I was assigned to the most crucial issue facing the college that year. At the end of December, when the students would be away for the holidays, the contract with the college's maintenance force was set to expire. This disparate group of men and women were invisible and unappreciated, but they performed the work needed to keep the college functioning. The men made the gas lights glow, cleaned the windows, seeded and mowed the Lawn. The charwomen took out the trash, swept the halls, and washed the blackboards. They went about their business without complaint and disappeared at the end of the day. No one had the slightest curiosity to know where.

It was a disorganized group, but they came together when the college posted new rules to extend their work hours with no increase in pay. The next day the leaves on the Lawn weren't picked up and the past days' blackboard scribblings remained. The maintenance workers had gone on strike, and I was assigned by the editors to find out how the college was going to get them back to work. After I made some inquiries, President Dwight invited me to tea that Saturday.

As I walked to his house on the southwest corner of the Lawn, we saw a group of men and women, no more than twenty, standing idly by. One of them shouted, "More work, more pay!"

A maid answered the door and showed me into the parlor where President Dwight was waiting. "Welcome, young man. I hope that rabble didn't disturb you."

I was surprised by this derogatory reference. "These men, and women too ... aren't they, shouldn't they be getting more work? I mean more money for more work."

Dwight looked down his nose and over his Ben Franklin glasses. "Dalton, is it? Are you the best they could send over from the college paper? Try to follow what I say. These people speak unrecognizable languages. They are unreliable and make up every excuse under the sun to miss work. The college isn't here to support them; they are here to support us. For a fair wage. If they think they should be paid more, they can find another employer. Now leave."

President Dwight intimidated me. I stood up to go but knew I had to ask at least one more question. "Can't Yale afford to pay them for the extra hours of work?"

Dwight stood in his white collar and full clerical gown. "You heard what I said," and he pointed to the door.

It took me twice the normal time to walk back to the *News* office. When I explained to Managing Editor Phelps what had happened, he exploded.

"You didn't ask whether they would negotiate with the workers; whether there was any flexibility on the pay scale; whether the leaders would be punished for organizing?" Then he yelled, "Peters!" When Simon came over to his desk where I was standing, Phelps said, "Dalton screwed up the interview with Dwight. Get over there and see what you can salvage." My humiliation was complete when Peters came back with answers to Phelps's questions and a couple of quotes that put the story on the front page of the next day's paper. If I couldn't stand up to a fusty college president, how was I going to cover the mighty steel men of Pittsburgh?

The *News* published near daily editorials condemning the college's position, but it changed nothing. By March, pressure from the president and the trustees, the faculty, and even some students for the maintenance crew to go back to work ended support from the *News*. I continued to cover the lack of progress in the negotiations, but I could see that the workers' resolve was waning. Fewer of the men and women stood on the street in front of the president's house, and I noticed some of the former picketers shoveling a late snow off the campus walkways and cleaning the classrooms. The "more work, more pay" flyers disappeared from the bulletin boards. The workers' organizing had accomplished nothing. This was my first lesson in the power management holds in labor disputes.

———

Something very good and something very bad happened that spring of my senior year.

A tea dance was scheduled with Smith in late April, and I was hoping that Rita Heinz would be there. I hadn't seen her since my awkward attempt at a kiss at South Fork, and then there was my rude refusal to say hello when she delivered presents the Christmas after my injury. I feared she had written me off but hoped that she could appreciate our many connections. We both came east to college from Pittsburgh, our families were close, and we had been in each other's orbit for four years. I'd had a special feeling for this lovely, spirited girl since the moment we met at the Westinghouse Christmas party. If she did come to the dance, I was determined to make a better impression.

The train bringing the girls from Smith to New Haven was due in at five, and the dance would begin a half hour later in the great room of Connecticut Hall. I arrived fifteen minutes early and paced until they began filing in. Many of them rushed off to men they knew while others made self-protecting circles and chattered away. I was about to leave when I saw Rita. She was the prettiest girl there, and I tried not to seem in a hurry as I walked over to her.

"Miss Heinz, it is so good to see you."

"You never seem to know what tone to take with me, do you, Jamie? At least you didn't call me Henrietta! But I am happy to see a familiar face."

"Welcome to New Haven, Rita. Let's try the dreadful punch and the dried-out tea cakes." I offered her my arm, and I was happy when she took it. At the refreshment table, I tried one of the cakes and crinkled my nose at the first bite. "Not up to Heinz standards," I said. Rita laughed, and I asked her to dance.

The irregular rhythms of the Eddie Wittstein Society Band made dancing difficult, but we managed a casual waltz.

"You Yalies sure know how to put on a party," Rita laughed. "But at least your dancing is better!"

I blushed. "Kind of you to say. You are as graceful as ever."

We talked about our friends from Pittsburgh, I told her about my work on the *News*, and she told me about her writing classes and the college's year-end riding exhibition. "In which you will no doubt win the blue ribbon," I said. Now it was her turn to blush.

Soon the lights flickered, announcing the end of the dance. "May I walk you to the station?" I asked.

"That's very kind of you, Jamie, but if I'm not in one of the carriages, old Miss Beldingham will make sure I don't leave my room except for classes and meals until the end of term."

We lingered on the Chapel Street sidewalk until the carriages pulled up. "I've enjoyed our evening, Miss Heinz," I teased.

"As have I, Mr. Dalton. Jamie, you have been a perfect gentleman. Perhaps we will see each other at South Fork over Decoration Day." Then she kissed me on the cheek, alighted the carriage, and was gone. I touched my hand to the spot of the kiss and was thankful that for the first time I had not acted the fool in the presence of Miss Rita Heinz.

———

But what happened next wiped out my elation over that happy evening and cast a pall over my final days in New Haven. Jason was spending more and more time in the dives on State Street, but I was so involved at the *News* that I hadn't confronted him. Late one afternoon I returned to find Peters flipping through a months-old issue of *Harper's Weekly*.

"Have you seen Jason?" I asked. I had left early that morning for class and assumed Jason was in his room because the door was closed.

"He hasn't been back since he left late last night."

That scared me because no matter what shape Jason was in, he always returned to our rooms before the next morning. Knowing where he was, I hurried to State Street to check out the dives he and I frequented. Seeing these places in daylight—and sober—was a shock. There were the repulsive smells, the sticky floors, and the pervasive grime, but worst of all were the patrons. The men were either hunched over their shots glasses or passed out with their heads in the swill on the bar. Then there were the women, the whores, just arriving for their evening's work, all older and blowsier than I cared to remember.

The bartenders at the first four spots I tried said they had seen Jason the night before, but he had left after a couple of shots. The other place he might have gone was the Oyster, and I hoped he wasn't there. It had a rougher crowd than any of the others.

The bartender at the Oyster was wiping down the bar with a dirty rag, and I asked whether he had seen Garland. "He's upstairs sleeping it off," he said, like it was the most normal thing in the world.

I shot up the stairs and hurried into the room with an open door.

Jason Garland was lying face up on the floor, his head in a pool of vomit that was still seeping out of both sides of his mouth. I was shocked to see a bloody syringe on the floor next to him. I turned him over and held him up by the waist. His head hung slack, and his breathing was labored and getting worse. Not knowing what else to do I pounded him on the back to clear whatever was clogging his throat. I didn't think it was working until Jason's body tensed, and he vomited for five minutes. I held him up, so he didn't fall face first into the mess.

I needed help and thought of the two young doctors who had treated me after my football injury. Jason was a lot smaller than me, and with his left arm around my neck and my right arm around his back, I was able to drag him the half mile up Elm to their house. He yelled to let him down the whole time, but I was too scared to stop, not knowing what I'd do if he passed out again. When we got to their house, they must have heard the commotion. A window was thrown open, and Dr. Jackson stuck his head out. "Who is out there? Dalton, what in God's name do you want at this hour?" He forgot his pique when he saw what kind of shape Jason was in. "Bring him inside here but be careful to keep his head upright. Dr. Lamb, get the door!"

"His pulse is very faint. Did he take something more dangerous than alcohol?" Dr. Jackson said. Dr. Lamb took off Jason's shirt, and that's when they saw the red marks on his arm.

"My God," Dr. Jackson said. "He's been injecting himself, probably with morphine. We need to get him to the college hospital."

"Doctor, you have to treat him here. The college can't know about this," I pleaded. "You and Dr. Lamb took such good care of me when I was hurt, and I told all the football players and crew men about you. I knew your practice has grown! Can't you do me this one favor? Jason Garland is my friend's name. We grew up together in Pittsburgh, and we've always watched out for each other."

Dr. Lamb and Dr. Jackson had an animated conversation in a corner of the room, then said, "Dalton, we don't work for the college, but the students are the mainstay of our practice. We will get your friend cleaned up; then he must stay with us for a week. This isn't the first drug problem we've seen. If anyone asks, tell them he has pneumonia, and we must keep him under observation. Not a word of the real problem. Agreed?"

"Thank you, thank you," I repeated as I pumped both their hands. "Tell me what I can do."

"Be here every afternoon while Dr. Lamb and I see our patients," Dr. Jackson said. "Your friend is not going to have an easy time of it, and someone will have to watch him every minute. For now, he needs to drink some water."

Dr. Lamb and I sat Jason up on their leather exam table, and Dr. Jackson coaxed some water into his mouth.

Jason coughed most of it back out, but his eyes were staying open longer. "Now we need to get him walking."

Around dawn, Jason was finally able to speak. "Where am I? Dalton? What are you doing here and who are these men?" He was trembling, but at least he was talking.

Dr. Jackson took Jason by the jaw and wrenched his face toward him. "Young man, I am Dr. William Jackson, and this is Dr. David Lamb. If it wasn't for Mr. Dalton, you might have died tonight."

"How could that be?" Jason said, looking down at his stocking feet.

"Mr. Garland, you are a morphine addict. I have seen the injection marks, so don't deny it."

Jason slumped again. We maneuvered him into a chair, and he started to cry. I stood beside him and patted him on the back. "These men will help you, Jason." He gave a shudder, and his hands started to shake.

"The morphine must come out of his system to make the craving and shaking stop. That's why one of us must always be with him," Dr. Jackson said.

That week was the most unpleasant of my life. When I wasn't in class, I spent every minute at the doctors' offices, wiping up sweat and vomit. The doctors took care of him in the evening. Jason was furious with me because his back ached from the pounding I gave it, and there was little the doctors could do for his pain.

After a week, Jason had recovered enough to have a coherent conversation. At first, we sat and stared at each other in silence. When I couldn't stand it any longer, I asked how he was feeling.

"How the hell do you think I feel?" he exploded. "I think you cracked my spine! This mustard plaster isn't doing a damn thing."

"Garland, you scared me to death. I thought you were dying, and I didn't know what else to do. I've been covering for you, but our friends are asking questions. You need to get treatment, and New Haven is the last place you should be."

"But I won't graduate!"

I laughed. "You should have thought about that a long time ago. When did you last attend a class? When did you last complete an assignment? You weren't going to graduate anyway. If you stay in New Haven, you will go back to State Street and the dope. The next time you won't be so lucky, and the college or the police will find out.

"You could end up in jail! Or dead! Don't you want a Yale diploma? Here's what I suggest—take it or leave it. Let's get you through the next two days; then you tell Dean Butler that the pressure to graduate has brought on nervous exhaustion and you must rest. Butler is a kindly old gent. I'm betting he will believe you and let you withdraw. You certainly look in bad shape, whatever the cause."

Two days later I walked Jason into Dean Butler's office in Connecticut Hall. Dr. Jackson did me one final favor and wrote a note saying that he recommended that Jason withdraw from Yale for his health, which he didn't object to doing because he 100 percent believed that was the right thing to do. He added that with rest Jason should be able to come back to New Haven in the fall to complete the courses he needed to graduate. Jason didn't have to fake being in distress. The dean took one look at him and said, "Mr. Garland, you have let things go too far. You should thank your friend Dalton here for looking after you."

Jason mumbled something incoherent, and the dean filled out and signed the various withdrawal forms. "Here you are, Mr. Garland. You bring these papers back in the fall when you are feeling better. Now I need to wire your family."

That's when I jumped in. "I've already spoken to them, sir. He'll be on the early morning train, and they will meet him at the station in Pittsburgh tomorrow evening." I had written a wire to his parents telling them he was coming home for a few days "to rest up before final examinations." They hadn't seemed alarmed.

I offered to accompany Jason on the long trip, but he declined. "It will be hard enough to explain to them what has happened after they see how I look." Since he was eating and past the worst of his withdrawal, I didn't insist.

The next morning, I helped Jason pack, and we took a carriage to the newly built New Haven station with its rounded Richardson arch and waited for the 7:30 train to New York. We both were drained from the emotional stress of the last ten days and said little as we kicked the loose stones on the platform until the train arrived. As it pulled in, I was shocked when Jason threw his arms around me in a tight embrace. "Jamie, I will never forget what you have done for me. I am forever in your debt." And with the help of a Pullman porter, Jason got himself up the steep steps to the train and was gone.

After the drama over Jason's near death, the rest of my time in New Haven seemed anticlimactic. I didn't hear from Jason, but his mother let me know that he had gone to the clinic at the Bedford Springs spa for a "rest." I was glad I had saved both his life and his chance for a Yale diploma.

The one bright spot in the run-up to graduation was the letter I received from Cleveland Brooks asking whether I intended to return to the *Sun*. Even after four years in New Haven, the East didn't feel like home to me. Pittsburgh was the center of innovation in America. There could be no place, not New York, not Chicago, that was more central to the country's growth, and as a newsman I could be there to see it all, but I was dreading another confrontation with my father. I was a better man than when I came to Yale four years ago but wasn't sure my father thought the same. One day at the *News* office, Professor Simmons asked me if I had spoken to Brooks. I said I hadn't. He looked at me with a scowl. "You have a real opportunity there, Dalton. Don't waste it." Chastened, I sent a wire to Brooks asking if we could meet the last week of May. I received an immediate answer telling me to be in touch when I was back in Pittsburgh. Even if I wasn't prepared for life in the real world, I was glad that my college days would soon be over.

3

The Flood

GLAD TO ESCAPE THE TENSIONS WITH MY FATHER, I ARRIVED AT THE South Fork Fishing and Hunting Club that late May weekend to contemplate my future. I was happy to see that Rita was there for the weekend as well. After dinner at the clubhouse, we walked back to her family's cottage, one of sixteen that had been built by club members beside the lake. We agreed to meet for breakfast the next morning, and I repaired to my room. The rain had let up that night, and I slept soundly.

I woke early and couldn't get back to sleep, as I wrestled with what direction my life should take. I didn't want to waste my work on the *Yale Daily News* and my summer internship at the *Pittsburgh Sun*, but a more lucrative career in the law or the steel business was tempting. Even though the rain had resumed, heavier than it had been the day before, I started on my usual morning horseback ride into the rolling countryside up past the Unger Farm. To get there I had to cross the top of the dam that had been built forty years earlier to create South Fork Lake.

My chestnut horse slopped along until we came to the bluff that led to the road over the top of the dam, which was less than a quarter mile long and very slippery. In the minute it took me to cross, I could see that the water had continued to rise overnight and was only six feet from the top. From there, I took the bend around the dam's spillway, then up the sharply sloped path to the Unger Farm. Mr. Unger was an early member of the South Fork Fishing and Hunting Club and had managed the club since its inception. He surveyed the lake from his front porch and shook his head when I cantered by. It was not long before I cut my ride short.

When I returned to his farm, Mr. Unger stood in the rain waving his arms for me to stop. "Jamie Dalton, you must not continue! The wind is driving the water over the top of the dam, and the road across isn't passable." A dozen or so people who couldn't get to the club that morning were huddled together on Unger's porch, eyes wide, jaws slack.

The lake had risen another two feet, but I insisted I could make it back.

"I'm sorry, but you must stay here with us. Your father would never forgive me if anything happened to you," Unger insisted.

I shoved my hands in my pockets and took my place on the porch with the others. We all stared at the rising water. Fallen trees, mud, and brush had piled up at the spillway around the right side of the dam where any excess water was supposed to flow.

But it wasn't emptying the way it should. When the club was founded ten years earlier, the lake had been stocked with bass. My father had told me the club had placed a screen over the spillway to prevent the fish from escaping downstream. It was an indulgence that could have tragic consequences because with the spillway blocked there was nowhere for the water to go but over the top of the dam.

"Mr. Unger, with all due respect, something must be done and fast, or this dam will collapse. Don't you have men working on the property?"

"Thirteen Italians are here for the season, strong as hell too. They're holed up in my barn." Unger finally took charge. "I'll take seven of them and try to raise the top of the dam with loads of soil. You take the rest and cut another spillway around the first one, then see what can be done about that damned screen."

None of the men could speak English, but I was able to pantomime what I wanted them to do. We shoveled hard and fast, but the sludge filled wherever we dug. The rain hadn't stopped, and despite my entreaties, the men soon gave up.

If I could get the screen off the spillway, the water would drain out. I asked the men to grab some plank boards that had floated down from a nearby sawmill and build a makeshift bridge from the hillside out onto the top of the spillway. They were able to do that, but when I motioned them to go across, they wouldn't budge. They looked at me like I was crazy, as I inched across the planks on my hands and knees to the narrow concrete ledge until I was right above the frame that held the screen.

Iron latches from the top of the frame were bolted into the concrete of the spillway's crosswalk, and I presumed there were similar attachments at the base. I needed to wrench it out from the top and hope the rush of the water would detach it. But as I looked down, I saw all that had washed up against the screen. I yanked the rusted fasteners back and forth until they broke, but it didn't make any difference. The debris had pushed the frame flush against the concrete, and nothing was going to move it. I slapped at the water in frustration but then began the perilous crawl back over the planks where the men waited. When I got there, they crowded around me, a momentary lift to my spirits among all the tumult. The seven of us made our way back to the farmhouse, and the Italians vanished back into the barn. Then I saw Unger trudging up the hill with his bedraggled group of men.

"We brought barrow after barrow to the crest of the dam, but the water swept it away faster than we could dump it," Unger said.

———

And then the dam was gone. Unger fell to his knees with tears streaming down his face. He looked up at the sky and cried, "Oh my God," over and over.

We couldn't see anything below the dam through the roiling spray, but behind us the level of the lake was dropping fast. One of the men standing on the bluff told me later that in thirty minutes all that was left was mud and shallow puddles where the precious bass flopped around in their death throes.

Standing on the hill at Unger's Farm, I looked down at where the dam had been and at the water rushing out of South Fork Lake down the Little Conemaugh Valley into Johnstown, fourteen miles away. My contemplative weekend was over. Nothing could prove to Cleveland Brooks my passion to be a newsman, and my abilities, more than a firsthand report of what had happened and why. Any second thoughts I had about my career choice had been washed away with the collapse of the dam. I mounted my horse and headed around the river and down the valley.

⸺⸻

As I rode through the rain, I thought of what my father had told me about the South Fork Fishing and Hunting Club and its lake.

To compete with the Erie Canal, Pennsylvania built one of their own in the late 1830s, but the promoters soon ran into a major problem. Not enough water from nearby rivers could be diverted into the canal, and the barges were running aground. They decided to create a reservoir by damming the South Fork Creek in the highlands above Johnstown.

Construction was slow and sporadic, and in 1847 the shoddy, half-completed first effort failed. Since there wasn't much water behind it, no one downstream was affected.

In 1852 the dam was completed. It was sixty-two feet high and 850 feet in length at the top with four hundred acres of forest cleared behind it. The South Fork Dam had created a reservoir, two miles long, a mile wide, and sixty feet deep in the middle. From a nearby tower a guard could regulate the height of the lake by opening and closing five sluice pipes at the base of the dam. On either side were spillways where flood waters could flow out.

But that same year the Pennsylvania Railroad completed the first all-rail run between Philadelphia and Pittsburgh, and by 1854 the Pennsylvania Canal was out of business. In 1857 the railroad purchased the canal's right of way and the South Fork Dam for $7.5 million. But they had no reason to maintain the dam. No repairs were done on it for the next twenty-two years, and the reservoir reverted to a shallow creek.

In 1879 Benjamin Ruff, a tunnel contractor and real-estate investor, bought the South Fork Dam for $2,000 and repaired it to create South Fork Lake. Then he promoted the South Fork Fishing and Hunting Club as a retreat for wealthy Pittsburgh men and their families who were looking to leave the Cresson Springs resort because it had no lake for fishing or sailing. The success of the project was assured when the twenty-nine-year-old Henry Frick, already a leader in the steel industry, bought three shares.

⸺⸻

The flood gained speed as it funneled down the valley. I would be behind the crest of the wave, but I needed to observe as much as I could and get to a telegraph and wire Cleveland Brooks. I stopped at South Fork and was told that the telegraph was out from Mineral Point to Johnstown. I hurried ahead knowing that I would not be in touch with Mr. Brooks anytime soon. Despite all the devastation I was seeing, it thrilled me to have the chance to prove myself.

Just below South Fork, there was a stone viaduct that had stopped the waters, and a lake formed behind it. That momentary pause allowed me to catch up with the surge. The clot of uprooted trees and mud had overwhelmed the bridge, and it was as though there was a second dam collapse. I stared in amazement as pieces of houses, even the stone from the viaduct, hurtled along. It looked like some kind of liquid battering ram. The waters were flowing even faster, and I had to urge my horse to a gallop to keep up. The flood looked like a giant wave hitting the shore, crumbling everything in its path.

The next town down the valley was Mineral Point. The townspeople had received telegraphed warnings, and hundreds of them were perched on the hillside above the river. They watched helplessly as the roiling waters obliterated their village. All the houses, even the town's sawmill, had been sheared away, leaving only soil and rock. The clapboard, the shingles, and the contents of their houses were now part of the rampage.

I spurred my horse along the ridge to East Conemaugh, and over the roar of the river, I heard the plaintive, steady wail of a railroad whistle warning people to escape. I arrived just in time to see a thirty-foot wave of garbage level the town. Residents were scrambling up the steep side of the valley. Passenger and freight trains were stopped on sidings because of track washouts, and the conductors and engineers were urging passengers to leave the cars and get to safety. When the three-story wave hit the town, I saw passengers that hadn't made it to the hillside disappear under the water. As the flood swept over the railroad yards, the freight and passenger cars were tossed about as if they were a child's train set. The water smashed the roundhouse and swept fifty-ton locomotives downstream. Now the waters were filled with scores of railroad cars and houses. Nothing could stand up to the force of the water and the lethal objects it carried. Even worse, I saw a sign saying "Conemaugh Wire" bobbing in the water and knew what danger that portended. The barbed wire that mill produced would entangle every bit of scrap along the way to Johnstown.

Below East Conemaugh was Woodvale, a village that bordered Johnstown on its eastern end. Larger than Mineral Point, it had been built as a model town by the Cambria Iron Company. Neat, white, Cape Cod–style homes lined its symmetrical streets. There had been no warning blast to rouse the residents. As my horse and I, both panting from our race down the valley, watched, the town was reduced to rubble in less than five minutes. Houses, a sawmill, and a streetcar shed, all gone. Townspeople tried to outrun the wave of water, then one by one they all disappeared in the boiling froth. There were horses from the streetcar shed craning their necks for air before slipping beneath the surface. Across the valley I could see a sign that said Gautier Iron Works. Steam from the water hitting the boilers plumed into the sky.

More dangerous than the speed and the lethal height of the wave was what it contained: telegraph poles, railroad cars, horses, human bodies, and miles of barbed wire, certain to catch up anything in its path. I shivered in fright and raised my eyes to heaven. I had never been one for prayer, but I beseeched God to spare all the innocent people in the flood's path.

The water was now headed straight into Johnstown, and I raced ahead to get an observation spot atop the headlands above the city. From there I could see hundreds of houses awaiting their fate. A steady stream of people headed up the paths to higher ground, but I could also see residents desperately trying to secure their property. Horses and dogs and cats ran free on the streets. Church bells tolled in unwitting anticipation of the death to come.

I could hear the roar of the waters, louder than it had been, before I saw the wave. The crest was at its highest, and the water was filled with all the detritus it had corralled on its way down the valley. It looked like a semi-solid moving wall, and I could only imagine the horror the people of Johnstown felt as they saw it bearing down on them.

The houses on the east side of the city were swept away, and from my perch I heard the cries of people clinging to their roofs and saw others swimming through the swirling waters. The flood seemed to sway back and forth on the sides of the valley, picking up speed and height with every movement. The next strike was against the solid-looking stone buildings of the downtown area. For the most part they fared no better than the homes had. The water hit them like an enormous wrecking ball. The three- and four-story buildings buckled at their foundations, the roofs tilted, then whole structures slipped beneath the waters. The First Bank of Johnstown and the Town Hall stayed standing, but that made the leveling of all the rest even starker.

Below the business area, the Little Conemaugh took a sharp right-hand turn a quarter mile before it joined Stony Brook to form the Conemaugh River. The flood raced across the peninsula created by the two streams and slammed into the side of Prospect Hill that rose up hundreds of feet from the banks of Stony Creek. There it seemed to hesitate, and the backwash lurched back into the town. It caught people by surprise who had thought they had weathered the worst and destroyed homes and buildings that had managed to survive the first onslaught. If people weren't knocked senseless by various hard objects that had been swept back, they were pulled below the surface with a gruesome finality. Ten minutes after the first shock, the town had been destroyed.

Looking at my watch I saw that the first wave of the water had hit Johnstown at 4:07, an hour after the dam collapse. The flood roared like a gigantic beast, and a hideous black spray blocked my view of the waters below. I could still hear the ineffectual cries of train whistles trying to warn people of the fate that awaited them. There was a ferocious wind that could be felt in my perch on the bluff. Freight cars were flipping through the air. It was like the town had exploded.

After the waters backed up Stony Creek and buried Johnstown again, the flood lost some of its momentum, but it found an outlet down the Conemaugh. I saw the railroad bridge with its seven stone arches less than a half mile downstream from the confluence of the Little Conemaugh and Stony Creek and wondered whether the viaduct would hold against the onslaught of water and debris. Even at the flood's reduced velocity, I didn't see how it could.

But it did. The debris began to form a barrier, and I could see drowned horses and cows caught up in it. People struggled for their lives in the rushing torrent while dead bodies were tossed around like dolls. With the river still pushing them into the pile of refuse, I could see that they had no chance of escape.

At this point I was torn. I knew that I should do more than merely observe the tragedy unfolding in the valley below. But I also considered the opportunity I had. I could be the first to give an account of the destruction by getting to a working telegraph and wiring what I knew to Mr. Brooks. That's what I decided to do but promised myself that I would return to the wreckage and help out any way I could.

My horse had recovered from our sprint down the valley and was munching the grass on the hillside. I jumped on his back and headed west along the ridge, hoping to find a town that had escaped enough of the flood to still have a working telegraph. I soon saw the Cambria Iron Works, less than a mile below Johnstown. I knew from Father's descriptions of the area during our summer vacations that Cambria was at one time the largest producer of Bessemer steel in the country, bigger than even Mr. Carnegie's Edgar Thomson works, but now the waters had swept through the entire first floor of the plant and steam was rising from the water that covered the scalding steel-making ovens inside. All the telegraph poles were gone, so there was no sense in stopping. Next, I came to Bolivar, the first railroad stop below Johnstown. The railroad bridge there was swept away, but I saw a path along the side of the hill rising out of the valley that I could follow down the river. When I got closer to the town, I was relieved to find telegraph poles still standing and the wire leading west intact. The streets of Bolivar were awash in filth, but I was able to urge my horse through the town to the train depot. The stationmaster was an elderly man with tufts of white hair poking out from beneath his cap and wire glasses perched on his pitted nose. He was hopping from one foot to the other, and when he saw me, he cried out, "Where you coming from, sonny? With all the water and even some bodies floating through here, we know it's something terrible. Johnstown is gone, some say."

"I'm afraid they're right, but before I can say more, I have to beg a favor. Will you send a wire off to Pittsburgh for me, sir? I work for the *Pittsburgh Sun*, and my boss is expecting to hear from me."

"It's Reynolds. Patrick Reynolds. I'll see what I can do for you, but no guarantees your message will get all the way there. Service ain't been reliable since the waters hit."

"Much obliged, sir. You will be doing a great service to help get this vital information out to the world!"

"Not so sure about that, but I'll do it anyway. Here's some paper to write your message. I'll tap it out straightaway."

This was my first dispatch:

To Cleveland Brooks, Pittsburgh Sun: Saw South Fork Dam collapse. Followed 30-foot wall of water that destroyed towns, factories, swept railroad cars and locomotives off tracks. Swirling pile of debris leveled all but two buildings in Johnstown. Stone viaduct below town stopped rubble. Hundreds, maybe thousands drowned. Need instructions soonest. J. Dalton. P.S. Pls tell Richard Dalton Carnegie Bldg I'm OK.

I waited anxiously with Reynolds as we watched more of the rubbish and remains propelled through the flooded streets of Bolivar. I was physically exhausted from my ride down the valley and mentally spent from the horror I had witnessed. Every minute or so a dead body floated by. Men and women clung to tree branches and shouted for help, but there was nothing we could do to reach them. It was a helpless feeling and made the wait last even longer. While I sat in the telegraph office, I thought how my getaway weekend had morphed into this terrible event that was giving me the opportunity to become a true newsman. But as the bodies, living and dead, swept by, I knew I had to be more than a reporter in the face of such an unmitigated disaster.

I wrestled with that conundrum for a long half hour, when the telegraph bell rang, announcing Mr. Brooks's reply:

Dalton: Type set for a one sheet describing events. On street within hour. Swank at Tribune will give you space. Get more raw info. Rewrite here. You're hired.

I was dizzy from what Mr. Brooks was asking me to do. I had graduated from college two weeks ago, and now I was responsible for the initial coverage of a story that would shock the nation. I steeled myself to the task, as I sat on a station bench rereading the telegram over and over. All that mattered was the last line—*"You're hired."* But there was little time to relish that accomplishment, and I wondered how to find Mr. Swank in the chaos left behind by the storm. Then I remembered the promise I had made to myself to aid the relief efforts, and after a sincere thank you to Patrick Reynolds, I rode back to the bluff above the Stone Bridge.

Incredibly, all the wreckage that had piled up at the seven-arch bridge had burst into flames, and there were people being burned alive. Hundreds gathered on the bluff silently taking in the horror below. Some of the younger men took the path down the hillside, and I joined them. By now it was nearly nightfall, but the fire at the viaduct lit our way. With the churning water, it seemed impossible anything could burn, but perhaps some gases in all that mess had ignited. When a dozen of us reached the shores of the lake that was forming back toward the town, we saw how helpless we were to make a difference. The people in the water were either dead or so far away from us that we couldn't reach them, but we waded in and extended planks, branches, anything we could snatch from the shore. For every person we managed to save, a hundred others, dead and alive, became tangled in the burning rubble. Watching people sink under the water was awful, but it was worse hearing the cries of agony from those in the flames. The lake formed by the new dam at the railroad bridge had spread out a mile wide and two miles back into the town. There was a terrible stench, fueled by burning carcasses, animal and human. It was appalling to see charred hands of now dead victims, reaching out of the rubble in a last, desperate attempt at salvation. Even as I tried to save those still alive, I wept.

We worked in shifts through the night. As I caught my breath on the path up from the lake of horrors, I looked back to see the remains of Johnstown churning in the backwash of the flood. People were perched in trees, stuck there because they were still surrounded by water and looked to be asleep. The roof of the Hulbert House, the finest hotel in town, was now part of the blockage at the bridge. Then came the parade of housewares—tables and chairs, ice boxes, even stoves—all driven into the flames.

I had no time to reflect on the causes and consequences of the flood, but I was letting the details sink in so I could report what I had seen to Mr. Brooks. As shocked and appalled as I was, I knew my firsthand account would be the first to reach Pittsburgh. As the night progressed, I went over the many horrors so I wouldn't forget them. When I was overcome with exhaustion, I found shelter beneath the branches of a tall evergreen and fell into a dreamless sleep.

Upon awakening, I realized how hungry I was and headed toward the campfires burning back beyond the offal-filled lake. I rode along the river and was relieved to find tables had been set up with the small amount of food that could be scavenged from the few houses that had escaped the direct blast of the flood. The coffee was rancid and the bread moldy, but the survivors and rescue workers and I gulped it down like it was a Thanksgiving feast.

With my stomach partially filled, I set out to find George Swank. The first ten people I asked didn't even know who he was. Then I came across a man sitting on a log, and he looked lost. His frock coat and flannel pants were caked in mud, and I took a chance he would know the editor of the town's paper.

"Sir, excuse me, but can you direct me to the offices of the *Johnstown Tribune*? I need to find Mr. Swank."

"My boy, you are speaking to a broken man. My family is gone, my house as well, and my law offices are flooded. I know Swank, but as to where he is, I haven't a clue and don't care neither. Out there in that disgusting soup, I reckon, but if he's alive, he'll be at his offices in the bank building. Now leave me be."

Even with the waters receding, I knew my horse couldn't navigate the saturated ground. I tied him to a tree and trudged out through the muck. The smell was overwhelming, but I managed to slog the mile down Main Street to the bank. It hardly looked like the major thoroughfare it had been two days before. All the wooden buildings had been swept away with only cellars and foundations remaining. At the corner of Franklin and Main, the granite bank building stubbornly broadcast its solidity. I looked up to the second floor where I saw "*Johnstown Tribune*" emblazoned on a window. The window was open, and behind it I saw a short, overweight bald man with a pen and pad of paper in his hand looking up and down the street.

"Mr. Swank?" I called up.

"Who are you, sonny?" he threw down.

"James Dalton. Mr. Cleveland Brooks sent me. I'm a . . . ," I hesitated, not knowing whether I should claim my new status, " . . . reporter for the *Pittsburgh Sun*."

"Why would Brooks send me a greenhorn like you? Can't you see I'm busy here?" he blustered. It didn't look like he was doing much more than looking out the window.

"I was able to give Mr. Brooks a firsthand account because I was already in the area, and now he wants me to work with you to follow the story."

"Come up if you must, but only because it's Brooks."

The door to the *Tribune*'s second-floor office was gone, and I tiptoed up the rickety stairs. Mr. Swank kept his vigil at the window, paper littering the floor around his straight-back wooden chair. Then he turned and eyed me suspiciously. "Your daddy a member of that damned South Fork club?"

"Yes, sir." I knew I shouldn't lie to this man.

"Well, him and all his rich Pittsburgh friends better watch themselves. Everyone around here knew that dam would burst someday."

Rather than defend the club, I took another tack. "That's what Mr. Brooks wants me to find out. How did this terrible thing happen? Why did the dam break? He knows of my connection to South Fork and hopes I can use that to get some answers."

Father would already be furious I had taken a job at the newspaper, and now I was digging into the private preserve of his friends and clients. But I was determined to pursue the story, wherever it would take me.

"They call me a fair-minded man here in Johnstown," Swank said. "Right now, I'm keeping a diary of all I'm seeing. I've got a good idea where the blame lies, but I won't jump to any conclusions. If you want to poke around, be my guest, but I'm not going to trust the son of a member of that infernal club until I see you won't bury anything."

I tried to sound more sure of myself than I was. "You needn't worry about that. I must get back up to South Fork as soon as possible and speak with Colonel Unger. He knows more about the dam than anyone."

On the way out of town, I saw the recovery efforts unfolding. Men with black armbands had been rounded up by a citizen's council to patrol the streets. There had already been reports of looting, a despicable comment on human nature. But some men searched for bodies, while others were helping anyone who look distressed. An outdoor mortuary had been set up on the east end of town, near the cemetery. As I rode by, I could see row after row of bodies. Men and women with bowed heads shuffled along, trying to identify lost family members. In the short time I passed by, I heard two cries of despair as bodies were recognized. One man lifted the corner of a sheet, then sank to his knees in silent agony. There was no question about the horror of this terrible flood. My challenge would be to sift through all the information and opinion and write my story on the disaster as thoroughly and accurately as possible.

The rain had finally stopped, and I was able to ride faster but still had to contend with fallen trees and swollen creeks. Down in the gorge to my right was the stark reminder of the flood's destruction. Nothing was still standing. Mills tilted on their sides and houses were reduced to kindling. The difference today was that I could see men, women, and children picking through what the flood had left behind in the vain hope of putting their lives back together. Nothing would ever be the same for them, even if they couldn't accept that gloomy conclusion yet.

My world wouldn't be the same either. In the last twenty-four hours, while the Little Conemaugh Valley suffered, my career as a newsman was decided for me. I hoped my parents, Father, in particular, would see that journalism was my destiny.

After a two-hour ride, I was back at the bluff overlooking the empty lake. It didn't look like there had ever even been a dam there. It was only two hillocks facing each other with nothing in between. The water had dug a quarter-mile-wide trench that was even deeper than the floor of what had been the lake. I could see dead fish littering the mushy ground, and an unpleasant smell wafted up to me. There were rotten stumps from the trees that had been cut to create the reservoir. It was unimaginable that I ever spent my summers rowing and sailing on this very spot. I wanted to describe the scene in my reports, but it was more important that I understand why the dam had failed. Colonel Unger was where I would start.

Colonel Elias J. Unger had been a fixture at the club for as long as we had been members. He was a short, stocky man, with brown hair that hung over his ears in a sloppy sort of way. I knew from my parents that he had risen to be a successful hotelier in Pittsburgh, and that's why the club partners selected him to manage the South Fork Club. To assure he would accept the job, the partners had also granted him one ownership share, so he was both a member and an employee.

I knocked on the farmhouse door. When there was no answer, I knocked harder. Unger peeped out. "Ah, Dalton," he said. "It's all so awful."

"Worse than you can imagine," I answered. Then I told him of the destruction the failure of the dam had caused. The whole time I spoke he was slumped over with his head in his hands, not saying a word.

I didn't want Colonel Unger to be fearful of me, so I eased into what I wanted to ask him. "You don't know this, but I was at the club this week-end without my family to do some thinking. I've been pondering a certain career, and my father and I had come to a disagreement. But after seeing these terrible events, I've made my choice. I now work for a newspaper." Unger sat bolt upright, but before he could say anything, I continued. "When we talked in your yard before the dam collapsed, I had not been hired yet, but now I have. Today I am speaking to you as a reporter for the *Pittsburgh Sun*."

With that revelation, Unger became even more agitated and struggled to find his words. "I-I-ah-I don't care how long I have known your family, you are not going to take advantage of me, Dalton. I was hired to manage the club by the most successful men in Pittsburgh. If it ever got out that I was supplying information to a newspaper, they would have my head. I may already be their scapegoat."

"No one is talking about assigning blame. I want to learn as much as I can about the dam and the club, and no one knows more about them than you. Having the facts known can only help you. I'll keep your name out of whatever I report."

Unger rubbed his temples while he weighed his next response. "This will all come out whether I speak to you or not. Ask your questions, and I'll decide which I'll answer."

The Colonel and I stared at each other before I nodded in agreement and ventured my first question. "I know the dam and the lake were owned by the railroad and that Benjamin Ruff got a hold of it to start the club. How did that happen?"

For the next half hour, Unger told me what he knew about the South Fork Fishing and Hunting Club. The sale of the dam. The creation of the club. The inadequate repairs and modifications to the dam. The concerns of the people in the villages in the Little Conemaugh Valley and Johnstown about the safety of the dam.

There was one thing that Unger didn't mention. "Colonel, tell me about the spillway. It was designed to let out the overflow from the lake. Was the water getting through before the flood?"

Unger gave me a guilty look. "I won't talk about the spillway!" Then he started pacing around the room, looking for a match to light his pipe. He found one and was annoyed when it wouldn't light. "Ain't that enough?"

"Please, sir, just one more thing. If the townspeople were so worried, why didn't they send anyone to inspect the dam?"

"That's not my tale to tell," he snapped. "You'll have to find that out for yourself. The place you might start is at the Cambria plant." I pushed him to explain, but the Colonel was done talking. After I thanked him for his hospitality and forthrightness, I rode fast back to Johnstown. I was thrilled with all the information I had for my dispatch to the *Sun*.

When I got back to the bank building around six Saturday night, I organized my notes from the conversation with Colonel Unger. When Mr. Swank read them, he drawled, "Not bad, pup. We still don't have a line back to Pittsburgh, but it's expected to be put through tonight. In the meantime, I'll send a runner down to Bolivar, and they will wire it from there."

"If it's all the same to you, I'd prefer to take it myself," I argued.

"Suit yourself, but get back here fast. When we get the wire repaired, I'll be in touch with Brooks. I've already started writing up the headlines by hand and posting them in the window downstairs. You can see all the people gathering there to see the latest news."

Without another word, I took off, sloshing down the street. With all the mud, I knew I wouldn't be able to ride. The most direct route to Bolivar was down the north side of town and then across a rope bridge that had been strung over the Conemaugh since the Stone Bridge was still impassable.

There was destruction everywhere and a pervading stench from the decaying bodies. It was unlike anything I had ever experienced and hoped never to again. Relief efforts were better organized, and men sorted through the piles of debris, trying to find the living. When they found someone breathing, they were taken on a stretcher to a makeshift hospital on an untouched field a half mile from the town up Stony Creek. Other volunteers hauled the dead to the outdoor mortuary I had seen the day before. Not everyone was pitching in. There were small crowds of men hanging around uncorked whiskey barrels, and they snarled at me as I passed by. No good could come of that, I thought, but didn't stick around to find out what.

The burning pyre at the Stone Bridge lit up the sky, and the forty-acre lake behind it was a disgusting mix of destroyed homes and lives. Again, I vowed to return and do what I could to help the people that remained, but I had to get my notes to Mr. Brooks. Men stumbled across the rope bridge that dangled over the river. With my time in boats and sculls, I slipped only once and managed to pull myself up with my shoulder strength. On the other side, a group of reporters from other newspapers in the area had gathered and pounced on me with questions. They didn't realize I was a working journalist, or they would have waylaid me. After a few short words, I was past them and on my way to Bolivar.

I was surprised to see all the debris and even an occasional body float-ing downstream from the bridge. Workers at the Cambria Plant were scurrying around the grounds, looking to repair the flood damage and get the big furnaces fired by Monday. When I reached the depot at Bolivar, I was thrilled that there was no one else in line for the telegraph. My notes from the interview with the Colonel and what I had picked up around town were wired to Mr. Brooks in less than fifteen minutes. His quick reply was succinct: "Good work. Keep at it." As I made my way back to Swank's office in the dark, I planned out my next few days. Passing the Cambria plant, I saw that the walls were still standing but there were no workers to be seen. Remembering Unger's tip, I would return there on Monday and see what I could find.

Tomorrow was Sunday, and I had planned to aid in the relief efforts. But I hesitated. Had I gotten all my facts straight? I wanted to impress Cleveland Brooks. Even more important, would my reporting show my father that I had picked the right career? But my humanity outweighed my insecurities. I needed to help the people of Johnstown.

When I arrived back at the *Journal Review* offices, I found Mr. Swank bent over the telegraph, furiously dotting and dashing, and I realized that the wire back to Pittsburgh must have been restrung. "Anything more you want to tell Brooks?" he asked.

"Nothing for now," I mumbled, feeling the effects of my long day of navigating the torn-up valley. "Mind if I get some sleep?" I asked, motioning to a couch against the far wall away from the windows.

"Rest up. New tracks are being laid overnight, and the Pittsburgh trains will be here by noon. 'Nother busy day," Swank said with a grin.

I threw myself down on the couch. In the few seconds before my eyes closed, I smelled the dank, pungent aroma of the wet clothes that I had been wearing for forty-eight hours straight.

—◡—

I made my way back to the tent city the next morning to scrounge whatever food was still available. Besides exchanging their tragic tales of loss, survivors talked of what was to come. Disease was the greatest fear, particularly the dreaded typhus infection that could become an epidemic in mere days. To prevent that, volunteers boiled pots of water, then waited for it to cool before ladling it out to the miserable-looking people lined up to slake their thirst. There was some good news. Robert Pitcairn, director of the Western Division of the Pennsylvania Railroad, was leading the relief efforts, and he announced that he had raised over $50,000 in less than an hour. He was calling for people everywhere, not just western Pennsylvania, to donate whatever they could to aid the victims of this massive tragedy. He cited a figure of 1,500 dead, a shocking but plausible number from what I had witnessed.

Mr. Pitcairn had mustered railroad crews, and ten miles of lost track had been relaid overnight. Not wanting to waver from my resolve to aid the relief efforts, I avoided the mass of wires that had come from Mr. Brooks. My exclusive was long gone. The Associated Press had broadcast the disaster to the world, and reporters from every big city in America were headed to a little town nestled away in the Allegheny Mountains. I wanted to stay on the story, but I joined the aid workers instead.

Efforts were more organized that Sunday morning. Troops had arrived from Philadelphia at the behest of the governor of Pennsylvania, and military discipline was taking hold. Wagons from neighboring towns brought food and other vital supplies, and the troops had organized fast-moving distribution lines for the starving townspeople. The talk now wasn't just of lost loved ones but of how people were determined to rebuild the town. Their indomitable spirit was inspiring.

The embers at the Stone Bridge were still glowing, but the troops were making headway in scattering the debris. That was allowing more water to escape downstream, and the lake that had formed back to the city had receded. What was left behind was even more repellent than the rubble-filled water had been. The unrecognizable streets were a morass of devastation. The simple remains of people's live were scattered everywhere: dirty dolls, snatches of clothing, shattered pieces of plates and glasses, splintered chairs. Most revolting of all were the body parts. I saw detached arms and legs, even a couple of heads, so covered in mud that they could have been a worn kickball. Lost, crying children wandered through the mess, until they were comforted by volunteers who tried to reunite them with their families. If they still had families.

Given my youth and size, I was assigned to pull out pieces of the houses and factories that were stuck in the pervasive mud. Working alongside the other young men, I felt a part of the effort to put Johnstown on the road to recovery. The reporting was important to me personally, and if I believed what I had told Colonel Unger, it was ever more important to alert the world why this tragedy had happened. But if I was honest with myself, at that moment I knew that I had to help the people of this devastated city.

After five hours of work, the crew took a lunch break. I headed to the reopened train depot to organize the arriving relief workers. It was then that I saw a familiar lilac dress alighting from the train.

"Mother, what in the name of God are you doing here?"

Throwing her arms around me, she cried, "Oh, Jamie, we were all sick with worry, knowing you were at South Fork. I had to see that you were safe."

"Didn't Mr. Brooks give you my message? I told him to tell you I was fine."

"He told your father. We were both surprised he's hired you as a reporter. That's why I stopped by the *Sun* offices on the way to the train. Mr. Brooks assured me he would not put you in any danger. I'm glad to have met the man you'll be working for. He seems like a gentleman."

He wasn't to be my third-grade teacher, but this was not the time to argue the point. "How were you able to get on the train? I was told it was for reporters and relief workers only."

She gave me a pout. "Don't you think I'm capable of being a relief worker? Our suffrage group and the Red Cross sent us here. See that tiny lady moving toward town? That's Clara Barton. With her work in the Civil War, no one knows more about field relief than she does. I will be working under her guidance."

My mother's pride and determination showed a side of her I had never seen before. "What a fine thing to do," I told her.

"Don't look so surprised. Now tell me what you are doing in Johnstown. I hoped you were safe up at the club."

Was I ready to explain to Mother my decision to become a reporter for the *Sun*? She had been more accepting of my inclination to go into journalism than my father, but I didn't want to justify myself right at that moment. "That's a very long story, Mother. Maybe we can find a quiet moment tonight, and I will tell you the whole saga. For now, suffice it to say, that I have cast my lot as a newspaper man. This flood, the devastation, the fire at the bridge, it was all too much to ignore. I got word to Mr. Brooks of the initial disaster, and he hired me on the spot."

"I was afraid of something like that. You know your father won't be pleased."

"Mother, when I saw the dam break at South Fork, I knew what I needed to do and followed the waters rampaging down the valley. I saw all the death and destruction and knew I could be the first to report this catastrophe to the world. Would you want me to ignore all that? Would Father?"

"Jamie, I'm not sure what your father will say, but I am very proud of you." She smiled, then looked around the camp. "What will you do with yourself today?"

"They have me lugging plumbing and roofs and anything else you can imagine out of the muck. Maybe I can bathe in a creek later on. I must be a little ripe. Let's plan on meeting at the food tables around sundown."

After another six hours pitching in to mitigate the sheer awfulness of the flood's destruction, I was exhausted and dragged myself to the makeshift commissary. When I didn't see Mother, I went looking for her closer to the Red Cross tent. I was shocked when I spotted her. Her dress was covered in mud and blood, and she was dressing the wounds of a steelworker who had been burned trying to rescue people from the fire at the bridge. Was this Eleanor Ricketson Dalton of Pittsburgh? I had not seen my mother except for vacations when I was at Yale, but this was a very different woman from the one who seemed so delicate when I was younger.

"How are you, Jamie? I forgot when we were meeting. Give me a few more minutes, and I'll come with you. I'm not hungry, but you must be starved."

The steelworker was in terrible pain, but he smiled up at Mother like she was an angel of mercy as she applied a salve and wrapped a cotton bandage around his leg that was burned from ankle to knee. "Young man, I'm sorry I don't have anything for your pain, but this ointment should keep your wound from getting infected."

He grimaced, not comprehending what she had said. Then in very broken English he mumbled a reply that sounded something like "Danke, danke. You help me, schöene dame."

"How gallant," Mother responded with a big smile. "Now if you will excuse me, I must dine with my son." We walked away, and Mother said to me, "Before we go, I need to check in with Mrs. Barton. Jamie, you can't believe what a marvel she has been. So calm, so organized. She seems to anticipate every new calamity. Stay right here, and I'll be back in just a minute."

She returned with Mrs. Barton, who was dressed in all black, except for a white cap emblazoned with the ubiquitous red cross. The tiny lady took both of my mother's hands and looked into her eyes. "Thank you for your extraordinary efforts in such difficult circumstances."

Mother blushed and said, "Thank you for the opportunity."

Mrs. Barton went back to her tent, and we walked the hundred yards to the commissary, where I filled a plate with beans and a thin slab of something that looked like meat. Mother chose a piece of bread spread with a dab of jelly, and we found a log to sit on. "Not much like the porch at South Fork," I said, trying to lighten the mood.

Mother paid no attention to the pleasantry. "How can something like this happen? I've heard of terrible storms and their devastating effect but nothing like this. Mr. Pitcairn has said there are over a thousand deaths. He has been so strong in organizing the relief."

"I am sure Mr. Pitcairn is sincere in wanting to help, but he may have other motives as well," I replied. Mother stared at me and didn't say anything, so I continued. "The railroad depends on the towns around here for its commerce, but there is another more personal reason. Because he is a principal shareholder in the club, he and others may be forced to shoulder the blame for all that has happened."

"Others? You can't mean the members! What does the club have to do with this act of God?" Mother asked.

It would not be the last time I would hear the phrase "act of God."

"Mother, don't you know? It was the collapse of the dam at South Fork that caused this," I said, waving my arm to indicate the death and destruction all around us. Then I told her everything I had learned from Colonel Unger: the removal of the sluice pipes, the shoddy repairs of the dam, the unforgivable screening of the spillway. I was bursting with pride that I would be the first one to tell the world why the Johnstown Flood had happened. I hoped she would tell my father what a good newspaper man I was. And that he would agree that I had made the right choice.

But I could see Mother was shaken by what I had told her and wasn't ready to admit any blame on the part of the club or any of its members. "Jamie, how could any of us have known about these problems? Your father and I, all our very closest friends, we were and are in the dark about all of this." Then I saw a look of panic in her eyes. "You haven't . . ."

"Reported any of it to Mr. Brooks?" Mother hadn't seen the extras on the streets of Pittsburgh. "I'm sorry, but of course, I have. This is my job now, Mother. It's my responsibility to find out the facts. I'm not looking to blame anyone, but I do want people to know what happened. They have that right."

"Do you have any notion of the effect this might have on all of us?" she answered. "People are just looking for a chance to cast aspersions on any of our class. Think of the shame. There may even be financial consequences."

For all her newfound progressive ideas, Mother was still loyal to the world of wealth that had engulfed her since birth. Was she blind to the contradiction? Maybe I could only expect so much from my parents. It worried me that Mother did not recognize her internal struggle and would drink to relieve the stress. And be back at Cresson Springs.

"Mother, I won't be the cause of that reaction because it already exists. Don't you know that the people around here call South Fork the Bosses Club? They will look for someone to blame, and it won't be God."

Mother seemed taken aback be my casual blasphemy. "To have you associated with the sensationalizing of this event! Jamie, this could be devastating for your future. And I don't even want to think of how your father may react." There were tears in her eyes.

I tried to reassure her. "I'm not going to exaggerate anything. I'll report it all as honestly as I can. Better for me to write the story and be more accurate than the New York and Chicago papers who only want scary headlines to increase sales."

"Oh, son, it's all so confusing. I know you will tell the truth, but I'm terrified where this might lead."

I leaned toward her and kissed her on the cheek. "You must trust me, Mother. I haven't become a rogue overnight." I thought for a second. "There are many questions to be answered. After talking to Colonel Unger, the one thing I don't understand is why the people of Johnston, the mayor, the town council, and the like didn't make sure there was nothing wrong with the dam when it was such an obvious threat. Mr. Unger said they used to laugh about the dam breaking as if it was something that could never happen. Even more curious, why didn't someone at Cambria Steel inspect it when their entire plant could be destroyed, as it almost has been?"

"Jamie, have you ever heard of Captain Bill Jones?" I hadn't. "I have never met the gentleman, but your father speaks well of him. He says he is the best steelman in the country. Before he worked for Mr. Carnegie at the Thomson works, he ran the Bessemer furnace at Cambria when it was producing more steel than any other plant in the country. I heard on the train that he has brought a carload of supplies and three hundred men with him. He must care a great deal for Johnstown and its townspeople. No one will give you better information about the workings of Cambria Steel than Captain Jones."

I immediately knew how important this was. "Do you have any idea where he might be?" Mother shook her head. "I must speak with him as soon as possible, but you shouldn't be alone. Do you have shelter for tonight?"

"Mrs. Barton has arranged a tent for me. That's what she was telling me when you saw us talking."

"As long as I know you're safe, I will try to find Captain Jones. Do you know what he looks like?"

"I've never met the man, but I've heard he is short and, some say, very handsome. Everyone in the steel business seems to be short," she said with a hint of a smile.

"That's a good lead, Mother. Now please meet me right here at noon tomorrow."

"My son worrying about me! I like that." We embraced, and I went searching for Captain Jones.

⎯ ⚬ ⎯

Everyone I spoke with in Johnstown seemed to know this legend. "He fought at Fredericksburg and Chancellorsville." "He made Cambria Steel a success." "Old Man Carnegie pays him the same salary as the president of the United States."

I was told Jones would likely be at the Cambria works. I got to the plant near midnight and despaired of finding anyone there, but the whole place was abuzz with activity. Then I saw one man standing on a pile of iron ingots speaking to the workers and knew he must be who I was looking for.

He stood ramrod straight, and that made him look taller than I expected. I guessed he was in his late forties with a worn but pleasant face. He had a high forehead and a long, straight nose. His hair was brown and thick without a touch of gray, and he was clean shaven except for a well-trimmed mustache. His eyes scanned the yard, and he looked very comfortable in his command of the situation. There was a group of men awaiting his orders.

Trying not to appear as out of place as I felt, I strode up to him and blurted out, "Captain Jones, you don't know me, but I'm James Dalton, a reporter for the *Pittsburgh Sun*."

"Don't have time for any newspapermen," he said, glaring at me.

"My father, Richard Dalton, is an admirer of yours. It's important for people to know the facts from someone as knowledgeable as you about Johnstown and its relationship with the South Fork Club." It was a quick decision to invoke my father's name that I hoped I wouldn't regret.

He turned and gave me a hard look. Was he weighing whether this was an opportunity to cast the bosses in a more favorable light? "Don't matter to me who your father is." At least I had his attention. "I can give you five minutes. No more!"

"Who's this rube, Captain?" one of his men said.

"Name's Dalton. Says he's a reporter for the *Pittsburgh Sun*," Jones told them. My name and the paper's name didn't mean anything to them, but they understood "reporter." And they didn't like it.

The men, a dozen or more, were all shapes and sizes, but they did have some things in common. There weren't any Eastern Europeans in the group, so I assumed they must be English or Scottish, maybe German. They wore dark and dirty caps and had massive shoulders. Most distinctive of all, each had a distrustful, unblinking stare. "Bah, one of those rich man's newspapers that tells us we are lucky to have jobs when the bosses be cuttin' our wages or tellin' us to work longer hours. We have no use for your kind."

Another worker started in. "Yeah, word is the rich man's club up the valley is the cause. Wanting to sail their pretty little boats and catch the fish they stock in their lake. Them's take no heed of the rest of us, but we're tougher and stronger and will outlast them." He spat on the ground, and the men around him clapped him on the back.

Their hostility made me sweat. The *Sun* often sided with the workers in their labor disputes with the steel interests, but this was not the time to argue. Captain Jones let me stew for a minute, then said, "You men get back to work clearing the debris out of the mill. Let me worry about greenhorn reporters."

The men gave me one last dirty look and walked away. Captain Jones led me to two metal chairs that had miraculously escaped the fury of the flood.

"Not much I can do about what they believe. I want them working hard as they can, and if they think I'm in the owners' pocket, they won't pay me no heed. But that's not what you're here about, is it?"

"No, sir, it's not. I have heard that you worked at Cambria Steel for ten years and are very well-respected here in the valley. What can you tell me about relations between the town and the club and the steel company? I've learned something about the dam and its history from Colonel Unger, whom you may know, but I have more questions."

He shook his head with displeasure. "Useless fellow." I told myself not to mention Unger again.

Despite my initial misstep, Jones was very candid. He told me how the townspeople over time stopped worrying about the water in the South Fork Lake looming over them. That the town had approved the removal of trees and the flattening of the riversides for new factories and homes, making the Little Conemaugh Valley an unobstructed funnel pointing straight at Johnstown.

His most important revelation was a negative report on the dam that Dan Morrell, president of Cambria Steel and the so-called King of Johnstown, had commissioned, but it was ignored after he became a member of the South Fork Club. Jones assumed that report was shown to club member Robert Pitcairn. Pitcairn again. The Pitcairns lived very near my parents in Shadyside, and both of our families attended Calvary Church. I hoped Mother would introduce me.

Captain Jones told me more than I expected, but I had one last question about a rumor I had picked up in the relief camp. "Workers in the camps are saying that the Carnegie crowd allowed this to happen. That they let the repairs go because they wanted the dam to fail, so the flood would wipe out their biggest competitor, the Cambria Works."

Captain Jones eyes flashed in anger. "That's the most damn fool idea I ever heard. The Thomson plant produces twice the steel of Cambria, and Carnegie sets prices for the industry. He don't need to worry about the competition The whole notion is beyond ridiculous. Don't put garbage like this in the *Sun* or you'll look as stupid as those big-city papers will when they run it."

"Captain, you have been very generous with your time. Many thanks."

We shook hands, and I felt his strength. This was a smart, skilled man, and I could see why he was so revered, both by his men and his bosses. Maybe when we were both back in Pittsburgh our acquaintance could land me a tour of the Thomson plant. I was already setting my sights on what I hoped would be my next assignment.

I shook myself out of my reverie. There was no time to waste. I needed to get another wire off to Mr. Brooks with the information Captain Jones had given me, then I would find Mother. I wanted to know she was safe, but an introduction to Mr. Pitcairn was also on my mind.

After a lengthy telegram to Mr. Brooks from the *Tribune* offices laying out all that Captain Jones had told me, his reply was most urgent: "RETURN PITTSBURGH IMMEDIATELY." I thanked Mr. Swank for all his help and headed back to the camp.

There I saw Mother comforting a group of children who had been orphaned by the flood. She had a consoling smile on her face, and I hesitated to pull her away from them. "Mother, I need to speak with you."

She told the children she would be right back; then we walked several yards away. "What is it, dear?" she asked.

"I must return to Pittsburgh to confer with Mr. Brooks, and I can't leave you here alone."

"I already had this discussion with your father before I left. I am a grown woman who has raised three children, and I am perfectly capable of taking care of myself."

I thought back to all the times that Mother did not leave her bed for days and would have to recover at Cresson Springs. She searched my face and seemed to know what I was thinking.

"James, those days are gone. I haven't had a spell of melancholy in more than a year. You can see how I have held up in these dreadful conditions. It's given me a purpose, and I will stay here until I am ready to go.

"But Father will . . ."

"Let me worry about your father. You say you have a job to do. Go do it. When I am no longer needed here, I will see you back at home."

We wrangled over this for more than twenty minutes, but I was getting nowhere. Resigned, I changed the subject. "Have you seen Mr. Pitcairn?"

"What do you want with Robert?"

"He's run the railroad here and in Pittsburgh for more than ten years, and he's a club member. He has to know something about the dam."

"Jamie, I've warned you not to venture into this dangerous territory."

"And I've told you that I am not looking to cast blame. I want to report the truth about what happened here, nothing more."

"I don't know whether he is in Johnstown or gone back to Pittsburgh," Mother answered. Since we were at an impasse over her return to town and my coverage of the flood disaster, I hugged her and made her promise not to take any thoughtless risks. Walking away, I felt the dread of what my father would say about leaving her here and my new job at the *Sun*.

I found my way to the depot in Bolivar, where I could be assured of a train back to Pittsburgh. It departed at 4 p.m. and was jammed to overflowing. I stood the whole way for the four-hour trip, twice as long as usual, but it gave me time to consider all that I had seen. As focused as I was on the story of the dam, it was impossible to ignore the sheer horror that the Johnstown Flood had brought to the Little Conemaugh Valley and beyond. Homes and business destroyed, families torn asunder, survivors searching in vain for their loved ones. But there was also the heroism of the men and women rallying to the aid of others and their indomitable determination to rebuild Johnstown and make it flourish. These good people deserved to know why the flood happened and who was responsible. But was I the one to tell them? Only weeks before I had been a Yale undergraduate with a little more than a year's experience on the college paper.

4

Who Is Responsible?

ARRIVING BACK IN PITTSBURGH FROM JOHNSTOWN, I DISEMBARKED AT the Central Station and went to the newspaper's offices on Fifth Avenue. I could see through the window that the pressmen were still working frantically to put out all the extras coming from the newsroom. Exhausted from the trip, I took the stairs with less than my usual vigor. Brooks spied me as soon as I hit the fourth-floor landing and brought me into his office.

"You've done good work, Dalton, but we have much to discuss."

We went back over all I had seen and what I had learned from Colonel Unger and Captain Jones. Brooks wanted to know all the basic facts about the flood and the destruction it caused, and I answered his questions as best I could.

How high was the crest? Up to 60 feet in spots, but 35 feet most of the time. How fast did the flood move? The waters roared down the valley at 20 miles per hour, taking only 45 minutes from the dam collapse to when it hit downtown Johnstown at 40 mph. Four square miles were destroyed. How many lives were lost? Thought to be more than 1,700 but more bodies were being found every day. Many of the dead were unidentified. Homes and businesses? More than 1,000 homes and 280 businesses lost, valued at over $15 million dollars, $1 million to repair the Cambia Plant alone. Looters? The self-appointed police force has had the city under control since the morning after the flood.

"You've done well in digging out the facts, but there are other things we need to talk about. First, you didn't file anything for twenty-four hours," Brooks said.

"But, sir, I was aiding the relief efforts. If you could have seen . . ."

"Very noble of you, Dalton, but when I hired you, I expected you to report, not become part of the story. I know it was hard seeing all those people in distress, but others were there to help them. You got the big picture, but you need to report the despair of the man who lost his home in the flood. The horror of the woman who watched her children sink beneath the waters. We need to tell our readers the stories of what people like them experienced. You missed that. You are young, and I hope you learn from this if I am to keep you on."

"But I thought I was hired," I said in a shaky voice.

"You have to prove yourself. There is also a question of whether you can report on the city's elite. That can't be a problem.

"I'll be honest with you, Dalton. One of the reasons I want you at the *Sun* is the contacts you have. You can get to people no one else on the staff could. But if you won't report on what they say or do, it won't do the paper much good."

I wanted to stand up for myself without seeming defiant. "I reported on the cause of the flood, even when it involved the South Fork Club, but I didn't want to draw any simple conclusions."

"I appreciate that you reported the straight facts, but now you're back in Pittsburgh. You will have to cover stories where your father and the men he works for are involved. Can you do that?"

When I didn't respond right away, Brooks continued. "Your mother told me this could be difficult for you. I don't want you to burn any bridges with the sources you already have, but you can't pull any punches either." It seemed that Mother's conversation with Cleve Brooks had covered more than just my safety in Johnstown.

I squared my shoulders and put on my most serious look. "Mr. Brooks, I assure you dealing with my father and his associates will not be an issue."

Brooks narrowed his gaze. "We'll have to see about that. For now, you need to find out how the club members plan to defend themselves. The 'yellow press' has already decided it's the fault of the South Fork Hunting and Fishing Club, pure and simple. There is a cartoon of Carnegie, Frick, Mellon, and the others with fishing poles in their hands sitting on top of the dam and laughing, along with a bit of doggerel: 'All the horrors that hell could wish/Such was the price that was paid for—fish!'"

"Mr. Brooks, I hope you realize from my reports that it is nowhere near as simple as that."

"Then you have to dig out the story. What will you do now?"

"I plan on talking to Robert Pitcairn. He's with the railroad and a club member. I'm sure he knows more about the situation at the dam than anyone else."

"Good man! Go get an interview with him. Otherwise he will be making vague pronouncements that all the other papers will report as well. We need exclusives, Jamie!"

But I knew the path to Mr. Pitcairn was through my father, and I wasn't sure he would be willing to acknowledge my new status with the *Sun*, let alone furnish the entrée I needed to meet with Robert Pitcairn. I left the office and hopped a streetcar back to Amberson Avenue for a proper bath, some rest, and a much-needed change of clothes.

Father was home around six and immediately went into his study. I didn't follow him because I didn't think he wanted to be interrupted, but then I heard him call out, "James," in a stern, annoyed tone.

Without any pleasantries he began. "You mother has wired me, and I understand that you intend to defy my wishes." We were both standing, glaring at each other.

"Father, you can't fathom what happened at South Fork. I saw as much as anyone, from the collapse of the dam to the burning bodies at the Stone Bridge. All I could think about was how I could best use my education, my talents to convey that scene with as much skill as possible. You can't deny me this opportunity."

"But I must try when I see what a mistake you are making," Father sputtered. "Why would you want to be a part of the newspaper rabble that never does anything more than stir up passions and inevitably gets the facts wrong?"

"Cleveland Brooks is a man of integrity, and he demands accuracy from his reporters," I answered.

Father scoffed at me. "How do you intend to support yourself? You want to be independent? Fine. See how far that meager salary will go when you need to buy your own food and find a place to live. You can't expect me to support you when you so disrespect me!"

I was shocked. Was my own father willing to cut me off so suddenly, so brutally? Not knowing what else to say, I turned heel and made for the door of the study.

"And don't expect me to introduce you to Robert Pitcairn. Heaven knows how you and Brooks will mangle and twist anything he tells you." Mother must have told him my plan.

I stopped and stared back at him. "I thought you would have more faith in me." I shook my head and left the room. On my way upstairs I ignored Wills, who had been kneeling on the landing taking in every word of my argument with Father.

I stayed in my room for the rest of the night, not even coming down for dinner. Why was Father so opposed to me working for a newspaper? At that moment I considered that he could fear what I might discover. After very little sleep I was up early and donned my best suit. I grabbed some toast from the kitchen, then was on the streetcar for my first full day as a reporter for the *Pittsburgh Sun*.

———

Mr. Brooks didn't seem fazed that my family's introduction to Mr. Pitcairn was not to be forthcoming.

"Jamie, you are going to have to learn that the rules of polite society don't apply here. We're the press, the fourth estate, and we have the right to question anyone we want. They may refuse to answer our questions, but we still have the right, I would say the duty, to ask them. I can understand why your father doesn't want to introduce you to Pitcairn. The members of South Fork aren't just a club for frolicking in the mountains. They are a serious group of men who protect their interests at all costs. If your father is seen as helping the newspapers that are inquiring about those interests, including their recreation, then he will be shunned, his career in ruins. I want you to become a good newspaperman, but you must learn that your family's connections, while an advantage, can be dangerous as well, for you and for them."

I wasn't so sure about that but asked Mr. Brooks how I could contact Mr. Pitcairn. For the first time, he showed his impatience.

"Like any other young reporter would! Use anything in your means to track him down. Catch him on the way to lunch or go to his office and tell them that you will wait there until Pitcairn agrees to see you. They won't like that but do it anyway. That's another part of being a reporter that you'll have to learn: your upbringing tells you to be deferential, but that only goes so far. If you are going to succeed you will need to be persistent, even obnoxious. Can you make yourself do that?"

"If that's what it takes to succeed, I can put my refinements aside."

"I hope so. I should introduce you to the newsroom," Brooks said. He stepped out from behind the railing that defined his office space and took some scissors and struck them against a lead pipe. Half a dozen reporters looked up, not wanting to be interrupted from the stories they were grinding out for the next day's edition. "Gentlemen, I want you to meet our new man. This is Jamie Dalton, who was here for a time last summer. He was on the scene in Johnstown and gave us the initial reports. Did a damn fine job too. I am sure you will give him your usual warm welcome." His sarcasm let me know that I would have to prove myself to this hard-bitten group. The men went right back to their work without giving me another glance.

There was a man speaking on the one telephone box across the room. When I approached, he hung up the mouthpiece and brushed by me without saying a word. I cranked the telephone and asked the operator to connect me to the offices of the Pennsylvania Railroad. After several rings, a young man answered brusquely, "Railroad."

Trying to sound as stern as possible, I said, "James Dalton for Robert Pitcairn." I had not mentioned my affiliation with the *Sun*, thinking it would hurt my chances of getting past Mr. Pitcairn's sentries.

"Mr. Pitcairn is not taking any calls."

"May I leave him a message?"

"If you must. I'll tell him you called, but no guarantees he will respond."

"Please tell him that James Dalton is seeking advice." I hoped "advice" would sound less threatening than "information." The railroad office man rang off without another word.

I wasn't ready to camp out in Mr. Pitcairn's office and told Mr. Brooks that I had reached the railroad offices and was expecting a call back. He snorted. He pointed me to my desk, the smallest on the floor in a windowless corner, and told me to start combing through the out-of-town papers for any information that I might have missed concerning the club and the dam. I scanned the *New York Times*, the *Boston Herald*, and the *Chicago Tribune* and saw they had all captured the spectacular devastation and the pathos of the human misery. But beyond the reflex revulsion at the culpability of the so-called Bosses Club, none had dug into the story behind the dam collapse beyond some superficial rewrites of what the *Sun* had already published.

I began to make notes of what I wanted to ask Mr. Pitcairn, but I kept coming back to the essential question: what had the club and its members known about the condition of the dam? I knew this line of questioning was dangerous because I might discover who else besides Colonel Unger knew how vulnerable the dam was. And did I really want to know who was responsible for not taking the necessary steps to fix the structure whose collapse had caused such untold devastation?

While I was worrying over how I would proceed with the investigation, I heard the phone ring and saw the closest reporter grab the receiver. He nodded a couple of times, then answered with a big grin, "I'll be sure to tell him." Then he looked at me and in a loud tone of voice announced, "Say, Dalton, that was Mr. Pitcairn's office. He will meet you for lunch at the Duquesne Club tomorrow at noon sharp. I didn't bother to tell them that you'd be there." With that the room erupted in hoots and catcalls, and over the din I could hear the words, "How fancy," repeated again and again. I tried to ignore them, but it was obvious that my last name had garnered me the invitation.

I grabbed an unhealthy dinner of a pickled egg and peanuts at O'Reilly's Bar around the corner on Third Street from the *Sun*'s offices, then took the streetcar home. It was past nine when I walked in the house. I went right up to my room and forced myself to sit on my bed and take notes about what I wanted to discuss with Mr. Pitcairn. I would have to explain to him that I was a reporter and I was there to discuss the causes of the dam collapse. How he would react to that would determine the tenor of the rest of our conversation. Would he give me a frank answer? It didn't matter. I had to confront the man who had the most information on the dam break. I scratched out some questions, then turned down the gaslight on my bedside table. When I got into bed, I rehearsed what I wanted to ask Pitcairn before I dropped into a fitful sleep.

———

I was up before six and dressed in my best suit for lunch at the Duquesne Club. Mother told me that my great-uncle John Ricketson had been the club's first president. When I was younger, Father said he couldn't take me there until I was a "grown-up." I wondered whether he thought I was grown-up enough now. Perhaps he did, and that was another reason he seemed so threatened by my choice of careers. If he knew of my lunch with Mr. Pitcairn, he would be aghast.

At the office that morning, I reviewed both the Pittsburgh and out-of-town papers again to see if anything new had cropped up. The firsthand accounts of the personal devastation kept rolling in, particularly from the local papers that had better access to sources, but I still didn't feel any of them were getting to the heart of the story, at least the type of analysis that Mr. Brooks and I had discussed. Wanting to be punctual, I left the office at 11:30 for the five-minute walk to the Duquesne Club.

I turned the corner onto Sixth Avenue and walked the half-block down to the club. Although it was only sixteen years old, the club's brownstone façade was tinged to near black because of Pittsburgh's omnipresent soot. I remembered my grandfather telling me that the grime was the hallmark of the city's success, and I was sure that the club members looked at the smoky patina as a badge of their achievements. I pushed through a revolving door; then a tall, liveried man, about my age, gave me a supercilious look, and said, "Good morning, sir." He was well-trained, but he wasn't about to show me the kind of deference he gave to the members.

After walking the ten steps up into the marble entrance hall, I was awed. The room ran the width of the building and was two stories high with a mezzanine balustrade and walkway. The floor was covered by a deep maroon carpet with the club insignia emblazed in blue at the center. At either end of the room were floor-to-ceiling oil paintings of Pittsburgh. The one on the right was an overview of all the iron and steel mills reaching up the Monongahela, with their smokestacks billowing black. The painting on the left was of the downtown area from the top of Coal Hill. The focus was on the Point, where the Allegheny and Monongahela flow into the Ohio. Together the two paintings explained Pittsburgh's fortuitous geography and how the men of the Duquesne Club had made the most of that opportunity.

A small older man with ruddy cheeks and a merry face, dressed in a miniature version of the uniform worn by the man at the door, chirped out to me from behind a narrow, upright desk, "May I help you, sir?"

"I am here to meet Mr. Pitcairn."

"Yes, sir. He will be here right at noon and asked that you wait for him in the first-floor lounge across the entrance hall on the left."

The room was staid and simple with an enormous but subtle Oriental rug. There was a fireplace at one end and a long and broad mahogany table at the other that was set with tea and coffee, biscuits, butter, and jam. In the middle of the room on another table were all the Pittsburgh and New York newspapers, as well as a new broadsheet with the presumptuous name of the *Wall Street Journal*. Overlooking the street were three oriel windows. In one of the alcoves stood a man assaying the scene below as if the people rushing by were there for his personal inspection. His sense of superiority was palpable.

After grabbing the *New York World*, which under Joseph Pulitzer's ownership now had the largest circulation of any newspaper in the country, I allowed myself to be swallowed up by one of the room's dozen leather chairs. There was an older man who had already succumbed to the comfort. He alternately nodded off, then roused himself to return to his reading. I reminded myself not to get too relaxed.

As the grandfather clock in the corner struck noon, I saw the man I knew to be Mr. Pitcairn stride into the lounge. Although I had never been introduced to him, Father had pointed him out to me at Calvary Church. It was hard to forget him. A heavyset man with a luxurious walrus mustache, he had a bullet-shaped head that made him look like he was charging into battle. A tiny pince-nez provided an incongruous accent to his aggressive mien. I popped out of my chair, and his voice echoed off the walls of the heretofore silent lounge.

"Young Mr. Dalton! It's a pleasure. What a fine family you have! Your father such an accomplished attorney. And your lovely mother. Please give them both my regards."

I extended my hand and said, "I will do that, sir. It's a pleasure to meet you. Thank you for seeing me."

"Always happy to help out the son of a colleague. Let's walk down to the Garden Room and order some lunch. I'm on a very tight schedule today, what with this terrible business up in Johnstown. I heard you were at South Fork when it happened."

"Yes, sir, I was." I wasn't sure what he meant by "help out the son of a colleague," but I doubted it was with information about the collapse of the South Fork Dam.

Taking my elbow, he escorted me down the hallway. On the left were a cigar stand and a barbershop, then a room with two billiard tables, just the kind of amenities these important men required. To the right was a colonnade of stone pillars and through them you could see some twenty tables, each festooned with fresh linen, gleaming silverware, and a small, narrow vase holding a pale pink rose. In the center of the room was a circular fountain with a sculpture of Diana pouring water into the pool at her feet. Above was a glass ceiling covered on the outside with a film of dirt that gave the room a gloomy feel. We waited less than ten seconds to be seated.

"Mr. Pitcairn, how good to see you. We have your table ready," the maître d' gushed.

"Henri, this is Mr. Dalton's boy, Jamie."

The man gave me a short bow. "Fine gentleman, your father."

Scanning the room, Mr. Pitcairn said, "Now there are two men any recent college graduate would be wise to know." As we approached the table, I was shocked to see it was Mr. Henry Clay Frick and Mr. Andrew W. Mellon, engaged in a serious discussion. I knew the business legends of both men. After working in his family's whiskey business, Old Overholt, Frick had bought up bituminous coal fields around Connellsville, thirty miles southeast of Pittsburgh, then built ovens to cook the coal down to the coke that fired Bessemer ovens hot enough to make steel. After years of being his biggest supplier, Mr. Carnegie made Mr. Frick president of the J. Edgar Thompson plant, named for the president of the Pennsylvania Railroad, the company's largest customer. Through T. Mellon & Sons bank, Andrew Mellon and his brother Richard had lent Frick the money to expand his business as they had with many Pittsburgh entrepreneurs.

"We must avoid blame," I heard Mr. Frick say. Then seeing me with Mr. Pitcairn, he changed his tone. "Robert, good to see you. Who is this young man?" Although Mother and Father were close to the Fricks, Mr. Frick didn't recognize me.

Handsome, with a full head of brown hair and a neatly trimmed mustache and beard in the popular Van Dyke style, Mr. Frick looked young considering the power he wielded in the nation's largest industry. For a second, I was mesmerized by the intense focus of his pale-blue eyes that were in sharp contrast to his genial greeting.

"James Dalton, sir."

"Yes, Richard told me you have recently graduated from Yale and want to find a career in Pittsburgh. This is my good friend, Andrew Mellon." I shook Mr. Mellon's hand as well and was surprised how frail he looked. His brown hair already showed signs of gray as did his mustache. His cheeks were sunken, and his sprightly eyebrows shadowed sad but kindly eyes.

"Robert, how are the relief efforts progressing?" Mr. Frick asked. "Mr. Mellon and I were just discussing how we might help."

"Gentleman, what we are most in need of are funds."

"This is no place to discuss specifics, but you can count on our generosity," Mr. Frick said. Mr. Mellon nodded in agreement.

"I understand there was a meeting on Saturday. What was decided?" Mr. Pitcairn continued.

Mr. Frick glowered at him but did not reply. Then he turned to me and said, "Good to meet you, young man." He and Mr. Mellon went back to their meal.

Henri, who had been hanging back, ushered us to Mr. Pitcairn's table that was tucked discreetly in a corner of the room, far enough from the fountain so the burbling of the water wouldn't interfere with conversation.

We arranged ourselves across the table from each other, then passed on the suggestion of an aperitif. "No need for menus, Henri. We will both have the soft-shell crab and creamed spinach." Looking at me, he added, "The crab is in season, and the chef sautés them to perfection. And the creamed spinach is a *specialité de la maison.*" I nearly laughed at Mr. Pitcairn's butchered attempt at a French accent but couldn't argue with his selections. My only thought was that in a few minutes I would have to tell Mr. Pitcairn I was working for the *Sun.*

The Duquesne Club had a reputation for impeccable service, and a waiter soon placed plates of three crabs, browned to perfection, before each of us and then ladled out generous portions of the creamed spinach. Picking up his fork, Mr. Pitcairn opened the conversation. "Now what can I do for you, young man? Where do your interests lie? My railroad? Mr. Frick's steel? Mr. Mellon's bank? I'm sure your father has extolled the virtues of the law." Despite Mr. Pitcairn's forceful style, he was a friendly man, and I felt guilty that he might think I had hoodwinked him into this lunch meeting.

I shifted uncomfortably in my chair, then forced myself to look straight at Mr. Pitcairn's smiling face. "Sir, I, ah, have decided on a profession. In newspapering. Mr. Cleveland Brooks at the *Pittsburgh Sun* has offered me a position."

The smile disappeared, and I was confronted with the angry visage of the man who ran the western division of the country's largest railroad with an iron fist. Mr. Pitcairn shook his bullet head. "Newspapers are nothing! Boy, you have no idea what this city is all about. We've built this palace for our business lunches, but outside its walls there is nothing refined about what we must do to run our operations and make them profitable. Do you know where I came from? Not some comfortable house in Shadyside where I live now. No, I grew up in Slabtown on the North Side in one of those dreary hovels, just like Messrs. Carnegie, Phipps, Lauder, and the rest." He paused for effect with his eyes smoldering. I knew about Slabtown from Grampa Willis. It was part of the Carnegie legend, but I didn't know Pitcairn had grown up there as well.

He continued. "We learned how to fight and claw back then, and we persist to this day, but dress in finer clothes, live in grander homes. But every day is a struggle, just like it was back then. We run giant companies with thousands of workers. The union men disrupt our businesses, and we must be strong, even brutal to remind them it's our property, not theirs. And we need to be thrifty so we can invest in the equipment we need to stay atop our industries. The competition is fierce for all of us." I thought back to what Grampa had said about the 1877 railroad strike and wondered what part Pitcairn had played in the death of the striking workers.

"What I'm telling you, boy, is that no matter how newspapers jabber, it won't mean a lick to these men. If you want to amount to anything in Pittsburgh, it won't be at a worthless newspaper."

"I'm sorry, Mr. Pitcairn, my mind is made up. I accepted Mr. Brooks's offer and have filed several reports about the flood."

He leaned back in his chair and said, "Since you are not seeking my advice about your employment possibilities, why are you here?"

This was the juncture Mr. Brooks told me I would reach and that I would have to persist. "Sir, I want to discuss with you the history of the South Fork Dam. From what I have gathered so far, you know as much about the dam as any member of the club." Before he could disagree, I reviewed for him what I had gleaned from my talks with Colonel Unger and Captain Jones. When I was finished, Pitcairn gave me a blank look. "I have no comment about any of that." I thought back to what he had asked Mr. Frick and kept on, trying to be as respectful as I could.

"Sir, didn't Colonel Unger submit a report to you on the dam's deficiencies?"

"I don't remember any such report."

"The Colonel told me that you ignored the report."

"That is his recollection, not mine. In any case, there were no signs that the dam was anything but adequate. During the normal spring rains in previous years, the problems had been minimal, in the valley and the city. What happened this year was unprecedented. An act of . . ."

"God," I interjected. It galled me that this would be the South Fork Club's sole explanation for the flood. Pitcairn stood up, pushing his big belly forward.

"It grieves me that the son of Richard and Eleanor Dalton would behave in such a fashion. Enjoy the rest of the meal. It will likely be the last you have within these walls." With that he turned his back and hurried out of the Garden Room.

I looked around to see if anyone had seen or heard what had transpired. I was glad that Mr. Frick and Mr. Mellon had departed, and there was no one else in the room that I recognized. I looked down at my untouched crab, but my stomach was in a knot, and I couldn't manage even a bite. I tossed my napkin on the table and walked out of the room, hoping I was invisible. I may as well have been because not even Henri glanced my way. It was not until I reached the front door that anyone gave me a hint of recognition when the young doorman gave me another mocking "Sir."

Back at the *Sun*, I slumped into Mr. Brooks's office. "That good, eh?" he asked. I recounted all that had occurred at the Duquesne Club, trying not to leave out any detail, including what Pitcairn had ordered for lunch.

"Tell me again what you heard Frick tell Mellon." I repeated Mr. Frick's statement about avoiding blame.

"They are hiding something," Brooks said. "Frick was right to ignore Pitcairn's question. Pitcairn can run his mouth when he's off guard. Now that he knows that the *Sun* is sniffing around, I'm afraid we are not going to get any more out of him. After the shock of learning you were a reporter, you should have calmed him down. Found out more of what he knew about the dam without threatening him. You can't be bullied by men like Pitcairn." I didn't feel I had been intimidated, but I had to learn the nuances of being a good reporter.

"You'll get there," Brooks said. "For right now, the best thing for you to do is take the first train in the morning to Johnstown. You need to find out how the city officials are coping with the city's recovery, and I want you to investigate why this catastrophe happened. There is no simple answer. We would be naïve to go along with the 'act of God' explanation. We need to know whether these men ignored the warnings. Maybe Pitcairn did, but he will never admit it. I can't believe Frick, Mellon, and, God help us, Mr. Andrew Carnegie or any of the other members like your father knew anything about the condition of the dam. Nevertheless, it's their club and their responsibility," Mr. Brooks said.

"I want to know what happened, regardless of the answer, but as a reporter it's not my place to assign blame. Perhaps I can find others in the valley who have some idea how this happened," I replied.

"Don't forget to get some good interviews this time around. You'll have to sift through a lot of very emotional reactions. People will be in a state of shock and will look for an easy target, and a rich man's boating club fills that void. The stories of the survivors are what people want to hear. I don't want to be accused of exploiting their misery, but we have to sell newspapers. For right now, my editorials will explain the magnitude of the storm and cheer on the money being raised for the relief efforts. Wire me when you get there."

Since I was already downtown, I decided to stop by my father's law office. I wanted to clear the air with him before I headed back up to the Conemaugh Valley but didn't hold out much hope. From the lobby of the Carnegie Brothers building, I stepped into the recently installed elevator. There was an elderly black man in a dark-green uniform who asked for my floor.

"The Knox & Reed offices," I answered.

"Third floor, it is," he said closing the folding metal door and pushing the hand crank forward. I knew from previous visits to the office that the Carnegie interests were on the top three floors of the building, right above the law firm.

Father's office was a bit more spartan than his library on Amberson with a heavy smell of cigars and shoe polish left behind by the man who shined boots. He was bent over some papers and a couple of law books, so I cleared my throat. Looking up, it took a second for his eyes to focus and recognize me. "James, this is a surprise."

I couldn't tell from his tone whether the surprise was welcome or not.

I took a seat in the big leather client chair in front of his desk, and for a moment we stared at each other. He made a show of pulling out a desk drawer and then flipping a telegram toward me. "It's from your mother. She is still in Johnstown, doing God's work, or so she thinks. She has a charitable heart, and I myself have contributed to the relief fund."

"You should have seen her, Father! No one worked harder to help people." Then I read the wire. All it said was, "Richard, he's our son."

Father smiled at me. "A husband and wife married as long as we have can communicate in very few words. She's asking, no, telling me, to give you your head. I can't fight both of you."

I was so surprised that I stood up and extended my hand.

He stood as well but didn't offer his. "Not so fast. There are conditions that aren't negotiable."

"You must first identify yourself as a representative of the press when calling on someone of your mother's or my acquaintance. And yes, I have already heard from Robert Pitcairn. He's very angry, but I mollified him by telling him that you would never approach him again for information about the dam.

"I understand that you are digging into the causes of the dam failure. This may be the first of many instances where you are examining issues that involve me, my friends, or my clients. I want you to show me anything that involves our circle of business or social acquaintances before it appears in your newspaper."

Our talk had started in a promising fashion but was devolving into another stand-off. I had to push back. "First off, it isn't my newspaper. Second, you and Mother know every important person in the city. Mr. Brooks would never agree to that type of restriction hanging over me, and it would be impossible to keep it secret from him. Father, the kind of scrutiny and censoring that you would give my reporting would make me useless."

Father shook his head, then looked down at his desk and rearranged his gold pen, his silver letter opener, and his crystal inkwell. Was he toying with me? He finally looked up.

"Your mother told me that's how you would respond. In another wire she also said we have to trust you. I know you will never tarnish our family name, but you must treat the hardworking leaders of this city fairly. Your mother said that Brooks is of good character, but you and he better be damned sure you have your facts straight. As to the flood, no one in this city is at fault, and no judge or jury in Pittsburgh will find otherwise."

"Thank you for believing in me, Father," I said with sincerity.

"I'd offer you a whiskey, but it is the middle of the day. Let's enjoy a cigar." And he handed me one from a humidor that sat behind his desk.

As we smoked, I told him more about the devastation in Johnstown and Mother's accomplishments. He asked me about the breadth of destruction and expressed compassion for the survivors.

I stood up to leave, but something Father had said before was bothering me. "Won't any of the flood lawsuits be filed in Cambria County?"

"The South Fork Club is incorporated in Allegheny County, not Cambria. It made sense since that's where the majority of the members live. And any civil suit for damages will find that the club has only $35,000 in assets with a $20,000 mortgage lien against that."

I hid my excitement. Father had given me crucial facts about the club that no other reporter had. This time Brooks couldn't fault me for not getting the most out of a source. I excused myself, telling Father that I had to get a train back to Johnstown.

—◦—

The train was filled with relief workers, but a new group had appeared: sightseers, replete with picnic baskets. How morbid, I thought, but acknowledged to myself that the press had more than a little to do with such inhumane *schadenfreude*. Along the way I read the *Sun*'s major competitor, the *Pittsburgh Post*. Long known as the mouthpiece of the established order in Pittsburgh, the *Post* was already absolving the South Fork Club of any culpability. They posited that the club had tested the reliability of the dam and found it no danger to the people of the Little Conemaugh Valley. The *Post* also claimed that the Cambria inspection declared the dam safe and that their assessment must be correct since the steel company had the most to lose in the event of a calamity. I didn't know how the *Post* could say either of those things since I had information that said just the opposite. The report from Cambria Steel's John Fulton that the dam posed a major risk was dismissed as inaccurate and alarmist. Perhaps the *Post* hadn't uncovered the same information I had. Or maybe they had been co-opted by the Saturday group that Mr. Pitcairn had mentioned to Mr. Frick.

Buried in the middle of the second column on the third page was an item anyone was likely to miss. A coroner's jury in Seward, downstream from Johnstown, where over two hundred bodies had been recovered, had been convened. They had already been to the lake to inspect what was left of the dam and to find out what they could about how well it had been maintained. There weren't many details, but one fact was mentioned: when there had been leaks in the past, they were inadequately repaired. I would have to see what else that coroner's jury had discovered.

Back in Johnstown, I looked for Mother, but when I found the banner of the Ladies Relief Society where I assumed Mother would be, I was told that she had already returned to Pittsburgh. I was happy she was out of any danger since the threat of disease was already in the air and in the water, but I was sorry to have missed her. I wanted to thank her for convincing Father to allow me to work at the *Sun*, but I still had questions about his motives.

To catch up on the firsthand reporting, I returned to the *Tribune*, where I found George Swank asleep with his head on his desk.

I put my hand on his shoulder and whispered, "Mr. Swank?"

He roused himself, put his half-moon spectacles back on, and tried to smooth out the fringe of hair around his bald pate. It took a moment for him to recognize me.

"Brooks sent you back, eh? We're up and running. Look at what we've been covering and let me know if you have any questions."

I read through the many special editions the paper had published. One piece of reporting on the first afternoon of the flood caught both the horror and the humanity.

Fathers gathered whole families on the roof of a house, only to see their children and their wives fall into the roiling waters.

Train cars flipped into the air with all the passengers either crushed or drowned. Orphaned children wandered through the relief camps crying for their mothers. But there were also tales of extraordinary bravery.

Muscled steel men with no regard for their own safety braved the rampaging waters with every manner of lethal objects flying around them, as they tried to fish out survivors.

One family scrambled onto a log and rowed their way to shore using mangled lumber as paddles. A grandmother refused to let go of her cat and stayed afloat on her rocking chair.

I admired Swank and his reporters for the depth of their coverage, but I wanted to move beyond the sensational. I understood that these were the kind of details the public wanted to hear, but I was more focused on the causes of the flood and how the town leaders were reacting to the devastation.

I explained my assignment to Swank, and he said I should interview Arthur Moxham. He told me Moxham was a Welshman who had come to Johnstown three years ago and whose company made steel rails for streetcar lines. "They're calling him 'the dictator' ever since he was appointed to run the city during the recovery. I'm sure he's holed up across the street." That would be Town Hall, the only other building left standing in Johnstown.

I found Moxham pacing around his office, muttering about the rescue efforts. The Welshman was compact, with wispy light hair and dark-brown eyes. When he noticed me, he said, "We need more food!" Then it dawned on him that he didn't know me. "Who are you?" he asked.

"James Dalton of the *Pittsburgh Sun* and I'm reporting on how Johnstown is dealing with the aftermath of the flood."

"Well, Mr. Dalton, maybe you can tell the world how much help we need." Moxham sounded exasperated, but the hard look in his eye told me he'd be undaunted.

"Insurance company inspectors are overwhelmed with the extent of the destruction and can't begin to calculate their exposure. Survivors and business owners are already chafing under the delay. And as you heard me say, food is scarce and what the railroads are bringing in isn't enough. There are breakouts of pneumonia and diphtheria, but very little medicine is available. Doctors have been prescribing whiskey." Then Moxham gave me a grin. "Miraculously, hundreds of barrels have survived intact."

I didn't want Moxham to get sidetracked. "I've heard there has been looting."

"That's been stopped but with brutality. Vigilantes tried to lynch one of the miscreants and shot and wounded several others. The state militia will be here tomorrow and use more civilized methods to guard what remains of the city."

With a catch in his voice, Moxham continued. "We don't even know how many are dead. There is wild speculation that it could be as many as twenty thousand, but the Red Cross thinks the count is closer to two thousand. Whatever the number, it's horrifying."

The friendly "dictator" put out his hand and I shook it. "Please spread the word, Mr. Dalton. We need all the help we can get." I was both surprised and reassured that an important official like Moxham was relying on me.

Before getting a few hours' sleep at the Red Cross's tent city, I heard rumors of trouble up at South Fork. Regardless of what the *Post* might have to say, there was nary a soul that I spoke with that did not blame the collapse of the dam on members of the South Fork Fishing and Hunting Club. It was hard to argue with their logic. The club had rebuilt the dam to create the lake. The club had been responsible for the maintenance of the dam for ten years and had not done enough to keep it from failing. Ipso facto, the club and its members were to blame. I knew the answer wasn't that simple, but I wasn't about to argue with anyone from the valley. Most had lost family, all had lost friends and acquaintances, many had their businesses destroyed. I was not surprised when I heard groups of men muttering that something should be done about the "richies" up at the now empty lake. When I heard that a group of men from the leveled town of Woodvale were on the way to the cottages and clubhouse of the South Fork Club, I knew where I needed to be.

After paying dearly to borrow one of the few horses remaining in town, I lit out for South Fork the next morning. Looking down into the valley, I saw that even a week after the flood the landscape looked like the scene of a major battle. The few trees left standing were denuded of their leaves. Rocks that had not been seen in centuries had been uncovered. There was standing water everywhere, giving it a swampy feeling. Along the ridge back to South Fork, I didn't see a single other horse. The lake looked much as I had last seen it, only emptier and more dried out. If I had any doubts before, I knew now that the South Fork Fishing and Hunting Club was finished.

I circled around the back side of the lake, the one farthest from the dam, and came upon the club's cottages. They looked lifeless. I had heard that anyone there for the holiday had gone to Altoona, forty miles east, and I assumed Rita was safe. Would any of the families ever return to these lovely homes? I doubted it. Expecting the houses to be empty, I was surprised to see some desperate-looking men looting the Heinz home. They were walking out with furniture, food, silverware, whatever they could carry, and all had stupid, inebriated grins on their faces. I was back at South Fork as a reporter, to observe, but Rita and her family were close friends. I had to try to stop these men.

"What are you doing?" I demanded.

The drunkest of the lot spit at me and shouted, "We're taking back what these people owe us! They destroyed our homes, our families, and we will take what we want, though it can't begin to pay us back. And where do you think there is any law around here? They wouldn't stop us anyway." There was a wagon on the road, and it was then I saw men emerge from the other houses and throw whatever they could carry into the back. Anything too heavy, they broke into pieces.

Realizing there was no way to stop them, I rode to the club, which was only a few hundred yards away. There I saw a mob of men carrying torches and yelling, "Lynch the bastards!" and "Burn this place to the ground!" They were passing around a whiskey bottle, and one of them had a thick hemp rope. This mob wanted revenge and whoever was inside the clubhouse was the target of their wrath. These men of the Little Conemaugh Valley had seen their homes destroyed, their livelihoods taken away. Could I blame them for being angry and drunk?

One of the men hung back. He seemed sober and wasn't shouting slogans. Getting him aside, I said, "I'm James Dalton and I report for the *Pittsburgh Sun*."

He snarled but didn't say anything.

"Please, sir, I understand how you and these other men must be devasted, but what do you hope to accomplish here today?"

"I ain't ashamed of what we set out to do," he said. "We chased Unger and his lackey Boyer into the clubhouse. We knew Unger was manager of the club and it was his responsibility to repair that dam. Everyone knew it was falling apart. Unger and Boyer do the work of the rich Pittsburgh men who didn't care a lick as long as they could sail and fish on their pretty lake. We'd have strung them up, too, but they all slunk away. They knew what the hardworking folks in the valley whose lives they have destroyed would do to them." He was as angry as the others, even without the drink.

By then a few of the men had stopped their shouting. They circled behind and glared at me. I drew myself up to my full height and tried not to sound frightened, although I was trembling. "You and these men have terrified whoever is inside. The dam collapse will haunt them for the rest of their lives. What would stringing them up accomplish? You would be branded as vigilantes and the law would hunt you down. Do you want that for yourselves, for your families?"

The man I'd been speaking to spat tobacco at my feet. "And who might identify us? Maybe we should get a rope for you too."

Ignoring the threat, I responded, wanting the others to hear me as well. "You and your families have suffered. I'm here to tell your stories and find out what happened with the dam, nothing more."

"Why should we believe you? The bosses have the newspapers and the courts in their pockets. We will never get justice. The hell with them and the hell with you. C'mon, fellas. Let's go down to the lake and trash their precious boats. They're never coming back anyway." I hoped I had given Unger and Boyer a chance to get away. "Now, remember, Dalton, you never saw any of us."

"Not a one," I said, able to breathe normally again. Now I needed to get back to Johnstown and send a dispatch to the *Sun*. The trashing of the homes and the lynch mob at the clubhouse was a big story, even if I didn't identify any of the looters.

I checked the clubhouse, and when I saw that it was empty, I went to Colonel Unger's farm. He and Boyle were very shaken and thanked me for distracting the looters while they escaped out the back. I wanted to know more about the Fulton report, commissioned by Cambria Steel, on the dam's deterioration, but Colonel Unger was in no shape to discuss that or anything else.

As I was about to mount my horse, Boyer came up to me, glancing over his shoulder to be sure the Colonel was out of earshot. "Mr. Dalton, there is someone you may want to talk to, but no one can know that it was me that put you on to him. The man's name is Herbert Webber, and he was a guard at the club for many years. He lives down in South Fork village. Don't tell him I sent you."

I didn't remember a Webber, but at least it was a lead. After a five-minute ride to the little town, I asked around for him. A woman standing on the front step of her flooded but intact home struggled to lift her arm and pointed out a man sitting alone on a stump.

Herbert Webber was staring at the ground with a jar of what I assumed was whiskey sitting at his feet. He looked baffled and said, "Mr. Dalton, what are you doing here? I thought all the members went to Altoona."

"I've been hired by the *Pittsburgh Sun* to report on the flood." Webber gave me a wary look, then took a long pull of whiskey. "I'm glad you are safe, sir. How were you able to get away?" I wanted to engage him so he would be open to answering my questions.

"At the clubhouse when the dam broke. Walked back to the village after the waters passed," he said.

It wouldn't be easy dragging anything about the club out of Webber, and I wasn't sure I had the patience. Between the horror of the flood, the trains back and forth to Pittsburgh, the confrontation with the looters, I was spent. Webber's hands shook as he brought the whiskey to his mouth. His eyes were red and unfocused.

"May I have a sip of that?" I asked. Besides wanting the whiskey to revive me, it wouldn't hurt to gain Webber's trust by sharing a drink with him.

We passed the whiskey back and forth for a few minutes, then I said, "Can we talk about the dam?"

"Don't know a blessed thing," he grumbled.

"Mr. Webber. You worked at the club for years. You've seen things." I was too exhausted to be anything but direct.

Webber drank from the jar, kicked at the dirt, drank again.

"You want to hear the truth. No one else ever has." His speech was slurred. "Now the families in the village, my own neighbors, blame me as if I was one of the club people."

"What do you mean no one wanted to hear the truth?"

"They paid me to be the watchman, walk the land to be sure no one was trespassing or fishing or stealing the boats. I patrolled the property day and night. I must have walked the top of that dam a thousand times. I saw things. The clogged spillway screen. Leaks patched with straw and manure. Big rocks from the face of the dam had fallen to the ground, and in the spring the water spurted out like a watering pot. I told whoever would listen that it was bound to fail."

"How did they respond?"

"Told me to keep my mouth shut. That it was the best built dam in the state, if not the nation. I knew a flood might happen and kept at them. I gave some of the members an earful. 'Oh, Webber,' they would say. 'You shouldn't bother yourself with things like that. I'm sure Colonel Unger has this well under control.'

"Unger threatened to fire me unless I stopped talking about the dam. But it doesn't matter now. The Pittsburgh people will never come back and I'm out of a job."

The cover-up of the shoddy repairs was the most damning evidence I had heard yet. But I had to be careful. I wasn't sure of Webber's motives, and I needed further corroboration.

"Besides Unger, who did you tell?"

Webber hesitated.

"Sir, I can see that you did what you could, but it's important for people to know whether others were responsible."

"You want big names, don't you? Mr. Frick, Mr. Mellon, Mr. Pitcairn, men of their stature. Can't remember who I talked to. Don't matter because I always got the same response."

After a last sip of whiskey, he threw the jar away and turned his back on me. "Mr. Webber, you have been very helpful. Thank you for your time." I wasn't sure he heard me.

By then it was too late to get back to Johnstown, and I collapsed on a bed in one of the abandoned cottages. Waking at first light, I rode down the Little Conemaugh Valley on the same ridge that I had taken the day of the flood a week earlier. Along the way I saw the amazing resilience of the townspeople. Everywhere they were clearing debris, making order out of chaos, putting their lives back together. Many were still grieving, but there was a purposefulness in their industry. They had resolved to move on. Retribution was not on their minds.

⁓

With fewer obstructions I was able to reach Johnstown in under an hour and was pleased to find George Swank already at his post in the *Tribune* offices above the bank. First, I wired Mr. Brooks about the local men destroying South Fork Club property, the near lynching of Unger and Boyer, and what Herbert Webber had told me.

"Those robbers are lucky the police up there are occupied saving lives and property. Here in Johnstown some looters have been shot dead," Swank answered.

"Send Brooks a wire telling him what you've seen, then get yourself back to Pittsburgh. I don't think there is much more you can learn here. The troops are going to dynamite all the debris that's still on fire at the railroad bridge in the next few days, but I'll get you an eyewitness account you can run in the *Sun*." I thanked Swank, then spent a restless night on a cot at the Red Cross camp.

With some foreboding I was on the 6 a.m. train. The devastation beyond the Stone Bridge was almost as bad as it was in Johnstown. There were seas of mud and trees tossed willy-nilly. No houses or buildings were off their foundations, but debris was caught up in the many bridges over the Conemaugh River. A week later the rescue workers were still pulling bodies from the waters downstream.

When I wasn't observing the awful toll of the flood, I was thinking about the wrap-up Mr. Brooks wanted because up until now the story had only come out in dribs and drabs. No question that I had enough material at this point to give a detailed account of why the Johnstown Flood had happened. I hadn't wanted to exploit the suffering of the survivors, but it occurred to me that I should have interviewed more of them. I wondered whether my father would be angry over my coverage of the flood. Could it hurt his law practice?

Lost in my musings, the trip passed quickly. Walking to the *Sun* office from the train, I worried over the first significant piece of my career.

Back at my desk, I looked over what I had: my official interview with Colonel Unger after the flood, the informative talk with Captain Jones, the truncated lunch with Pitcairn, the background George Swank gave me, my own observations of the rescue efforts, the dangerous run-in with the looters at the cottages and the club. And the bitter rantings of Herbert Webber.

Despite the evidence on the ground in Johnstown, others disputed that the collapse was caused by the neglect of the South Fork Club and its members. The rainfall was the highest to ever hit the Conemaugh area, and some claimed that it was the sheer volume of water, not the poorly repaired dam, that caused the break. Some club members said the South Fork Dam didn't collapse or it was another dam that broke.

But I had more information than any other reporter on the scene. This will be easy, I thought, bucking myself up with false bravado.

But the words didn't come. I sat there staring at the typewriter, tearing out the copy paper, then threading more back in. I tried to put my notes in some semblance of order, only to rearrange them in a different fashion. After snapping a third pencil, I needed to get out of the newsroom and walked down Smithfield Street to the Monongahela wharf. The iron Smithfield Bridge loomed off to my right. Past it I saw the cars of the Duquesne Incline make their slow and steady way up and down Coal Hill, and I thought of Grandfather Willis. I remembered that he told me the big men of Pittsburgh—Carnegie, Phipps, Pitcairn, men whom he had grown up with in Slabtown—had not treated him fairly. The family indulged Grampa his rants, thinking he was merely envious of all the money those men had made.

As I stared down into the dirty Monongahela, it came to me what was at the core of my grandfather's anger, and it wasn't the money. In their eyes he wasn't important enough to worry about, and they ignored him. Their focus was on the construction of the next mill, breaking labor strikes, amassing profits. According to the ethos of the day, their successes justified whatever they had to do. Outside their businesses and their families, these men were careless.

Having reached that conclusion, I knew how I would shape my article. These titans of Pittsburgh's industrial colossus had paid no attention to what was happening at South Fork. It was a place for their wives and children and an occasional respite for them from the unrelenting grind of their demanding businesses. South Fork was convenient, a short ride in their private railroad cars. They had hired competent management, or so they thought. It was a simple two-month-a-year club, and it was unnecessary to give even cursory thought to its operation. If money was needed, the members provided it and didn't ask questions. And they didn't want to be bothered with warnings about the condition of the dam.

When I got to the newsroom, I sat down at my typewriter and didn't look up for another three hours. It was two weeks since the flood, and I had the story cold. After handing my copy to Cleve, I waited at my desk, impatient and nervous in anticipation of what Brooks would say about my piece.

A half hour later, he came out of his office and waved me over. His stern visage made me even more nervous, but when I stood in front of him, he broke into a big grin. "I'm going to run this on the front page, far left column in the Sunday edition, which has over forty thousand readers, twice the circulation of weekdays. And I'm going to write a page-four editorial right under the masthead to accompany it."

I was proud of what I had written. I had done my best to collect and state the facts. All the work I had done, all the horror I had experienced, all the exhaustion I felt had paid off. My piece on the Johnstown Flood would appear in the Sunday *Pittsburgh Sun*!

"Thank you, sir. Thank you, Mr. Brooks," I repeated as I pumped his hand.

"Call me, Cleve," he said.

———

From the Editorial Desk
Responsibility

The big-city papers have jumped to the conclusion that the members of the South Fork Fishing and Hunting Club should be bankrupted, then strung up for causing the Johnstown Flood. While we don't advocate such extra-legal methods, the Sun *is of the opinion that the members of the club are legally and morally responsible for the failure of the dam that caused this historic tragedy.*

As stated in our exclusive front-page story in this day's edition, the collapse of the dam was the cause of the flood, and any arguments to the contrary are trivial and absurd. The question of why the dam failed is also well-established.

Members have refused to comment on the causes of the dam collapse. This cabal of moneyed interests has closed ranks to avoid any public or legal reprisals. With insurance companies slow to pay their meager benefits, the cry for compensation will increase and be directed at this same group of wealthy men.

We urge Allegheny and Cambria Counties to investigate, but past probes of the actions of the rich and powerful have come to naught. That echelon has sophisticated legal counsel that public authorities cannot afford. And don't expect our local politicians to provide any leadership. The party machines, which control judgeships and sheriff's offices, have come to terms with the industrialists—we won't bother you, if you don't bother us.

Then there is the local press. No one in Western Pennsylvania will pay attention to what is being said in New York, Chicago or St. Louis, but they will take notice of the Pittsburgh papers. The consensus of our city's self-interested journals has been to absolve the South Fork Fishing and Hunting Club and its members of any wrongdoing. The Sun, as its name implies, wants to spread light on all vital issues in the public domain. Nothing could be more important than our right to know whether individuals or an organization should be held responsible, either criminally or financially, for the death and destruction in the Conemaugh Valley.

Some have argued it was an unavoidable, random act of God and nature. Others have pointed out all that has been done to change the contours of the Conemaugh Valley. There is no question that there was a record rainfall or that the excavations in the valley contributed to the fury of the flood. The fact remains that if the South Fork Dam had been properly maintained, this catastrophe would never have happened.

Maybe the club employees didn't do enough to warn the members. Maybe the members refused to listen. Andrew Carnegie expressed his sorrow for the devastation the flood caused but never mentioned that he was a club member. We will likely never know if men such as Carnegie, Henry Frick or Andrew Mellon were aware of the threat the dam posed. But whether they had forewarning is irrelevant. They are the club's owners, and they are responsible for any damages caused by a failure to maintain that property.

Public opinion has already convicted them. Whether the courts will do the same is doubtful. Can an Allegheny County court be expected to bring a judgment against any member of the South Fork Fishing and Hunting Club? Regardless of legalities, these men shut their eyes to the potential catastrophe. A city has been devastated, and over two thousand people have paid with their lives. That is unforgivable.

5

The Labor Beat

I WAITED IN THE NEWSROOM UNTIL I COULD GRAB COPIES OF THE SUN-day edition as they came off the press. Leaving several on my desk, I took one with me as I flagged down a hansom. It was past the time the street-cars ran, so I allowed myself the indulgence of a private service, some-thing I never did but felt was justified by the lateness of the hour and the publication of my first major piece in the *Sun*. I would have to remember to send a clipping to Harlan Simmons, my mentor back in New Haven.

But my ebullience was more than offset by the thought of Mother and Father's reaction to my article and the paper's accompanying editorial. My earlier flubs bothered me, but I knew I had written a professional piece of journalism; otherwise Cleve would never have published it. Two weeks ago, hiding behind a wall of professionalism might have carried the day with Father, but no more. He was very clear that he expected me to be "fair." I didn't need a legal education to know that meant fair to his clients, not fairness in a grander, metaphysical sense.

Since it was nighttime, I wasn't able to read as the cab jostled over the Liberty Avenue cobblestones, but that didn't matter since I could recite my whole article from memory. I thought over everything I had written and couldn't find a sentence that I wouldn't be able to defend. I had either witnessed the event or spoken to those who had. Any statistics I cited had been verified with town or company officials. I was on solid ground.

But I could not be sure whether my "facts" would matter to my father. Would he care that I had gotten the story right, or would he think that my reporting had led the *Sun* to be the only Pittsburgh newspaper calling for an investigation into the collapse of the South Fork Dam? Would he accuse me of betraying him? I hoped that Mother would support me since she had been in Johnstown and had seen how awful it was. I knew that she had become more confident and independent, but would she buck my father on an issue he saw as so fundamental to the welfare of our family?

I handed the driver four bits for the ride, then stumbled up our front walk. I was happy that there were no lights on but went around to the back door anyway, not wanting to run into anyone on my way to bed. Between exhaustion and dread of Father's possible reaction, my mind was overwhelmed, and the last thing I wanted was to engage in any conversations. I made my way up the backstairs, and when I was safely in my room with the door closed, I gave an audible groan and collapsed on my bed.

Sunday morning, I woke at daylight. I shrugged off the clothes I had worn the day before, put on fresh linen, and fell back asleep. It felt like minutes, but it was three hours later when I heard the family stirring. I knew I would be expected to attend church with them and put on my Sunday church suit.

But when I got downstairs, I had a rude surprise. Father was standing there and said, "You are not coming to Calvary with us. I will speak to you when the family returns from church."

We stood staring at each other; then Father turned his back and went out to the carriage. The rest of the family followed. Wills looked back and stuck his tongue out at me.

They were back in an hour, and Father called out to me, "James, in my study." I walked past him into the room, and he closed the door behind me. I was nervous and kept my shaky hands in my pockets.

There was a copy of that Sunday's paper on his desk that he rolled up and slapped against the side of his leg.

"James, you have betrayed our family! There is nothing you can say that will make up for the fact that you and that dreadful Brooks have as much as accused the South Fork members of criminal negligence. How dare you tell the world about the incorporation? I had no inkling that you would use that against me, us."

"Father, it's a fact that the club is organized in Pittsburgh. I verified that with one quick trip to the courthouse."

"It was a private conversation! I am disgusted with you."

"But I didn't use your name. And don't you want me to tell people the truth?"

"The simple, logical explanation is that it was done merely for convenience's sake. You as much as accused me of violating the law. We asked for an exception, and the clerk filing the papers granted it. The implication was that it was done to avoid liability or to get a more favorable ruling in case of any lawsuits. It had nothing to do with that! No one could imagine any trouble. South Fork was a simple club. You were there for years. Did you see any problems?"

"You don't believe what you just said, Father. You're a better lawyer than that."

"You can read my mind now with your new reporter skills? Don't be so insolent." He composed himself, then looked straight into my eyes. "I've had enough of this argument. You have made your choice, and now I've made mine. You want to defy my wishes about your career, then you must live on your own! I can't be seen to tolerate you under my roof when you are reporting half-truths about the men and industries that make this city what it is and provide this family with its daily sustenance. You are to leave immediately!"

I steeled myself. "You'll regret this, Father."

"I doubt that!" He slapped the newspaper against his leg once more. Did I see his eyes watering as he turned his back to me? Feeling the sweat on my face, I left the room. I did want to find my own place someday, but this felt so abrupt.

Mother was waiting for me in the front hall. She took me by the arm and pulled me into the parlor. After the gloom of Father's study, the light décor and sunlight were welcome. Mother embraced me, then stepped back. "He told me that he was going to demand that you leave. I argued, but he was insistent. Given how he feels, it may be for the best. I love you, and your father loves you. You can't forget that!" Mother was in tears.

"He seems more concerned about his relationship with his powerful clients."

"My darling, you must realize that these men could ruin his career, our life with a snap of their fingers. There would be no sentiment involved. 'Business is business.' They all say that again and again."

I thought back to New Haven and how independent I felt there. "I'm going to Jason's. I'm sure I can sleep on his floor."

"Oh, Jamie, I'm not sure about you living with Jason." Mother knew of Jason's troubles at Yale.

"Right at the moment I don't have another option."

I went up to my room and gathered some clothing in a satchel. When I returned, she was still standing by the front door.

"Good-bye, Mother. I'll come around when Father has cooled off." She embraced me, kissed me on the cheek, and I was out the door.

After his delayed graduation from Yale, Jason had returned to Pittsburgh, sober and energized. He impressed my father with his newfound determination, and Father secured him a clerk's position with Carnegie Steel. He was living in rooms above Schiller's Pharmacy on the corner of Walnut and Aiken, a short walk from our house on Amberson.

After I knocked, he opened the door, looking a little the worse for wear. Had he been slipping? Eyeing my bag, he said, "This isn't just a social call, is it?"

I explained my situation and asked if I could stay with him for a couple of days.

"Jamie, I will always be indebted to you for what you did for me in New Haven and how your father has helped me. Stay as long as you like," he answered.

But I didn't like imposing on him, and the conditions were less than ideal. I tried to consume a big lunch at the eateries near my office because there was never any food at Jason's. I would get home late and make myself as comfortable as I could on his one sofa with only a thin blanket and a bolster as a pillow.

By the end of the week, I was already considering other options. When I got back to Jason's on Friday night, there was an envelope with my mother's handwriting. The note had two words: "Aunt Leila."

Leila Ricketson was the family renegade, and I couldn't remember the last time I had seen her. She was my mother's older sister by three years. When Mother and Father talked about Aunt Leila at the dinner table, I picked up the few scraps I knew about her. She professed to be an artist but had never sold a thing. She wore all black: most times, a capacious blouse with puffy sleeves and bloomers under a knee-length skirt with ratty old leather sandals on her feet. When she wore pants, a total scandal, Grandmother Ricketson wouldn't let her in the house. She lived in Regent Square, only three miles from our house on Amberson. Was Mother suggesting that Aunt Leila might give me a place to live? What else could she mean? But I had never been to my aunt's house and had no idea what I was in for.

But anything was better than Jason's garret. That weekend I told him my plans. He was sad but understanding.

"I'm sure you will be more comfortable at your aunt's, but I still owe you and your family a great deal." Then he stopped and said with a sly grin. "I know what you cover for the paper. I may be able to help you from time to time." I nodded but didn't say anything. Did he know what he was saying?

On Sunday I caught a streetcar on Fifth to Penn, then past all the East End mansions belonging to the richest families in the city. First was the Heinz home on the left, the pillars of its circular driveway at each end of the block. It reminded me that I hadn't seen Rita since the night before the flood, and I resolved to call on her as soon as I was settled in at Aunt Leila's. Just north of the Heinz place on Thomas was the sprawling estate of George Westinghouse, replete with wooden natural gas derricks on the broad front lawn. Never one to squander an opportunity, Mr. Westinghouse sold the gas to his neighbors and delivered it through specially installed pipelines. At the corner of Homewood Avenue, we came to Clayton, the French chateau-style house that Henry Frick had expanded as befitting a coke baron who was also president of the Thomson steel plant. Further on there was the squat, stolid home of Durbin Horne, the scion of the department store family. Horne's had been a Pittsburgh institution for fifty years. Next were the inauspicious brick gates that led up a tree-lined alley to the home of the Thomas Carnegie family. The house had been built by his brother Andrew for their beloved mother Margaret, Thomas, and himself. Andrew and his mother began spending more and more time living in hotels in New York City, and the house became Thomas's after he married Lucy Coleman and started having children, eventually nine in all. Both Margaret and Thomas died in 1886, but Lucy and the children continued to live in the house off Penn. Across the street from the Carnegie's was the impressive home of their cousin and business partner, George "Dod" Lauder, another one of the Slabtown boys.

Passing all these estates made me realize how much my life was changing. I had led a very comfortable life for twenty-one years, and now I was leaving it for what? These sprawling homes were also a reminder of what I might be up against in taking on the Pittsburgh establishment.

I left the car at Braddock Street. Regent Square was south of Point Breeze and east of Squirrel Hill and nowhere near as fashionable as either of those neighborhoods. The homes became less and less grand as I walked along. About a mile past the intersection with Forbes, I came to 357 South Braddock, the number I had found in the Pittsburgh directory for Leila Ricketson.

The four-square house was more modest than ours and was built with the narrow yellow Monongahela brick that was unique to western Pennsylvania. Seated on the porch behind an easel was a woman with straight black hair that hung unpinned down to her shoulders. She looked deep in thought and paid no attention to me. I didn't want to break her concentration and didn't say anything. Instead, I watched her ease with her brushes, how she mixed the bright paint colors, and how the shapes and shades appeared on the canvas as if by magic. I leaned in, and she must have caught sight of me.

"Who the hell? Wait. James? Jamie? Nephew?" I nodded, and she looked me up and down as if appraising a piece of furniture. "What a handsome man you have become, Jamie." Aunt Leila's opened her arms to embrace me. Seeing that her smock was covered with paint splotches, I tried to lean in with only my head and shoulders. "Fastidious like your mother," she laughed. Then she squinted and said, "I doubt this is a social call. Let's go inside and I'll get you a glass of juice. You look a little peaked."

—◦—

"Now tell me what brings you all the way out to Regent Square? I hear you're a newspaperman," Aunt Leila said.

"So you have talked to Mother."

"We are very different people, but she is my sister."

"Then you know why I'm here?"

"I do, I do," she laughed. "I hear your father is not thrilled with your new profession and you may need a place to live. Well, I'm not thrilled with his profession, and I'm happy to take you in."

"Thank you for making this so easy, Aunt Leila." And this time it was me who opened my arms to her, damn the paint splotches on my jacket.

"I'm happy to have another Bohemian in the family!" she said. We hugged; then she gave me a mischievous grin. "And I don't mind getting under Richard's skin. So self-important, but I know he loves Ellie." Mother hated that nickname and that's probably why Leila called her that.

"Now, no more of that aunt business. It's Leila from now on." Her happy smile and bright eyes made me feel like I'd already found a home—at least a temporary one. "Now, young man, I need to get back to work. There are no formalities here. You can come and go as you please. I won't bother you and, in return, I'll ask that you don't bother me. I'm leaving for Paris in a month to show my paintings. The Philistines in this dirty city don't appreciate anything but portraits and landscapes. Such dreary stuff."

I looked at what Leila was painting and saw a hazy, satanic scene of the iron and steel mills along the Monongahela from the perspective of the hill overlooking the town of Braddock. I hadn't seen anything like it before, but it appealed to me.

She showed me to my bedroom, which was up the back stairs over the kitchen. It had been a maid's room, but Leila had no need for a maid. She showed me the back door as well. "Don't bother using the front. I don't need to know when you come in or who you bring home." Leila led a very different existence from our structured, proper life on Amberson. "There's coffee, toast, and jam if you want some breakfast. If you want eggs and bacon, you'll have to get it at one of the grim little places downtown." I thanked her and retired up to my room. I read over my Johnstown notes for an hour or so and fell asleep.

As I walked down Grant Street late the next morning, I saw Cleveland Brooks step from a carriage, kiss the gloved hand extended out the window, then dash into the *Sun* building. As I got closer, I was surprised to see what I thought was my family's horse and buggy, but it darted away before I could catch up. By the time I had walked to the fourth floor, Cleve was already at his desk, reviewing the wire copy that had come in overnight on the rattling teletype machines. He motioned me into his office.

"Dalton, we need to discuss our coverage of the flood."

"Mr. Brooks, was that my mother I saw you speaking with on Grant Street? I thought that was our family's carriage."

"Those old buggies all look the same. I was saying good-bye to a cousin visiting from the East." Then he hurried on. "We have work to do. The flood coverage is all about the court cases now. No criminal charges are being filed and the civil suits could drag on for months. The fix has been in from the start, and the South Fork men are going to skate on this."

I didn't think I had been mistaken about the carriage, but it was clear Brooks didn't want to discuss the matter. I forced myself to think about the legal consequences of the flood, particularly about what part my father might play in any of those matters. I couldn't imagine him browbeating public officials, but I could see him defending the club against any possible financial damages. Besides the advantageous locus of any proceedings, the club had the ancient common-law precedent of an owner's right to manage his private property as he saw fit. And then there was force majeure, the act of nature argument. I agreed with Brooks that little would come of the civil suits. What I most feared was that I would have to cover my own father in court. Brooks disabused me of that notion.

"Of course, I can't have you anywhere near a courtroom where your father will be defending the mighty men of South Fork.

"I want you to learn about Carnegie Steel and the unions. At first you will only be gathering information. Your writing is fine, but you have to prove to me that you can report the truth, that you have the discipline to check information and not rely on the first thing you hear. You will work with Gus Sullivan. No one knows the labor beat better. Learn from him. If you master the reporting, I'll let you write some of the smaller pieces yourself." Then Brooks laughed. "He's a little gruff."

This took me aback. With all the strikes and lockouts making headlines, this was the most important beat on the paper and put me between the men that I had known my whole life and what they considered the rabble that was trying to destroy their businesses. It was an exciting challenge, but remembering what Grampa Willis had told me about the Railroad Strike of 1877, I knew there could be physical danger as well. Besides that snippet of knowledge, I knew very little about the unions and the history of their relationship with the steel companies. Not wanting to seem lost, I said, "I'll start with the back issues."

I spent the rest of the day with the bound, crumbling old copies of the paper. The first sign of unionism in Pittsburgh came in 1874 when the Knights of Labor organized the puddlers at all the town's ironworks. They were successful at the start because owners of the many small firms couldn't afford to lose business if the workers went on strike. Opinion turned against labor after the violence of the strikes in the anthracite fields northwest of Philadelphia and the Railroad Strike of 1877. Since then, it had been a constant battle between the management of the Carnegie Companies on one side and the Amalgamated representing the skilled workers and the Knights of Labor representing the unskilled on the other. The owners had recently become more provocative by hiring Pinkertons who spied on the workers and escorted scabs into the plants to break strikes.

The *Sun*, as I expected, had kept a middle course in its coverage, calling out the excesses of both sides. In his editorials Cleve had made it clear that the workers were at a disadvantage, and it was getting worse. He had begun warning that if labor continued to get nothing from their negotiations, they would get frustrated and angry, and that could lead to violence.

My apprenticeship was unexpectedly short. I had seen Gus Sullivan in the newsroom but had never dared to disturb him. Not a large man, he had a bald head and fluffy white whiskers. His eyes were beady, but I rarely saw them because he would seldom lift his head. His pen would fly across the copy I turned in; then he would hand it back to me without saying a word. After so many years, he had a sixth sense. At first my copy was covered with questions marks and "ck," meaning check. Even when I thought I had it right, he found things to correct. Soon my copy returned with fewer and fewer marks. I even got an occasional nod of the head in approval when he returned pieces and I was allowed to take them to the print shop to be set.

I was beginning to enjoy my collaboration with Sullivan when I came into the newsroom early one day and found him alone, slumped over his desk, his big black pencil still in his hand. I knew enough to run down to the street and find a policeman who summoned a doctor. Gus Sullivan was dead.

His funeral service the following week was attended by every journalist, steel and union executive, and city official in Pittsburgh. Afterward I returned to the newsroom, not knowing what my next assignment would be. Brooks called me into his office.

"Sullivan had been giving me good reports on your progress. You'll be our lead reporter on labor. I'm not sure you are ready for it, but I don't have anyone to spare. Don't disappoint me."

I stuttered my assurance until Brooks interrupted. "Enough. Prove yourself to me with your copy. To get you more background, I've arranged for you to meet with Captain Jones at noon tomorrow at the Carrie Iron Furnace, before going on to the Thomson steelworks. No one can tell you more about the steel business than Jones. He was in the military, so be on time.

"And you should go down to Homestead. Get to know men of the Amalgamated and the Knights. They are preparing for the coming negotiations over a new contract." I was glad Brooks had trusted me with such a crucial assignment but worried whether I was prepared for it.

⟜⟝

I met Captain Jones right at noon that Tuesday. He did remember me.

"Young Mr. Dalton, good to see you again. Mr. Brooks is an old friend and treats me and my men fair. You want to learn about the steel business? I'm mighty proud of what we've built here and down the road at Thomson."

"It's so good of you to do this, Captain Jones. I've always lived in Pittsburgh but know so little about how steel is made."

We walked through the Carrie furnace yard, then up the stairs to a platform where rail cars, filled with iron ore, stretched back as far as the eye could see. Upon arriving each tipped the ore down to the yard below.

"First the raw iron is mixed with limestone and heated to burn away the carbon. Then it flows into the blast furnaces," Jones explained.

We walked into an enormous shed, and I saw a three-story vat. A whistle blew and Jones shouted, "They are forcing air into the mix. Everyone needs to be on their toes, so they don't get burned by the debris." Right then jets of fire shot out of the vat, and hot cinders fell to the floor. The men moved in slow motion on wooden shoes that kept their feet from being scalded.

Jones continued. "The process used to stop here. The hot iron would flow right into the rollers that made wrought-iron rails. But those brittle rails cracked, and trains went off the tracks. Steel solves that because it's flexible in its way, and the Bessemer process makes it economical enough for railroads and bridge builders to afford it. Let's head over to Thomson, and I'll show you how steel is made."

I was captivated, seeing these strange, dangerous places that made Pittsburgh the center of the industrial world.

On the way out, Jones pointed down to something that was shaped like a gigantic cigar, tapered at both ends with a protruding hatch in the middle. "These vessels get filled up with the pig iron, then are brought by narrow gauge to the Thompson plant."

We rode in the engine of one of those small trains a mile east. The mill's soaring chimneys poured black smoke into the sky. Captain Jones explained what had made the Bessemer process so revolutionary.

"The pig iron twists through all these giant pipes, then is poured into the Bessemer Converter. Look up." I saw a pear-shaped, 12-feet-tall kettle, and Jones shouted above the deafening noise. "This convertor holds 15 tons of molten iron that is fired by Mr. Frick's coke that heats the mix to 4,000 degrees. After all the impurities are cooked out, we add just the right amount of carbon to strengthen the steel."

I saw sparks coming out the top of the processor, then a whooshing sound. "That's cold, forced air," Jones said. The sound grew louder and louder until there was a piercing shriek and an explosion of white light above the convertor. "That means the steel is ready to be poured," Jones added.

I could see men scrambling to get the spout on the convertor into position to pour the pure steel into the various molds for rails, beams, and plate that were scattered about the floor of the mill. The millworkers seemed oblivious to the suffocating heat and deafening noise from the blast.

"Time was you had to work wrought iron for hours to get steel. It took fourteen hours to get fifty pounds of steel. A Bessemer oven produces several tons in just a half hour, but they aren't the last word in steelmaking. Now Mr. Carnegie is switching the Homestead mill to open hearths, invented by a German named Siemens, that are even more efficient than the Bessemers. And they can use the lower-grade iron from the Mesabi Range, the largest deposit in the country.

"Mr. Carnegie is a smart man. He knows that by using the most advanced processes he can make steel faster and cheaper than any other steelmaker. Even if he has to lose money on each rail or beam, Mr. Carnegie will cut his prices until he forces his competitors to the wall, no matter any previous 'agreements' he might have made. And when the economy slows down, he can buy 'em up cheap!"

I wasn't sure I understood the technology, but I was familiar with Carnegie's business tactics. Father had touted them over the years.

Jones then pulled me into the shade of the mill wall. "Mr. Dalton, if you're going to be covering the unions here in Pittsburgh, you should understand that I'm a steel man first. It has been well reported that I have disagreed with Mr. Frick and Mr. Carnegie over the men's working hours. It's bad enough that the men work twelve straight hours, seven days a week. But when they switch from the day to night shift or vice versa, they have to work twenty-four straight hours in all that heat and noise. They call it the long shift. The men are too exhausted to be aware of what's going on around them. That's when they get hurt.

"I convinced Mr. Carnegie we could get more out of the men if they worked fewer hours. The men had to swallow a pay cut, but the shorter shift was more important to them."

Even in the shade, the sweat dripped off my face and onto my notebook, but I scribbled furiously so I wouldn't miss a word.

"Mr. Dalton, I need to be getting back to work. Hope I've given you some idea how steel is made." Before I could thank him, he was already headed to the mill floor. I had a lot more to learn, but in a very short time, Captain Jones had given me the basics of the steel business.

— ⁓ —

After returning to the *Sun* offices, I thought about how all-consuming the labor beat would be as my involvement with the Johnstown Flood, both as a reporter and as a part of the South Fork Club, wound down. I knew it would be difficult to get any information from the owners as adamant and secretive as they were. I tried not to let it show at the paper, but with the uncertainty over my new assignment and all the changes in my personal situation, I was experiencing an anxiety that I had never felt before. It wasn't so much that I was no longer in the comfortable confines of Amberson Avenue. What bothered me most was the falling-out with my father. I wanted to stand on my own two feet, but at the same time his rejection was painful.

I left the *Sun* offices around six, and rather than take the Forbes streetcar, I took the Fifth Avenue line. I still had a hankering to drop in at Amberson Avenue, but by the time I got to my accustomed stop, I thought better of it, sure that Father would not be welcoming. Rather than dwell on all the complications I faced due to my new career, I decided to stop at the Heinz estate. It had been too long since I'd seen Rita, and I hoped she would understand how busy I had been.

Approaching the front door of the sprawling Moorish stucco structure, a departure from the usual dark and upright Pittsburgh home, I realized that I didn't have a calling card to present, *de rigeur* for any social visit, let alone one that could be considered a courtship. I needn't have worried. Before I could even lift the outsized, polished brass knocker, the door swung open and out bounded Rita in a light muslin dress, devoid of the ungainly paraphernalia of a ridiculous bustle and constricting whalebone stays that most women wore. She looked sporty, as she always did.

"Jamie!" she exclaimed. "I'm glad you are still alive. After the flood, we were all packed away to Altoona, and I wasn't sure what had happened to you." Then she frowned. "Why haven't you been in touch until now?"

I gave her a brief rendition of all that had happened at Johnstown and my new job with the paper. "Jamie, you and I have had our ups and downs. I shouldn't have to remind you never to take me for granted. Have you come all this way past Amberson to see me?"

"I was on my way out to Braddock Avenue. It's a short walk from there to where I'm living in Regent Square. With my Aunt Leila Ricketson."

"Your father threw you out, didn't he?"

I nodded, casting my eyes down to the floor. Rita didn't let me indulge in any self-pity. "Good for him and good for you, Jamie. You're doing what you said you wanted to do. Someday he will have to see the importance of that and how it will make you a better person than one who is forced into some precast mold."

I took Rita's hand right there on the Heinz porch and realized how much she meant to me. I wasn't sure of her feelings, but I knew I wanted us to see more of each other.

She was standing close to me now. For a moment we looked right into each other's eyes without saying a word. I was the first to speak. "I know I am going to be very busy with the job. Troubles at the Homestead plant will keep me hopping, but I want to be able to see you when I can. What are your summer plans?"

"Nothing as momentous as that. It's odd, the steel mills are no more than five miles from this very spot, but my father has never as much as let me take a carriage ride by them. They could be on the other side of the moon. At least Daddy takes me to the Heinz plant. He is proud that women work there, canning all his pickles and vegetables."

I asked when I might see her again. "I'm sure you will be busy with your new job this week; then I'm going fishing with the Mellons this weekend. They have a new farm on the Loyalhanna, near Ligonier. They say it is filled with rainbow trout!" she answered.

Rita always surprised me. Without question this was the first time I had ever conversed with a woman about fishing, heretofore a male preserve. When she saw me smile, she said, "Not you too! My mother is positively scandalized that I would be wading in streams with older men, when I should be 'tending my knitting.' But, I mean, it's Richard Mellon, and he assures me there will be a household full of people. Of course, none of the other women will be fishing. I hope we will do some shooting as well," she added.

I loved her independence and readiness to flaunt all the tired social strictures of what was appropriate for young ladies of her social sphere. When you were as naturally athletic as Rita, you should be allowed to participate in activities more demanding than dancing around a maypole.

"I will call you at your office when I'm back from the country. It should be late Monday or early Tuesday. We can make a plan for the following weekend. Maybe a ride. Or even better, let's go to a ball game! The Alleghenys give Daddy a box because he supplies all the relish and ketchup they throw on the hot dogs they sell."

"You are quite a girl, Rita," I said.

Rita took a step toward me. "Jamie Dalton, I am twenty years old and nothing less than a grown woman." Then she got up on her tiptoes and kissed me on the mouth. "Now you get out of here before my mother shoos you away. Say hi to your Aunt Leila for me."

And she was gone back into the house as quickly as she appeared. She seemed so light and delicate in her muslin dress, but from what little I could see, the muscles of her arms and legs were defined, not puffy like the other girls her age. Buoyant but tightly wound, her first two years at Smith had made her confident and self-sufficient—and very appealing to me. I loved the taste of the rouge from her lips and savored it as another streetcar took me down Penn to my stop at Braddock. Omnibuses ran all the way to the Thomson plant on the Mon but not at this time of night, and I had another fifteen-minute walk to Regent Square and Aunt Leila's. As I strode along, it occurred to me that my new address afforded me convenient access to Braddock as well as the Homestead plant that was only a short way across the river, reachable by a ferry or a walkway on the 23rd Street iron railroad bridge.

When I came in the back door to the kitchen, Aunt Leila was busy making herself coffee, dressed in something that looked like a tent with a hole cut out for her head to pop through.

"You've never seen a kaftan, have you?" Leila loved nothing better than to shock.

"No. If it's not offered at Horne's, Mother has never worn one."

"I found this at a street bazaar in Casablanca, Morocco. You should go there someday."

I had never been out of the United States, let alone to Morocco. "Maybe someday, but right now I'm going to bed! See you in the morning."

"I doubt you will. I do most of my work late at night and don't awake until noon, if I can help it." I laughed and went up to my narrow bed. As I lay there, I thought about what I had seen the other morning. Could Mother have been shopping at Horne's, seen Cleve Brooks on the street, and given him a ride to the Sun Building? Maybe I had been wrong about the carriage. Maybe Brooks did have a cousin in from out of town. It took me some time to get to sleep.

Tuesday, June 20, was an important day for both my beats. That morning the Allegheny County Sheriff's office was announcing the status of their investigation into possible criminal charges against the South Fork Club for negligence in the maintenance of the dam. And that evening there would be an organizational meeting of the Amalgamated to prepare for what could be a protracted battle with Carnegie Steel over the next three-year contract at the Homestead works. Since my father wasn't involved in the announcement, Brooks put me back on the case.

The Sheriff's Office was in the year-old Allegheny County Courthouse, already the most renowned building in the city. I had taken a tour of the courthouse the previous summer, and even with my limited appreciation for architecture, I could see what a special structure it was. After a year in the smoke, the polished sandstone, quarried from Coal Hill, had lost its luster, but it was still brighter than any other building downtown. The four turrets and the ten-story campanile gave it the appearance of an Italian fortress and broadcast its seriousness of purpose. Everyone's favorite feature was the bridge that linked the courthouse to the county jail across Forbes. It was modeled after Venice's Bridge of Sighs and served much the same purpose. It was the last free steps convicted prisoners would take before their incarceration.

The massive front doors opened into a cavernous entrance hall. I asked the vacant young man in a too-tight suit, no doubt a son or nephew of a member of Boss Magee's political organization, to point me to the Sheriff's office. He could barely be bothered to point to the stairs on the south end of the hall, then drawled, "Segund."

When I reached the second floor, I could see immediately where the office was because there were already five or six newsmen jockeying for a spot outside the marbled-glass door. I recognized a couple of them from Johnstown, but the others were likely from the many out-of-state papers covering the story. "Make way for the new man," the guy from the *Post* said, laying on the mock deference.

"Making sure your daddy and his friends ain't going to jail?" It irked me that they questioned my ethics, but I wanted them to accept me.

"Trying to get the story, same as you fellas. Give the rookie a break, eh?" They shook their heads, but the taunting stopped.

The lumbering sheriff with a reddish walrus mustache and a florid face flung the door open. "Move back, guys. Let me breathe. I'll be quick.

"I've just come from the three-judge panel. I'll read from their official statement. 'There is no evidence of any culpability. The spring storms have flooded the upper Conemaugh Valley to an extent never observed in recorded experience. The dam has held for ten years, and it would have again this year if such historical weather conditions were not experienced. Further we have accepted the statements of Colonel Unger, president of the South Fork Club, that the dam has been maintained and all reasonable precautions taken. The club and its members cannot be held responsible for an act of nature and the County cannot indict God. As to any criminal action the County of Allegheny sees no need to bring an indictment that can never be proven against any individual or entity.' End of statement."

The newsmen began shouting questions as soon as the sheriff had finished. "Was any testimony taken from the members?" "How can the death of two thousand people be ignored?" "Where's the justice?" "Name these fool judges!" "Does the Sheriff's Office take orders from Chris Magee?"

With that last outburst, the sheriff began waving his arms and shouting. "That's enough. I won't be answering any questions, and neither will the judges that I won't name. You pack of jackals best be gone or I'll have the deputies throw you out, and they won't be gentle about it." With that he stepped back into the office and slammed the door in our faces. A couple of the guys began pounding on the door, but they stopped after a minute when there was no response.

Being the new man and already under some suspicion as a club accomplice, I didn't say anything. The guys grumbled for a few more minutes, but realizing that their questions were going to go unanswered, they dispersed, presumably back to their offices to write scathing diatribes against the injustice of the Allegheny County legal system. Rather than just rail against the opaque judgment of the court, I resolved to write a straight piece about today's announcement but then try to discover who might have influenced the court's decision. It was then that I saw a door opening down the hall, and the familiar figure of my father emerged and headed down the far staircase before any of the remaining reporters caught a glimpse of him. But knowing Father had been at the judges' panel and getting him to tell me what was said were two very different matters.

I went back to the office and wrote a brief story of today's events, then discussed them with Cleveland Brooks. After reading the judge's statement, as I suspected, he had chosen "Cannot Indict God" as the headline over my story.

❦

I headed out Penn to Rita's that Saturday, not expecting her to be there. I was happy when I saw her sitting on the front porch in a broad straw hat with a blue and maroon band. She was wearing a light-yellow cotton dress with a pitcher of lemonade on the table beside the chair and was reading a Dickens novel, *The Tale of Two Cities*. When she saw me, her face brightened with a big smile. "And here is my very own Sydney Carton!"

Dickens wasn't in the Yale curriculum in those days, but I assumed this was a compliment. I swept off my homburg and bowed low. "At your ladyship's service." Rita's kidding, affectionate manner always put me at ease.

"To what do I owe this surprise pleasure?" she asked.

"Can't I drop by for no particular reason?" I laughed.

"I suppose so, but I don't want to sit on this porch a minute longer. Let's take a ride. You look like you could use the exercise. I'll put on my riding habit, and we'll be off. You can use one of our horses." In a matter of minutes, she was back in her jodhpurs, boots, and a ruffled shirt with a diamond stick pin. Her hair was pulled up and her face shone. This was a sweet, lovely woman. More than ever, I wanted Rita Heinz in my life.

We rode down Penn, then turned right at Mr. Frick's home. You could already see the outline of the steel-framed addition and the new French-chateau detailing. On our right was the new Hilliard place, built with the money from coal fields in Ohio that would soon rival Frick's Connellsville operations.

At the south end of Homewood Street was a virgin forest with bridle paths for the adventurous. I had never been there myself, preferring the Schenley property that was closer to Amberson. I didn't want Rita to see any hesitation on my part, so I cantered along with her. We skirted the ten-year-old Homewood Cemetery, which had been created out of William Wilkins's 650-acre estate of the same name. Wilkins was buried there, and many prominent Pittsburgh families such as Rita's, the Fricks, and the Schoonmakers had purchased plots. I wasn't superstitious, but I was glad we stayed out of the cemetery. Riding in a graveyard seemed at the very least sacrilegious.

After we worked our way down into the valley that ran all the way to the Monongahela, Rita broke into a gallop, and I struggled to keep up. Rita had a confident seat, and I could see she was enjoying my discomfort. She guided her horse easily over fallen trees and trickling streams, while I had trouble navigating every obstacle.

She was drawing farther and farther ahead. I was barely staying in the saddle, when my horse balked at a squirrel that crossed the path and I went flying over his head, landing on my back in a pile of muck. Rita looked back with some exasperation and shouted, "Jamie, are you all right?" Then seeing that I wasn't stirring, she grew concerned and headed back toward me.

I was still lying on my back, but I wasn't hurt because I landed on soggy ground. Rita jumped off her horse, but when she looked down at me, I couldn't resist a smile. "You big faker! There is nothing wrong with you at all."

I brought myself up into a sitting position and started rubbing my legs and chest to make sure she was right. "Only my pride is wounded," I said.

"I fall all the time," she said. "Particularly when I have to ride side-saddle with all those bulky skirts and petticoats that Mother insists on. I'm too modern for that! Now let's get you up and walking around."

We tied the horses to some saplings, then walked onto a small path that led deeper into the trees. At an old fallen maple that crossed the path, I gestured that we sit down.

"What a clod you are, Jamie Dalton," she said with a laugh. The dappling light through the trees gave a glow to her face, and without replying I pulled her toward me. She didn't resist, and the kiss became increasingly passionate. There was no one around, and we both sensed this could end much differently than that brief embrace on her porch.

We slid off the log onto a bed of dried leaves. Her eyes sparkled with encouragement, and my hand strayed over her blouse, moving down her body. After a moment she reached down and pulled my hand away. "I'm sorry, but I'm not ready for that."

"To be honest, I don't know whether I am either." Then we both laughed. I momentarily flashed back to the nights of drunken carousing in New Haven. In my mind the State Street whores had no faces. Those experiences hadn't prepared me for this kind of intimacy with a woman like Rita, so alive, so complete.

We lay there for a time holding hands and looking up at the canopy of trees, not at all self-conscious about what we had almost done. "We need to be sure of this, Jamie," she told me. I knew what she meant. Neither of us had any notion of marriage and knew things should wait until we did.

We didn't say much as we walked our horses out of the park, but it didn't feel awkward. When we started up Homewood, Rita looked at me and said, "I very much enjoyed our day, Jamie." Her face was pink, but I didn't hesitate to kid her.

"You sound like we've merely been for a trot in the woods on a sunny day."

"Don't be a rat! You know what I mean," she said, regaining her sauciness. Back at her house, we resisted an embrace, but I did take her warm, soft hand.

"I will see you very soon," I said.

"You'd better," she replied, smiling up at me.

As I waited for a streetcar to take me back to Regent Square, I mused about Rita and our abbreviated passion, but thoughts kept coming back to what might happen at Homestead in the coming week.

———

I continued to monitor the legal situation concerning the flood, but with the criminal suit dismissed and the civil suits still being prepared, there wasn't much new to report. Without any shocking headlines, the story was already fading from consciousness, at least outside of the Cambria Valley. Relief workers there were still finding bodies, and the townspeople faced the enormity of rebuilding their city.

I had been excited and a little intimidated about covering the contract negotiations at Homestead, but it was less of a story than I anticipated. There was an initial confrontation where the plant workers repelled a contingent of scabs escorted by the county sheriff's men. Then the company posted sharpshooters on the ramparts above the plant entrances and the workers were locked out. For the next few weeks, I was expecting further confrontations at Homestead, but nothing happened. On Monday, July 31, I found out why.

William Abbott, president of the Homestead works, issued a press release that morning hailing the resolution of the Homestead lockout. Wages were based on a per ton scale of steel produced, and the Amalgamated had agreed to a cut of $1.50 to $26.50, with possible adjustments every six months. The workers were already back on the job.

I was shocked. Hugh O'Donnell of the Amalgamated had seemed so confident in the strength of the union's position after repelling the sheriff's men and the black sheep. I hurried to O'Donnell's office to speak to him before anyone else did.

I found him on the second floor of the union office, leaning back in his chair, smoking a cigar with a big smile on his face. "Mr. Dalton, what can I do for you today?"

"Frankly, sir, I'm surprised to find you in such good humor. Hasn't the Amalgamated capitulated on its wage demands?"

"Hardly, my boy. This cut is small potatoes, and only the most skilled, less than 20 percent of the workers, will be affected. When the demand for steel comes back, so will our wages. What's important is that the Amalgamated still represents the men at the Homestead mill. They haven't chased us out like they did at Thomson and Duquesne."

I went out to the Homestead plant the next morning. The men on the morning shift were back at work, and the others paraded around the town, drinking beer and slapping each other on the back. The big whistle at the plant blew in celebration. Their jobs and, for most, their wages were secure for the next three years, and they had renewed confidence in the Amalgamated's ability to represent them against the Carnegie men.

The company put out positive statements about the wage concessions, but two months later, it announced that Abbott was being replaced by Henry Frick, who would now manage all the Carnegie steel plants.

The message to the company's workers and its competitors was clear. Carnegie had found the man he wanted. Frick would be relentless in opposing the unions and ruthless in competing with other steel companies. What Carnegie hadn't gauged was how Frick would one day fight him for control of the steel and coke businesses.

There was another message that Cleveland Brooks made very clear to me. "Dalton, we, and by that I mean you, should have had this story a month ago. You have to get sources inside these companies. We can't sit on our hands waiting for the company to announce their plans if we are to be the top paper in Pittsburgh. Dig deeper, kid."

6

On My Own

A MONTH WENT BY, AND ALTHOUGH I WAS SETTLING IN AT AUNT LEI-la's, it bothered me that I didn't feel welcome on Amberson. I left the office early and took the streetcar out Fifth, hoping to speak to Mother before Father got home.

It was a hot day, and all the awnings were unreeled, giving the porch plenty of shade, and I was surprised that Mother wasn't sitting out there. When I went in the house, everything looked the same but still felt foreign. My relationships with both my parents had changed, and this didn't feel like my house anymore. I knew I was welcome, but it occurred to me I might be intruding. And I wondered if Father was home from work. I wasn't ready for another confrontation.

I found Mother alone, sitting in the stuffy parlor. Her head was down, and there was a glass of sherry on the table next to her. "Mother, it's too hot to be inside," I said. "Won't you come out on the porch with me?"

She was twisting a lace hanky, and when she looked up, I could tell that she had been crying. "Jamie, what a surprise," she said in a dull tone.

"What's wrong?" I asked.

"Nothing at all."

"Mother, I can see . . ."

"It's something that I have to work out for myself." Then she stood and spread her skirt down her legs. "How is my handsome boy?"

I could see there was no use pressing her any further. "Very busy, but I like it that way," I answered. "I stopped by to see how everyone is."

"And when your father isn't around. All is well here. Wills and Kat are looking forward to a summer trip, but since no one is returning to South Fork, we must make different plans. The train lines are so improved, perhaps we can think about going somewhere new. Canada? New England? How does that sound to you?"

"That sounds wonderful for all of you, but I will be working," I laughed.

Mother and I looked at each other for a moment, neither knowing what to say. "How's Father?" I finally asked.

"He won't admit it, but he's very worried about you. As am I. No one has forgotten what happened with the railroad strike twelve years ago. I don't want you to be in the middle of any union violence. Not for the sake of a newspaper story."

I decided not to take offense at that last remark. "Mother, the contract at Homestead has been settled and won't be up again for three years. Nothing to worry about!" Despite my light tone, she wasn't convinced.

"I'm imploring you to be smart and safe."

I shook my head. "I'm not a union organizer, for God's sake!" Mother's glare told me that she didn't appreciate my profanity.

Then her eyes closed, and I could see was trembling. "Mother, are you well?"

"It's just one of my moods. I thought they had passed after becoming involved with the suffrage movement. The aid work at Johnstown was very fulfilling, but I've been a little down since I've been back. Don't worry, my son; there will be no more trips to Cresson."

She tried to get me to stay for dinner, but I wanted to avoid an argument with Father. I had reported that the Amalgamated got what they wanted in the new contract at Homestead and was sure he'd take exception to that. He thought that anyone who was not in full agreement with the company was the opposition. I'd explained to him again and again that it was not a newspaperman's function to take sides, but he would never listen. I gave my mother a hug, then walked back to Regent Square enjoying the leafy confines of Homewood.

～❦～

By the end of September, I was getting anxious because I hadn't had a story that made the front page in weeks. Cleve assured me that my job was safe and that was just the nature of the news business. He told me not to be impatient and that things would change.

And they did. On the afternoon of September 26, 1889, I heard the phone ring in Cleve's office. I perked up because no one called him unless they had something important to say. His brow furrowed. All he said was, "We'll get someone down there right away." Then he yelled for me.

"Dalton, there has been an accident at the Thomson plant. They've taken Captain Jones to Homeopathic. Run there as fast as you can!"

I grabbed my bowler, a notebook, and a pencil and within five minutes was at Pittsburgh Homeopathic Hospital, the largest in downtown Pittsburgh, four stories high and covering a city block. Every newsman in Pittsburgh, as well as a wire service reporter, was at the hospital. After a long hour, Dr. William Nimick came out into the lobby.

"Gentlemen, Mr. Jones has serious burns from a plant explosion. I am happy to report that we have treated him with the most modern of medicines. We have given him a draft for the pain, and he is sleeping. All the doctors who have examined him agree that he will make a full recovery. There will be no new announcements until morning."

I was back at the hospital the next day. Around noon Friday Dr. Nimick told us that Captain Jones's condition hadn't changed and didn't say when he would talk to the press again. With nothing new to report, I dawdled around the office for the rest of the day, then checked in at the hospital on the way back to Aunt Leila's.

"He's dead," the reporter from the *Post* told me as he scrambled out the door. I found Dr. Nimick for a quote. "His wound became infected, and sepsis set in. At five this afternoon he lost consciousness, and he died at 9:30 tonight," he told me. Then I hustled back to the *Sun* to get the death announcement and obituary in the next day's edition.

I got back to Regent Square after midnight, and Aunt Leila was still painting. She could see I was shaken by Jones's death, and we stayed up until three talking about that amazing man.

Tuesday, September 30, was the day of Captain William Jones's funeral, and it was the biggest the city of Pittsburgh and the town of Braddock had ever seen. More than two thousand people from all walks of life gathered at the downtown station to see the casket loaded on the train. A throng of ten thousand greeted the cortege in Braddock and escorted Captain Jones's family to the Washington Avenue Cemetery, just three blocks from the Thompson plant where Captain Jones and his inventions had changed the course of steelmaking in America and made Andrew Carnegie one of the richest men in the country.

The people lined the streets on the approach to the cemetery, but few made it inside the gates where the service and interment would take place. There were only chairs for two hundred people, and they were filled by the family of Captain Jones and the many Pittsburgh dignitaries who had benefited from his genius. The press area was cordoned off at the back of the seating area, but I was able to see and hear everything. The now-widowed Harriet Jones had to be helped down the center aisle and was seated in the front row, right next to her son and daughter and various cousins and friends. In the pew behind them sat Carnegie, Frick, and Charles M. Schwab, Charlie to everyone who knew him even slightly. He was Carnegie's protégé and had already been chosen to replace Captain Jones as superintendent of the Thomson works.

Hugh O'Donnell of the Amalgamated sat up toward the front. The union leadership had been invited to sit in the private section, which made sense given the close relationship Captain Jones had with workers at the plants. I didn't recognize the two people next to him. One was a short and unsmiling man, early forties, with beady eyes and a nose that looked like it had been broken more than once. The other was a striking woman with high cheekbones and full lips. She had raven hair down to her shoulders and was much taller than the man. I guessed her to be in her thirties. How were they connected to O'Donnell?

The Reverend Harold Williams of the First Methodist Church of Braddock was the first to speak. He extolled Captain Jones's faith, humanity, and generosity. "Without Captain Jones, our house of worship in this little town would never have been built. Without his leadership, our pews would not be filled each Sunday. His passing is tragic, but Our

Lord will welcome him with open arms, and you can be sure Captain Jones will soon be advising our Savior on how heaven can be made more productive."

This last drew a smile from his widow, and the crowd laughed, breaking the somberness of the occasion. Then Mr. Carnegie rose and took his place behind the lectern. His head was barely visible. I had never heard Carnegie make a public speech before and was surprised by how much of his Scottish brogue remained. I suspected he could modulate it at will depending on the circumstances. His rolling Rs lent dignity to the service.

Mr. Carnegie extolled all that Captain Jones had done to make steel so much cheaper to produce and profitable. He closed by saying, "The only decision of Captain Jones that I ever questioned was his refusal to take a partnership share in Carnegie Brothers, choosing instead a salary equal to that of the President of the United States." Mr. Carnegie's face was flushed and streaked with tears.

O'Donnell was the next to speak. He towered over the pulpit with his broad shoulders and thick brow. He emphasized how Captain Jones was a true steel man that understood the value of his workers. "He spent his days on the floor of the mill, not in an office downtown, not in the castles of Europe. He fought the long shift and for that every steel worker in Pittsburgh is forever grateful."

The steel bosses were getting restless, but this was not the time to answer O'Donnell and it would have been cowardly to walk out. The crowd felt the tension and seemed relieved when O'Donnell took a less confrontational tone but not without a not-so-subtle warning. "As Mr. Carnegie and I can attest, Captain Jones bridged the divide between management and labor while maintaining the respect of both. I fear what may happen in future negotiations without his calming hand."

After some final words from Pastor Williams, the crowd began to disperse. I knew I should get back to the *Sun* to file my story, but I wanted to find out more about the brooding man and his lovely companion. While he was speaking to a small group of men, she was hanging back out of his sight.

"Captain Jones was a great man, wasn't he?" I said.

"I would not know," she replied. "I am here today because Hasçek is here."

"And Hasçek is ...?"

I saw her eyes look at her companion's back, then return to me, her head thrown back. "Miloš Hasçek is the leader of the Knights of Labor. If you are a reporter, as I believe you are, you should know that I have nothing more to say to you."

"At least tell me your name. You don't want me to think of you as Hasçek's woman."

"Majefski, Zofia Majefski," she said in a strong voice, looking me straight in the eye. "And I am no one's woman." Then she strode down the steps of the church and stood alone. After a few minutes, Hasçek, who walked with a noticeable limp, joined her, and they set off. I hoped to see this intriguing couple again, particularly Zofia Majefski.

———

Two weeks after the memorial service in Braddock, Cleve Brooks called me into his office.

"With Captain Jones gone, we have to see what the family intends to do with the patents he filed while working for the Carnegies. The company wants the patents back under its control. That's your next story."

The following day I was at the Jones home on Kirkpatrick Street in Braddock to speak to his widow. It was a rangy, wood Victorian, dark but elegant, befitting the town's most important citizen. As I came down the street, I was happy not to see any reporters.

A well-appointed carriage stood in front of the Jones home. I was shocked when I saw Henry Frick walk out the front door but aghast when I saw who followed him—my father! I gathered myself and walked straight up to Frick. I couldn't appear to be afraid of him.

"Mr. Frick, respectfully, there has to be more than concern for the widow Jones to bring you out here on a workday."

Frick held up his gloved hand. "I am here to offer my condolences to the captain's widow. I understand you are a newshound, but let me offer you some advice. In most cases there are simple, not nefarious, reasons for people's actions. It will do you or your paper no good to make something out of nothing."

"Mr. Frick, may I have a few words with my son?" Father asked.

"I will wait but not for long. There are important issues that require my attention," Frick said as he climbed back into his carriage.

Father stayed behind. "James, I am surprised to see you here."

"No more so than I am to see you."

My father took me by the arm and urged me back towards the Jones's front porch, out of ear shot of Mr. Frick. "Father, why . . ."

"Don't start interrogating me, James," Father said with a scowl. "I will give you a very brief explanation of why Mr. Frick and I are here, and that will have to suffice." Had my father and I become adversaries? I nodded so he would continue.

"Mr. Jones holds more patents for steelmaking than any man in the United States. Mr. Frick wishes to pay his respects but also to encourage Mrs. Jones to give due consideration to the company's generous offer for the purchase of Captain Jones's patents."

I gave Father a skeptical look. "But why are you here? Wasn't he capable of presenting the offer to Mrs. Jones himself?"

"I am the Jones family attorney."

My jaw dropped. "Father, how can you represent both the company and the Jones family in this patent matter? It is a clear conflict." Had we drifted so far apart? Maybe I didn't know my father as well as I thought.

Father's eyes narrowed. "I am very capable of representing Mrs. Jones in this matter. I have told Mr. Frick that he must not submit an unfair offer from the company or I will not approve it. I have given her and the family my word, and that is good enough for them, whether it is for you or not."

"What is this fair offer you have given her? Those patents are extremely valuable!" My face was red, and it was hard to keep my voice down. This was about more than a newspaper story now.

Father looked me in the eye and didn't blink. "Thirty-five thousand dollars."

I stared back at him. "Those patents have made the Carnegie companies millions."

"James, I have become reconciled to the fact that you are pursuing this frivolous career, but in this case, you don't know what you are talking about. There is no need to discuss this any further." His words were defiant, but he gave me a sad look before he joined Mr. Frick in his carriage.

Father hadn't said that the $35,000 offer for the patents was off the record. I wrote up my exclusive but left out the warning from Mr. Frick. In truth, the man frightened me, and to incur his ire even further would not help me or the newspaper in covering Pittsburgh's steel industry.

The day my piece on the patent offer appeared, I was sitting at my desk at the *Sun* when I looked up and saw my father charging across the newsroom, brandishing a newspaper like a sword. "How dare you?" he shouted.

"Father, calm yourself."

"I won't be calm until you explain why you have violated my trust."

"This is no place to discuss this." And I took Father by the arm and led him down to the stairwell on the floor below. Now it was my turn to be angry. "How dare I? How dare you come into my place of work and accuse me in front of the whole newsroom? You never said I couldn't use the price the company was paying for the patents."

"And I never said you could!"

We wrangled like that for several minutes until Father said, "You have taken advantage of our relationship. And lost my respect." Then he flew down the three flights to the street.

＿＿

On October 24, the Carnegie office issued a brief statement that it had acquired all of Captain Jones's patents for $35,000, confirming my reporting. In the editorial column, Mr. Brooks vented his outrage. "Carnegie's meager payment to the Jones family is unconscionable." I knew it would be a long time before my father and I were back on speaking terms.

Cleve continued his rants for several days, but the family was mum. After the furor died down, Brooks called me into his office.

"Jamie, I'm impressed with your work on the Jones's patents. It took guts to use your father as a source. It's not easy reporting on people that are close to you, especially when I'm roasting them in my editorials. Feeling any pressure?"

Brooks had caught me off guard. Did he think I had a bias? "Is there an issue with my reporting, sir?"

"No, none at all." He paused. "I know what families can be like."

"To be honest, my father is not reconciled to my new profession and my coverage of the Jones patents hasn't helped. But my mother has been supportive."

"You've done a fine job, Jamie. Congratulations. You are the *Sun*'s official reporter on the steel beat."

My words tumbled out. "Thank you, sir, you won't be disappointed, sir, I'm totally dedicated, I'm ..."

Brooks cut me off with a laugh. "I'm counting on you. I'm sure your father will come around. I've only met him in passing at the courthouse, but I did have the pleasure of spending time with your mother at a very dull benefit for the Newsboys last year. Not sure where your father was, but I was very grateful when she rescued me from two catty old sisters who were pumping me for gossip. What a charming woman she is! But, of course, you know that. She is very proud of you, Jamie."

Not being sure what to say next, I was happy when we returned to the safe topic of the steel business.

———

The years 1890 and 1891 were relatively quiet for me. The presidential election was two years off and so was the new contract at Homestead. At the paper I learned my craft. My job consisted of attending sessions of the various city boards and councils. There was little discussion—issues had already been voted up or down in camera. The scheming and corruption were behind the scenes, and no matter what I uncovered it didn't seem to change a thing. Boss Christopher Magee was in full control of Pittsburgh, and the Carnegie partners got anything they wanted from him. Magee's greatest feat was how he kept the common man behind him. He reminded them that despite its fealty to the rich and powerful, the Republican Party was a friend to the working man. The Grand Old Party's protectionist tariffs kept the steel and glass businesses thriving and secured their jobs, the party argued, conveniently ignoring the rise in prices for basic goods. The bosses at the plants encouraged the Eastern Europeans to vote the way they wanted them to. The Irish and the Germans knew the patronage they relied on for favors big and small flowed through Magee and the GOP. Despite the Democrats' support of labor, Pittsburgh managed to stay solidly Republican year after year.

The many misdeeds of the political class were an endless source of copy, and Magee's cocky corruption sold more newspapers than the futile efforts of the self-righteous good government types, goo-goos, who promised, but never delivered, reform.

I was working long hours at the paper, and with Rita at Smith, we had had little contact, even when she was home for vacation. And to be honest, I was just out of college and decided I didn't want to be serious about anyone. There were too many distractions in our boisterous city. I stayed out late with friends, and while I was never drunk at work, I was often hungover. I felt guilty that I was not at my best on those days.

In the fall of 1890, Rita's senior year, she had sent me a couple of cross letters, upbraiding me for my lack of attention. They had stopped by the spring, and I wrote her a letter of apology that she never answered. It was one evening in June when I took the Fifth Avenue streetcar home and disembarked at the intersection with Penn. I knew she had recently graduated and was back in Pittsburgh, but I was intending to walk the rest of the way to Regent Square in the long summer twilight. I stopped to look at the Heinz home when a horse and rider stormed out of the drive nearly trampling me.

"You should be more careful. . . . Oh, it's you, Jamie." Rita wasn't smiling when she said this. With perfect posture on her horse, the tailored riding habit, and a face even lovelier than I remembered, she looked more mature, more desirable. I had made a mistake in ignoring this very special person.

"I was hoping I would see you. Please accept my apology for not staying in touch. It's been a busy time at the paper and . . ."

"Oh, save it, Jamie. I'm sure you have your reasons, just don't feed me excuses. I'm a grown woman, and if you think you have broken my heart after our brief tryst in the park, you are even more conceited and self-centered than I had supposed."

She deserved to be angry. My face flushed in embarrassment, and I kicked at the pebbles on the driveway. Rita was and would always be the brightest, most fun, most attractive women I knew. She shared my interest in Pittsburgh politics and business, and I missed our long conversations about the city we both loved.

"You mean a great deal to me, Rita. Can you forgive my inattention? It was not deliberate."

"No, I do not. Why do I waste my time with you?" With that she gave a shake of her reins and headed up South Murtland to the Wilkins Woods, her horse kicking gravel back against my trousers. With that abrupt dismissal, Rita put me on notice that she wasn't going to be taken for granted. I resolved in that moment to prove how much I cared about her and that she could rely on me.

I knew my family had been invited to the Heinz Fourth of July picnic. I was no longer living with them but was sure no one would object to me being there. I hoped to speak with Mr. Heinz and Mr. Westinghouse about how they treated their workers, such a contrast with the steel men, but now it was more important that I be there to repair whatever was left of my relationship with Rita.

— ⁓ —

July Fourth was the following Friday. I arrived at the Heinz home a little after five, and the picnic was in full swing. I lingered on the back veranda to look over the field where there was a large tent, dozens of picnic tables, and a long buffet laden with a munificence of food. Turkey, duck, and pheasant, all shot and dressed at the Heinz property in Sharpsburg. Clams, shrimp, and oysters that had been shipped from the Chesapeake Bay on overnight, ice-cooled trains. Racks of beef and ham still on the bone. And, of course, all the sides and garnishes that were the staples of the Heinz food empire: horseradish, the company's first product; tomatoes, peppers, squash, and every other kind and color of vegetable; eight different flavors of mustard; and, of course, jar after jar of pickles, maybe not the fifty-seven varieties claimed in the Heinz advertisements but enough so the true number didn't matter much. Keeping sentry every few feet on the picnic tables were clear glass bottles filled with the rich, deep red of

Heinz Ketchup, the company's best-selling product, which I knew from my conversations with Rita was made from an old family recipe passed down from generation to generation back in Bavaria.

I spotted Rita near the buffet, but as I approached her, she walked off in the opposite direction. Even as I admired her white muslin dress and shining brown hair, I worried that she wouldn't speak to me.

I followed her across the lawn where she was in conversation with Mr. and Mrs. Thomas Purnell, friends of my parents. "Hello, Mr. and Mrs. Purnell. Rita, may I speak with you?"

"Please excuse the rude Mr. Dalton," she said to them. "I will return shortly." She moved away, then turned with her hands on her hips. "What are you doing here, Jamie? Wasn't it obvious that I didn't want to see you?"

Before I could say anything, she gazed back at the buffet where her father was speaking with Mr. Westinghouse. When she turned back to me, her eyes were narrowed and her lips pursed. "I know the reason you are here! It's to speak to Daddy and Uncle George, isn't it?"

"Rita, I hoped you and I could talk. Of course, I'd welcome a chance to speak to your father and Mr. Westinghouse, but I can do that later."

"I knew it!" And she walked off. As I looked after her, Mrs. Purnell gave me a knowing smile.

I'd lost my appetite, but the kegs of beer chilled in tubs of ice looked inviting. On each barrel "Iron City" was painted on the side in the same gothic type as used in the official seal of the city of Pittsburgh. As I drank from my schooner of cold beer, I noticed a large group at the other end of the lawn that by their dress and demeanor looked different from the other guests. I hadn't noticed the approach of Mr. Heinz and Mr. Westinghouse.

"You look puzzled, Mr. Dalton. Do you think it odd that I would invite my employees to celebrate the birthday of our country, theirs as well as mine?

"Mr. Heinz, Mr. Westinghouse. No, sir, I think it's a fine thing for you to do."

"Young man, I understand that you are working for the *Sun* and covering the steel industry. Perhaps you would like to hear about the different philosophy of labor that Mr. Westinghouse and I share. Shall we sit in the shade of the tent?"

As we took our seats, I thought about what I knew of these two men who were second only to Carnegie in the successes they had brought to Pittsburgh. Both were of German extraction but were very different in appearance. Mr. Westinghouse was the taller of the two and had straight brown hair, streaked gray at the temples and parted on the right side, while Mr. Heinz had black, curly hair parted in the middle. Both had flowing handlebar mustaches with luxurious sideburns, a jolly contrast to Carnegie's close-cropped white beard and Frick's aggressive goatee. Mr. Westinghouse's open face and friendly eyes gave him an intelligent, welcoming look that must have served him well in his many business ventures. Mr. Heinz's eyes were more restless and never stopped scanning the tent to see what might need his attention.

George Westinghouse was an undeniable genius. The air brake he invented in the 1860s made the railroads safer and more profitable. His latest project was the dispersal of electricity via alternating current. His proposal was more scalable than Thomas Edison's direct current because it could travel longer distances from one central plant. The fight was bitter and involved patent litigation that threatened the financial future of both men. Mr. Westinghouse maintained a calm, cheery demeanor in the face of the terrible pressures he faced and loved speaking to the press. Mr. Heinz was more reticent, but he had much to be proud of. He had invented the food-processing industry.

"Sirs, thank you for this opportunity. I am curious as to why there are so few labor problems at your operations. Mr. Heinz, I understand that you pay less than the average hourly wage for industrial workers. Why do they accept that? Why haven't they organized into unions?"

Mr. Heinz was blunt in his answers. "I suspect you don't report good news, James. The reason we do not have problems with our employees is that we treat them well. I'm a religious man, and I manage my businesses as I manage my life. 'Do unto others,' the Bible tells us. I treat my workers with the same respect that I hope they have for me. The wages I pay them may be lower than other businesses, but the men and women in my employ receive many other benefits."

"Such as?" I asked.

"Workers have only so many years when they can be productive. They support their families and there is nothing left over for savings. What are they supposed to do after they stop working? Rely on their children? Beg alms from the church? They have worked hard and deserve some dignity. I have set aside money for them, a pension, for their retired years. We also provide medical care for all our workers and their families."

"We do the same," Westinghouse said. "Does that surprise you, Mr. Dalton? It only makes sense. Healthier people mean fewer absentees, and our production lines keep moving. They work more years, and we have fewer new people to train. My workers become part of the Westinghouse family. It's much the same for Mr. Heinz."

"What's most important is that our people work eight-hour shifts," Mr. Heinz added. "You can't expect anyone to labor for twelve straight hours, as Clay and Andrew demand. Yes, there is more expense to having three rather than two shifts a day, but it is more than offset by increased productivity and fewer injuries. I understand Mr. Frick wants to force the Thomson workers back to the twelve-hour day. A mistake in my estimation."

Mr. Westinghouse was beaming. "The answer to your original question is simple. We have fewer labor problems because our workers are happy. Why, we have put in a baseball diamond at our Fifth Street plant. In the winter, we set aside space inside for a boxing ring and gym apparatus. Much better for the men than heading straight for a tavern, I say."

"Gentlemen, this is quite a revelation. I know that good news does not get its due, but what you have told me today is in stark contrast to the contentious state of affairs at the steel mills. Our readers should be aware that driving men to the breaking point is not the only way to make a business thrive."

Mr. Heinz smiled in appreciation, and Mr. Westinghouse said, "James, we trust you will accurately report what we have told you. That will be a service to the city and all its citizens. Now, I am sure you would prefer spending your time with Mr. Heinz's lovely daughter." I did but couldn't tell them how cold my earlier reception had been.

❧

Another month went by without going back to Amberson Avenue, and I felt guilty about not checking on how Mother was faring. I was nervous about seeing my father, and I wondered how upset he was about my coverage of his purchase of the Jones patents. When I got there, Mother was wearing a broad straw hat and tending the flower boxes. Did I hear her whistling?

"Jamie, I'm thrilled to see you. Let me finish with these petunias and we will go inside. No one else is home."

"You seem much happier than you were at my last visit."

"Oh, don't pay attention to my silly moods. I'm attending suffrage meetings, and it has given me so much to do. Today I need to organize leaflets for the rally we are holding in Oakland next week on that large piece of land where Western is moving.

"The rally will be on September 1," she continued. "We're hoping for good weather. These women I have come to know in the movement won't be deterred, rain or shine."

"I'm pleased to see you in such fine spirits, Mother. How many are you expecting?"

"Over one thousand," she answered. "But I am worried about what is drawing them. More and more we are sharing the podium with women who want to prohibit the sale of alcohol. They argue that they want to defend women from working-class husbands who come home drunk and abusive. I understand the rationale, but why should women get the vote only to take away others' right to drink?"

"Mother, it seems to me that the women advocating some sort of prohibition are acting on their own moral sense and using the lot of the mill wife as a convenient argument. You don't see too many Hungarians or Irish at the rallies, I'd imagine?"

"I suppose not. In any case, I must ignore that issue and put my shoulder to the suffrage wheel. It's so basic. Men and woman are all created equal. I'm sure that's what Mr. Jefferson would say today!" Then she added, "I had hoped we would get better coverage of women's issues in the *Sun*."

"I'll be sure to mention that to Mr. Brooks,"

"He seems like a man that would rally to a progressive cause."

I laughed. "He speaks highly of you as well." I was surprised to see Mother blush, and I changed the subject. "Have you read any of my articles about the steel companies' purchase of Captain Jones's patents? His family deserved so much more!"

Mother paused before she answered. "It's useless making that point with me. Your father is disappointed. He feels you took advantage of him."

"Please don't tell Father I even brought up the subject with you. Our relationship doesn't need any more strain."

She patted my face. "I won't say a thing. Now can I tempt you with some cakes? I don't think you're getting enough to eat, living at Leila's."

7

Zofia

THE LABOR QUIET AT THE CARNEGIE COMPANIES ENDED ABRUPTLY ON New Year's Eve, Wednesday, December 31, 1891. That afternoon I was at the *Sun* when Cleve waved me into his office.

"Jamie, I hope I'm not interrupting any plans you have, but I'm hearing there may be trouble at Thomson tonight. I want you to get out there as fast as you can and find out what's going on."

"I thought about going to the Monongahela House ball, but I can skip it." I had been hoping to see Rita there. When I had seen her at various functions that fall, she hadn't been as frosty as at the Fourth of July picnic, but she hadn't agreed to have dinner or even take a carriage ride when it would be just the two of us. I made sure she knew I wasn't interested in anyone else, but I didn't know whether we would ever be a couple again. "I'll catch the next train," I told Brooks.

When I got to Braddock, I sensed there was trouble brewing. Small knots of laborers, the unskilled Eastern Europeans, were huddling on street corners. Then I saw Miloš Hasçek walking down Washington Street, approaching each group. The men nodded their heads in agreement as he spoke to them. I was disappointed his lovely companion was not with him.

Various groups marched down Fourth Street to the Thomson plant. Many were weaving, and all were shouting, "No twelve, no twelve!" and "Knights forever!" But when around two hundred men occupied the stockyard, they didn't seem to know what to do besides pass around flasks.

At that point a young man positioned himself on a coupling of one of the narrow-gauge cars that plied the yards. It was Charlie Schwab, who

Frick had promoted to superintendent of the Thomson works after the death of Captain Jones.

"You men don't belong here tonight," he shouted over the din.

"We have every right to be here," Hasçek yelled back. "You want to yoke us to a twelve-hour day when your Captain Jones agreed to eight. We will never allow it!" The men cheered.

"We will discuss that in time," Schwab replied, "but tonight this drunken rabble is here illegally. Mr. Frick notified the sheriff, who has sworn to uphold the law. Look around you." There were more than a dozen men cradling rifles and positioned at high points around the yard. "He won't hesitate to order his deputies to shoot unless you leave immediately."

That quieted the workers. Hasçek tried to rally them, but they began to shuffle out of the yard. Schwab's show of force had worked.

Masking his humiliation, Hasçek shouted, "The Knights shall return. Count on it!"

But would they dare challenge the power of Frick and the Allegheny County sheriff?

With the end of the demonstration, I returned to the *Sun* and filed my story. I thought about heading to the Monongahela House but took the Forbes Avenue car back to Regent Square instead.

———

The aborted occupation of the Thomson yard on New Year's Eve proved to be a single outburst. Sheriff's men and company guards patrolled the plant, ready for a "Hun attack" that never happened. The workers returned to the mill, and the furnaces were at full blast within a week. The twelve-hour shift was back, and the Knights were no longer a factor at the Braddock mill.

A series of violent events kept roiling through 1892, providing me a series of page-one pieces in the *Sun*. In late January a horrific explosion at Frick's Mammoth Mine #1 killed 107 workers. I got out to Connellsville in time to see the recovery efforts. There were men that were blasted beyond recognition being brought up from the mine. Their bodies were dumped into an open trench dug near the town cemetery.

The newly formed United Mine Workers took ten thousand men out on strike to demand better working conditions. A defiant Frick instead announced a pay cut, with no promise of any new safety measures, and refused to negotiate. In an initial confrontation, a combination of sheriff's deputies and Pinkertons that Frick had hired killed seven men and wounded dozens more. The strike dragged on another two months, but the fight was out of the mine workers and the union called it off.

My reporting had fueled public outrage against Frick but, as usual, to no effect.

The Duquesne works, five miles up the river from Braddock, was the next trouble spot. Frick had acquired Carnegie's top competitor for a bargain price during a slowdown in demand that had crippled the company. But now the Amalgamated had organized the skilled workers to seek pay equivalent to what men in other iron and steel mills in Allegheny County were making.

Frick's spies gave him the names of the strike organizers who were fired and blackballed at the other Carnegie plants. He even wheedled a court order enjoining union men from interfering at the mills under the threat of jail. The strike was over in a month, and the Amalgamated was through at Duquesne. One by one Frick was bringing the Carnegie mills to heel. The only unionized plant left was Homestead.

In March I attended the Amalgamated's first meeting in preparation for the Homestead strike that was sure to come when the current contract ended on July 1. The union hall was merely functional. Flickering gas lights on bare wood walls illuminated a space filled with two blocks of ten benches that could seat no more than two hundred men, but twice that many had jammed in the back of the hall and down the side aisles to the stage. I stood in the back, taking it all in.

There was clearly a divide between the two seated groups. On the left representing the skilled workers were the Amalgamated men, all speaking English, many with Scottish or Irish accents. The men on the right spoke a polyglot of languages that were undecipherable to me, but I knew they were the Knights of Labor, men from Eastern Europe who were filling the unskilled jobs in the automated Bessemer plants. In the back the two groups mixed easily, some even greeted each other as acquaintances. This camaraderie spoke to the difficulties the Carnegie interests might have in splitting the solidarity of the two labor groups.

I heard a stir at the front door and saw Hasçek limp into the hall. His dark eyes scanned the crowd with a nervous fixation. He wasn't smiling but was greeted with warmth by every Knight he approached. Zofia Majefski walked beside him with her shoulders back and her head held high. I was surprised when she looked right at me. Before I could react, she turned away. When the pair got close to the stage, two of the men vacated seats on the aisle of the third row. I wondered about the nature of their relationship. Colleagues? Friends? Lovers? When the meeting concluded, I would seek them out.

Hugh O'Donnell of the Amalgamated, dressed in an ill-fitting brown suit with a short, garish tie, approached the dais and held up his arms up for order. Calls of "Quiet!" filled the hall, and the room grew silent.

"Boys, Carnegie and his flunky Frick want to run us out of here, like they did at Thomson. Wants us signing 'yellow-dog' contracts that we won't join unions. If we don't stop them here, we might as well close up shop. So what are we going to tell them?"

"Hell, no!" erupted from both sides of the house.

O'Donnell stoked the outrage. "To my Amalgamated brothers, they think they can cut our wages 10 percent. I have to say, Mr. Carnegie was smart to convert the Homestead plant from rails into structural steel for the skyscrapers and steel plates for the war ships. But they can't be crying poor when business is slow. Old Andy always cuts his prices to keep the orders flowing, but is that our fault? We won't let him wring out the profits so he can lease out another castle in Scotland, when our workers are living in dilapidated company shacks and buying what can barely be called food at the company store until they are so in debt they owe the company more than they get paid in a year. We won't allow that!

"They don't want us to organize, but the steel companies band together to set wages and prices across the industry. They expect the government to protect them with tariffs and send out militias to break our strikes. Then they buy off the politicians to pass laws that cripple unions."

Cries of "Cowards!" rang out.

"To my many Hungarian friends in the Knights of Labor, I have another message."

Exaggerating his enunciation of each word, O'Donnell said, "You have come from Hungary, where you were serfs, and found jobs in the land of opportunity. Do you want Carnegie and Frick to take away those jobs?"

There was grumbling among the Knights. Then Hasçek stood up. "Mr. O'Donnell, don't treat these men like fools." The right side of the room nodded in agreement. Hasçek had a slight accent, but his English was fluent.

"Ah, Mr. Hasçek from the Knights. Would you introduce yourself to the gathering?" O'Donnell asked.

Hasçek turned to the room. "I am an organizer for the Knights of Labor, but for ten years I was a steelworker, until a falling rod mangled my hip." That got the notice of everyone in the room. Whatever his nationality, a man injured at the plant was in the fraternity of steel men.

O'Donnell acknowledged that. "Continue, brother."

"Thank you, sir, but you must understand something." He waved his arm to include the men on his side of the room. "These people are from many countries, not just Hungary. Bulgaria, Russia, Poland, Slovakia, all over Eastern Europe. I know it's easier to call us all Hungarians. They may not understand that you have lumped them together, but they deserve the dignity of you acknowledging they are not all from one country. And don't call us 'Hunkies.' It's the same as 'spic,' 'wop,' 'nigger.' An insult. You want us to join you in this resistance to the oppressors, then give us our due."

I was struck by his use of the word "oppressor." It smacked of the kind of class struggle that Marx and Engels advocated in their *Communist Manifesto* that I'd read at Yale, and I wasn't sure the Amalgamated leadership was headed in that radical a direction. But Hasçek had read the room and knew when to pull back to the topic at hand.

"We are with you, Mr. O'Donnell. We must be stronger than we were at Thompson in January. These men want their jobs; they want to bring their families here from their old countries. We will stand with you against the capitalists, but don't take us for granted." Hasçek sat back down to the cheers of the Knights of Labor, and many of the men around him clapped him on the back. He shied at their touch but endured it.

O'Donnell took back control of the meeting. "We are partners to the steel men, not their slaves. We know better than the men in the offices downtown what is needed in the mills. They should heed us about who to hire and how to run the shop. And we deserve a share of their profits as well." I thought to myself how the owners would never take demands such as this seriously.

"The bosses think they can break us by bringing in their damn scabs. But we won't let their cursed black sheep into the plant, no matter how they threaten us. Frick is a dangerous man. He gunned down the strikers at his coke works, and he will do the same here in Homestead.

"Remember that management wants to be rid of the unions altogether, the Amalgamated and the Knights both. They even plant spies and try to bribe union officers. At Duquesne and Thomson, the men can't even organize to demand new safety rules. We must make our stand here in Homestead.

"They think it's their God-given right to cut our wages and extend our hours." Then O'Donnell shouted, "Wad'r we gonna tell the bastards?"

The seated men all rose, stomped their feet, and again chanted, "Hell, no!" They kept that up for five minutes until O'Donnell left the makeshift stage, and the men dispersed, exuding the confidence and determination O'Donnell and Hasçek roused in them. I waited on the cobblestone street outside the hall to speak with O'Donnell.

While I stood there, I saw Hasçek leave the hall, surrounded by several of the larger Knights. I hoped I could talk to Zofia, but before I could approach either of them, the group moved down the sidewalk away from the hall. There was a Polish American club down Main Street, and I presumed they were headed that way. I considered following, but then O'Donnell came out, and I knew my first responsibility was to find out whatever I could from him.

"Mr. O'Donnell, James Dalton, the *Sun*. You and I spoke during the '89 labor talks."

"Can't recall every newshound poking around." He tried to walk past me, but I didn't move.

"All I want is to ask you a couple of questions."

"The Pittsburgh papers always take the side of the owners. Why should I believe you are any different?"

"The policy of my paper is to give both sides a fair shake." He gave a snort of disbelief, but I continued. O'Donnell could be an important source, and I needed to get him to talk to me.

"What are you going to do if they hire guards to escort the new hires into the plants?"

O'Donnell took a step back, and his face got red. "Then there will be a battle royal. Every man, woman, and child will be out to stop them. You heard what I said at the meeting. No black sheep!"

"What if they bring in the sheriff and all his deputies to protect the scabs?"

"Not even if the devil Pinkertons escort them will we allow anyone to take our jobs. And you saw today that the Hungarians are on our side as well. Those brutes won't stand aside!" he exclaimed.

"What do you make of Hasçek?" I asked.

"Don't know him particularly. Not sure I trust him, though. I fear it's more than wages and the right to organize that he wants."

"And the woman?"

"She's always with him. Never speaks to a soul except Hasçek. Word is he found her on the streets, abandoned by her family and doing who knows what to survive. The man is right tetchy about her. He's pulled a knife on men who dared approach her. I'd stay away if I was you."

O'Donnell's warning piqued my curiosity, but I tried not to let that show. "Mr. O'Donnell, I hope I can count on you to keep me abreast of what is happening with the Amalgamated." He didn't reply but hadn't refused me either. I headed back to the newspaper's office, hoping I had made a reliable contact on the labor side.

—◆—

The next week I was headed down Eighth Street in Homestead when Hasçek and Zofia came out the door of the Amalgamated headquarters in the Bost Building. I stuck my hand out and said, "Hello, sir. I'm James Dalton from the *Pittsburgh Sun*. I heard you speak at the rally the other night."

He didn't take my hand. "Hasçek," was all he said.

"I was impressed with what you said that night. What do you think will happen with the labor contract at Homestead?"

"The anger is building."

"About Mr. Frick's planned lockout?" I asked.

"We will fight Frick and Carnegie, but it is the whole capitalist system that must be destroyed. Have you seen where the workers live? Have you seen their children taken to the plant after four years of school? They are ten years old and are worked as hard as adults, and without more education that will never change. But this one contract means very little. Win or lose, the struggle will continue until the workers of this country and the world unite to end the system that exploits them. I lead the Knights as a first step towards that end."

I was taken aback. "You sound like a communist, an anarchist!"

He looked at me in a condescending fashion. "You think you are a truth seeker as a newsman. You know nothing of the world."

Since I suspected he was right, I didn't argue.

Instead, I turned to Zofia, who had been at his side saying nothing, and offered my hand to her. "I believe we have met, Miss Majefski."

Hasçek was about to cut her off when she answered, "I have no recollection." But I saw that her dark eyes were not as hostile as her words. Perhaps she would speak to me after all?

As she walked off, I admired her shapely figure, not disguised by the very full black blouse and long black culottes she wore. Hasçek tried to take her arm, but she shook off his hand. It didn't surprise me that Hasçek was so protective of her, and that made her all the more mysterious and intriguing to me. And I thought back to what had almost happened with Rita when I had fallen from my horse that day in the woods. I had to respect her limits, but that didn't mean my desires had vanished. I felt a primal attraction to Zofia. Might she be more willing?

As I headed downtown to write up that day's events, I decided not to include any of Hasçek's comments. I might need him as a source for whatever was to come at Homestead. And I would have to be wary of him if I was to have any further contact with Zofia.

Then O'Donnell came out the door of the Bost Building. "Let's go down to the plant, Dalton."

We walked out onto Eighth Avenue and took a left toward the sprawling mill. You couldn't appreciate the enormity of the operation until you saw it up close. You were dwarfed by the looming, blackened walls and roofs of the sheds and perplexed by all the enormous cylinders and tubes that twist into every configuration imaginable. There was the constant flow of trains carrying coke up from Connellsville that stopped only long enough to deposit their contents before they steamed back for another load. Even the trains looked small in comparison to the mill. The sheds sprawled up and down the south side of the Monongahela for more than a mile in each direction. There were four thousand men working at the Homestead facility, but they were swallowed up by it. The only time you were aware of their numbers was at the shift change.

At that close range you were assaulted by the black, choking smoke and soot. Your eyes itched, and you couldn't breathe through your nose. It was no exaggeration to say that you were chewing on the air and the taste was vile. You couldn't help but be aware of the filthy air in other parts of the city, but at the plant, it was infinitely worse. I had to wonder what the long-term effect would be of breathing such a toxic mixture this close to its source.

Noticing my discomfort, O'Donnell said, "You get used it. What bothers the men is when that black smoke ain't pouring out of the stacks. That means a strike or a lockout and no pay, while the wife and kids survive on scraps. That's why they this next contract is crucial. Frick is ruthless, and he is determined to be rid of the unions. It may get bloody, but we have to stand firm."

I was thrilled over the prospect of such a sensational story, but it worried me as well. I had never witnessed the kind of violence he was anticipating. How would I react?

Every night that spring when I got back to Regent Square, I thought about staying on the tram that took a big left turn into Braddock, then stopped at the Thomson works. From there I could look for Zofia in the workers' gathering spots. Hugh O'Donnell and I shared a language, but I wasn't sure how I would be received by the Eastern Europeans. After the inhumane twelve-hour shifts, these tough men would wash away the dirt in their throats and pain in their bodies with shots of elixirs that might have been called whiskey on the bottle but did not deserve the name. Some would return to the hovel they shared with other men. Others would stagger back to the shack where they lived with their wives and children but in no condition to be either a husband or a father. At best a worker would shovel down some food and fall to the floor onto a hard mattress shared with his wife and at least one of his children. At worst he would be violent. Maybe the suffrage ladies who advocated prohibition had a point.

I knew this much about the lives of the steelworkers but little more. There were many barriers besides language that would block me from entering one of their social clubs. My height and build would serve me well, but I doubted they would trust me. It would help my reporting if I could get to know some of these men and understand their lives and hopes, but if I was honest with myself, I was there for the chance to see Zofia. Rita was always on my mind, but I was discouraged by how dismissive she had been the last time we spoke. I knew our connection was real, but the lure of Zofia, someone so different from any woman I had known, was overwhelming. And I couldn't forget her friendly eyes at the union meeting.

That spring I made several trips to the working men's bars in Braddock and Homestead. I told myself I was gathering background on labor's side of the upcoming strike, but I always asked about Hasçek and Zofia. That would bring the conversations to an abrupt end.

But I persisted. On Decoration Day in late May, I stayed on the streetcar out to Braddock. A small parade came down Washington Street and skirted the mill property. Men stood with their families, who all waved tiny

American flags as an oompah band and a horse-drawn calliope added some gaiety to the procession. When I approached them and announced that I was with the *Pittsburgh Sun*, they stared in blank incomprehension or waved me away. Either they didn't want to interrupt one of the few days they could spend with their families or didn't want to be seen talking to a reporter.

Feeling useless, I wandered farther up the street until I found a ramshackle, one-story building that had a faded sign on the front that announced it as the Polish American club of Braddock. I entered the hall with some trepidation. On the left were several broad sheets of plywood on three-foot-high trestles that served as a bar. On the floor were brass spittoons overflowing with tobacco juice. Men were standing shoulder to shoulder looking down into their beer and shot glasses, paying me no mind. In this place drinking was a serious business with no frivolity or joy. The barman gave me a dirty look and asked what I wanted.

"I'm looking for a young lady. She's involved with the Knights of Labor."

"See any women around here?" he scoffed.

It was then that I saw a man limp from the shadows in the back of the club. He challenged me right away. "Dalton, are you such a fool to think I wouldn't hear about your inquiries? I am the leader of the Knights, and I can understand you asking for me. But there is no reason for you to speak with Miss Majefski. She will not see you." Miloš Hasçek had his hand in his pants pocket, and I thought back to what Hugh O'Donnell had told me about the knife.

But that didn't deter me from responding to him. "Mr. Hasçek, I am writing a color story about the union leadership, and I'm sure my readers would love to know more about a woman who is involved in the labor movement. My interest is purely professional."

It was then that Zofia walked into the room. "Miloš, let me speak for myself?" Hasçek look displeased but let her by.

"Mr. Dalton, I have made it very clear that I have nothing to say to you or the *Pittsburgh Sun*. This club is for workingmen. You need to leave."

I heard her words, but at the same time she was moving her eyes toward Hasçek. "But, madam, don't you think it is the working man's point of view that should be represented in my newspaper?"

"You are a young and inexperienced boy. Why should I waste my time with you?"

"All I need is a half hour," I answered.

Hasçek stepped between us, and he had his knife in my face. "Go. Now," he growled.

I didn't think; I reacted. I knocked the knife out of Hasçek's hand and pushed him hard. He sprawled against one of the tables and started to come at me again. Zofia grabbed his arm.

"Get out of here, Dalton, before you get hurt," she said. Men were lined up behind the two of them. She had a scared look. Might she be concerned for my safety? In any case, I thought it best to heed her warning.

"Miss Majefski, Mr. Hasçek, I am very sorry to have interrupted you on this day of celebration. I will be going." Before I could turn, I saw Zofia nod her head imperceptibly. I did the same.

I didn't get a story out of my Decoration Day excursion, but at least I had spoken with Zofia. My interest in this woman was greater than before, but I resigned myself to being discreet. Another meeting with her under Hasçek's baleful gaze would end badly. I needed to find a way to see her alone.

<hr>

It was a week later when I arrived at the *Sun* to find a hand-folded envelope on my desk with the word "Dalton" scrawled in barely legible script. "Meet me tonight on the Smithfield Bridge at 10." It was signed "ZM." My heart raced. It was from Zofia Majefski, and she wanted to see me. For what reason I didn't know and didn't much care. It was enough that she had agreed to a meeting.

The hours dragged by while I fidgeted with a story on how the two sides were preparing for the possibility of a strike at Homestead. At eight I went to O'Reilly's on Stanwix and stayed for an hour and a half, scarfing up corn beef and cabbage and downing a couple of cold beers to calm my nerves. At 9:30 I made my way down to the end of Smithfield Street and walked up the iron stairs to the walkway across the bridge. There was a dark figure in the middle of the bridge. It had to be Zofia.

As I drew near, she dropped her head scarf and said, "Dalton, I wasn't sure you would come."

"Why would you doubt that?"

"You don't seem like the adventurous type to me, never venturing out of the cocoon of your bourgeois society." In the darkness, I couldn't tell whether she was teasing. "Do you have no humor, Dalton? I'm serious about our cause, but even I realize how ridiculous we can sound." She pivoted. "Why have you come here tonight?"

"Why have you? You are the one who set up this rendezvous."

"You have asked to write about me in your capitalistic newspaper, but I suspect there is more to it than that." I stared out at the river rather than respond. She followed my gaze, and we both looked up the Monongahela towards the twenty-four-hour glow of Homestead and Braddock. I saw the source of Pittsburgh's wealth. I assumed she was seeing something very different—the choking smoke, misery, and exploitation.

I turned her to face me. "You are a woman who sees men as they are. I won't bother to dissemble. I'm not sure my editor would even accept a piece in the *Sun* about you—that is not the real reason I'm here. You are a beautiful woman, and I want to spend time with you. Learn about you, from you." I knew no one like Zofia. Her beauty and strength captivated me.

She looked at my hand on her arm, and I let go. "Mine is a simple story, Dalton. I was born in Poland. My mother died giving birth to me. My papa and I immigrated to America, and we came to Pittsburgh, where he shoveled coke to fire Carnegie's furnaces. In a few years he died as well, burned to death from an explosion in one of those hellacious mills. I fended for myself until I became involved in the movement and met Hasçek."

"Fended for yourself?"

She stared at me for a long minute. Was she wondering how much she wanted to reveal? Or maybe she was thinking that I wasn't worldly enough to understand a life so foreign to my own.

"Dalton, I cannot blame you for the sheltered life you've led, but you know nothing of the depths. After my father died, I stayed in the same boardinghouse where he and I had lived. When I matured, I walked up and down Washington Street in Braddock at any hour of the day. One night a man pulled me into a dark alley and raped me. The woman who ran the boardinghouse said I had brought shame to her and her family, and she threw me out.

"After sleeping under a bench in the town square for a few nights, a woman in a gaudy dress approached me and said, 'You are a pretty young girl. I can help you.' I didn't know it at the time, but she was the madam of the most notorious house in Braddock. For the next three years I lived that life." She paused. "Are you shocked, disgusted?"

"Not at all," I said too quickly. I was shocked, but nothing about her could disgust me. "How did you escape?"

"Hasçek came into my life. He bought me out of that horrible place and was kind to me for a time. I was grateful and maybe even in love with him.

"That all changed after the rod at the plant shattered his hip. He could no longer perform in bed and blamed me. He tried to abuse me, but I am the stronger one. We still live together but apart."

"Zofia, you don't need him."

"My dedication to the cause of the people is absolute, and we work together, even though I disagree with the violent tactics he and others espouse. People say he controls me. No man will ever control me. Hasçek knows this and fears that if I want you, I shall have you."

She stepped closer to me, and I could see in the dim light of the bridge her dark, deep eyes. "I believe in the same class struggle that he does, and I owe him my life. But tonight, he has gone east for another meeting with the anarchists. Their way is not the answer. The capitalist troops are too many and too well armed. That is a fight that will always end in disaster for the worker.

"You are very bold, Dalton. I arranged our meeting because you are the only man brave enough to challenge him. I'm thinking you are twenty-five years old?" I nodded. "I am thirty-two, but in experience I am many years older than that. I hope you are not set in your thoughts. The press is mighty in your country. Perhaps I can convince you that our cause is just." She was smiling at me.

"Use me however you like," I answered with more confidence than I felt.

She stepped toward me and kissed me on the mouth. She pulled her face back from mine and said, "I owe Hasçek much, but I will take physical love as I please. I want you to fuck me, Dalton."

I was shocked by her boldness, saying a word I had only heard from the whores in New Haven. But I was ready to do what she asked. As she unbuttoned me, I lifted her skirts and soon was inside her—right in the middle of the Smithfield Bridge, for all to see if there happened to be anyone about at that late, cold hour. Our coupling was hungry and quick. Her guttural urgings in a language I did not understand inflamed me, and I responded with an animal lust from a place in me I didn't know existed. Our cries peaked; then we were quiet. Leaning against the railing of the bridge, we slowly untangled. She broke the silence.

"Dalton, you perform better than I expect."

She kissed my neck and licked the ridges of my ear, and I shuddered. She made me nervous and delirious, all at the same time. I kissed her on the mouth and enfolded her in my long arms, feeling her breasts flatten against me. She knew I was ready again, but she pulled away.

"Enough for tonight, Dalton. Maybe again, maybe soon, but I guarantee nothing. I will contact you; you may never try to contact me. If I see you, I will acknowledge you, nothing more. Understood?"

I started to object, but she put a finger to my lips. "I enjoyed our evening, Dalton. Don't spoil it." She turned and walked toward the south side of the river. I watched her until she disappeared down the walkway; then I walked the opposite way back downtown. Even if I did see her again, would we ever share another moment like this?

8

Homestead

THE WEEK BEFORE THE CONTRACT DEADLINE, I MADE THE ROUNDS OF the Eastern European bars on both sides of the river trying to talk to the strikers but with the hope I would see Zofia, even if I had to interview Hasçek to do it. I wanted to catch a train back downtown after an unproductive night, but first I stopped at the last tavern on Eighth Street, Homestead's most infamous saloon, Margaret Finch's Rolling Mill House.

The place was dark, my shoes stuck to the floor, and the smell was awful. Besides stale beer, there was the manure the workers brought in on their boots and the stench of urine from the screened hole in the back of the room that served as a latrine. There were men lining the bar hunched over their boilermakers. They had become used to the putrid air. I never would.

I stood with my back to the bar, trusting only the watered-down lager they had on tap. That's when I saw Hasçek in a booth in the back.

"Mr. Hasçek, sir, may I have a moment?"

Hasçek turned and looked me up and down. "The rich Mr. Dalton who plays at newspapering. I have no time for dilettantes."

"But you should have your point of view represented in the *Sun*. On my honor, I will not distort a word you say. Doesn't the Knights' position deserve to be heard?"

"You will misrepresent me. There is no honor in the ruling class. Nothing but lies and deceit."

"After my piece appears, if my reporting is not accurate, come to my editor and demand my resignation. I'm sure he will be happy to oblige you if I am in the wrong."

Hasçek looked at me and shook his head. "What a lot of garbage you spew, Dalton. I don't care what you write. These negotiations are a charade. You are a fool if you think the Amalgamated will serve the interests of the common laborer. Carnegie will buy off the unions with his millions, and we will be left with nothing, again. By destroying the labor movement, Frick wants to take away what little control the men have over their miserable lives. At least he is not a lying hypocrite like Carnegie who writes books and makes speeches about the nobility of the working man. He preaches that no worker should take another man's job, and all the while he is telling Frick to bring in as many scabs as he needs to run his plants."

"Then why are your men sympathetic to the strike?" I asked.

"Do you expect them to lay down for their oppressors? At least they can take pride in their resistance."

I thought of all the suffering and misery in the villages of Braddock and Homestead, back to the time Mother had taken me to the church-sponsored Thanksgiving dinner. My sympathies were with the workers and their families, but the best I could do was report the truth and hope that spurred others to action. Hasçek seemed to be speaking for a doctrine that was an end in itself. Did he care about the people or was his dedication to an ideal?

Hasçek was off on one of his socialist screeds. My eyes searched the room as he spoke. "But you're not here to report, are you? You're looking for her!" Hasçek snarled. "Miss Majefski wants nothing to do with you. 'What do I care about that silly boy?' she says."

That sounded like Zofia's proud bluster, and I hoped she'd said it to throw Hasçek off. Hasçek and I stared at each other for a few moments. "I must file my story. Goodnight, sir," I said, then left to catch my train.

The Homestead contract was due to expire June 30, 1892. By the end of 1891, Carnegie had announced that he would be seeking new terms, not giving any details beyond insisting that the workers be paid on a sliding scale based on the price of steel, with a lower minimum amount per ton. He offered a year-and-a-half contract, half the length of the last, knowing full well that an agreement ending in the middle of the winter was anathema to the union. With the cold weather, higher food prices, and fewer orders at that time of the year, steel companies would be in a much better position to withstand a strike.

From time to time I had taken Jason up on his offer to give me information on the workings of the steel company. When I asked about Carnegie's stance on the Homestead negotiations, he told me that Carnegie was waffling on whether Homestead should be non-union. After insisting on an announcement that there would be no unions at Homestead, he confused Frick by saying that the plant could stay unionized but that workers must negotiate individually for their jobs and their salaries. Later he told Frick to break the union however he could.

In mid-May Frick began construction of a wooden fence, replete with barbed wire, shooting towers, and searchlights, that surrounded all but the river side of the Homestead works. It was inevitably dubbed "Fort Frick." He ramped up production of steel plate so the company would have plenty in reserve if the workers went on strike. At the end of May Frick met with William T. Roberts, head of the Amalgamated's Advisory Committee, who was in charge of the union's negotiations. Roberts told him in no uncertain terms that the $22 minimum and the December 31, 1893, contract end date were unacceptable.

On June 2 I got word from Jason to meet at the sausage stand on Fifth. I saw him approach, but he brushed by, slipping me a note that read, "Frick 300 Pinkertons July 3." The plant owners did not intend to be outnumbered as badly as they had been in 1889. With "Fort Frick" and the Pinkerton men, Frick would be ready for a long siege and could bring in as many black sheep as needed.

Brooks felt we had reported enough on the Amalgamated but needed an interview with Henry Frick. "It's damned important that we get to him before anyone else, but he despises the press and never gives interviews."

The Fricks had endured a terrible tragedy. A year ago their five-year-old daughter had died of infection, four years after swallowing a pin on a family trip to Europe. Mother told me she had stayed with them every day for a month, but that her friend Adelaide had been bereft, and Clay, as she called him, had slipped into a deep depression. I knew Mr. Frick would never show his feelings to the public, but perhaps my mother's help to his family would soften his stance on giving interviews.

I wondered whether it was cynical and exploitive to use his gratitude for Mother's kindness to my own advantage. But I was a reporter for one of the city's major newspapers, and why wouldn't I approach the president of the company confronting a major labor dispute? My future at the paper could depend on it. "Let me think how I will get him to speak to me," I said to Brooks. And before he could respond, I left his office and walked out onto Grant Street to consider my dilemma.

It was a hot June day, dirty as always, but with my head down, I strode away from the business area, paying no attention to other people on the street. What kind of reporter was I going to be? As I had grown into my job at the paper, I had proved that I could report the facts. Cleve had given me every break imaginable, but I could sense he wanted me to be more aggressive, to challenge the establishment, not just rely on my access for the occasional morsel of news.

But this situation was more delicate. I was sure Mr. Frick would see me, but how would he react when I asked him the hard questions any committed reporter would ask? His stern, angry demeanor scared me, and I had to consider how the interview might affect his relationship with my father or my mother's friendship with Adelaide Frick.

As I walked beside the Pennsylvania Railroad tracks, I thought back to what Grampa Willis had told me about the railroad strike and the slaughter of so many men. My concern over social niceties seemed trivial beside the life-and-death struggle at Homestead. An interview with Mr. Frick could shed light on what was at stake, maybe even save lives. That night I thought through all the questions I would ask Mr. Frick and barely slept.

The next morning, I walked the two flights down to Frick's offices, which coincidentally were in the same building as the *Sun*, Frick having refused to move into the Carnegie Building where the rest of the steel offices were housed. No one was at the front desk, and his office door was open. I approached with some trepidation but heard myself say, "Good morning, Mr. Frick." He looked up from his papers and gave me a thin smile.

"James, what brings you here today? Still scrounging for news?" he asked in a diffident tone. Mr. Frick had a haggard look and had aged since I last saw him. Not surprising, considering the stress he had been under in both his personal and professional life. As he stood to greet me, I saw that he was as immaculately dressed and groomed as ever, but there was more gray around his temples and in his beard and more lines around his bright blue eyes.

"Let me be forthright, sir. I want to interview you for the *Sun* regarding the current labor situation at Homestead." I hoped my voice didn't sound as nervous as my stomach was.

His eyes narrowed. "Cleveland Brooks has been no friend," he said.

"As you might imagine, sir, I have very little influence over what Mr. Brooks writes in his editorials. If I am to succeed in my job, I must be faithful to the facts."

He gave me a long look before he motioned me to the chair in front of his desk. "I can give you fifteen minutes."

"Mr. Frick, thank you for this."

"I am grateful to your mother for her help in our time of need."

I took out my pencil and notepad where I had scrawled the questions I wanted to ask. At this point I was too anxious to refer to them and started right in.

"What are you hoping to accomplish with the new contract?"

"We are in a competitive business," he answered, "and have to keep our costs as low as possible. Since labor is the largest component of our costs, we can't afford to pay more than the market. The surveys we have conducted show that the Homestead plant pays a higher wage than any other metal company in western Pennsylvania."

"But isn't that the price Mr. Abbott negotiated on the company's behalf in 1889?"

"Abbott," Frick scoffed. "A weak leader, intimidated by the union rabble. It's our right to pay what we want."

"Don't your workers have the right to a decent life?"

Frick bristled. "We provide a fair wage. It's up to the individuals to make their own lives. We are the owners of these properties and have the right to manage them as we see fit. The Amalgamated and the Knights are interfering with our property rights. They want to tell us who can be hired and fired. They insist that new men join their association before they can start work. Do they think they are the owners? I won't have it."

At this point I worried Mr. Frick was seeing me as just another obnoxious reporter. Maybe he resented that I knew there was a tenderness behind his tough, unbending public persona. But I had to ignore my misgivings if I was to ask the questions I had prepared, regardless of the consequences to my family's relationship with Mr. Frick.

"Isn't the real intent of these negotiations to break the union?" I asked.

"If the union gives their men bad advice and they strike, they will be very disappointed when others take their jobs," he shot back.

I could sense his growing anger. Was I pushing him too far? What would be the repercussions? I knew Father would hear about what I had asked Mr. Frick. Would he at least give me begrudging respect for doing my job? With some trepidation I asked what would be my last question.

"What about your insistence that the next contract expire at the end of the year? Isn't it unfair to force the men to negotiate in the middle of winter? The Amalgamated will never accept that."

"Fair or unfair isn't the point. The issue, as I have said before, is that we have every right to operate our business on our property as we like. Without interference. If a man isn't agreeable to our terms, he can seek employment elsewhere. Now, Mr. Dalton, I have afforded you enough time. Good day."

I thanked him and extended my hand, which he ignored. As I turned to leave, he said, "You know why I agreed to see you today. From here on, don't expect me to treat you differently than other reporters."

Looking back at Mr. Frick, I nodded in silent understanding of what he was telling me. I had made a choice. I couldn't make men like him so angry they wouldn't speak to me, but I wasn't going to handle them with kid gloves because they were friends and associates of my parents. My career as a newsman was too important for that.

———

Events in June moved swiftly with no hint of compromise on either side. In a show of solidarity, three thousand workers overflowed the Homestead

Opera House on June 15, 1892. To loud cheers Hugh O'Donnell, the head of the strike committee, told them they had every right to defend their jobs and their families but not to destroy any property.

After what was the final negotiating meeting, the Amalgamated told the press the two sides were only $1 apart on the per ton minimum but that Frick insisted the new contract end in the middle of the winter. When the union refused to accept that, Frick announced, "This ends our negotiations." He had the confrontation he wanted all along.

Both sides prepared for battle. Sensing this could be an even bigger national story than the Johnstown Flood, I spent each day patrolling the Homestead plant and the streets of the town. I was scared and excited by the tense atmosphere. Violence could break out any minute. I did consider my safety, but I wanted to be in the middle of everything that happened.

The company had positioned water cannons on twelve-foot platforms around Fort Frick. On Saturday, June 25, all over town there were notices, signed by Henry C. Frick, that the company would no longer negotiate with the Amalgamated. He also told reporters he had hired three hundred Pinkertons to "protect our property." I knew there would be trouble but couldn't imagine the death and violence to come.

The following Wednesday, June 29, Frick closed the Homestead Mill, locking out 3,800 workers, and announced that he would no longer recognize either the Amalgamated or the Knights of Labor. The workers pledged not to leave the plant grounds until a new, favorable contract was signed. They warned that not a single black sheep would enter the plant. I could see that neither side would back down.

❧

That Sunday I decided to visit Father and waited until after church to go to our house on Amberson. It was a hot summer day, and Father sat on the porch in his shirtsleeves, smoking a cigar. I gave him a wave as I came up the walk. I couldn't tell if he was happy to see me or not.

He wasn't. "Have you become a radical? Mr. Frick told me the questions you asked."

"Do you and Mr. Frick have any idea what is about to happen in Homestead? The town is prepared for war!"

"It's out of our hands now. Mr. Frick is allowed by law to do as he sees fit with his property, and he intends to hire people that will work on the company's terms."

"Does that include mowing down the workers and the people of Homestead?"

"I hope it doesn't come to that, but if the people destroy or block access to company property, they will be dealt with. They are the law-breakers, not the company."

"You should be glad I won't quote you on that," I answered.

—◆—

On Tuesday morning, July 5, I watched as the workers forced a contingent of the sheriff's deputies out of Homestead. The confrontation was peace-ful, but Mr. Frick had the excuse he needed to bring in the Pinkertons. That night I roamed the outside of Fort Frick. At 2:30 a.m., whistles began blowing all over town, warning that the hired detectives were on their way up the river. I followed the leaders of the Amalgamated as they gathered at the top of a forty-foot dirt ramp that led down to the river wharf below the squat, yellow-stone Pump House, the worker's favored rallying spot. From there I could see the lights of a tug pulling two barges. The workers fired warning shots from their own boat.

Most of the mob was still on the top of the hill overlooking the boat landing, but when the barges drew near land at 4 a.m., Mother Finch of the Rolling Mill House tavern yelled, "Those dirty black sheep will never land." Not knowing or caring whether the men on the barges were Pinkertons or scabs, hundreds of men and women, most of them armed, rushed down the ramp to the landing. Initially it was a standoff, but then Captain Heinde, the leader of the Pinkertons, shouted that they intended to take possession of the mill and would shoot anyone who tried to stop them. Then a union man carrying a pistol came near Heinde, who rapped him on the head with a billy club.

It was a starless night, and from my perch on the hill above the wharf I could see very little, but I heard the first shots. I couldn't tell which side fired first, but for ten minutes bullets flew; then the shooting ended as abruptly as it began. An eerie silence followed as workers brought the wounded back up the ramp. My stomach heaved as I saw all the blood. I had witnessed the fury of nature in Johnstown, but the fury of men killing each other was more horrifying. I struggled to compose myself and made an assessment of the casualties. Three Homestead men and one Pinkerton were dead, and many others wounded.

After wiring a report to the *Sun* from the Bost Building, I hurried back to the top of the ramp at the Pump House, where the standoff continued. Despite the carnage the workers would not disperse. The Pinkertons were pushed back onto the boats, where some had already taken cover. Sharpshooters on a nearby bridge shot at the invaders. The tug had towed the barges away from shore but was receiving so much fire that it fled. The Homestead men pushed an oil-soaked wooden raft that had been lit aflame into the river to sink the barges. They threw sticks of dynamite and bottles of grain alcohol with burning wicks. The Pinkertons were besieged, and after another of them was shot, they tried to surrender, but the workers refused.

The scene was terrifying. I was drenched in sweat and my hands shook, making it impossible to take notes. Before the showdown, my sympathies were with the workers, but the attacks of the crowd even after the Pinkertons had laid down their arms were appalling. And in the long run self-defeating. If the workers continued to riot, they would face city, maybe even state, troops.

I returned to the Bost Building, where I made myself inconspicuous as Sheriff McCleary negotiated with Hugh O'Donnell of the Amalgamated.

"The Pinkertons are beaten and pose no further threat," McLeary said. "Let them leave Homestead with the promise never to return."

O'Donnell laughed. "Why should we believe Frick won't just send twice that many tomorrow?"

"I'm a man of my word. Let them go, and you will see no more trouble from the Pinkertons. I guarantee it, and so does Chris Magee."

O'Donnell only laughed again. "That promise is worth nothing, but let's get these thugs out of Homestead," he said. "We need to prepare for whatever else that damned Scotsman and his toady Frick send our way."

"I will lead them to the Opera House," McCleary insisted. "In the morning we will put them on a train back to Pittsburgh, but you have to guarantee their safety until then."

There was no way anyone could assure their free passage with all the anger still brewing in the town. Through a clenched jaw, O'Donnell bit off his words. "We will do all we can to see that they are not harmed. March them up around seven."

Word got out that the Pinkertons had surrendered and would be moved from the barges to the Opera House and then put on trains to Pittsburgh in the morning. But the townspeople were in an ugly mood and clamored for revenge. The violence wasn't over. I didn't want to see any more of it, but that was my job.

Men, women, and children lined both sides of the road up from the river and onto Eighth Street, forming what became known as the Gauntlet. As the Pinkertons came off the barges, they were attacked with bats, rocks, sticks, or any bit of scrap metal the crowd could find. I watched in horror as women, some with babies in their arms, struck at every detective that passed them. The sheriff's men did very little to protect them. Many were cut and bleeding, and some had been knocked unconscious. As far as the people of Homestead were concerned, the Pinkertons were scabs who would take away their jobs and homes, and they deserved the worst.

And I wasn't immune from their rage. The townspeople didn't know me, and I was dressed a good deal more like a Pinkerton than a steelworker. I stayed close to the buildings but still had to ward off several blows.

When the Pinkertons reached the small square in front of the Opera House, the beatings became even more vicious. The fallen detectives were slashed with knives and forks and struck with brass pots and iron skillets. Children cracked them with baseball bats. Dogs bit them. As they were being led inside, I could see that every last one of them was injured in some way, but miraculously none were killed on that bloody march through the Gauntlet. The first day of the Battle of Homestead was finally at an end. I was tired and hadn't had a thing to eat and little to drink for twelve hours. My adrenaline was pumping from fending off the attacks, and it was hard to think. I wandered back up Eighth Avenue with the vague intention of getting a launch back over the river to Braddock when three young steelworkers blocked my way.

"You Pinkertons need to get back to the square," one of them said.

"Let me by. I'm with the *Pittsburgh Sun*."

"Not likely," he said.

Then I heard someone come up behind me and my world went black.

———

"Where am I?"

"Oh, thank God!" Mother exclaimed. She, Father, Kat, and Wills were all standing around my bed. "You're at the Homeopathic Hospital. The doctors said you have a concussion, probably from a sap or a billy club. Ambulance workers went to Homestead after the rioting had stopped. We were told that they found you on the street and a dark-haired woman was with you. She left as soon as they arrived."

I let that sink in and changed the subject. "I need to get back to work. What have the doctors said?" I asked, trying to get out of the bed.

"Son, you're not going anywhere for at least twenty-four hours, maybe more," my father said. "We have to keep you safe. You were in real danger."

"Mr. Brooks had heard what happened and called the house," Mother said. "I'm sure he will stop by later today. We are going to let you rest, but there is someone else that would like to see you."

I lifted my head and was surprised to see Rita Heinz in the doorway of my hospital room. "Please, don't be long, Rita dear. The doctors want him to rest," Mother said, and my family filed out of the room.

Rita stood at the foot of my bed, smiled, and said, "You didn't have to go to such extremes to get my attention."

I laughed. Rita could always make me laugh. "I thought it might have been you that bopped my noggin."

"Would you blame me?"

"I guess not." I grinned. "Rita, thank you for coming. It means a lot to me."

Rita took the chair closest to my bed, and we began chatting like the old friends we were. But I wanted Rita to be more than a friend. Landing in the hospital made me take stock of what my life had become. I was totally immersed in my job, and that had led to my dangerous but thrilling obsession with Zofia. I was realistic enough to know that neither of those extremes was healthy. I would have to make Rita my priority, if we were to have any sort of serious relationship.

After a pleasant half-hour of conversation, she came to the head of the bed and took my hand. "I've overstayed my time, but I'm happy to know you will be up and around soon." Then she added in a lighthearted tone, "You may call on me if you wish."

That was just what I wanted to hear. "You can count on that, Miss Heinz."

—•—

Cleve Brooks did stop in that afternoon and told me what I had missed. "This morning the Pinkertons were loaded onto a train at the Central Depot for Philadelphia. A representative of Governor Pattison announced at the station that all charges against them had been dropped. It's an outrage that there will be no consequences to the Pinkerton Agency for the violence they incited at Homestead."

"Has Mr. Frick said anything?" I asked.

Brooks looked disappointed. "He's refused to talk to the Pittsburgh papers, but he did give an interview to the *Philadelphia Press*. He said he would have no further negotiations with the Amalgamated or the Knights and was calling on the state to enforce his property rights. Governor Pattison has called on Major General George Snowden and 8,500 troops to be at Homestead in two days."

"And that's where I'll be," I assured him.

Brooks looked down. "Son, I'm afraid I can't let you do that. The doctors want you to rest. I spoke to your mother, and they are going to take you back to their house for a few days to recuperate." I started to argue, but Brooks held up his hand. "The doctors and your family have made the decision. If you listen to them, you'll be up and around in a few days, no more than a week." It might as well be a month, I thought.

The next morning, I had a small headache but otherwise felt fine. By noon I had pestered the doctors enough that they agreed to discharge me. I called my family, and Mother and Father picked me up at the hospital and took me to Amberson Avenue. The first thing I did was eat a decent meal after all the hospital food. It was good to be home. The sheets were finer, the bed softer, the food better than at Leila's. I had a chance to catch up with Kat on her college plans—her heart was set on Radcliffe—and Wills told me of his burgeoning animal and insect collection. Mother and I talked of my experiences during what was already being called the Battle of Homestead. I spared her some of the more gruesome details, even though she had likely read them in the papers.

As much as I enjoyed all the creature comforts and the time I spent with the family, I was restless to get back to my newspaper life. After I insisted for two days that I was perfectly well, Mother mercifully released me. I arranged for a hansom back to Leila's, where she tried to get me to drink some Mideastern plant concoction that I politely declined. The next morning, I was back at the *Sun* offices.

But I had missed the story. I had to read another newsman's account of the troops escorting scabs into the plant, without any resistance from the workers. All that was left for me was to regurgitate Frick's statement that he would rehire only workers that were not part of the July 7 violence and that they must sign individual contracts. He closed with the solemn declaration that the government of the great Commonwealth of Pennsylvania was fulfilling its duty to protect the property rights of all its citizens.

Frick had won. I sympathized with the workers that were losing their jobs, but I couldn't forget the barbarity of the Gauntlet.

—◆—

On Thursday, July 21, the strike leaders and the Homestead mayor were indicted for murder. Two weeks after it had begun the Battle of Homestead was over. The workers had lost, even if it would take several more months for them to realize it.

It had been a horrible two weeks. I was shaken by my injury and appalled by the hatred I had witnessed on both sides. And I hadn't written the front-page pieces on the Battle of Homestead, the biggest story of the year—at least so far.

—◆—

Cleve Brooks told me to work half days when I returned, at least for the first month. Since I was leaving the office before supper rather than late at night, I took that opportunity to call on Rita. We would sit on wicker chairs in the Heinzes' backyard and drink lemonade.

One day she said, "Jamie, I know covering the strike has been an ordeal for you, but you seem to have grown up over the last few months."

I wasn't sure about that given what had happened with Zofia, but I was encouraged that she had seen a difference.

"You seem less restless, less anxious. I hope the change isn't temporary," she said with a smile.

I loved when she teased me. I raised my right hand. "I pledge to you that is my new permanent state." Later when I got up to leave, she kissed me good-bye. She hadn't done that since our near tryst in the park, and that had been years ago.

⟞⟝

That Saturday my assignment was to submit a recap of the week's events for the Sunday edition. I slept until 11 and got to the *Sun* offices just after noon. Cleve Brooks wasn't there. Two other reporters were in the office, both of whom had been assigned to obtain interviews from the families of the workers that had been killed.

Without any deadline pressure, I was dawdling over my copy, when I heard two quick pops, followed by a third, that all seemed to come from the floors below. I knew it was gunfire and had to be coming from Mr. Frick's office. I took the stairs two at a time, down to the second floor.

I rushed into Frick's office and was aghast at what I found. The president of Carnegie Steel and John Leishman, his vice president, were wrestling with a third man who was waving a .38 revolver. Frick was covered with blood, and I could see wounds on both sides of his neck. The three were grappling in front of the large plate-glass window that faced the street, and a crowd had gathered below.

Then the assailant pulled out a dagger and stabbed Frick three times, twice in the hip, once in the ribs. Leishman had grabbed his arm, and I knocked the knife out of the would-be assassin's hand. Mr. Frick slumped against his desk, blood covering his shirt front. Two men from the office staff wrestled the maniac into a chair.

"The Cause lives. Frick dies!" he screamed out.

One of the office men punched him until he stopped his ranting. From the time of the first shots to the would-be assassin's restraint had taken only a minute.

Frick struggled to his feet to confront his assailant. "He has something in his mouth!"

Another man pried open the man's jaw and removed a capsule that we later learned was filled with fulminate of mercury. If he had bitten down on it, we would have all been blown to hell.

The police arrived and took the man away through a cordon of onlookers that were screaming for his death. Mr. Leishman had fainted and was being helped from Frick's office. I sat on the floor next to the bloody but conscious Henry Frick and held a glass of water to his lips.

He was weak but rallied when he saw me. "James, why on earth are you here?" Frick asked, forgetting I worked two floors above. Before I could answer, Frick said, "A drop of Overholt would serve me well." How could he jest at a time like this? I rose to retrieve the whiskey bottle and a glass from the sideboard when Dr. Frederick Litchfield arrived. He was my family's doctor, and I assumed he was Frick's personal physician as well.

"Mr. Frick, my God, what has happened? It wasn't a half hour ago that I saw you lunching at the Duquesne Club."

"Doctor, I will be fine. Just get these damn bullets out of me," he coughed.

By this point several other medical men had arrived on the scene. One of them had cleaned the blood away, and Dr. Litchfield examined the wounds. Then he turned to the others and shook his head.

I couldn't bring myself to leave. No one in the steel business had been closer to my family than Mr. Frick, and Mother and Mrs. Frick were best friends. It was impossible to forget his cruelty to his workers, but I couldn't ignore what a brave man he was. Offering him the only comfort I could, I held his hand and said, "The doctors will take care of you, sir." He gave me a surprisingly strong squeeze in return. I opened his shirt collar so he could breathe better and fanned him with some papers from his desk.

Dr. Litchfield interrupted my thoughts. "Sir, we must sedate you with chloroform before we can retrieve those bullets. I fear how close they may be to your arteries."

"The hell you will," Mr. Frick said. "I won't inhale your noxious gas. If I'm insensible, how can I tell you where the bullets are?" No one in that room had ever won an argument with him and wouldn't try now.

One of the larger fellows and I gently moved Mr. Frick to his office sofa. A doctor who told us he was a surgeon probed his neck with a long thin instrument. He was amazed, as we all were, that Mr. Frick directed the exploration. "To the right, a little deeper, now to the left," he said in an unwavering voice. Suddenly he exclaimed, "There! That's where it is." Within seconds the doctor had retrieved the bullet and did what he could to close the wound. The same procedure was repeated on the other side, while a second doctor tended to the knife cuts. Throughout it all, Frick never cried out. He grimaced from time to time but was composed, complimenting the doctors on their skill and efficiency.

After the doctors closed his wounds, Mr. Frick announced that he had papers to sign before taking his carriage home.

Dr. Litchfield's face flushed scarlet. "Mr. Frick, I must insist that we summon an ambulance from Mercy Hospital. It can be here in a matter of minutes."

"If you let me attend to my business, I will comply."

With glazed eyes he looked at me for several seconds, then said, "Jamie, I beg a favor. Please ask your mother to get to Clayton and inform Mrs. Frick that my wounds are not serious. My wife has been confined to her bed after the difficult birth of our son last week, and this is the anniversary of our daughter's death. I want her to be treated with the utmost delicacy. Your mother will handle this task with her usual discretion."

I looked down at the man who bestrode the steel industry and thought back to his threat when I had confronted him about the Jones patents. The flyers he had posted on Fort Frick. The barges pulled up to the wharf below the Homestead plant with three hundred Pinkertons aboard. The terrifying gun battle. But that was the public man. I couldn't deny the private man my help.

"Of course, sir. I will telephone her straight off," I said.

Then Frick bent his head to the papers on his desk.

As I left the room, Dr. Litchfield grabbed my arm. "Have you ever seen such courage?" We were both awed by what we had just witnessed.

I reached Mother at home. After her initial shock and hurried questions as to the particulars, she said, "Jamie, please escort Clay home in the ambulance. You see him as this powerful steel magnate, but he has a fragile side as well. His family is in such a distraught state. It is only one year since their precious daughter Martha was taken. Now their baby may not survive, and Adelaide is overcome. A family friend will be of comfort to him." I wasn't sure Mr. Frick considered me any kind of friend, but I promised Mother I would do what I could.

Mr. Frick assured everyone in the office that he would be back at work on Monday. They smiled in disbelief, but none doubted that he would make the attempt. Since there was a growing throng at the front of the *Sun* building, the ambulance had been told to come around to the alley in back. Mr. Frick could walk, but he leaned on me as I maneuvered him down the stairs.

Cleve appeared at my elbow. "Can I be of any help?"

"No need, thank you. When I get him home, I'll call in the story. I know the Fricks have a telephone."

Brooks shook his head. "I'm sorry, Jamie. You were a participant. I've already assigned another reporter. He may want to interview you."

First Homestead, now this. I shook my head in frustration. But I had promised my mother I would look after Mr. Frick and couldn't stop to argue. Brooks knew better than to say anything else to me.

When we got to the ambulance, Mr. Frick said, "Thank you, James. You have been most kind."

"My work is not complete," I said, trying to disguise the bitterness I felt about missing the story. "Mother has insisted that I accompany you home. You wouldn't want me to disappoint her."

He was too weak to argue. I took his arm and lifted him into the back of the ambulance, where an attendant laid him on a stretcher. I knelt down and tried to distract him with small talk as we embarked on the long, bumpy ride along Pittsburgh's cobblestone streets back to Homewood. "I hope this trip is 'off the record,' as you newsmen say? Don't want the whole city reading of my difficulties," he said.

"Mr. Frick, you must understand that there will be extensive reporting of the attempt on your life and your courage in fighting off the man who tried to assassinate you. Anything you say to me now will be confidential, if that is what you want." Unfortunately, I wouldn't be the one to write that bylined story.

"No, no, I understand the nature of your work, James," He grew more serious. "Please don't report on the extent of my injuries. I have already instructed my office to issue a release. I want everyone to know that a deluded anarchist could not bring me low, and neither will the criminals at Homestead. With or without me, the corporation will win this struggle. We will associate this coward with the trade unions. Public sentiment will shift in our favor." At least I could contribute a couple of quotes. To someone else's story.

"Now James, let me rest before arriving home. I do not want Mrs. Frick to see me in distress."

Arriving at the Frick home at the corner of Penn and Homewood, the ambulance attendant and I carried Mr. Frick up to the second-floor landing. I had been with Mother when she visited Mrs. Frick, but we always stayed in the parlor or dining room. I was being given a glimpse of the private man, even though I knew better than to think I could use that information in my reporting.

Mr. Frick asked us to stop at the entrance to his wife's bedroom. "Ada, do not disturb yourself," Frick called softly. "My wounds are superficial. I am more concerned about you, my dearest. We will rest together and be well soon."

Mr. and Mrs. Frick's bedrooms were joined by a well-appointed bath. On the door frame into Mr. Frick's room, I noticed several marks with dates and initials beside them. We had something very similar on Amberson Avenue to show how much my brother and sister and I had grown each year. The loving informality of those pencil scratches were incongruous but reassuring in the home of a man who was feared by so many. When we had settled Mr. Frick in his bed, he thanked both me and the attendant profusely, then added, "I won't be needing your services any further, as I intend to be back in the office Monday morning."

With that we exited via another door that led into a bright, spacious room with a large table in the center that was covered in toys and children's drawings. Flanking either end of the table were two desks, one for

Mr. Frick, the other for Mrs. Frick. I had never seen an arrangement like this. In my home and the homes of my friends, the fathers had their own well-defined space and the children theirs, but Mr. and Mrs. Frick wanted their family together when all were home. These signs of devotion to his family showed a gentle side to Mr. Frick that the public would never see. I was sure he didn't want them to.

⸺❧⸺

Right after the shooting Mother spent most of her days at Clayton comforting Mrs. Frick. The extent of his injuries did not allow Mr. Frick to return to work on Monday, but he had a telephone installed next to his bed, and a revolving array of secretaries took dictation and read wires, letters, and newspapers to him, she told me.

Mr. Frick's trials were not at an end. On August 3, his son and namesake, Henry Clay Frick Jr., barely a month old, died. The church services were the next day, and Mother spent that night with Adelaide. She called me the next day. "Clay took the trolley to work this morning. Adelaide is worried sick about him, but you know what he's like."

With the aftermath of the strike to cover, I rewrote wire service reports that quoted Mr. Carnegie, still ensconced in his leased castle in Scotland, as saying that he "deplored" the violence and had hoped for a "negotiated" settlement with the unions. I imagined how furious Mr. Frick was. Mr. Carnegie had previously and publicly pledged his "unwavering support" for whatever Frick needed to do to break the strike and drive the unions out of the Homestead plant.

But public and editorial opinion swung Mr. Frick's way. The would-be assassin was identified as Alexander Berkman, a known associate of the radical socialist Emma Goldman. His attack on Frick was conflated with the workers' violent abuse of the Pinkertons during the Gauntlet and doomed labor's chance of achieving its goals. Even the leaders of the Amalgamated told me they supported Frick. Any voice to the contrary was dealt with harshly. When W. L. Iames, a union man, shouted to a crowd that he wished Berkman was a better shot, the soldiers guarding the plant strung him up by his thumbs. Across the country newspapers extolled Frick as a "man of steel" and a "super man."

The tide had turned against the workers. By mid-August the Homestead plant was up and running, manned by more than 1,500 scabs. As the days grew cold, I watched as the men trudged back to work but not before they signed individual contracts and agreed not to participate in union activities. On Sunday, November 20, I covered the meeting of the Amalgamated where less than two hundred members, all that was left of the union, voted to go back to work on the company's terms. Cleve Brooks editorialized that the labor movement in the Pittsburgh steel industry was finished due to the violence on the shores of the Monongahela July 6, the Gauntlet July 7, and Frick's bravery July 23.

With her encouragement I did call on Rita that summer. On weekends we would take walks around her Point Breeze neighborhood, play golf at the Schenley course, or eat dinner at various hotels and restaurants in Oakland and downtown. We always enjoyed ourselves, and the more time I spent with her, the more I felt that she should be the one woman in my life.

But it was impossible to get Zofia off my mind, and on the nights that I wasn't seeing Rita, I would go to bars in Homestead and Braddock, have some boilermakers, and ask about her and Hasçek. Since people knew I was a reporter, no one thought that was strange. One night at the Czech American Club in Braddock, I bought Tomáš, one of the regulars, a few pilsners.

"Have you seen Hasçek and the woman recently?" I asked.

"Not since the strike. Want me to ask around?"

I decided not to press any further. "No need," I answered and bought him another beer and a shot. We talked for a few minutes about how the union was losing its hold on the workers who couldn't afford to stay out on strike; then I left the bar and took the trolley back up Braddock.

Leila was in the kitchen cooking an unrecognizable stew. "Care for some couscous, Jamie?" I politely declined and went up to my room. The room whirled around when I lay down in bed.

I slept fitfully that night, pondering whether it was a coincidence that no one had seen Zofia and Hasçek since Berkman's attempt on Frick's life, but I was suspicious that he may have had some role in the failed assassination. I couldn't imagine Zofia did, given her vehement aversion to violence.

Several days later I received a note at the *Sun* office. "Heard you were asking for me. Meet me at eleven o'clock tonight on the bridge. Not like last time. Z."

It was a late summer night, with a gentle breeze wafting up the Ohio. Through the nighttime mist, I could see the smoldering glow of the furnaces along all three rivers. It was a beautiful, otherworldly sight, if you could forget the human cost of keeping those fires banked.

Zofia stood at the center of the bridge with the wind blowing through her long dark hair. I opened my arms to her, but she put up her hand. "I have come to say good-bye, Dalton."

"Now wait just a minute. I have to know whether you or Hasçek played any part in Frick's shooting."

"You know violence is not my answer to the class struggle! As to Hasçek's part in the shooting, I know nothing. He went into hiding the night after the Homestead battle. He didn't tell me where he was because he was afraid that I would come to him, and company spies would follow. Three weeks later he felt it safe to emerge. He would not tell me anything that happened since I had last seen him. In any case, I had nothing to do with Berkman."

"But if Hasçek aided Berkman in any way at all, your association with Hasçek could put you in jail as well."

She put her hand to my face and said, "You are a sweet boy, Dalton, but I am very able to care for myself. The labor movement in Pittsburgh is dead. Hasçek and I go to New York to protest against the greedy banks and the criminals on Wall Street. That's where the true evil lies."

She turned to leave, but I grabbed her arm and pulled her toward me. "I care for you, more than I should. I know how dedicated you are to your cause, but you can't control what others may do. If you are ever in trouble, promise that you will contact me."

Zofia kissed me on the cheek. "I don't need anyone's help. Best fortune in your life, James." She turned and walked away. This time I was certain I would never see her again.

—◆—

Rita had gone east to visit friends from Smith, and for the next several weeks, all I did was work during the day and go to downtown bars at night. I wasn't getting sloppy drunk, but it was enough to make me jolly and chat up the other patrons. When I told them I worked at the *Sun*, they nodded their heads and smiled. I guess they expected all newsmen to drink too much. But the real reason I was drinking was to get Zofia off my mind. I had never been infatuated like this, and when I wasn't concentrating on reporting and writing, she was all I could think about. And as much as I tried, I wasn't finding a solution in beer and whiskey.

—◆—

When I returned to Regent Square after another night in the bars, Aunt Leila was sitting cross-legged on her brightly colored Persian rug with hands on her knees and her eyes closed. She had told me that was her meditation pose, and I tried not to disturb her on my way up to bed.

I was surprised when I heard her say my name just as I put my foot on the stairs. "Jamie, come sit with me."

I was tired and a little drunk but did as she said.

"I doubt any of my herbal concoctions will help whatever is bothering you. I'm a lot easier to talk to than your parents, you know."

I looked at Aunt Leila in her flowing red and gold robe, her dark-blonde curly hair tied up into a top knot, and gave her a big smile. "No question about that."

"From now on it's Leila. Talk to me! Where have you been going these nights? I hear you stumbling in! I know you're not going to visit Rita Heinz in that condition."

Should I confide in Aunt Leila? I was tired and didn't want to concoct some specious story about attending union meetings. She would see right through that. Everyone in Pittsburgh knew that the unions had been crushed.

She rearranged her robe, then said, "Jamie, I have been all over the world and have seen and done more than you can imagine. There is little you could say to shock me. And it goes without saying that anything you tell me stays between us. My guess is that it's about a woman. That's what usually distracts men your age."

I wasn't getting anywhere resolving my feelings about Zofia on my own, and there was no question that Aunt Leila ... Leila had a unique perspective—on everything! And I trusted her.

For the next thirty minutes, I told her about Zofia. Seeing her at Captain Jones's service, the union meetings, her ties to Hasçek. Her striking, dark looks and my fascination with her.

"I think there's more," Leila said softly. I had been staring at a Far Eastern painting on her wall while I had been speaking, but now I faced her. I shook my head and said, "There seems no sense in trying to hold anything back from you."

She nodded her head, and I told her about receiving the note from Zofia and meeting her on the bridge. What Zofia had told me about her early life, her pride and resolve in support of labor and the socialist cause. Her independence from Hasçek despite appearances.

Leila looked at me to continue. When I didn't, she said, "And you made love to her. On the bridge that night."

"I did," I said with a wary pride.

Then Leila did something unexpected. She laughed.

"So you're infatuated with a mysterious woman from—where did you say?—Poland, and you're thinking you want to run off with her and become a socialist agitator. Jamie, you're a smart young man. How do you think that will end?"

"But I can't stop thinking about her."

"Then don't, but be honest about what she means to you. It's less about her than what she represents to you. A side of life you've never known. Freedom and passion that you have never experienced. She is a thrill, and being with her may shape you in some way. But do you believe in your heart that she is your destiny?"

I knew the answer was no, but I couldn't say it.

"What about Rita? Jamie, I have always been unconventional and was never going to fit into the mold my parents wanted for me, the path your mother chose. It's right for her but not for me. And you are more like her than you might care to admit." She paused and gave me a quizzical look.

"But I have to say that your mother has been outright giddy of late. She loves being part of the suffrage movement. And she's very impressed with your boss, Mr. Brooks. Very appreciative of the articles he writes about the suffrage lectures."

She smiled at me, but I didn't want to be lured into any speculation, so I didn't respond. After a moment Leila continued.

"Jamie, after all my travels, I came back to Pittsburgh. I'm happy with a quiet life where I can paint and enjoy the beauty of the Homewood forest at my doorstep. The most important thing I have learned is to appreciate what's right in front of you. I can't think of two people better suited than you and Rita, even if you're both too headstrong to admit it.

"If you remember one thing that I have said to you tonight, remember this. Don't ignore the obvious! Now you get some sleep and let me get back to my meditation!"

With all that Leila told me, falling asleep wasn't easy. I thought about how monotonous my existence at Aunt Leila's had been. My life had been commuting, working, sleeping, endlessly repeated. Seeing Rita had made a difference, and what Leila said made sense to me. My infatuation with Zofia was hopeless. Part of me had always loved Rita, ever since we met many years ago at the Westinghouse Christmas party. She was smarter and lovelier and more fun than any woman I knew. And we had so much in common—our families and friends, our shared interest in sports like fishing and shooting and riding. We both loved reading, history, and politics.

I boiled my thoughts down to the two things I knew to be true. Zofia, my fantasy, was leaving Pittsburgh, and unless I was willing to live in New York, which I wasn't, she was out of my life. Rita lived where I lived, and she was the only woman I had ever loved. Obvious.

9

Jason

BESIDES RECONNECTING WITH RITA, MY OTHER PRIORITY THAT SUM-
mer of 1892 was to repair my relationship with my family, specifically
with my father. His concern at the hospital had been sincere, but other
than that we had barely spoken since our confrontation over his involvement with the purchase of Captain Jones's patents. I had been appalled
that he had taken advantage of the man's widow; he was disgusted that I
had printed the details of the transaction in the *Sun*. The one most hurt by
our standoff was Mother, and I wanted to spare her that pain. Although I
wasn't aware of any problems since then, she had seemed so down in the
weeks after her Johnstown relief work, and I didn't want to be the cause
of a relapse. One Sunday I suggested to her that I come to the house for
the after-church Sunday dinner. I even offered to meet the family for the
11 a.m. service at Calvary.

Living at Aunt Leila's, I had seen very little of my brother and sister.
Kat and Wills had school, and I had my work at the *Sun* and couldn't join
the family on summer getaways, even if invited, which was seldom. When
I had been home after my injury at the Gauntlet, I was still a little foggy
and hadn't noticed how much they had changed. Kat had blossomed and
was an attractive young lady, not as tall or as pretty as Mother, but her
erect bearing and sober mien telegraphed her confidence and intelligence.
Wills was tall and gangly and pimply, as restless and energetic as ever. I
shook hands with Father, kissed Mother on the cheek, then took my place
between my sister and brother.

Wills spewed questions as soon as I sat down. "Where were you when
the gun battle with the Pinkertons started?" "Was the Gauntlet as awful

as everyone said?" And most insistently, "Did you really save Mr. Frick's life?" I tried to shush him, but it wasn't until Mother reached over and pinched him on the leg through his gray flannels that he quieted down. "I'll tell you everything over lunch," I whispered.

We all wedged ourselves into the family's phaeton, pulled by two sleek Cleveland bays—Father must be doing well at Knox & Reed, I thought—and soon we were back at Amberson Avenue. Before we sat down at the table, the adults enjoyed a sherry, Kat and Wills ginger ale. The heavy linen tablecloth, the sparking silverware, and the gleaming china told me that the family was richer and more formal than I remembered.

Father intoned a brief grace. "Bless this food to our use and us to Thy service. We ask this in Christ's name. Amen."

Then a servant in livery brought out a large roast of beef surrounded by boiled red potatoes and an assortment of vegetables. While Father carved, a young Irish girl, in a black dress covered by a white smock, poured wine into sapphire-infused crystal. Kat's and Wills's glasses were filled halfway.

Wills resumed his questioning, and with as little embellishment as possible, I told the family of my part in the events concerning the Homestead lockout, the battle with the Pinkertons, the Gauntlet, and my injury. As to the attempt on Mr. Frick's life, I downplayed my involvement. After I told them all how heroic Mr. Frick had been, I stopped my monologue. Father hadn't said a word the whole time.

Mother was the first to speak. "Mrs. Frick wanted me to thank you for how brave you were that day. We're very proud of you, Jamie. Aren't we, Richard?"

For the first time since we sat down, Father and I looked each other in the eye. "Son, you were courageous in reporting on the Homestead riots, and the Frick family will never forget how you came to Mr. Frick's aid when he was almost killed. But I have issues with what you've written in the *Sun*."

From there followed a very familiar argument about the company's right to do what it wished on the property it owned versus the right of the workers to organize, the company's right to make a profit to expand their business and provide jobs versus the workers' right to a decent standard of living.

I tamped down my annoyance at his narrow-minded view of what was happening in the streets of Braddock and Homestead and tried to be as rational as possible. "But when Mr. Frick brings in the Pinkertons to escort scabs into the plants, how do you expect the townspeople to react? Isn't there a different way to manage a labor force? Look how successful Mr. Heinz and Mr. Westinghouse have been."

"Son, you have learned a great deal, but the subtlety of business still eludes you. Those men have been successful with borrowed capital, and unless they show the kind of profits their bankers expect, they will soon lose control of the companies that bear their proud names."

I drained half my wine glass, then answered him. "Be that as it may, Father, unless the steel companies change their ways, the government may do it for them. Demand safer working conditions, a minimum wage. The Progressives have even called for an income tax."

"The government doesn't know how to run these businesses. Steel men do. They need to keep their hands off!"

"Mr. Frick seems happy when Chris Magee and Governor Patterson brings in troops to stop the strike. Or when the government in Washington votes for the high tariffs to shut out any foreign competition. Do they only approve of government interference when it benefits them?"

Father's face flushed, and I could feel myself getting angrier.

"I won't have this unpleasantness at my dinner table," Mother interjected with tears welling in her eyes.

Like fighters sent to their respective corners, Father and I glared at each other. Was this what I wanted? Not to be on speaking terms with him over these unsolvable societal issues? I decided to back away from any further confrontation and offered an apology of sorts.

"Father, I have my own views on these matters, but I hope my reporting has been evenhanded. As you and I are demonstrating here today, there are at least two sides to every issue. I hope I am presenting those sides equitably."

"But that damned Brooks is roasting us daily."

I could see red streaks rise up my mother's neck. "Richard, Cleveland Brooks has been to several of our suffrage rallies, and his reporting is always fair." I had seen small pieces in the paper about the suffragettes, but it had never occurred to me that Brooks had written them. I let Mother go on. "Richard, this is not about a newspaper editor. This is about you and your son. You both owe it to each other and to all of us to cease your quarrels. Find some common ground or avoid these divisive issues altogether."

"Eleanor, my love, I don't wish to upset you and neither does Jamie. Son, let's repair to the library and smoke a cigar. Very good for the digestion!" I was surprised but stood right up. We left Mother, Kat, and Wills at the table.

When we were in the library, Father handed me a glass of brandy and a Monte Cristo, which he lit with his sterling-silver desk lighter. "See here, we both have our jobs to do. Don't think I haven't seen the streets of Homestead, but my job is to facilitate the wishes of Mr. Carnegie and Mr. Frick." I looked at him skeptically. "I don't break the law. But we do stretch the meaning of the statutes in our favor and make sure the legislatures pass laws that will benefit us as much as possible. Don't be naïve, son. That's what business, capitalism, is all about, taking advantage of every opportunity."

"Don't shun me just because I have a different opinion," I answered.

"I see socialism and the end of the American way of life in your sympathies. You see oppressive capitalism in mine. I doubt we may ever agree, but at least we can treat each other in a civil fashion." Father stopped, then with narrowed eyes asked, "Just don't become one of those radicals that wants to kill a great man like Mr. Frick and blow up the whole system. I could never abide that."

I thought of Hasçek and Zofia, then laughed. "I'm no bomb thrower, Father; I'm a reporter. What I believe in is telling the truth, as accurately as possible." I knew that was more of an aspiration than a fact, but for my own pride, I wanted to let him know that I was serious about my job.

"You're as dedicated to your profession as I am to mine. For your mother's sake, I believe we can give the appearance of cordiality." Then he smiled. "Perhaps the more we know about each other's businesses, the better we will do our jobs." Father extended his hand, and I was happy to shake it. For all our differences, he was my father, and I wanted him to be as proud of me as I always had been of him. He refilled our glasses, and we both tossed back the brandy.

Mother was hovering at the door. When she saw the handshake and the toast, she burst in. "I knew my men would find their way." Then she kissed both of us on the cheek.

But she wasn't done with her guidance, at least for me. "I know you and Rita have been seeing each other. I hope you're serious this go-round."

"I always see her on my days off. Sometimes even for dinner on weekends."

Mother laughed. "Do you think a meal here and there is enough to win her heart? She's a bright, accomplished young lady and has the pick of every eligible bachelor in Pittsburgh." She would be appalled if she knew about my involvement with Zofia. Mother may have become more enlightened from her work in the suffrage movement, but she would never be ready to welcome a Polish radical into the family.

"I intend to call on her this afternoon," I answered. Bidding the others farewell, I strode out Fifth to the Heinz home, enjoying the fine cigar that Father had given me. As I walked along, I took stock. My late-night conversations with Aunt Leila had focused my thoughts, and I knew my life was better with Rita in it. Trips to the mill towns to find Zofia were over. Despite not getting the first bylined stories of the strike and the assassination attempt, I was considered Pittsburgh's top reporter on the steel beat. And I was reconciling with Father. All seemed well.

I hoped Rita was home. After I dropped the big brass knocker on the Heinzes' front door, the butler answered the door. "Hello, Winfield," I said. "Is Miss Rita home?"

"I will see, sir," he answered.

His officious, British-butler style made me nervous, and I paced around the entrance hall until he returned several minutes later. "Miss Rita is unavailable," he announced, then turned and walked to the back of the house. I didn't believe him. Why was Rita ignoring me? With my head and shoulders slumped, I walked back up the winding gravel path to Penn Avenue. Halfway there, I heard a voice.

"Are you lost?" Rita said.

I approached her for a kiss on the cheek, but she pulled away. "Let's walk," she said.

As we headed out Penn Avenue, I tried to make small talk, but it wasn't working. After a noisy trolley went by, I turned to her and asked, "Rita, is something wrong?"

"Nothing at all," she snapped.

There was a cool evening breeze, but we were both perspiring. "Am I supposed to guess?" And I regretted my sarcasm as soon as it came out of my mouth.

"Jamie Dalton, you are infuriating. Do you think I will always be waiting for you?"

She turned back toward her home. I caught up with her and said, "But ever since you visited me in the hospital, we have been seeing each other."

"Some Saturdays, some Sundays." By the time we were back at the gates to the Heinz home, she wasn't as piqued. "Jamie, you need to figure out what you want."

I didn't hesitate. "It's you I want."

"I'm not convinced," Rita said. It was obvious she didn't want to argue the point. She walked back up her drive, and I didn't stop her.

With that, Rita dashed the cockiness I felt earlier. Remember the obvious, I told myself on the walk home. Rita was a special woman, and I would have to treat her that way. Rather than tell her of my intentions, I would have to show her. I knew what was expected of me. At first, I made sure that I would see her or call her several times a week, and it became understood that we would enjoy some activity on the weekends. Daytime we would ride to the hounds in the appropriately named Fox Chapel, just north of the sprawling Heinz property in Sharpsburg. We played golf in Schenley Park and tennis on the court Mr. Heinz had built at the Penn Avenue house. In the winter we attended concerts put on by traveling symphonies or played endless games of mahjong and bridge with friends. Some evenings there were weddings and charity balls. After several months, we began to see each other or talk on the telephone every day.

One night after dinner and dancing at the Schenley Hotel, Rita and I were sitting outside her home in the back of the carriage I had rented for the evening. In the previous months, we hadn't progressed beyond a quick kiss hello and good-bye, and I was surprised when Rita took my face in both her hands that night and said, "Well done, Jamie. You're off probation." Then she kissed me on the mouth and didn't recoil when I returned the kiss and held her tight in my arms.

When we broke the embrace, I wanted to be serious. "I am so happy when we are together. Rita, I love you. Do you love me?

"Let me think about that." My mouth dropped open. "Don't want you to get too cocky," Rita laughed. "Of course, I love you, Jamie Dalton. I think I always have."

From that night on, Rita and I were never apart. We were Pittsburgh's brightest young couple.

For the next two years, my life took on a sharply contrasting dual nature. I was an aggressive newspaperman covering the country's largest, most innovative industry, but I was also squiring one of Pittsburgh's most sought-after women to all of the city's most exclusive events. Those worlds could overlap for me, but I tried my best to keep them separate. My credibility as a reporter was already questioned by my peers given what they considered my privileged background. My continued entrée into the world into which Rita and I had been born depended on the perception that I was at least fair in my reporting and not out to get anyone. It was tough to balance my place in those two worlds, but I managed it because my ability to be first with a story for the *Sun* often depended on the subtle cultivation of my connections with the top men in Pittsburgh's business world. Being with Rita so much, I watched my drinking. Work hangovers were infrequent.

I enjoyed living at Aunt Leila's with her entertaining travel stories and wise counsel, and I was even getting used to her exotic cooking. But my trips to see my family had become more frequent, now that Father and I had reached an understanding. I spent most of my free time with Rita, and that meant I saw more of her father, as well as his good friend and neighbor George Westinghouse. There was an unspoken understanding that nothing I heard from either of them would wind up in the paper, but the background I gleaned from them about the inner workings of the city's industries was invaluable. It was also my understanding that I could pursue leads from what they discussed as long as I found out the facts for myself and nothing led back to either of them.

Mr. Heinz was taciturn, but Mr. Westinghouse loved to talk, even gossip. Where Mr. Heinz had built his business on an incremental, industrial approach to the messy business of food processing, Mr. Westinghouse was renowned as a genius. His leaps of imagination came from a buoyant, outgoing nature. He loved to roam over any subject under the sun, and there was nothing he enjoyed more than to share his insights into the whims and foibles of his fellow captains of industry.

One afternoon while we stood on the porch of the Heinz home watching the women and children of the two families enjoy games of badminton and croquet, Mr. Westinghouse laughed and said, "I hear Mr. Carnegie and Mr. Frick are running afoul of each other. Again!" I had a question on my lips, but he gave a big puff on his cigar and walked away.

I was about to leave as well when I heard Mr. Heinz cough. I looked around, and he was pointing to a wicker chair. "May I have a word with you, James?"

"Of course, sir."

"You are now a man of twenty-six and established in your profession," he began in his gruff, formal way. "Rita is not a girl anymore, just two years younger than you. I need to know your intentions."

In the two years we had been together, Rita and I had, of course, discussed marriage. We had both concluded that we were enjoying our carefree life and didn't feel any urgency to formalize our arrangement. And up to this point our families had refrained from putting any pressure on us.

For me there was another factor. I was serious about journalism, but I wasn't making much money from the *Sun*. Rita's family was very wealthy, but I didn't want either of our families supporting us. My reporting on the steel business had received some attention, and I was being paid generously for freelance pieces I wrote for *Harper's* and *McClure's*. Rita and I had agreed that I would put that money away for the future, but I wanted to save more before we would take the next step.

"Sir, I can assure you that I love Rita with all my heart and have the best of intentions."

"Your courtship has been, shall we say, protracted. Certain things are expected. I have always been fond of you, James, but my patience is not infinite. Do I make myself clear?"

"Clear as a bell, sir. We ... I will not disappoint you." I wanted to marry Rita, but this was not the time to make any promises.

Henry Heinz looked me up and down and said, "I will trust you. For now." Then he motioned to the lawn. "Please feel free to rejoin the festivities." I could feel my shirt clinging to me and was very glad to be released. I headed straight to the kegs of Iron City.

———

The pace at the *Sun* had slowed. I was working just as much but with less urgency since the Homestead upheaval. Through the middle of 1894, there was little drama surrounding Carnegie Steel. The only scandalous event was an investigation into defects in steel plating that had been sold to the Navy. The inquiry was prompted by a letter that was sent anonymously to the Pittsburgh newspapers as well as to Washington. I dug into it for about a week, but no one at the company wanted to talk. Then the company announced that they had come to an agreement with the government that their profit would be shaved on the next big contract. Jason told me that Mr. Carnegie had sailed back from England and trained down to Washington to talk with officials about the inquiry. It seems the voluble Scotsman's salesmanship worked as well with the Democratic Cleveland administration as it had with the Republican Harrison.

With Rita and I together, we made plans with other couples, but I felt badly that I had only seen Jason when I had questions about Carnegie Steel. He had taken me in when Father had kicked me out of the house on Amberson, and in the two years since he had warned me of the coming conflict at Homestead, I had sought him out for information, but we hadn't seen each other socially. I still worried about how much he drank and hoped that he hadn't slipped into using drugs again. He was always sober when I saw him during the day, but his eyes were bloodshot on occasion, so I had my suspicions.

I was surprised that he seemed reluctant when I asked whether he would have dinner with Rita and me.

"You don't need me along on one of your romantic evenings. I'll be in the way."

"Nonsense. Rita thinks you're a fine man. Do you want her to get a friend to join us?"

Jason's face reddened. "No, no, I don't want to put her to that much trouble."

If he didn't want Rita's help in finding a dinner companion, I wasn't going to push him. "Then say you'll join us. We all have lots to catch up on, and I don't mean about the company or the paper."

I could see that I was wearing him down, and he finally agreed. "Next Saturday, it is," I said with an enthusiasm that I hoped would make him feel more welcome. Rita and I picked Jason up on Fifth at Aiken in one of the Heinz carriages, then drove to the Schenley Hotel for dinner. Soon our table was laden with all manner of delicacies. We started with oysters, followed by filets of veal, surrounded by glazed carrots and Brussels sprouts, then an arugula salad with Dijon dressing. The wine steward was very attentive, refilling our glasses with a red Bordeaux. For dessert we all ordered chocolate soufflés, accompanied by champagne and tiny cups of espresso.

We laughed louder and were less inhibited in what we discussed as the evening wore on. Even knowing Jason's history with drugs, I supposed a little wine wouldn't hurt him, and I matched him glass for glass so he wouldn't feel uncomfortable. Jason was a good dinner companion, steering the conversations in new and interesting directions. Since Mr. Frick had moved to the Carnegie Building after the assassination attempt, Jason had been working with him on his burgeoning art collection.

"I research pictures for him in art books and keep abreast of recent auctions, so he knows what to buy and what price to pay when he and Mr. Mellon go to Europe on a buying spree. With the number of paintings they are acquiring, they are going to need a museum to house all of them." We all laughed at that notion.

Rita and I kept the conversation on the light side. She told us how many trout and pheasants she had bagged in her last trip to Westmoreland

County. She was also proud that she had taken only thirty strokes to complete the six-hole Schenley Park course.

"I can beat all the women and most of the men," she announced with a satisfied smile. "The game is getting so popular with our set that there are plans to lease another hundred acres from the city to build twelve new holes. That will give us eighteen, just like the old courses in Scotland. Daddy and Mr. R. B. Mellon and Mr. John Moorhead will be the founders of what is to be called the Pittsburgh Golf Club. They will recruit other members and build a clubhouse. Willie Anderson, a professional from Scotland, has been hired."

Then I talked about the newspaper, in particular the cutthroat competition for stories as well as the increasing trend to emphasize society scandals. "I have the utmost respect for Cleveland Brooks, but even the *Sun* is dredging up some of this smut. The owners tell him to keep up with the competition and sell more papers. 'If that's what it takes to keep my job, that's what I'll do,' he's told me. It's too bad Messrs. Frick and Carnegie are so stuffy. Can't sell many newspapers talking about how Frick is a good family man or how devoted Carnegie is to his mother."

Jason gave me a Cheshire-cat smile, then said, "They may be dull in their lives outside the company, but I bet the public would like to know a lot more about the personal relationship between the two tiny giants." The wine was making Jason less disciplined in his comments about the two men than I had ever heard before.

Glancing at Rita, I offered that I had heard that they had had a falling-out. "But I don't know what it's about," I said, hoping Jason would fill me in.

I wasn't disappointed. "It started with Homestead. In the aftermath Mr. Carnegie told Mr. Frick how much he supported him, then told the board of directors he would have avoided any violence. That slight got back to Mr. Frick, and he was furious.

"Now Mr. Carnegie wants to bring a new partner into the coke business, a competitor named William Rainey. Mr. Frick loathes the man for undercutting his prices and is livid that Carnegie is using his majority ownership to insist on the merger."

Jason seemed to realize he was being indiscreet. "You can't write of this, Jamie."

"You know I never attribute anything to you."

"Jamie, you will get me fired someday if you don't find someone else to give you information about the steel company, particularly about Mr. Frick. I see him every day, and he knows that you and I are friends. He doesn't like the *Sun*'s editorials, and it makes him question where the paper gets its information. You need to find a new source and let me be for a time."

I knew Jason was right, but it worried me that I would lose my inside track with Frick and the Carnegie Steel Company. When Rita saw that I was about to argue with him, she grabbed my arm to restrain me.

"But there is something I think you should know. Your father has been working exclusively for Mr. Frick for the last six months. I've heard talk that he may be leaving Knox & Reed to take a permanent position as Mr. Frick's personal attorney."

I couldn't hide my surprise that Jason knew something about my family that I didn't. "There is no way you could have known anything about this," Jason reassured me. "The only reason I know is because of all the letters I have transcribed for Mr. Frick that have been sent as 'Confidential' to your father. I deliver them by hand, and when he receives them, he puts them in a drawer of his desk and locks it. They don't want any of this to leak out."

Rita could see that both Jason and I had drunk too much wine, and when he ordered brandies, she said, "Jason, I hate to call it a night, but I promised Mummy that I would go to early service with the family tomorrow."

"And I have to go into the office to file a story for Monday before meeting my family at Calvary," I said, not mentioning that I couldn't wait to question Father about his new relationship with Mr. Frick.

Jason looked disappointed when I waved away his drink order and asked for the check, but he perked up when I said I was paying for dinner. "No matter how much the company's profits grow, our meager salaries don't increase. You're most kind," he said with a slight slur. The truth was that I made little at the paper, and even with what I was paid for my freelance articles, I wasn't exactly flush. At the moment I wasn't spending much either, but with Aunt Leila returning at the end of the summer, I knew it was time to get my own place and pay rent for the first time in my life. Most important, I was determined to show Father I could live on the money I made from reporting and writing. For Rita, the pickle heiress as I teased her, it was a very different story, but she never carried money. In any case, a lady never picked up the check.

We were just about to board the carriage to head back up Fifth, when Jason announced, "Thanks for a lovely evening, my friends. I'm going to take that streetcar to meet a friend at the Mon House," he said.

"You sure that's a wise idea, old man?" I asked.

"I'm not a college boy anymore, Dalton." Then he took off at a trot for Forbes Street. Rita looked puzzled, but I didn't want either one of us speculating about what Jason might be up to. Instead, we stepped up into the carriage and talked about the get-together Rita's family had planned for the following weekend. It would be a formal affair, she said, with dinner in their ballroom and dancing until well after midnight.

"Do you think your father will ask me again about our being married?" I asked.

"Don't worry about Daddy. I will convince him to trust you as I do." She kissed me and laughed, "But don't expect me to wait forever, Jamie Dalton." Then she nestled her head in my shoulder.

After church and lunch the next day, I took Father aside.

"I have something important to ask you. I have heard that you are leaving Knox & Reed." There was no doubt that this was the last thing he expected to hear from me today.

"No one is supposed to know anything about that," he snapped. "I want to know who told you!"

I gave him a look that said he should know better than to expect I would tell him my source. "Your newspaper ethics are laughable when I see what gets printed by your holy Mr. Brooks," he rejoined. Then he paused to look at me. "I suppose it doesn't matter much where you heard it, but what I'm about to tell you is between us. Understood?"

I knew he would ask me that, and I readily agreed. Being back in Father's good graces was important to me. It had occurred to me that he could be the source to replace Jason, but that was secondary for the moment. "I am your son. I will be a reporter when we agree it's appropriate."

He looked relieved. "It has made me and your mother so happy that we are a family again. I do trust you, but the changes in my law practice are so sensitive and secret that I must be very careful. There are enormous sums of money at stake for Mr. Frick. For me as well.

"Mr. Frick wants to work with me, not Mr. Knox, who will always be Mr. Carnegie's man. He has recently asked me to handle both his businesses and his personal affairs. His interests and Mr. Carnegie's are diverging, and Mr. Frick wants his attorney to represent him alone, not the steel company."

"Aren't Mr. Frick's and Mr. Carnegie's interests aligned? If Carnegie Steel does well, so does Frick Coke. What could change that?" I asked.

"Carnegie's incessant meddling! He is rarely in Pittsburgh, but he is never out of touch. For public consumption he tells one and all that 'Mr. Frick has my full, unqualified support,' but that's not the reality. Every decision is questioned and not just about Homestead. Mr. Frick becomes infuriated when others tell him of Carnegie's complaints. I will tell you more, but you may not use any of it until I say so. And I warn you that will be when it is to Mr. Frick's advantage."

I ruminated for a minute, then asked, "Isn't this a great risk to you? What if Mr. Carnegie decides to rid himself of Mr. Frick? If he is your only client, where will you be if his portfolio is dismantled?"

Father laughed. "Mr. Frick will still need abundant legal advice. He owns 6 percent of Carnegie Steel. No one knows what that is truly worth, but it is in the tens of millions. Plus, there is the 20 percent he still owns of the H. C. Frick Coke Company. Mr. Frick is the smartest businessman I have ever known. Even Old Andy won't be able to cheat him out of what he's owed."

"I've heard that Mr. Carnegie wants to merge Frick Coke with a competitor, William Rainey."

Father looked at me with a wary respect. "You do have your sources. Remember, this is the company he built from nothing, what saved him from running his family's whiskey business. No matter how many shares of the company Mr. Carnegie owns, Mr. Frick won't tolerate the interference."

"Father, this is an important story, and I already have one source. May I use you as confirmation?"

"As long as it is an anonymous confirmation."

"Father, I think our understanding serves us both well." I had seen a new side of my father, a man more ruthless than I had imagined. And the information he gave me could advance my own career. We were more alike than I had imagined.

———

Mother was hovering by the front door as I was leaving. "I hope you're pleased with the *Sun*'s coverage of your suffrage meetings?" I teased. "Mr. Brooks seems to have taken a personal interest."

"Yes, I have seen him there on occasion, and I was right about him being a Progressive. But what's more important is how well you and your father are getting along. I'm so delighted that this family is whole again." Mother clearly didn't want to talk about Cleve Brooks, so I gave her a big smile and a hug and was on my way.

———

"What do we know about the current dispute between our two lords of steel?" Cleve asked me as I settled into the hard wooden chair in his office the next morning.

"It's been building up for years," I began. "Frick stays at his desk in Pittsburgh, managing all the minutiae of running this enormous company, while Carnegie is in Scotland, buying castles, shooting grouse, and playing golf. He fires off the occasional telegram telling Frick how supportive he is but then always ends by making what he considers to be 'one small suggestion.' He is solicitous of Frick's health and in a condescending fashion suggests he should take a trip to Europe or Egypt to settle his nerves. Frick has tolerated it all up until now, but I hear he is getting angrier and angrier. He thinks Carnegie is trying to drive him out of the coke company."

"Where are you getting all this?" Brooks asked.

I hesitated. I had begun to stop off at Amberson Avenue on my way home from work to speak with Father, who I knew would be in his study enjoying a cigar and a brandy after the family dinner. He spoke to me with more ease as time had passed and was nowhere near as insistent that what he told me couldn't appear in the paper. The new implicit agreement was that, as long as his name was not attached to it, I could use anything he told me unless he told me I couldn't.

But if my father was to be a new source, I didn't want to do anything to jeopardize his position with Mr. Frick or in the tight-knit community of the Pittsburgh steel families. Brooks sensed my reluctance.

"C'mon, Jamie. It's for your own protection that you share your sources with me. As good as you are, I have years more experience in this business, and I can steer you away from the pitfalls. If you write something careless, it will hurt both you and the *Sun*. It's in all of our best interests, and you well know that anything you tell me will stay between us."

"I trust you, Cleve, but this is very sensitive. It's my father we are talking about."

He looked at me with something akin to admiration. "Your father? I thought you weren't speaking to your father."

"Let's say we have had a reconciliation. I worry that it is based on self-interest, but that's my issue, not yours, not the paper's," I answered.

"I need to understand what you mean by self-interest."

I sighed, knowing I would have to reveal more than I cared to if Brooks was going to allow what Father had been telling me to make it into the pages of the *Sun*.

"At the start I wanted peace with my father for Mother's sake." I noticed Brooks sat up straighter at the mention of my mother and looked more attentive. "I took him at his word that he had decided to let me reunite with the family because that's what my mother wanted, but it soon became clear that was not the only reason.

"My father is going to work exclusively for Mr. Frick. We have been talking more and more, and I'm learning a great deal. But it is clear that he wants me to get that information into the paper when it is helpful to Mr. Frick."

Brooks shifted in his chair. "We have to be very careful here, Jamie. I'll be damned if the *Sun* is going to become a mouthpiece for Frick."

"I understand that, but tensions between Frick and Carnegie could be one of the great stories of the decade," I said, leaning forward. "What's at stake is control of the largest industrial concern in the country and millions and millions of dollars. Plus, there is nothing readers like more than the inside story on the rich and powerful."

Sitting back in his chair, Cleve said, "I admire your diligence, but we have to be sure we report the Carnegie side of these events, even if it's a 'no comment' from one of his minions. Don't think I'm going to send you off on a ship to Scotland!"

"I didn't expect you would. I will have to catch him when he makes one of his brief stops in the town that has made him all his money." I was relieved to see that Brooks was going to accept Father as a source.

"Go after the coke company rift," Brooks told me.

Buoyed by Cleve's confidence in me, I strode out of the newsroom with my head held high.

It was the holiday season, 1894, and Rita and I seemed to be going out every night to another ball at another East End mansion. I liked these affairs up to a point. While it's hard to complain about the sumptuous meals and the dazzling decorations, with each hostess trying to outdo the last, I got Rita to agree to take a night off and have a quiet dinner at the Monongahela House. I was almost as happy that we would be alone as I was that I didn't have to don white tie and tails for the fifth night in a row.

As Rita and I walked into the dining room, I looked over to the bar and saw a group of toughs surrounding a man loudly and drunkenly holding forth. It was Jason Garland.

Rita grabbed my arm. "Jamie, I know it was supposed to be just us tonight, but we have to get Jason away from that group. They don't look like suitable companions."

I knew they weren't suitable at all because I had seen a couple of them at Pittsburgh's gaming clubs. They were hangers-on, boys who would eavesdrop on conversations to enrich themselves, maybe overhear a stock tip, lift a wallet, or supply more than just the alcohol being served. I didn't want Rita to know I was familiar with these men, but I agreed that we had to get Jason away from them.

"Jason, old man, fancy seeing you here tonight. Rita and I would love to have you join us." The men surrounding him were rough customers, and even though we were at the best hotel in town, I didn't want to do anything to draw their ire.

Jason gave me a vacant look, like he didn't recognize me; then his eyes focused. "Jamie Dalton, my old friend and college mate. Surprised to see you here. Why aren't you and your debutante out at one of your fancy-dress balls?" he said, slurring every word.

One of the men, clearly their leader, glowered at me. "Leave him be. He's with us tonight." I drew myself up to my full height and tried to look as menacing as I could. Rita had come up behind me and was pulling me away, but I shook off her hand.

The man had on a rakishly tilted bowler hat and wore a black suit, buttoned up to the collar. All of them wore the same uniform, down to the polished black ankle-high boots. Their greasy dark hair that hung down over their collars and their thin mustaches did little to make them appear older than they really were. Nineteen, maybe twenty. I feared that each one carried a switchblade, maybe even a derringer.

"Mr. Garland here can do as he please, dontcha agree?" the man asked with a threatening, thin smile. Then he took a step toward me and leaned his face close to my ear. "If your friend is looking for more than they serve here, we are happy to provide it. He pays, he gets what he wants."

I could feel the adrenaline surging but kept my voice low and certain. "Find another mark. He's going with me." Jason was slumped on a barstool looking distant and befuddled. Rita was imploring me to come back to our table. The hooligan and I were chest to chest, with the others close behind him. Neither of us was giving an inch, and I could smell his breath, a mixture of beer and the free pickles from the jar on the bar.

"Do we have a problem here, gentlemen?" A man in a disheveled suit showed us his badge, then turned to the thug and gave him a shove. "Danny Doogan, I follow you and your gang all over town and mostly leave you alone. But you ain't gonna be bothering the good folks in a respectable place like this."

Two uniformed cops, brandishing nightsticks, had appeared in the entrance to the restaurant, and the detective motioned them toward us.

Speaking in a quiet but commanding tone, he told them, "I'll be giving you and your cronies an escort out. Don't do nothing to disturb the diners, or you'll get a beating and spend the night in jail. Just march straight out like the little cowards I know you to be."

They strutted out single file with Doogan bringing up the rear. When he passed me, he spit a stream of tobacco juice at my feet.

"No doubt I'll be seeing your friend again." He tipped his hat, gave a mocking bow, and was gone.

"Dalton, get your drunk friend out of here," the detective said. "My men have seen him staggering out of the bars along the wharf, but he doesn't seem to be harming anyone but himself, so we've left him be. What I won't abide is him bringing Doogan and the Boilers into a fine place like the Monongahela House. Next time he does it, he is going into a cell along with the others."

I thanked the man for his discretion and told him I would do all I could to keep Jason out of trouble. Then Rita and I took Jason by the elbows and walked him as discreetly as we could out of the restaurant. I noted several familiar faces among the patrons and knew that the story of Jason's drunkenness would be all over town by the next day. I hoped there wasn't any further speculation about why he was there with a gang of street toughs.

We propped Jason up between us in the carriage and rattled our away back to Point Breeze. He immediately passed out against my shoulder. It was quiet, just an occasional undecipherable mumble from Jason, while Rita and I said very little. I think she was shocked to have found Jason at the hotel with a street gang. I was aware of Jason's problems with drugs at New Haven and wasn't so surprised. But it made me sad. The confident, talented young man who I got to know on that first trip to New Haven was long gone.

Our first stop was the Heinz home, and I walked Rita to the door. "He needs help, Jamie. I know you will be a good friend, as will I."

I kissed her good night and wondered how good a friend I had been to Jason. With my ravenous appetite for information from the Carnegie Company, had I put him under too much pressure?

Jason was still sleeping when we arrived back at Schiller's. I wrestled him up the stairs to his bed, then threw a blanket over him. Not wanting to leave him alone, I sat in his one easy chair and fell asleep.

I awoke to the sounds of retching in the bathroom. When Jason returned, we sat there in our underclothes, not unlike how we often greeted mornings after in New Haven. Jason avoided my gaze, plopped down on the couch, then put his face in his hands. Not knowing what to say, I merely coughed.

Jason groaned, then looked up. "I don't remember a thing after getting to the bar at the Mon. How bad was I?"

I didn't know knew where to start. "You were very drunk, and I don't know what else. I have seen you worse but not for a long time. What worries me more than your drunkenness were your companions. How in God's name did you get hooked up with that gang of hoodlums? Are you back on the dope?"

Jason held his head in his hands and mumbled, "I need it."

"The hell you do!" I answered, raising my voice. "The detective at the Mon House told me his men have been watching you. Said he will arrest you the next time he sees you roistering about with those toughs."

With a weary, despairing voice, Jason answered, "I can stop drinking, but getting off the opium and the cocaine won't be so easy." I was surprised that he could admit his drug use so casually, but perhaps that was a sign he could reform. "If I stay away from the Boilers, maybe I can get off the dope. I know it's no excuse, but I've been under pressure at work . . ."

"What about work?" I asked.

"Nothing," he answered.

I didn't want to push him. "You should call in sick, then stay here and sleep it off. I'll check in on you later. My advice is to talk to your mother. She's a smart, strong woman and will help you decide the best path forward. You may have to go back to Bedford."

"I will talk to Mother, but I'm telling you what I will tell her. I am not going back to that clinic. Never again." He answered in such an emphatic tone that I thought he might be coming around, until I saw that his hands were shaking uncontrollably.

"Will you be all right?" I asked.

"I'll be fine. Thank you, Jamie, you are always there when I need you most, but you should get to work." With that, I gave Jason's arm a gentle squeeze and left, not without some misgiving, for the *Sun* office.

⸻ ⸻

I had intended to check in on Jason, but as I was leaving work the next night, I was handed a telegram. It was from Jason and said that he had told the steel company that he was taking his mother to White Sulphur Springs for the holidays. I was happy that he had left Pittsburgh, but I wondered how I would get any new information about the infighting at the Frick Coke Company.

Although Rita and I worried about Jason, we did enjoy the biggest event of the season, Mr. and Mr. R. B. Mellon's New Year's Eve Ball at their magnificent twenty-acre estate on Fifth, which stretched all the way from Bigelow Boulevard to Shady Avenue. Mother invited the Heinzes to Amberson Avenue for a New Year's Day lunch. I hoped no one was expecting an engagement announcement. I had spoken to Mother about what Rita and I had discussed, and she seemed to understand.

Work began again in earnest on Wednesday, January 2, 1895, and when I arrived at the *Sun*, I found an envelope waiting for me. I could see it was in Jason's handwriting with a West Virginia postmark. There was a note inside.

"Jamie, you are a good and true friend, and I can't begin to thank you for saving me from so much hurt and embarrassment. I'll never be able to repay you for all you've done, but this is a start. I've been entrusted with some sensitive correspondence that I know will be of interest to you. Do what you want with it, but don't use my name. I'll be back in the office January 9, but after that we will have to keep our distance. Mr. Frick has spies everywhere, not just in the plants. Maybe in a month I'll be able to talk to you more, but right now I need to concentrate on my job and staying away from the booze and the junk."

The significance of what Jason had sent me was apparent. The top document read in part: "You have gone behind my back to discuss a merger of H. C. Frick Coke with William Rainey. Mr. Rainey is well known to me as he has been a competitor for many years in the Connellsville fields. He is a no-account and not to be trusted in the least, let alone as a partner in such a vast enterprise as our coke business. If you insist on interfering in my management of our businesses, I will be forced to reconsider my position with Carnegie Steel."

Mr. Carnegie replied with his usual bland assertion. "You will always have my full support." From there the letters grew more and more acrimonious. In one Mr. Carnegie suggested that Mr. Frick "take a long ocean cruise, maybe to the Middle East whose delights and timelessness are a balm to even the most troubled soul."

The final straw was a short letter from Mr. Carnegie to Henry Phipps that inexplicably had been delivered to Frick by mistake. "Mr. Frick is unwell, and I don't believe he can perform his duties as the president of my steel company any longer," it said.

Frick's response was blunt and to the point. "I am tired of your charade about my health. If you want me out, be a man and purchase all my shares." This last was dated December 31, 1894, and was the final paper in the file Jason had given me.

I sat at the table pondering what I should do with this trove of new information. These harsh words between the two most powerful men in Pittsburgh were dynamite. Jason had to know I would report on them. But he had been through a serious trauma in the last month. Had he thought through the possible consequences? How angry Mr. Frick would be that his private correspondence was public knowledge?

I weighed this all out and decided to ignore that small voice of caution. This story could affect the lives of tens of thousands of coke and steel workers and the financial fortunes of the entire city. I would write it, and the *Sun* would publish it.

The piece appeared on Monday, January 28, 1895, under the sensational headline "Battle of the steel magnates—Carnegie, Frick fight to the death?" It caused a furor that left the other Pittsburgh and national papers scrambling to catch up. Mr. Frick's office was besieged by reporters, but he would push pass them as he entered the building each morning and exited it that night. His office issued a terse statement. "Carnegie Steel and Frick Coke have no comment on these spurious press reports." Mr. Carnegie was in his suite of rooms at the Manhattan Hotel in New York and said nothing.

By Friday, February 1, all the speculation was confirmed. The reporters at the front of the Carnegie Building were suspicious that something was afoot when Mr. Frick did not arrive right at eight o'clock. I was surprised to see that there was a guard posted at the front door, and I decided to join the scrum down on Smithfield Street.

At noon a man I didn't know but recognized from all the time I had spent at the Carnegie offices opened the front door of the building with a sheaf of papers in his arms. "This is the raw meat you jackals have been waiting for all week." True to form we all scrambled to pick up copies of the release he dropped on the street.

The first sentence read, "Henry Frick has resigned all executive positions with Carnegie Steel." As soon as they saw that, the newsmen sprinted away in every direction, hoping their paper would be the first on the street with this momentous news. I finished reading the announcement on my way back to my office. Frick was resigning, effective immediately, and would be replaced by John Leishman, the man who had saved Frick from being killed by Alexander Berkman. Frick would be appointed chairman of the board of directors, which sounded like a meaningless title. I knew that the minority partners on the board were under the sway of Carnegie and did little besides affirm anything the majority owner asked of them. The press release concluded by saying that Mr. Frick would take a "well-deserved" leave of absence.

I wrote up the story, then headed back to the Carnegie Building to see whether I could get any further comments. The guard had gone, and the office was empty expect for one man behind a stand-up desk. He knew who I was and started in on me. "I have nothing to say to you or any other reporter. It's the damned press with all their speculations that forced Mr. Carnegie and Mr. Frick to take such a drastic step." I wanted to argue that our reporting of the facts had nothing to do with the decisions they had made but thought better of it.

"Has Mr. Garland left for the day?" I asked as innocently as I could.

The man squared his shoulders and gave me a disgusted look. "Mr. Garland was terminated today for his disloyalty to Mr. Frick. You bear some responsibility for that."

Before he had finished the accusation, I bounded down the stairs and out to the street and ran to the Mon House, hoping Jason was at the bar merely drowning his sorrows. The bartender told me he had been there earlier but staggered out after drinking three double shots of gin. He's off on one of his tears, I thought, and with dread I headed to the wharf.

There were already police shooing away onlookers. "Let me through; I'm press," I shouted to the first man that tried to stop me, and he backed away with a begrudging look. Then I recognized Sheriff McCleary, who I knew from the Homestead strike.

He saw me and said, "Dalton, you don't want to see this. It's not a pretty sight."

"I may know the man, Sheriff. You must let me see him."

The scene was worse than I imagined. There was a body face down in the street with the back of his head blown apart, but despite the shattered features and all the blood, I knew it was Jason. Then I staggered toward the river and vomited. Still numb, I asked the sheriff what he knew about Jason's murder.

"He was shot from close-up by a small pistol, likely a derringer. I don't know for certain, but my guess is that he was down here looking for drugs, and when he met up with Doogan and his men, they rolled him, then killed him. His money was gone, and we didn't find a pocket watch. But don't expect an arrest anytime soon. Half the Hill will testify that Doogan and his boys were having a nice Irish stew with them tonight."

I walked back to the *Sun* and typed up the account of Jason's murder. I left the copy on Cleveland Brooks's desk with a note attached. All it said was, "I quit."

10

Back in the Game

I FELT RESPONSIBLE FOR JASON'S DEATH, NO MATTER HOW MUCH MY family and Rita tried to convince me otherwise. If I hadn't pushed him for information about the Carnegie companies, maybe he wouldn't have felt the need to take drugs again. Seeing how drunk he was the night Rita and I went out to dinner with him, I should have insisted he get help, regardless of his protestations. I should have gone to Mrs. Garland with my concerns. I should have been more of a friend and less of an ambitious young reporter.

Cleveland Brooks was understanding about why I wanted to resign.

"You should take a month off and think through your decision," he said.

In that state of mind, I was incapable of resuming my position as the lead reporter investigating the complex machinations of Pittsburgh's steel industry, the driver of the country's burgeoning wealth. The battle for sources, the drive to be first with every piece of news was too intense for me to give it my full attention. My heart wasn't in it.

Not knowing what else to do, I took long walks all over the East End of Pittsburgh—out past Highland Park to the shores of the Allegheny, through the leafy beauty of Woodland Road with all its grand homes, even over Squirrel Hill all the way to the Monongahela. I came to realize, obvious as it might be, that the worst thing I could do was nothing. A month after Jason's death, I presented myself at the *Sun*'s offices, not knowing what I would say.

Cleveland Brooks was sympathetic. "I know how devastating this must be for you, but you are too smart, too valuable for the *Sun* to lose. I think you should look over the other departments of the paper, then come back to me and tell me what interests you. Someday you will want to cover the steel business again. The struggle between Frick and Carnegie will be epic."

I nodded in agreement, but I wasn't listening. At that point all I could think of was how hard I had pushed Jason and the devastating consequences. I couldn't take advantage of anyone like that again, and I knew I might need to if I were to maintain my position as the top reporter on the steel beat.

For weeks I stewed and got nowhere. And I was drinking more than I ever had in my life. After my crazy days at Shady Side and Yale, and knowing the problems in the family, I had tried to control my drinking. I had a great capacity for alcohol and was never falling-down drunk, but there were the awful hangovers. I told myself they hadn't affected my job, so I didn't need to stop drinking.

But after Jason's death, I would have a couple of beers at lunch, whiskey before dinner, wine during, and brandy after. When we were out for dinner, Rita would try to get me to slow down, then say very little in the carriage on the way home.

At least I was sober enough to know that something had to change in my professional life, and I took Cleve up on his suggestion to explore the publishing side of the business.

The complexity of the daily operations astounded me. As the printed papers rolled off the noisy, enormous presses, they were scooped up by a noisy rabble of newsboys who ran all over downtown hawking the latest headlines. "Frick defies Carnegie." "Bloody battle in the coal fields." "Pirates trounce Redlegs." Making two cents on each paper they sold was a great incentive. For home delivery our teamsters would deliver the paper to central spots around the city, and newsboys would deliver the papers in time for the Mr.'s breakfast.

Even more profitable for the paper was the sale of advertising space that on any given day might take up over half of the paper's ten pages. The largest buyers of advertising space were the big department stores: Horne's, Kaufmann's, and the upstart Boggs and Buhl, which was making inroads against its larger competitors with the catchy headline "Ladies and Gentlemen, Horses and Mules, Buy Your Clothes at Boggs and Buhl." Although the ad salesmen had a justified reputation for carousing, they were fierce competitors that would never let one of these profitable accounts slip away from the *Sun*. I enjoyed tagging along when they entertained the stores' top brass.

The department stores weren't the only advertisers. Home fixtures, furniture, jewelry, and patent medicines all needed to be sold. Even doctors touted their services: "Guarantee a positive cure," set in large type, then below that in smaller print, "in all curable cases." There were also many columns filled with personal ads at one penny a word: help wanted, lost and found, commercial and residential real estate, even corporate announcements of dividends and annual meetings. The advertisements, big and small, showed the panoply of what made the city thrive.

I found the business side fascinating, and it occurred to me that my ultimate position at the *Sun* might be publisher, but I wasn't willing to give up journalism, at least not yet.

Cleveland Brooks honored my request for less taxing assignments. To ease back into the daily cycle, I rewrote wire service copy from all over the world. I had never envisioned that I would be relegated to such a mundane task but working on these international dispatches gave me insights never afforded to me in my formal education at Shady Side or Yale. Another new area for me was business news. This was closer to my old assignment than I may have liked, but it was straight reporting on financial markets both in Pittsburgh and New York with no investigative work. It was about the numbers, not the people, and that was just fine with me.

When the spring came, I volunteered to cover baseball, the sport that in twenty years had become a national obsession. Pittsburgh's team played across the river in Allegheny, which was still a separate city, much as Brooklyn was separate from New York. The Alleghenys were in the American Association until they jumped to the National League for the 1887 season. In 1891 they became the Pirates when the Philadelphia Athletics of the Association claimed the Pittsburgh team "stole" one of their best players, second baseman Lou Bierbauer.

When the Pirates were in town, I walked on the covered Union Bridge over the Allegheny River and took my press box seat in the third incarnation of Exposition Park, which was located just east of the poor Slabtown neighborhood that produced many of the city's successful steel men, including my father. The games began at three o'clock and didn't last more than two hours. It was convenient for a man working downtown to slip out early, watch a game, drink a beer, and be home by dinnertime. During the week the attendance was around two thousand and would climb to five thousand for weekend games.

The game was rough-and-tumble back then. From my seat next to the dugout, I could see the players taking quick sips from flasks between innings, and with the stimulus of alcohol, fights would break out on the field after brush-back pitches or hard slides with sharpened spikes that slashed at the infielders. Being around the team all season—I sometimes accompanied them on the road to St. Louis, New York, and Boston—I got to know the players well, and that allowed me to give a personal touch to my reporting, although I knew better than to mention the drinking. Baseball had nowhere near the same consequence as the city's steel industry, but all strata of Pittsburgh doted on the Pirates and looked forward to reading about their exploits in the newspaper. Cleve gave me more and more space for my baseball write-ups, and during the season the newsboys always sold more papers.

With some embarrassment I contributed to the Society News that appeared in the paper each Sunday. Millicent Van Buren, the lady who edited that section, knew my family and, of course, Rita's, and every Thursday afternoon she would ask me to tea at the New Century Club and pump me for any bits of gossip I may have heard. At first, I resisted her entreaties, but after a time, it became a game to me. She would say something like, "I heard the Frews were leaving on the *Mauretania* and will spend the winter in Cap d'Antibes." "Will young Tom Hilliard attend Princeton this fall?"

I would laugh and either confirm what she said or tell her I knew nothing about it. Then I would dish a few morsels of my own, with the understanding that she would have to confirm the leads I gave her.

That was my life, dabbling in the business side of the newspaper, writing what the serious reporters disdained, and trying to ignore the lingering feelings of guilt over Jason's death. After a year of that, I still couldn't admit I was adrift. Rita wouldn't see me as often as I'd have liked, and I knew it was because of my drinking.

It was Mother who roused me out of my self-indulgent torpor. One Sunday in the spring of 1896, the family had finished a heavy lunch of roast beef and Yorkshire pudding, and I went out on the porch to smoke a Havana blunt when Mother appeared next to me at the porch railing.

"Jamie, you must know I have been right where you are now. Maybe for different reasons, but the result is the same."

I attempted to look confused, but she wasn't fooled. "Don't pretend you are past your guilt about Jason. You keep yourself busy, but I know you are unhappy, and your drinking is to the point of being out of control. You need to talk about what happened. If not with me, then with someone. Keeping it all to yourself will kill you—and that is no exaggeration. When I've gone to Cresson Springs"—I was shocked she would even mention that—"what helped me most was to simply talk, and it really didn't matter who I talked to. It could be a nurse, it could be a doctor, even some of the kitchen staff. The more I was able to express what I was thinking and feeling, the easier it was to deal with what seemed overwhelming. The people I spoke with would ask some simple questions, and my answers would lead me to look at my life from a different perspective. I can tell you from experience that the more you keep bottled up, the worse it will get. Your father and I knew there was more to Jason's withdrawal from Yale than exhaustion. He was a troubled young man, Jamie. You couldn't save him from himself."

"But I knew he was fragile. I pushed him too far," I said with a catch in my voice.

Mother put her hand on mine. It felt warm and reassuring. "You may have, but you were doing your job. He didn't have to reveal anything about Clay's business. He made his own choices, Jamie. He was so fond of you. Think what you did for him at New Haven."

Her concern was moving, and I felt tears on my face. "Momma, I should have been a better friend to him."

"You can't change the past. You are smart and capable with so much to offer." She held her arms out to me. We embraced, and she left me to my thoughts.

That summer Rita and I took long rides in the Homewood forest on weekends. During the week I would stop off at her house after work, and we would walk through the streets of Point Breeze, sometimes roaming as far as Shadyside. We had grown up in these neighborhoods, and this was where we both felt at home. Rita would never press me to talk about what I was dealing with. She knew when to ask questions or let the conversation drift along. One night we decided to challenge our endurance and walked up Negley Hill, the longest, steepest hill in the East End. I was winded but calm as we reached the top.

"You have been so dear, Rita. I know I have been poor company ever since ..."

"Jamie, I want the best for you, for us. Maybe it would help to talk, but I can't when you've been drinking."

"Soon," I promised.

After that night I tried with moderate success to limit my drinking to an occasional beer and wine at dinner. I wanted to talk to her about what was on my mind—the guilt over Jason that I couldn't shake, the ebb and flow of my many conflicts with my father, my stalled career. I didn't need to talk about Zofia. She was a memory, not a consideration.

Rita would let me ramble, then prod me to be self-reflective when I drifted too far off course. It was difficult for me to admit that my new role at the paper was comfortable but not fulfilling. Talking to Rita helped me think clearly, like I would find my way sooner rather than later. In the back of both of our minds was that I needed to resolve my issues, all my issues, if we were to marry. I was lucky to have such a sensitive, intuitive woman in my life.

<hr>

One September Saturday after a Pirates game and several Iron City beers, I stopped midway on the Union Bridge and took Rita's hand. We looked past the Point, crowded with warehouses at the confluence of the rivers, and down the Ohio. With all the noise and industrial dirt, it may not have been the most romantic spot, but I knew what I wanted to say.

"Rita Heinz, I love you. Will you marry me?"

Rita took a step back, then shook her head. "Jamie Dalton, you know that I have always loved you, but you aren't ready for marriage." Rita had been patient with me, but she had reached her limit. "You aren't sober enough long enough to take this next step."

"But I don't want to live my life without you, Rita. I want us to have children. Isn't that enough?" My commitment was absolute. I had always known in my heart that Rita was the right woman for me. My love for her and the loneliness I had felt in my solo existence at Aunt Leila's made the supposed strictures of marriage irrelevant.

"I'm sorry, but something has to change. We are a long way from having children together." We said very little on the long streetcar ride back to Penn Avenue.

Rita and I didn't see each other for the next month. She wouldn't answer my calls and would not see me if I presented myself at the Heinz home. At night I moped around Leila's house but kept on drinking. Leila had been to New York, but she returned one night and found me asleep on the couch with a glass of whiskey balanced on my chest.

"Is this what you do at nights?" I had never heard Aunt Leila take a tone like that with me. "You are pathetic."

I started in on my guilt about Jason, my troubles at the paper, then Rita's rejection of my proposal.

"Poor child! You come from one of the finest families in Pittsburgh, you work for its best newspaper, and until recently you have been the beau of the most sought-after women in the city. It's time for you to wake up! And the first thing you should wake up to is that you will never be happy unless you stop drinking. You must know that it's a problem that runs in our family. Why do you think I was gone all those years?"

I tried to argue with Leila that I was different from her, my mother, my grandmother. But she refuted me at every turn, and eventually I stopped talking altogether. "Figure out what you want, Jamie. A fulfilling career? A lovely wife and a happy marriage? You know the answer. Now I'm going to bed."

For the next week, I cut back until all I drank was one glass of wine with dinner. That Sunday, I presented myself at Rita's. The butler said she was not available, but this time I told him I would not leave until she saw me. After an hour of kicking the stones on the driveway, she appeared on her front porch. She looked at me and didn't say a word.

"Rita, please listen to me. I love you and I will do anything for us to be together. And that includes not drinking. All I have now is an occasional glass of wine."

"And why that? Jamie, I've heard your promises about alcohol before. I won't believe you will stay sober until I see it with my own eyes."

Every Sunday for the next month, I would appear at the Heinz house at nine in the morning. Every Sunday, I told Rita that I hadn't had a drink that week. She would nod at me, say she had to get ready for church, then return to the house. On the fifth Sunday, I asked her to go for a walk around Point Breeze that afternoon. She hesitated but said yes.

I still had to prove myself to her, and for another five months, I stayed away from liquor, even beer. The pharmacist at Schiller's told me about a sweet brown fizzy water called Coca-Cola that came in little green bottles for only a nickel, and that became my new drink. Nothing addictive there, I thought.

I felt better than I had in years. I didn't miss the next-day dry mouth and headaches after drinking. One Sunday late in the fall, we were taking a horseback ride in what was becoming known as Frick Park, and I took a deep breath.

"Rita, I hope that I have proved my devotion to you by changing, by being sober." She looked at me with a hint of a smile. I continued. "You know how much I love you. Please marry me. You can be assured I know my own mind." I decided not to mention children again.

Rita had a serious look that worried me, but it turned into a big, beautiful smile, and she said, "I've never stopped loving you, but now I believe in you." Then she threw her arms around my neck. "Yes, Jamie Dalton, I will marry you. But please know I will hold you to your word about liquor."

"Your love is worth everything to me," I answered.

"Before anything else, you will have to speak with Daddy."

The next Sunday, I presented myself at the Heinzes' home just after three when I knew the family would be finished with their formal Sunday lunch. The butler greeted me at the door. "Winfield, I was hoping to speak to Mr. Heinz." As he showed me into the library, I saw Rita just outside the door, and she gave me a wink.

Whatever confidence I had evaporated when I saw Mr. Heinz waiting for me. My palms were sweating, and I clenched my hands in front of me.

"Please sit, James. What can I do for you today?" he said with a smile.

"Mr. Heinz, I seek your approval to marry Rita," I blurted.

His face took on a more serious demeanor. "I'm not sure this is the right time, James. What are your prospects if you stay at the *Sun*?"

"Right now, I am learning the business of newspapers, but my goal is to return to reporting on the steel industry. I have the respect of Cleveland Brooks and can have my pick of assignments."

"I understand that what you are writing about now is, let us say, beneath your talents," he answered. "Young man, Rita will be a wealthy woman someday. I don't want you to exploit her fortune to take the easy path. There are many more lucrative careers than journalism in our not-so-fair city."

"Mr. Heinz, I promise you I will strive to be the best in whatever field I choose. I will admit that due to personal concerns I slowed my ambitions, but that will change in the near future. Please trust me on that."

"And your problems with drink?"

That question I feared but was ready for. "I hope Rita has told you that I haven't touched a drop in over six months."

Mr. Heinz hesitated, then looked me square in the eye. "My daughter will not marry a slacker. I will hold you to account if you make Rita unhappy," he harrumphed.

He let that sink in, as he watched me squirm. "But I have always been fond of you, James, and your father and mother are fine people. If you will agree to a long engagement with a wedding date toward the end of next year, I will give my blessing."

We both heard a cough from outside the room.

"I beg your pardon, sir, but I know Rita was counting on a summer wedding. Could we agree on September?"

Mr. Heinz knew whose cough that was. "You may as well come in, my child, since you are already a part of the conversation that I thought was to be private between James and myself."

Rita walked into the library with a sheepish look. "Don't be mad, Daddy. I do love Jamie so. Please give us your blessing."

Moving out from behind his big desk, Mr. Henry J. Heinz looked me up and down, glanced over at Rita, then opened his arms. "September it is! You will be a fine addition to our family, James Dalton." He pulled us into his embrace.

"As I will be a great addition to the Dalton family," Rita added. "Father, may we be excused to give them the happy news?"

⸺ ⸺

And the whirlwind began. My parents were thrilled. Their renegade son was marrying into one of Pittsburgh's finest families, and they both loved the irrepressible Rita. My future bride was smart and efficient, and though it infuriated her mother, she was able to dispose of the marital minutiae with dispatch. She spared me from organizing bridal showers and engagement parties, and I didn't have to hear about the sticky negotiations over her wedding trousseau and what the bridesmaids would wear.

Father and I tried to stay out of the way, but there was one conversation about the wedding I was looking forward to. I waited until after Christmas dinner when Father and I were happily ensconced in his library smoking cigars and drinking port. "I've been thinking about who my groomsmen should be," I said, then listed off five friends, two from Shady Side, three from Yale.

"I have more of a dilemma about who should be my best man. I suppose it should be Wills."

"That seems logical," Father said with an impassive poker face.

I couldn't hold back my excitement a second longer and stood up and took a step to where he was sitting. "Father, you are my best man. You always have been and always will be."

Father stood, and his stern visage cracked. "I am honored, my son." We both started to cry, then opened our arms and embraced. It had been a long eight years since I went to work at the *Sun*, but we had weathered the storms.

———

With my light responsibilities at the paper and Rita and her mother overseeing every imaginable detail of the ceremony and reception, soon it was our wedding day, Saturday, September 7, 1897. Some of my old friends from New Haven had arrived by train on Friday, and that night my parents hosted a dinner for the wedding party at the University Club in Oakland.

The next day I stood nervously beside my father in front of the simple altar of the Shadyside Presbyterian Church. When Mendelsohn's familiar "Wedding March" filled the church, I looked up the main aisle and saw Rita walking slowly down the aisle on her father's arm. I had never seen a more beautiful woman and was reminded of what Aunt Leila had said: Obvious!

Rita's dark-blonde hair was pulled up into a tight chignon that allowed the fine features of her face to capture the room. Her sparkling blue eyes, her bright and deep dimples gave her a classic beauty. Atop her head was a finely woven lace veil that I knew had been Mr. Heinz's mother's back in Germany. Her wedding dress was of a fine satin that molded perfectly to her slim body. My face broadcast my love and awe of this lovely woman that was to be my wife. I was proud and happy, more than I had ever been or expected to be.

The ceremony and reception were glorious. I felt Father's strong presence behind me as I looked into Rita's beautiful blue eyes and we took our vows. I looked back to the first row and saw Mother standing with Kat on one side and Leila on the other. Mother wore a fitted mauve dress with long sleeves and a high collar. Kat wore the same cut but in gray. I wasn't surprised to see Aunt Leila in a voluminous orange and green caftan. What did surprise me was that she held my mother's hand throughout the service as they both cried.

After riding back to the Heinz home on Penn Avenue in their most well-appointed brougham, Rita and I stood in the receiving line to receive our guests, all two hundred and fifty of them. It had worried me that I would be tempted by champagne and beer at the reception, but I made sure that the buckets holding kegs of Iron City and ice would be stocked with my little green bottles. The time passed quickly, and soon we were released for our first dance as a married couple.

I led with confidence, and Rita whispered into my ear, "You are a much better dancer than when we met at that long-ago Christmas party." I held her close and whisked her around the dance floor with a flourish. I had to admit we were a very handsome couple.

The next dance was with Mother. "I've never been prouder of you, Jamie. You've been a fine reporter, but more important the breach with your father has been healed. And that's to your credit, as well as his. Rita Heinz is lucky to have you as a husband. You are even luckier to have her as a wife!"

When Father cut in, I knew who my next partner would be. Seeing her standing next to Wills, I approached. "Aunt Leila, may I have this dance?"

"I'd be honored," she said with a mock curtsy. "Will I ever get you to drop the Aunt? It's Leila!"

The orchestra picked up the tempo, and Leila and I twirled to the rhythm. As we walked off the dance floor to find a glass of champagne, I turned to her and said, "You have been so good to me. For taking me in and all your wise counsel. I can never thank you enough."

"I never worried about you, Jamie. But you did need a kick in the right place from time to time!" We toasted each other, her with champagne and me with Coca-Cola. By this point I was enjoying myself so much that it didn't occur to me to take a drink.

The rest of the evening was a blur. I remember that Kat, twenty-six now and a curator at Mr. Carnegie's new art museum, was never off the dance floor. Wills, who had just graduated from Williams and was apprenticing at Father's law firm, gave a very funny toast, teasing his older brother for always being in the middle of whatever disaster befell Pittsburgh and his undeserved luck in getting such a fabulous woman to marry him.

Rita and I didn't leave the party until midnight, when we rode in the brougham to the Schenley Hotel where Mr. Heinz had arranged a suite for us. The next day we boarded a train bound for California.

We were astounded by the West. Neither of us had crossed the Mississippi, and the open spaces and the clear skies seemed miraculous. But coming east I grew anxious about my return to the paper and spoke about that one night as the train rolled across the Great Plains.

"I know why I took the assignments, but I'm getting restless covering the Pirates and Pittsburgh society."

"It's still about Jason, isn't it?" Rita asked. I didn't say anything, and she continued. "You'll know when you are ready. I believe in you, my dear."

"I want you to be proud of me." There wasn't much more to be said, and we returned to the enjoyment of our meal and the scenery.

I stayed with my old assignments when I returned to the *Sun*, but by the next summer I wanted to get back into hard news and thought about attending one of Mother's suffrage meetings. But what were my true motives? To see firsthand the importance of this movement? To be proud of her participation and leadership? It was both of those things, but I also had suspicions about her and Cleve Brooks. I noticed when Cleve wasn't in the office, and he was often out in the late afternoon. I dithered over my decision until it was past the time the meeting was supposed to start; then I hustled out the door to get a Fifth Avenue streetcar out to Oakland.

After I got off at Thackeray Street, I strode up the hill until I was in front of the Colonial Dames' clubhouse, an unpretentious two-story clapboard structure. I loitered on the sidewalk for a minute, still not sure whether I wanted to go inside. That's when I saw the front door open, and Mother and Cleve Brooks emerged, engrossed in conversation. Mother was shaking her head, and Brooks was gesticulating with his hands. Before they could see me, I hustled back down Thackeray, hoping they weren't headed toward Fifth. I looked back once, and they were still standing in front of the building. Mother's head was down, and her shoulders were shaking; Brooks's hands were on her arms in an intimate gesture of comfort, but he had a very sad look on his face. I shouldn't have come.

I struggled with whether I should say anything to either Cleve Brooks or my mother about seeing them together that afternoon. I rationalized that Mother was attending the meeting and Brooks covering it. Nothing nefarious about that. But what about their animated conversation that seemed to end with Mother crying and Cleve trying to console her? That part I couldn't put out of my mind. It didn't allay my suspicions when Brooks was unusually short-tempered over the next few weeks, barking out caustic edits to the newsroom. After about a month, he seemed back to his unflappable self, and he asked me to have lunch with him at the Pittsburgh Club, where Brooks was a member as were many of Pittsburgh's Fourth Estate. After we traded superficial pleasantries and ate the trout almandine, Brooks wiped his mouth with his napkin and began.

"Jamie, more will happen in the steel industry in the coming years than anything that has occurred since Homestead, and no one will be able to cover these upheavals better than you. Frick and Carnegie are tangling over the price the steel company pays for coke, but that's a pretext. The Old Scotsman wants Frick out, but they are entangled in the Iron-Clad Agreement that limits what partners get paid for their shares. There's a lot to dig into.

"It's even rumored that Carnegie might sell the company. That would be the biggest story in the country, and it would be all yours!"

He had my interest. And I was very glad that my mother would not be the subject of the lunch.

"You've done fine work at the paper," he continued. "You have the curiosity and the need to uncover truths and make the public aware. I've been impressed with how you've learned the business of newspapers, and your ideas about getting the newsboys paid faster have made them work harder and sales are up. Your sports writing has been first-rate. You're even a good gossip columnist," Cleve said with a laugh.

"But I know that's not where your heart lies. The Carnegie-Frick battles and a sale of the steel company will attract even more attention than that phony war in Spain. You want to be on the inside, don't you?"

I looked down into my coffee cup, like it was there I would find an answer. I was torn but not ready to admit that to Cleve. With Pittsburgh's growth, there were a raft of job options, in steel, banking, law, even accounting. But I had stayed with the *Sun* because I loved newspapering and had stuck with my pledge not to ask my family for financial help with our household expenses. I knew that Mr. Heinz was supporting Rita's sporting activities, but that was their business. Rita and I were very comfortable in our new house on Kentucky Street, still in Shadyside, halfway between her parents and mine. I didn't feel any pressure to bring in more money. I could indulge my misgivings.

"I shouldn't have gone into newspapering in the first place. If it hadn't been for the flood, I doubt I would have."

Brooks scoffed. "You know that's not true. Are you forgetting how you loved writing for the paper at Yale? The Johnstown Flood showed you, showed me, that you had the stuff to become a good reporter. I know what's happened, but guilt over your friend's death does you no good. It certainly won't help Garland."

I knew he was right, but I couldn't bring myself to say it.

"Imagine what you might accomplish as a newspaperman! If you want another career, you will have plenty of time."

"This is a lot to take in. I need to think it over," I answered. It was obvious that I didn't want him to push me any harder. What I couldn't speak of was my mother's fragile condition as of late. Whenever I visited, she was never without a glass of wine in her hand. Maybe it wasn't fair, but I couldn't help but hold Brooks responsible, and doing his bidding seemed disloyal. I needed to be sure Mother was well before I took on the all-consuming steel beat.

We soon left the table and walked back to the *Sun* in silence.

***

After work I headed back to Amberson Avenue to talk to both Mother and Father. I was shocked to see my father helping my mother up the stairs. She tripped over every step.

"James, I need help with your mother. I've never seen her like this."

I took Mother in my arms and carried her to her bedroom. She kept mumbling about a suffragette meeting.

"I am very distressed," Father said when we were back in the library. "When I came home, Agnes was fluttering around, saying she didn't know what to do. She pointed to the parlor, and I found your mother slumped in a chair with an empty bottle of sherry on the table next to her. She has had more wine than usual in the evenings, but I didn't know she was drinking in the afternoons. Son, she needs to go to the clinic at the Bedford Springs Hotel. They have had remarkable luck with these, er, situations."

"Father, let me accompany her."

Father seemed relieved. "You know the demands on my time. Agnes is devoted, but you will be a greater comfort to her." I sent a wire to Cleve that said Mother was sick and I needed a couple of days to take care of her. Let him think what he wanted.

The next morning Mother was still shaky but understood when Father explained that it was for the best that she go to Bedford Springs for a few days. "I'm sorry I have disappointed you," was all she said.

Agnes packed for her, and Father went with us down to the station. "Take good care of her, son." I assured him I would, and Mother and I boarded the train. For most of the three-hour trip, she stared out the window. Time to time she would reach for my hand and mumble a thank you. It was sad to see her reduced to this, but she had been down before and had always rallied herself. Eventually.

At the front entrance of the Bedford Springs Hotel, I was told to pull down to the clinic, a separate building on the grounds. The hotel was tucked in a serene valley. The leaves on the hillside were just past their peak but still gave off a warm glow in the sunlight. At the front door of the clinic, a doctor in a frock coat and a nurse all in white were waiting for us.

"Good day, Mrs. Dalton. I am Doctor Harold Hunsiker." Then he turned to me. "I was told you are her son, James. Please know she is in the best of hands."

Mother had relaxed. "I will be fine, Jamie dear. Please come see me in a week." I looked at the doctor, who gave a nod of assent.

"You couldn't keep me away. Please be well, Mother. We all love you very much." We both had tears in our eyes as we hugged. I took my leave and went back to the station for the train to Pittsburgh.

That night I was comforted by Rita and our house on Kentucky. I had refused the Heinzes' gracious gift of a larger home in Point Breeze.

Between my salary and a small trust of Rita's, we were able to cover our rent and living expenses. During the day, Rita was occupied with riding, tennis, and, in season, golf. I had regular hours at the paper, and weekday evenings we would enjoy cooking for each other, a good fire, and any new novels we could find. On weekends we would see our friends at social functions. I enjoyed our regular life and loved Rita more every day. And she would listen patiently as I mused about my prospects at the paper, all the while guiding me on the path we both knew I should take.

—◦—

But Mother's problem had shaken me, and in a week I was back at Bedford Springs as promised. Dr. Hunsiker showed me into a sunroom where Mother was lying on a chaise reading the latest issue of *McClure's* magazine. The first thing she said was, "They talk about corruption, but nothing about suffrage!" I knew she was feeling better.

"You mother is doing well," Dr. Hunsiker said. "Good food and the clear mountain air will do wonders. And we have the patients talk to one another in a group setting. It helps them to know they are not alone. You may not be surprised that your mother has become a leader in these sessions. Now, I'll leave the two of you alone." We both thanked him before he left.

I pulled up a wicker chair. "You look wonderful, Mother." Her eyes were bright, and her hair shone from brushing.

"Much better than the last time you saw me! Oh Jamie, I am so sorry for what I've put you and your father through."

"Don't think about that now. We are all happy you are doing better."

"And I am going to stay better. Dr. Hunsiker is a fine, understanding man. He knows better than to prescribe fake medications that only make the problem worse. He has convinced me that I shouldn't drink. More important, that I don't need to. If I can face my problems, even talk about them, I won't resort to liquor. He has suggested a colleague in Pittsburgh for me to speak with."

I admired her resolve. "Father and I were surprised about your relapse. Can you tell me what's been bothering you?" I twisted in my chair and whispered my next question. "Does it have anything to do with Cleveland Brooks?" I couldn't say that I had seen them outside the suffrage hall and that she was crying.

She smiled, but her eyes narrowed. "I love your father and you children more than anything in the world, and that's all that needs to be said. Now I wish to devote my life to my family and the suffrage movement. Dr. Hunsiker says I can go home in another week."

I took Mother's hands. "Aunt Leila said you and I are more alike than either of us will admit. I have had my own temptations, but no woman is more right for me than Rita. I love her, and I hope I am deserving of her love. That's why I stopped drinking, for Rita!"

"But, Jamie, you have to do things for yourself as well. I'm glad you're not drinking, but what are you going to do about your career? You can't be satisfied with going to baseball games or writing about the frivolities of Pittsburgh's elite."

I thought of Cleve's offer to cover Carnegie Steel again but wasn't sure I should bring up anything about the *Sun*.

"You don't have to avoid the topic of the newspaper with me," Mother said with a confident smile.

Hearing that, I didn't hesitate. "I have been offered my old assignment, covering the steel business, but I want to hear what you and Father think about that."

"How could we possibly object?" she said with a wave of her hand. "Jamie, let us make a pact that we will pursue our dreams—with no further distractions. You be the best newsman in the city of Pittsburgh, and I will see that Congress passes the suffrage amendment! Are we in agreement?"

I laughed, happy that Mother had regained her equilibrium and the latest slip was only that. "Mother dear, as they say in the business world, you have a deal!" As we said good-bye, our tears were of joy and thanks, not sadness. Mother was back at Amberson Avenue a week later.

❦

The next morning, I went to Father's office and assured him that Mother was doing well and would be home soon. Then I brought up the possibility of a new assignment.

"Cleve Brooks wants me back on the steel beat."

He reacted with surprising calm. "I have been expecting this," he said. "I know you have enjoyed what you have been doing at the *Sun* for the last few years, but you seem very restless."

"I can't keep hiding in the sports and society pages," I replied. "There are momentous events coming that could change the steel industry and the whole city of Pittsburgh. I want to be in the middle of that and report on it. I've been on the bench long enough!"

Father was drumming his fingers on his desk. "There is more at stake here than allowing you to trust your instincts. As chairman, Mr. Frick is still involved in the company. I don't know how he will react to this news, but he may fear that you will learn something from me that will harm his interests. I want you to be fair and truthful, but I cannot be an on-the-record source. Please don't embarrass us both by asking me to be."

"Father, you know I would never betray your trust. I only want your respect."

"You shall have it, my boy, as long as you write the truth."

But what if the truth was inconvenient or even injurious to Mr. Frick? I thought.

Father went on, "I will assure Mr. Frick, if he asks, that you have the utmost integrity. He trusts me to keep his legal concerns confidential."

Was Father giving me an opening?

"I understand, but can you give me some background on the coke price dispute?"

Father laughed. "It's all a canard. The Old Man insists they agreed to a price of $1.35 a ton. Frick says that's what it costs to get the coal out of the ground and cook it into coke. He wants Frick Coke to show a profit. It's ridiculous. What one part of the company pays another doesn't mean a damn thing to the overall business."

"There must be a reason Mr. Carnegie is forcing the issue," I said.

Father hesitated before he responded. "This is very delicate. My future, and by extension yours, will depend on the outcome of this struggle. Understood?" I nodded, and he went on.

"The Iron-Clad Agreement specifies that by a vote of three-quarters of their shares, the partners could force any partner to leave the firm and sell his shares back at the book valuation. Since he holds the majority of the shares, the Iron-Clad protects Carnegie from a revolt by the partners, but it leaves the minority partners vulnerable, like Mr. Frick is now. Carnegie has had to increase the book value in the last five years due to the rising profits, but if Mr. Frick is forced out, he will not get anywhere near what his shares are truly worth."

"What can Mr. Frick do?" I asked.

Father smiled. "That's where I come in. I intend to prove in court that the Iron-Clad Agreement is invalid. Mr. Frick owns 6 percent of the partnership. That will be worth millions if he is allowed to get market price for them."

It occurred to me that there was much at stake for Father as well. He seemed to know what I was thinking. "This is important to me, too. In payment for my legal services, I have accumulated 1 percent of Carnegie Steel as well as shares in Frick Coke."

"How much could that be worth?" I asked.

"A hell of a lot but think what I have done for those gentlemen. The courts blamed the Johnstown Flood on an act of God, not the members of the South Fork Club. I stood by Mr. Carnegie and Mr. Frick as they weathered the initial reaction at Homestead and made sure the unions were banished from the mills for good. Profits have soared! Then there were the Jones patents and much more that must remain private. You may not agree with those outcomes, but you must admit I have earned every dime of whatever that 1 percent will be worth.

"There are many things I'd like to do with that money, son. I want to take care of you and Kat and Wills and your children, but we can't put it all in dreary railroad bonds. I've had my eye on the Dilworth lots up Amberson at the corner of Fifth, and George Oliver has been telling me about a beautiful little town called Coburg on Lake Ontario. A perfect place to get away from Pittsburgh's hot, dirty summers. And I've been speaking to some other gentlemen about starting a specialty steel company. Pittsburgh Steel has a nice ring to it, don't you think?"

I had never heard Father talk about buying homes or starting businesses, but I imagined having that much money at your disposal would widen your horizons. I fiddled with a pencil on his desk. I wasn't thinking about the money. I was thinking whether Cleve Brooks would allow me to cover this story.

"What will happen next between Mr. Carnegie and Mr. Frick?"

"They'll keep wrangling over the coke price, but there are more important issues to consider."

My mind filled with questions, but before I could open my mouth, Father raised his hand. "You are on your own from here on. Now, let's spend some time with the rest of the family." He led me out of the library with his arm around my shoulder. The next day I was back on the steel beat.

—◦—

Rita and I had settled into a life of quiet domesticity. We saw friends on the weekends for dinners, concerts, and even the occasional play in out-of-town rehearsals before heading to Broadway. Rita was always occupied either with riding, golf, or tennis, and her father had asked her to organize the Heinz Charitable Foundation.

And I had my work at the paper. For the next several days after my conversation with Father, I speculated about what was happening at Carnegie Steel. If Carnegie was finding Frick to be more and more difficult, maybe he wanted to walk away. He was sixty-four, an old man in the world of steel. Or maybe Frick wanted out too, tired of dealing with Carnegie's constant badgering. Any rupture in the partnership would cause a big stir. But if Carnegie Steel was for sale, that would be the story of the new century!

As peripheral as it was, I thought the dispute over the coke pricing could lead me to more important information about the company. That Thursday I went to the Carnegie Building to see whether anyone would give me a comment. I was acquainted with the young man at the front desk and knew our conversation wouldn't be pleasant. "Good to see you today, McKay." I tried the hearty approach.

"Dalton, you would think you would get discouraged. No, Mr. Carnegie is not in Pittsburgh. Mr. Phipps and Mr. Lauder are not available, and no one else in our offices is authorized to speak with you or any other member of the press. The only reason I'm speaking to you is because I'm the office guard dog."

I tried not to show my distaste for his smug officiousness. "C'mon, friend. I only have one simple question." I blurted it out before he could stop me. "Is there a disagreement on the price of coke that the steel company is paying to the coke company?"

McKay looked rattled. "The Carnegie Steel Company has nothing to say on this matter."

I was about to chip away at his stonewalling when I saw a round, bald head stick out of one of the offices in the back. I knew it was Henry Phipps, even though I had never spoken to him. After Carnegie and Frick, he was the most important figure in the steel industry. He was a self-effacing man and never sought the limelight. He was short like most of the other men in the steel business, but unlike Carnegie and Frick, who managed the business from on-high, Phipps was the detail person, the one who knew where every penny was coming from and where it was going. His meek look belied his reputation of being as ruthless as Frick and as demanding as Carnegie. Not even they dared to question Phipps's command of the company's financial details. He was another of the Slabtown boys, and only Carnegie had a bigger partnership share.

Knowing his penchant for staying behind the scenes, I was surprised when he gestured me into his office. "Come in, Mr. Dalton. I overheard what you asked McKay. Maybe I can be of some assistance. I'm Henry Phipps."

"Thank you, sir. I know who you are."

"And I know who you are from your byline in the *Pittsburgh Sun*," he said. "What interest could your newspaper have in something as arcane as our internal pricing of coke?"

"Sir, I understand that Mr. Frick and Mr. Carnegie are not in agreement on the matter. You must admit that would be of interest to our readers."

"I'll admit no such thing," he answered with some asperity. "Mr. Dalton, you have been around long enough to know how complex a business steel is. We coordinate suppliers from all over the nation. The competition is fierce and unrelenting. The technology changes by the month, and our capital demands never cease. There are hundreds of decisions that have to be made each week. You wouldn't expect that Mr. Carnegie and Mr. Frick would see eye to eye on each one of them, would you?

"These two fine men discussed the issue last year. Perhaps their recollections of that conversation don't jibe, but that will all be worked out over time. It always is. Nothing newsworthy here. If there is nothing else, I need to get back to my ledgers."

"Very kind of you to see me, Mr. Phipps," I replied, accepting the brush-off, but as I left his office, I smiled to myself. Phipps had confirmed the disagreement, and his seemingly causal decision to speak with me underscored its importance.

But in the following months, I could learn little more about the supposed rift between the two men. We ran a blind item in the gossipy "Around the Industry" column on the inside business page, and no one paid any attention. All it said was "Is the price of coke causing friction between Henry Frick and Andrew Carnegie? And why should that matter to either of them?"

11

The Bitter Fight

TRYING TO CRACK EITHER CAMP FOR MORE INFORMATION WAS FRUS-
trating and futile. I wished for all the wrong reasons that Jason was still
alive. My luck changed when I got a telephone call at the *Sun* on a blus-
tery day in early March 1899. It was my old roommate from New Haven,
Sam Lawrence. We hadn't spoken since graduation, but I was happy to
hear from him. I was surprised when he said he was in Pittsburgh.

"What brings you out here, Sam?" I asked.

"I'm staying at the Monongahela House. Meet me for drinks at six?
We have plenty to discuss."

At six Lawrence and I greeted each other in the Mon House bar with
hearty handshakes and slaps on the back. Then we settled into two easy
chairs, and the waiter brought us each an old-fashioned. We caught up on
all we knew about the men of the class of '89; then I told him about my
newspaper career.

"I've landed on my feet as well," Sam said. "I'm with the Morgan
Bank and have become Mr. J. P. Morgan's personal secretary," he said.

"Congratulations," I replied, though I knew he had used his family
connections to get the job. But I sensed an opportunity. "Is Mr. Morgan
here in Pittsburgh? It would be a real coup if I could interview him."

"He's not," Sam answered, "but maybe we can help each other. Ask
me any question you want about the bank; then I'll ask you about the steel
business."

I was wary but plowed ahead. "Out here in Pittsburgh, it's impossible to get any information out of Carnegie Steel. There are rumors of a
split between Carnegie and Frick, but I can't verify it. My job depends on

uncovering new stories, every day if possible. I'm getting a lot of pressure from my editor to produce, and I'm coming up short."

"Funny you should ask. I'm looking for something very similar. As you can imagine, Mr. Morgan devours information. That's why he sent me out here. He thinks Carnegie is getting restless."

"That's what I'm talking about! You and Morgan must know more than I do."

Neither of us spoke. I wondered whether I could believe anything Sam told me, and he was undoubtedly thinking the same about me.

As if reading my mind, Lawrence said, "Dalton, let's trust each other. New Haven, the Old Blue, and all that. Nothing ventured, nothing gained, I say."

"Sounds reasonable. Let's start with what Morgan knows about Carnegie and Frick, shall we?"

Lawrence nodded. "Last fall we were hearing that Carnegie is distracted. He had his first child, Margaret, last March and is enchanted with her. Then there is Skibo Castle in Scotland. It hasn't been touched for a hundred years, and he wants to make it very grand. And golf, of all things. Carnegie is obsessed with it, even though he can't break sixty on his own nine holes."

"What does this all have to do with Morgan?"

"Word was with all those changes in his life, the old Scot was thinking about selling Carnegie Steel. The coke company too. There was some back-channel contact with our bank and the Rockefeller interests, but neither would bid. Then Carnegie changed his tune. He told people he didn't want to sell after all and that he would run the business until he was eighty!"

I thought of asking Lawrence where he was getting all this information but thought better of it. Let him keep talking; maybe it would become obvious.

"We hear that Frick is unhappy that Carnegie doesn't want to sell." With that disingenuous remark, I now knew that Henry Clay Frick had been feeding information to J. P. Morgan.

When I didn't respond, Sam said, "I'm sure Mr. Frick will be speaking to Mr. Morgan in the near future. They share a love of fine old

European masters, and I hear Mr. Frick wants to concentrate on his picture collection."

Then Sam changed the subject. "What do you know about Federal Steel?"

"I understand that Mr. Morgan is financing a combination of Illinois Steel and several finishing companies, but I hadn't heard it referred to as Federal Steel," I said. "That's a very grand name for a steel company. I doubt that will sit well with Mr. Carnegie."

"But it may solidify Frick's thinking that this will be the best time to get his money out of Carnegie Steel," Lawrence answered, then hesitated before he went on. "Now you didn't hear this from me, but there may be a man named William Moore involved. I've heard Mr. Morgan mention him with disgust, but that's all I know about him. Tell you what I'll do. If I hear anything about Moore, I'll wire you, but don't expect anything soon." After I agreed to do the same for him, we settled into the innocuous chatter of two college chums.

———

With this new lead, I scoured the back issues of the *Sun* for any mention of William Moore. No luck. For the last five years, Cleve had made sure we also had the *New York Times* and the *Wall Street Journal* on file. It was in the *Journal* where I saw mention of William Moore, and it wasn't complimentary. It seemed that William and his brother, Charles, were railroad stock speculators. They weren't men that wanted to run roads; they saw them as a way to make a quick buck. Time and again, the *Journal* reported that the Moores had acquired a major stock position in a railroad; then they would fuel rumors of expected expansion, while quietly divesting their holding at a substantial profit. By the time the new stockholders discovered the railroad they had bought was bankrupt, the Moores were off grabbing up paper on their next unwitting target. One fiasco followed another—the last was the looting of Diamond Match.

In reading that they were coming after American Can next, I saw a familiar name, John H. Gates. He was better known as "Bet-a-Million" Gates, a legendary gambler and stock jobber who reputedly once bet a million dollars on which raindrop would first fall to the bottom of a window on a speeding train. No one believed that, but Gates was infamous nonetheless.

The stories about the Moore Brothers and Gates were titillating, but would stock men like them have the audacity to come after the Carnegie companies? Lawrence told me as much as he knew, and I hadn't heard from him in weeks. No one in Frick's or Carnegie's offices was saying a word. When I asked what they knew about William Moore's interest in Carnegie Steel, they would look at me blankly and say they had never heard of the man. I believed them, knowing how secretive speculators always were.

I was sure my father would know about the Moores, but what, if anything, would he tell me? Concluding that it would be best to talk to him at home, I called Mother and invited myself to dinner.

It was early May 1899, and from the streetcar that took me out Fifth Avenue, I saw spring in bloom. The fresh green of the oaks and maples along Amberson made the fire and smoke of the mills along the rivers seem far away. Mother, wearing light leather gloves, was cutting flowers from the window boxes that were hooked to the front porch railing.

"Jamie, I'm so glad you've come to dinner. Your father asked me to make something light and quick. 'The men have business to discuss,' he told me. He's so self-important," she said in mock exasperation. "I've laid out some cold salmon and a lettuce and tomato salad with Mr. Heinz's latest innovation, bottled dressing."

"Believe me, Mother, our cupboards are stocked with it!"

Father and I ate quickly, then retired to the front porch and sat on the wicker chairs. I got right to the point. "I have heard rumors about William Moore and John Gates. They seem to be rather unsavory characters." Father steepled his fingers in a prayerful position at his lips but didn't respond. He wasn't going to make this easy. I decided to bluff to see how Father would react.

"They are coming after Carnegie Steel." My assertion was less than convincing.

"You don't know that for a fact, do you? Mr. Frick has said little to me," Father answered.

"You must know more about it!"

"Since you have already heard their names, I will confirm that these men have made inquiries, nothing more. But if you print even that, he will know it was me who told you."

I shifted in my chair. "I do have other sources."

"Fine, as long as nothing can be traced back to me. There is nothing certain, but you can't imagine what is at stake," Father explained. "I have warned Mr. Frick that Mr. Carnegie will never agree to sell his company to men like Moore and Gates with their dreadful reputations. This will be ten times any deal they have done before."

"Do you have an idea what they are offering?" I asked.

Father gave me a thin smile. "I don't know the exact number, but I've heard it could be at least $300 million. That, however, is mere speculation and off the record, to the paper, to the rest of the family, to anyone."

I stared at Father and couldn't speak a word. Father had told me he had a share of the partnership, but hearing such an enormous sum astounded me. Our family had always been comfortable but not truly wealthy. Rita's family was one of the richest in Pittsburgh, but since all the Heinz money was wrapped up in the company, she couldn't touch it. What would money like this mean for my family? For Rita and me? For all the other Carnegie partners and lawyers? For the city?

"What will happen next?" was all I could think to ask.

"We have to wait and see. Mr. Frick and Mr. Phipps are in this together, and neither is telling me much. But let me warn you. A deal is never done until the sale documents have been signed and the money is in the bank. Now, James, let us rejoin your mother."

After we didn't see her on the first floor, we went upstairs and found her laying out clothes on her bed.

"Are you taking a trip, Eleanor?" Father seemed surprised.

"Not until next week. I'm sorry we haven't had a chance to discuss it. The Suffrage Association wants me to speak to the regional groups. I'll be going to Cincinnati, Cleveland, and Buffalo. You can manage on your own for a few days, can't you, Richard?"

"I will make do." Father beamed.

It had been a long time since I had seen them both this happy.

———

Sitting at my desk the next day, I realized how little I knew about the Moore-Gates offer. Father didn't have any more to tell me, and I hadn't heard anything new from Sam Lawrence. Without another source about the current state of the negotiations, I could only file a story speculating that Moore and Gates were taking an interest in the steel industry and mention their reputations as stock speculators. Since speculator and swindler were nearly synonymous, people would see that as a warning.

Frustrated by the lack of new information, late that afternoon I repaired to O'Reilly's. Even though I wasn't drinking, it was always good to frequent a place where so many colleagues and rivals congregated. As I drank a soda water, I looked around the dimly lit bar and saw a man in the middle of an animated conversation with several other patrons. Although we had never met, I knew him by sight and reputation. It was Charles Schwab, who ran all the mills for Carnegie Steel.

With Mr. Carnegie's backing, Schwab had a fast rise from his first job as a roller at the Thompson works. He became the plant manager there, and after the 1892 strike, he moved to Homestead. His engaging personality and knowledge of the steel business won the trust of the men, and the productivity and profits at the Homestead works soared. And he had stayed in the good graces of both Carnegie and Frick and now was in line to be the next president of the steel company.

He also had the reputation as a carouser and raconteur, and he was proving it that night in the tavern. From what I could hear of the stories he was spinning, discretion was not one of his many assets.

"Frick says to Carnegie, 'How do you expect me to run this business, when I'm forever answering your wires concerning the most mundane matters?'

"'Oh Mr. Frick, you know I value you above all others. There is no better executive in the whole of the country,' Carnegie answered.

"'Then, for god's sake, leave me be!' Whereupon Frick stormed out of Carnegie's office, slamming the door behind him.

"Scenes like this happen every time Andrew is in Pittsburgh," he concluded with a grin. The men around him, foremen from the plants, all laughed and slapped their boss on the back in appreciation of a glimpse at the foibles of the two giants of the steel industry.

I was happy when Schwab walked back up to the bar, looking to refill his glass. I was about to speak with him when he turned to me and said, "Dalton? From the *Sun*?"

"Yes, sir," I replied. Schwab may have had a few, but he was a very perceptive man and saw I was surprised that he knew me.

"Call me Charlie! I've seen you nosing around the offices, and I make it my business to know the men covering our company. Never hurts to have a good relationship with the press."

"I would be grateful for a private conversation, Charlie. Perhaps in the back?"

Schwab gave me a quick appraisal. "I know what you want." He put his arm around me and led me to a booth in the darkest part of the bar. There was a short, stubby candle on the table, and we could barely see each other's faces.

"I like to gab, Dalton, but I'm no fool. If we are going to remain friends, which will be good for both of us, you must agree to whatever terms I set. If I give you information that I don't want to see in the newspaper, you won't print it until I tell you to. Got it?"

I could see Schwab was used to getting his way, particularly in his relationships with reporters. He wasn't asking anything of me that I didn't agree to with every other confidential source, but I wanted him to feel he had the upper hand. "Mr. Schwab, Charlie, I'm happy to comply with any terms you wish. Will that allow me to pick your brain from time to time?"

"Pick away," he said with his engaging laugh.

I hesitated like I was gathering my thoughts, but I knew what I wanted to ask him. "I've already written a piece for tomorrow's edition saying that William Moore and John Gates at the behest of Mr. Frick and Mr. Phipps are organizing a buyout of Carnegie Steel and Frick Coke." Another bluff.

Schwab stared at me, then went on. "I'm not going to ask you where you found that out, but I have a pretty good idea. That doesn't matter. Fact is, Frick and Phipps are getting ahead of themselves. I know for certain that Mr. Carnegie don't want the deal to go through, and if he don't want it, it ain't gonna happen. But I doubt it will get that far."

"What do you mean?"

"This is too big a deal for Moore and Gates. Now you didn't hear that from me or this neither. One of Moore's biggest investors, Roswell Flowers, has died, and his family has pulled the money out of the deal."

"I won't quote you, but if this deal fails, I want to be able to say why."

"Go right ahead; just keep my name out of it."

I was gratified he agreed to that, but it made me wonder why he was so willing to talk to me. To gauge his credibility, I had to know what was in it for him.

"Charlie, it doesn't sound like you want this deal to happen. Why is that?"

For the first time that night, Schwab raised his voice. "Because the Old Man knows that Carnegie Steel and Frick Coke combined are worth a damn sight more than those two grifters can scare up.

"Frick and Phipps want out, and they have their reasons. Henry Phipps is the same age as Mr. Carnegie, and he wants to enjoy whatever years he has left. With Frick it's more complicated. He's afraid Mr. Carnegie may force him out of the company, and then his shares will be worth the book value, nowhere near what a reputable investor would be willing to offer."

"Is that because of the Iron-Clad Agreement?" I asked.

"I know for a fact that Mr. Carnegie is looking for any excuse to be rid of him. Don't say anything about that as of yet. It will get both of those gentlemen mighty upset to read about any of this in the papers. These are crucial times, and everyone needs to think clearly"

I decided not to push him any farther. "How can I contact you?"

Schwab laughed. "The last thing I need is Frick thinking I'm blabbing to the papers. Tell you what we'll do. You come by here every Thursday around this time. If I have anything to tell you, I'll be sitting in this booth. If I'm standing around with my men, don't come near me. Just drink a beer and leave." Or a soda.

It seemed a little cloak-and-dagger, but I readily agreed.

For the next four weeks, I returned to O'Reilly's each Thursday, but Schwab was never in the booth; sometimes he wasn't even in the bar.

When I saw him making jolly conversation with his steel men, he wouldn't acknowledge me. Maybe he didn't intend to talk to me any further. But on the third Thursday of June, I peered into the dim light in the back of the bar and saw Schwab sitting there.

"Long time," he joked. "Did ya think I had forgotten about you?" I gave him a phony hurt look. "I've been waiting for something important to happen, and now it has. The deal is off."

"That fast!" I exclaimed. "What happened?"

"With the Flowers investment gone, Moore and Gates went to George F. Baker at First National Bank in New York, but that was never going to work because Baker is a staunch ally of Morgan, who may have intentions of his own."

"There's something else, isn't there?" I asked.

"Isn't that enough?"

"C'mon, Charlie, give me the full story."

"OK, but you can't use it until I say so. Agreed?" I saw a stern look on Charlie's face and imagined how he could cow even the toughest union man.

"That's our agreement," I said.

"The final rupture between Frick and Mr. Carnegie is coming. The Old Man wrote me a letter from Scotland. He didn't go into detail, but he's mad as hell. 'Mr. Frick has betrayed me, and I won't have him in my company a moment longer.' Frick won't go quietly, and there is bound to be a battle royal."

I was itching to get all that Schwab had told me into the *Sun*, but I knew I would have to be patient. "What happens now?" I asked.

"There will be a showdown at both companies' board meetings at the end of the year. But don't bet against Mr. Carnegie coming out on top. He's the majority shareholder of the steel company, and he owns the most shares of Frick's coke company and controls that board."

I leaned on the table. "You are tying me up, Charlie. I may not be able to hold this until then. You know how fierce my competition is. I've made promises to you. Now you have to make one to me. I need to know what happens at those meetings. It could be any one of the board members giving me information. You won't have to worry about being caught out."

Schwab gave me that grim look again. "Let's see what happens between now and then. No guarantees."

— ~ —

Charlie and I met throughout the fall, and he continued giving me morsels of information that I was able to use in our gossipy business column. "Carnegie wants to make the $1.35 per ton coke price permanent, but Frick laughed at him." "Frick proposed that the book value of the companies should be doubled, and Carnegie refused." I was making it obvious that the management of the Carnegie properties was in turmoil and the worst was yet to come.

I was disappointed that I didn't see Schwab right after the November 20 meeting of the Carnegie Steel board, but I continued to go to O'Reilly's every night for the next two weeks. Rita was put out that I was coming home late and reeking of beer and cigars, even though it was only from the all-pervasive smell of the barroom. My feeble explanation of having to go to a tavern for work was falling on increasingly less sympathetic ears.

On December 4 I was hanging around O'Reilly's when Schwab came stumbling in. Supporting himself on the bar, he ordered a double shot of rye.

"Anything but Overholt," he growled at the bartender.

"My God, Charlie, what has happened to you?" I asked.

After throwing back the whiskey and ordering another, Schwab motioned for us to go to the back booth. He was still wobbly but managed to navigate the slick, sawdust-covered floors. We slid into the booth, and he took another slug and gave a heavy sigh. "Dalton, I've just been cursed out so loudly and obscenely that I will never forget it. I knew Frick had a temper, but the man was unhinged."

Now he had my full attention. "You need to tell me what prompted this outburst. I thought you were on good terms with Mr. Frick."

"I thought so too," he said, as he looked down into his glass. He finished off the second shot, then continued. "At the board meeting, Frick said Mr. Carnegie had mismanaged the business. Brought up that damned coke price again. Mr. Carnegie grew more and more agitated, but Frick wouldn't let up.

"The next day Mr. Carnegie was boiling mad. Told me to write a letter to Frick saying that he would recommend that the steel company board abolish the office of chairman. If Frick is out as chairman of the board, it will be easier for Mr. Carnegie to invoke the Iron-Clad Agreement and send him on his way with a pittance of what his shares are truly worth."

I gave a nod to encourage him to go on.

"I must have rewritten that letter five times, trying to be as polite and conciliatory as possible. I decided Frick was owed more than a letter delivered by post, and earlier this evening, I had my driver take me out to Homewood Avenue.

"The maid showed me into the front parlor, and there was Frick sitting in a comfortable chair, reading the evening papers. I hemmed and hawed, until Frick says in a friendly sort of way, 'What brings you out here tonight, Charlie? Mr. Carnegie send you?'

"I looked down, pawing at the rug with the tip of my boot, then handed him the letter. 'What's it say?' he growled, his fierce blue eyes flashing.

"I stood up straighter, then choked out, 'Mr. Carnegie intends to abolish the office of chairman of the board of Carnegie Steel at its next meeting.'

"Before I could say another word, Frick jumped up and screamed, 'That son of a bitch.' Then he started in on me, called me Carnegie's lackey. He was inches from my face, and even though I'm a good bit taller and heavier than him, I was afraid he would attack me. I'm not ashamed to say I turned tail and ran right out the front door and jumped in my carriage. I told the driver to take me back downtown as fast as the horses could gallop."

Schwab wiped his red face with a handkerchief. "Easy now, Charlie," I said. "Can I get you more whiskey?" Charlie held out his glass to me. When he finished off his third double, he had regained some of his composure.

"Guess I'm not so tough after all," Schwab said with chagrin. Then he shook his head. "I can't imagine what will happen next."

It didn't take long to find out. There was an envelope on my desk the next morning addressed to Mr. James Dalton, the *Pittsburgh Sun*. I ripped it open and read the one-sentence press release. "As of this day, December 5, 1899, I formally resign as Chairman of the Board of the Carnegie Steel Company, effective immediately. H. C. Frick." He resigned before Carnegie could fire him. I ran out of the office and sprinted the two blocks to the Carnegie Building. When I got there, the corridor was jammed with reporters from the other papers. A big man was blocking the door to the company's office. He held his arms up to get our attention, and we quieted down.

"Mr. Frick is not in his office today, and we cannot tell you where he might be. Other than that, we have no comment."

Shouted questions rang up and down the hallway, but the big man ignored them all. "No comment, I said, and I mean it." In the ensuing lull, I gave it one last try. He was turning away when I shouted, "Will Mr. Frick remain chairman of Frick Coke?"

That stopped him. He looked back over his shoulder with an annoyed look and grumbled, "This is the office of Carnegie Steel. Ask your question to the coke company. It's in Connellsville," he added with a snide look. That meant Frick *would* remain as chairman of Frick Coke. Then the man went back into the Carnegie offices and slammed the door behind him. We all rushed back down the stairs to file our stories. People all over the country were shocked by Frick's resignation and shares on the New York Stock Exchange wobbled for a few days before righting themselves.

There was little news out of the Carnegie or Frick camps through the rest of December and the holidays. Carnegie played off his passing resemblance to St. Nicholas and distributed turkeys and hams throughout Braddock and Homestead. He also announced with his usual pomp and magnanimity that he would build a new library in Homestead, saying the gift was "from one working man to another." He didn't seem to notice or care that it would be built where the state militia had encamped when it broke the 1892 strike. From my mother I learned that Mr. Frick had taken his family east to their home in Lenox, Massachusetts. He wasn't due back until the next meeting of the Frick Coke board on January 9.

I was glad of the news lull because it gave me a chance to reconnect with Rita after all the late nights at O'Reilly's waiting for morsels of information from Charlie Schwab. We had the usual rounds of dinners and dances but spent some quiet evenings on Kentucky Street in front of the fire. It was around the middle of the month that Rita prepared a special meal of lamb chops with mint sauce, followed by an almond torte from Lutz's Bakery on Walnut Street. I wondered what the occasion was but didn't let it concern me as I ate the delicious dinner.

After the meal, I settled into my high-backed, upholstered chair in front of the fire, and Rita brought out two demitasses of coffee, handing one to me. Despite my post-meal lethargy, I knew something was up. I looked at her as she arranged herself on the settee and said, "Rita, my darling, is there something on your mind?"

"Now why would you say that?" she asked.

"You don't cook my favorite meal followed by my favorite dessert and espresso coffee on just any night."

"It's because I'm happy we've been spending more time together, Jamie dear."

"And what else?"

"Oh, all right, don't interrogate me like you would one of your newspaper sources." Then she gave me a beatific smile. "I want us to start a family."

I stood and opened my arms. "I've been hoping for you to say that for so long."

We embraced and kissed passionately; then she pulled away. "Why haven't you said anything, if this is what you wanted?"

My cheeks flushed. "I guess I thought that this was a woman's decision."

"You are an old Victorian, Jamie Dalton. If there is something you want, ask me for it. I can always say no," she said.

We kissed again and soon were in our double bed, where we spent all our free time for the next three weeks. It was the best Christmas I could remember.

It was December 31, 1899, and the celebration of the new century at the Monongahela House was spectacular. More than five hundred people attended, the men all in white tie and tails, the women in their finest ball gowns, many imported from Paris. I was proud that the dresses of the women in our party were all made in America, albeit New York. We had a table for twenty with the whole Dalton and Heinz families, which included some cousins and, of course, Aunt Leila, in a bright-red ball gown. It didn't matter that she was unescorted because every man there wanted to dance with her.

Ten courses were served at a candlelight dinner. The newly formed Pittsburgh Orchestra played from eight o'clock on, and the jubilant crowd danced the mazurka, the waltz, and the two-step. At midnight the guests filed out onto the hotel's roof garden and watched an hour-long firework display that lit the skies brighter than any of the mills along the river ever had. The spectacular show was befitting the most important industrial city in America, we all agreed.

There was a sense of anticipation in the air. For several years there had been rumors that Andrew Carnegie might sell his steel company, and that talk had intensified. Such a sale could make many of the people in that room richer than they could imagine. I knew more about that possibility than anyone else there, except the top Carnegie managers, and I was swept up in the excitement. After the fireworks, Rita and I danced together until the music stopped.

The meeting of the Frick board was Friday, January 5. I dropped by O'Reilly's after work, hoping to run into Charlie Schwab, and wasn't disappointed. Charlie was sitting up at the bar and soon followed me back to a booth.

He started right in. "You can't use this yet, but the coke company's board approved the $1.35 per ton price by a vote of five to two. Frick stormed out of the meeting right after the vote."

He had a smug look. Schwab was on Mr. Carnegie's side, plus he knew that Mr. Frick was the only man capable of blocking his ascent to the top of the steel company.

"What's Mr. Frick's next move?"

"All I know is that Frick was hopping mad when he left Connells-ville last night, muttering that 'I'll whip the old bastard yet.' He can try," Schwab scoffed.

—❦—

Events moved quickly from that point. On Monday, January 15, the Carnegie Board voted 32–4 to invoke the Iron-Clad Agreement and buy out Frick based on the $82 million book value for Carnegie Steel. That was less than $5 million for his 6 percent share, and it was likely worth four times that.

Ten days later, Henry Frick filed suit to block his removal from the steel partnership. The court filing was public record, and that was when I was able to post an article on the final breach between the two titans of the steel industry. I didn't get a beat on the other papers, but I knew my piece had many more background details.

The trial began on March 12, and my father, as Frick's lead attor-ney, pleaded his case. As much as Cleve Brook trusted me to be a steady, objective reporter, he couldn't allow me to cover the trial. But nothing could keep me from being in the gallery, and Father secured me a seat in the back of the courtroom. Mr. Carnegie's defense was led by Philander Knox, my father's former mentor. It was not to be a jury trial—Judge Josiah Calhoun would decide the outcome. Judge Calhoun was tall and broad-shouldered with a sweep of reddish graying hair. He had a reputa-tion for decisiveness and disdain for any lawyers or clients that tried to hoodwink his court.

Frick and Carnegie were sitting with their counsels though they weren't expected to testify. Behind Frick and my father sat the finan-cial wizard Henry Phipps. Because of his encyclopedic knowledge of the workings of Carnegie Steel, Phipps could be a devastating witness for either side.

The reporters from the Pittsburgh papers took chairs in the press gallery, and the men from the big-city papers crowded into the standing space behind. The seats for the public were filled, and there were lines of people outside the courtroom waiting to get in.

In his opening remarks, Father contended that Mr. Carnegie was trying to defraud Mr. Frick of what was due him as the man most responsible for the growth of the Carnegie Steel Company. Knox countered that Mr. Frick had betrayed Mr. Carnegie by going behind his back to sell the company of which Mr. Carnegie was majority partner. And that gave Mr. Carnegie the right to invoke the Iron-Clad Agreement and force the sale of Mr. Frick's shares at book value. Since Mr. Frick brought the suit against Carnegie Steel, Father called Henry Phipps as the first witness.

"Mr. Phipps, what is your position with Carnegie Steel?"

"I am the company treasurer, sir. Have been since Mr. Carnegie formed the partnership in 1869. We go all the way back to Slabtown."

"Sir, what were the company's profits for 1899?"

Although it was in his interest to disclose that information, Phipps hesitated. Profits had always been a closely guarded secret. "Twenty-one million dollars, and the forecast is for double that in the current year," he said in a quiet voice.

There was an audible gasp from the assembled. The financial affairs of the company had never been made public. Mr. Carnegie looked horrified. He had protected that information at all costs because he could foresee the consequences. The workers would claim that the company could well afford to pay them a decent wage, and it would make a mockery of the Republican Party championing a protective tariff for an industry that clearly didn't need protecting. These profit numbers would be national news.

"One more question, sir. What is the current book value of Carnegie Steel?"

"Eighty-two million."

"With an estimated forty-two million in profits for one year, wouldn't the company be worth many times $82 million?"

"Undoubtedly," Phipps said in a strong voice.

"And shouldn't Mr. Frick's 6 percent share of the company be much greater than 6 percent of $82 million?"

"Without question." What Phipps didn't say was that his 15 percent would be worth even more.

"No further questions, your honor, but we reserve the right to recall Mr. Phipps later in the proceedings."

Knox stood up to ask Phipps a question, but Mr. Carnegie pulled him back down and whispered something in his ear. "The defense has no questions for Mr. Phipps at this time," Knox said.

Father had won the first round, but he seemed reluctant to make his next move. He looked at Carnegie and Knox, then up at Judge Calhoun. "I call Henry Clay Frick to the stand," he said.

Another gasp. I knew this was a dangerous strategy because of Mr. Frick's volatility, but I was sure my father had warned him to control his temper.

"Mr. Frick, what are your positions in the Carnegie Steel companies?"

"I am founder and president of H. C. Frick Coke. Until recently I was chairman of the board of Carnegie Steel."

"In the last year, have you and Mr. Phipps sought out a buyer for these companies and why have you done that?"

"Yes, we have. With the profits Mr. Phipps has cited that are projected to double in the upcoming year, we felt this would be the optimal time to realize the true value of the company."

"And did you find a prospective buyer?"

"We did. The respected New York bankers William Moore and Henry Gates."

I heard the crowd titter when Frick said "respected."

"And did you present their offer to Mr. Carnegie?"

"Yes."

"And what was that offer?"

"Three hundred twenty million," Frick answered. "Two hundred fifty for the steel company, seventy million for the coke company."

For several seconds, the courtroom stayed quiet. Then it erupted with cries of "Oh, my god!" and "That's not possible." Reporters for the out-of-town papers ran for the exits, but I knew there was more to come.

"Mr. Frick, was the offer accepted?"

Frick shot a dirty look to the defense table "No, sir. Because of Mr. Carnegie's vacillations, the offer was withdrawn."

"Didn't that offer prove that the company was worth a great deal more than $82 million? And that your shares would be worth much more than $5 million?"

"Irrefutably," Frick said and gave Carnegie a triumphant look. Carnegie didn't seem shaken in the least by this latest revelation.

"Your witness," Father said.

The shock of the $320 million offer was still rippling through the crowd. Father and Mr. Frick had made the point that Carnegie was understating the price of the company, and the only possible reason was so he would not have to pay out a higher figure if he was to buy out Frick's shares per the Iron-Clad. I was proud that my father had presented such a compelling case.

But now it was Mr. Knox's turn to cross-examine Mr. Frick. Mr. Knox was respected as the consummate corporate lawyer, but he hadn't been in a courtroom in years.

"Mr. Frick, you said Mr. Carnegie vacillated. Did he have a reason for that?"

"You'll have to ask him."

"Are you aware of Miller's and Gates's reputation as corporate raiders, flipping their acquisitions for short-term gains?" Father objected, and the judge sustained his objection. Frick didn't have to answer, but the point had been made.

"Isn't it true that Miller and Gates couldn't come up with the full amount of the down payment?" Frick took his time to say yes.

"And wasn't it the case that these men had never done a deal even one-tenth the size of this one? And that Miller and Gates never had a prayer of raising close to $320 million?"

"I wouldn't know," Mr. Frick answered.

"I doubt that," Mr. Knox said. "In any case, you should have known."

"No testifying, Mr. Knox," the judge said.

When Knox walked back toward the table where Mr. Carnegie sat, Mr. Frick looked relieved. He started to rise when Knox turned and in a very calm voice asked, "Mr. Frick, were you to receive a commission if Miller and Gates had succeeded in acquiring Carnegie Steel?"

For the first time, Mr. Frick looked shocked. I leaned forward in my seat.

"I don't know what you mean," Mr. Frick sputtered.

"It's very simple, sir. If the deal was consummated, were you and Mr. Phipps to receive a fee from Miller and Gates for helping them acquire Carnegie Steel and Frick Coke?"

Mr. Frick stared straight ahead. "Yes, we were."

Father looked at Mr. Frick with his mouth agape. Was this the first he had heard of this? But the worst was yet to come.

"And what was the amount of that fee?"

I held my breath along with everyone else in the courtroom.

Frick didn't answer right away. Was he savoring or dreading the moment?

"Five million dollars," he announced in a firm voice.

At that point Father asked for and received a fifteen-minute recess.

—◆—

I rushed out to the lobby of the courtroom and saw my father huddling with Mr. Frick and Mr. Phipps. I gave Father a nod of reassurance when he looked my way. Frick's testimony had been devastating. His attempt to extract a fee from Miller and Gates looked like a clear violation of the company's partnership rules about self-dealing. Frick had his finger in Father's face and was speaking too loudly. I approached them, and before he waved me away, I heard Father say, "Mr. Frick, please be calm."

"It will never work," Mr. Frick growled.

Did Father have a stratagem to counteract the shock of the five-million-dollar fee?

The consensus of the other reporters was grim. The commission Frick and Phipps had negotiated with Miller and Gates was damning, and the Carnegie board of directors had every right to invoke the Iron-Clad Agreement and pay Frick based on the book value of $82 million, not the purported market value of over $300 million.

I filed back into the courtroom and kept my gaze on Father and Mr. Frick. Even if Brooks didn't want me to be the lead reporter on the trial, at least I could take notes and share them with the other *Sun* reporters. I wanted to be sure what we ran would be as objective as possible and didn't want our coverage to affect the outcome of the trial. Father's legal reputation could suffer if he lost the case.

"Another witness, Mr. Dalton?"

"We recall Henry Phipps."

There was a stirring in the courtroom. What more had Mr. Phipps to add? I thought.

After Mr. Phipps settled himself in the witness chair, Father didn't waste any time with pleasantries. "Sir, when did the Iron-Clad Agreement go into effect?"

"It was first signed by the partners in 1887."

"And it needed to be renewed every five years after that?"

"Correct."

"And the partners signed it again in 1892?"

"Yes, sir." Mr. Phipps took a second, then said, "But one of the partners, John Vandevort, never signed the agreement, and he is now deceased."

"No one questioned its validity from 1892 to 1897?" Father asked.

"No one did," Mr. Phipps said.

"The last renewal was in 1897?"

"Yes."

Speaking in a firmer voice, Father asked, "Mr. Phipps, did you sign the 1897 agreement?"

"No, I did not!"

"And why not?"

"Because no one knows better than me what this company is worth, and the book value is absurd. As much as I've always loved Mr. Carnegie, I can't wait forever for him to dispose of the company in a proper fashion. We are not young men, sir."

That got a laugh from the crowd. I was still focused on my father. Had he regained the upper hand?

Father turned from Mr. Phipps and looked at Mr. Carnegie and his lawyer.

"Without your signature, do you believe the Iron-Clad Agreement is valid?"

"No, I do not," Mr. Phipps said with a smile.

Philander Knox pulled himself out of his seat. "In not signing, Mr. Phipps was voicing his disapproval, nothing more. Whether he signed the agreement in 1897 or the now-deceased partner signed in 1892 is immaterial. The intent was clear, and the 1887 agreement remains in effect. Carnegie Steel and its board of directors have operated under its strictures since then."

Father responded directly to Mr. Knox. "The agreement says all partners must sign. And they didn't."

"The board is in its right to invoke the expulsion clause for Mr. Frick's solicitation of the fee," Knox retorted.

From there the lawyers devolved into arcane legal wrangling. Judge Calhoun let them go on for several minutes, his face getting redder and redder. When he cracked his gavel, Father and Mr. Knox broke off.

"I've heard enough! If I could sanction both sides, I would. Mr. Frick, in seeking to maximize the value of your share of the company, you got too greedy. The fee you tried to extort, and I use that word deliberately, was unconscionable. I don't blame the Carnegie board for trying to rid themselves of you.

"But Mr. Carnegie, your so-called Iron-Clad Agreement is equally egregious. You have held your partners in thrall for too long. Your partners can't share in the success of what is their business as well as yours because of a document whose legality is in question.

"I am telling both of you to come to your senses and negotiate. It shouldn't be hard if you can get your egos under control. I expect to see both parties back here in a month. With a settlement!"

Mr. Frick was red-faced, and Father and Mr. Knox looked perplexed as to how any agreement could be reached between these two implacable foes. But Mr. Carnegie leaned back in his chair with a sly grin on his face. As Mr. Frick walked out of the courtroom, Mr. Carnegie stopped him.

"Mr. Frick, perhaps we can meet again when we have put all this unpleasantness behind us."

"I'll meet you in hell!" Frick snarled.

This was the last time the two men would ever speak.

The next day the *Sun*, along with every paper from the *New York Times* to the *San Francisco Chronicle*, ran the story of the trial on the front page. "Battle of the Steel Men" was common. The more sensational went with something like "Death Match in Pittsburgh." The *Sun* took a middle course: "Carnegie and Frick Square Off."

The public reaction was instantaneous. Based on its profitability, Carnegie Steel was the second-largest company in the country, after only Standard Oil, and the economy could ill afford the chaos of a protracted legal battle over its future. Charlie Schwab told both sides that the whole steel industry would suffer if they did not mend their differences. Christopher Magee warned that the city of Pittsburgh would be crippled. Mark Hanna, the richest, most powerful politician in the country, offered to mediate, as did George Westinghouse. The problem was that the personal hatred between the two men knew no bounds and wiped away their usual clear, dispassionate rationality. Neither would back down; neither would accept mediation.

What broke the standoff was Father's personal appeal to Philander Knox. Father told me on February 15 that he had met with Knox and convinced him that the Iron-Clad would not pass legal scrutiny. Knox agreed to share that conclusion with Mr. Carnegie. He must have convinced Carnegie to settle because Father told me that he and Henry Phipps were taking the train to New York the next day to meet Mr. Carnegie in his home at 5 West 51st Street. He asked me to not print anything until the final details were in place and promised me the exclusive before anything was released to the public.

<center>~~~</center>

Father was true to his word. Late the night of the meeting with Mr. Carnegie, he telephoned me at the *Sun* office and laid out the surprisingly simple terms of the agreement. The two companies would be consolidated at a new book value of $320 million, $250 million for Carnegie Steel, $70 million for Frick Coke, the Moore-Gates evaluations. Frick's share in the new company would be worth over $20 million. The ridiculous battle over the price of coke was finally resolved at $2.40 per ton, halfway between the price the two men had claimed. And in return for relinquishing any management position in the new company and withdrawing his lawsuit, Frick would not be required to sell his shares back to the partnership.

Judge Calhoun had been right. This agreement benefited both sides. Frick would receive a fair value for his shares. Mr. Carnegie had rid himself of Mr. Frick. And he had lost nothing by revaluing the company.

But I knew the battle for Carnegie Steel was far from over.

12

The Speech

RITA GAVE BIRTH TO A NINE-POUND, TEN-OUNCE BABY BOY ON SEPTEMber 30, 1900. Her pregnancy had lasted two weeks past her due date, and we engaged the services of a midwife, the one our mothers deemed the best in the city. It was a difficult delivery, and her skill brought Rita through the agony of birthing a child that large. Richard Heinz Dalton came into the world with a piercing cry that early fall morning.

Needless to say, I was thrilled, and my father was proud to have his first grandchild named after him. Mother took on a glow that I had never seen before, and she doted on all of us, making sure we were comfortable and well-fed and that Rick, as we called him, was immune to any infant mishaps.

I wasn't surprised when Rita was up and about after a three-day recuperation. With our mothers' vast network of possible servants, it was easy to find a nursemaid, Margaret McNertney, for the baby, and she took up residence on the third floor of the Kentucky Avenue house. Assuming that we would have more children and I would keep getting raises at the *Sun*, Rita and I began considering a larger home. There were many new, substantial houses being built on Northumberland and Ayelsboro Streets in Squirrel Hill, and we started looking a month after the baby was born. And it wasn't long before Rita resumed her routine of riding and golf before the chilling winter weather began.

❦

Although the daily stories that had blossomed from the bruising fights between the two most notorious men in the steel industry had abated,

I sensed that the fate of Carnegie Steel was still not decided. Charlie Schwab couldn't or wouldn't tell me what was happening on the inside, and Father was consumed with tying up the loose ends of Mr. Frick's agreement with the Carnegie partnership. What seemed obvious to me was that there were only two men who could afford to purchase the company—J. P. Morgan and J. D. Rockefeller. Rockefeller seemed determined to rule the world of oil and wasn't interested in the steel business. For the present, he was keeping a close eye on A. W. and R. B. Mellon, who were financing their nephew, William Larimer Mellon, to drill along the Gulf of Mexico, so I decided to concentrate my efforts on Morgan. He had created Federal Steel, and Carnegie had already responded to the threat by purchasing and building finishing plants of his own.

Although I understood his reasoning, it irked me that Cleve hadn't allowed me to cover the courtroom battle between Carnegie and Frick, and I resolved to break any story on the sale of Carnegie Steel. That meant I needed to go to New York to find out what Morgan was planning. With a new baby, I thought twice about traveling, but Rita understood my frustrations and told me to go. She assured me that between her and Margaret and the grandmothers, Rick would be well taken care of.

On the first of November, I wired Sam Lawrence that I wanted to get together when I was in New York from the fifth to the seventh, staying at the University Club.

The week before my trip, I received a telegram at the *Sun* office that caught me completely off guard. It was from Zofia. "Must see you. Most urgent. Wire me at Western Union, Spring Street."

It had been seven years without a word from her. My life had changed, and I didn't want to stir up old passions. But knowing her involvement with Hasçek and Goldman, I couldn't ignore what sounded like a cry for help. I wired her back. "Will be in city next week. Where? When?" Within an hour, I received her reply. "Gramercy Park. 3 p.m. Wednesday." I'd have to ask at the University Club for directions.

❦

To keep myself busy on the train, I read up on J. P. Morgan's banking career.

Morgan made his reputation as an investor in railroads. He used the leverage of his capital to rationalize the chaos of competition and speculation and had pulled the Northern Pacific from the verge of bankruptcy after it was plundered by J. J. Hill and Jay Gould. To his enduring credit, in 1893 Morgan had propped up failing banks, and the country avoided a years-long financial collapse as had happened after the Panic of 1873.

With photography now a staple of newspapers and magazines, Morgan's image came to symbolize the power of the New York financial community. Morgan looked like what he was, the most powerful banker in America. His large head, always topped with a beaver-skin top hat, and his natural bulk made him stand out, and his beady, close-set eyes looked as if they could see through steel. But it was his bulbous, hideous nose, scarred by rosacea, that defined his face. One had to ignore it, lest you offend the colossus of the economy.

I stopped at the concierge desk when I arrived at the University Club that Tuesday. "How do I get to Gramercy Park from here?"

"It's about thirty blocks south, sir. Easiest way to get there from downtown is the Third Avenue Elevated Railroad. You take that to 18th Street, and Gramercy Park is a short walk west on 20th St. Or we can arrange a carriage for you, sir." I thanked him and said a carriage wouldn't be necessary.

After I dropped off my valise in a cramped, shabby room on the fourth floor, I took a hansom down Fifth to 36th Street, then walked to Morgan's granite home on Madison. Sam met me in the front entrance hall and gave me a tour. The living quarters were modest, but the two large square rooms on the south side of the building, attached by a long corridor filled with pictures by Old Masters, were spectacular. Morgan's library displayed hundreds of books, all rare and priceless. The room was surrounded by a balcony with a wrought-iron balustrade that was lined with original manuscripts. In the center of the room in glass cases were his most prized possessions, two Gutenberg Bibles. At the west end of the corridor was a cavernous room that could fit more than one hundred people where Morgan would sit alone at the end of hectic days at 23 Wall Street and inspect his books on an outsized mahogany desk.

Sam told me of Morgan's business philosophy as he showed me around the house. "What Morgan believes is that mindless competition prevents industries from fulfilling their potential and becoming more profitable. His threats to cut off financial support squelched the battle between Commodore Vanderbilt's New York Central and the mighty Pennsylvania Railroad. His latest project is the merger of the Northern Pacific, Great Northern, and Burlington lines into Northern Securities. If he can steer clear of the trust busters."

"Will we get a glimpse at the great man himself?" I asked.

Sam laughed. "These events are for the little people like us to marvel at his wealth and power. Mr. Morgan has other, more diverting activities to occupy him." He gave me a wink to seal his meaning. Even in Pittsburgh, there were rumors of Morgan's love of the New York nightlife and the women that went along with it. I wondered how Carnegie and Frick, men whose personal reputations were above reproach, might react to that side of Morgan if they were forced to do business with him.

"I'm glad to have had a chance to see Morgan's lair, but this levee is a bit stuffy, don't you agree? Maybe we can find a livelier spot, as long as we don't cross paths with the lion of Wall Street," I said.

Sam perked up. "I know just the place. It's a saloon called the Rouge, and they have a piano player who plays what's called honky-tonk. Very lively and it attracts a smart, young crowd."

"I'm in!"

"That's the old New Haven spirit."

I was excited to see the Rouge. Pittsburgh didn't have any honky-tonk bars, at least none frequented by whites. We stopped on Greenwich Street and took the five steps down to the door of the club that was in the basement of what was someone's brownstone home thirty years before. When we stepped inside, it was a full-out sensual assault: the smoke and liquor, the blinking lights around the stage, and the clinking piano and raspy voice of the colored man playing it. What most surprised me was the crowd jammed into the small low-ceilinged room. Some of the men were dressed formally like Sam and me, and the women with them smoked and gulped champagne from narrow flutes. There were other couples that wore what looked like hand-me-down clothes. I could hear at least three different languages being spoken: French, Italian, and a garble that might have been Russian or Hungarian. Off to the side was a group of Negroes, dressed in garish imitation of Fifth Avenue swells. I loved the place immediately and wondered whether I could find anything like it in Pittsburgh's Hill District.

We found the last open table, and Sam ordered a glass of scotch.

"The best you have," Sam demanded of the waiter.

The first sip made him cough—was this the best they had?—but he managed to down it and called for another round.

While I tapped my foot to the lively beat of the piano, I took in the polyglot scene and thought about the next day. Sam and I hadn't made plans, and I wanted something to do before meeting Zofia at three.

"Could you take me on a tour of the stock exchange tomorrow?"

"I thought you were going back to Pittsburgh?"

"If I'm going to be writing about all you money men, I ought to at least have a look at where your earth-shaking transactions take place." Sam gave me a funny look but told me to meet him in front of Trinity Church at the corner of Broad and Wall Streets at ten the next morning.

The next day, I caught the Broadway train downtown and met Sam at 11 Wall Street, where the New York Stock Exchange was located. From a perch high above the floor, it was fascinating to watch all the traders in their swallow-tail coats yelling bids to the specialists who controlled the trading in individual stocks. Sam tried to explain to me all the intricacies, but the chaos was overwhelming.

Leaving Sam at the Stock Exchange, I rattled up Third Avenue on the El to 18th Street and easily found Gramercy Park. It was deserted, and I found Zofia sitting under the statue of Edwin Booth. She stood and said, "Dalton, it is good to see you." There was a confident tone in her voice that was belied by the shaky hand she extended.

Her touch brought back appealing memories, but I had enough self-control not to let that overwhelm my better judgment. "You as well, Zofia. You said it was urgent."

We sat back down on the bench; then Zofia turned to me and said, "For the first time since I have been with Hasçek, I am frightened. Not of him hurting me—he wouldn't dare. He is scheming with Emma

Goldman, and they are keeping it very secret. They ask me to leave the room when they start any serious discussions. Most of the time he sees her without me.

"I believe in many of the same things as Goldman," she continued. "The capitalistic system is built on the on the backs of the working class. Carnegie makes four thousand times the salary of a laborer. The politicians are corrupt, and the vaunted free press doesn't expose the inequities. But I fear she and Hasçek are planning something terrible."

"Why do you think that?"

"Hasçek told Goldman he wants to strike at the top. He talks about making headlines all over the world, that he wants to create chaos, overthrow governments. He says violent acts are the only solution, but then Goldman hushes him and says they will talk of these things at another time. I know she means when I'm not there. More than that, I do not know.

"James, you know I abhor violence, and I don't want to be caught up in Goldman's web. Have you seen all the orphaned children on the streets that are either ignored or abused? Though I am but one person, maybe I can help them. All Hasçek and Goldman want to do is blow things up, maybe literally. They must be stopped!"

"Zofia, I see you are frightened, but these are vague suspicions. Do you have any idea what they intend to do?"

"You doubt me? I trusted you when we knew each other in Pittsburgh and thought you would trust me now. I have misjudged you, James Dalton." She got up to leave.

I stood and said, "Zofia, please don't go. If you want me to help you, I will, but I need more information. When you know more, we should go to the police."

"No government man will believe what I have to say! They are always on the side of the wealthy and powerful."

"I will believe you. Wire me at the paper when you get more information. I will take the next train to New York if you suspect anything is about to happen. In any case, I will be back in the city with my family on December 15, staying at the Savoy Hotel. We should talk then." Father had mentioned that he would attend a speech of steel and financial executives and wanted to bring the whole family along to enjoy New York City at Christmastime.

"Thank you, James. I didn't know where else to turn." I said good-bye with a chaste kiss on the cheek, and she left the park. As I walked back to the University Club, I speculated about what Goldman and Hasçek could be planning. The next morning, I was on an early train to Pittsburgh.

———

Rita gave me a big hug and a kiss when I got home the next evening. My son seemed curious when I approached his layette, but I didn't think he recognized me. Even a few weeks after he was born, his little eyes had crinkled and his tiny mouth smiled when he saw me. Had I really been working and traveling so much that he had lost that memory? I resolved to spend as much time with Rick as I could—be sure to stay for his breakfast before going to work and be home early enough not to miss Rita feeding him before he went to bed and, of course, take him for proud strolls in his baby carriage up and down Pittsburgh's Fifth Avenue on Sundays.

We had dinner with Mr. and Mrs. Heinz that Sunday, and they had graciously included my family as well. The grandmothers made a great fuss over Rick, hugging and kissing him, while the grandfathers stood back, beaming proudly as they shared cigars after the meal. He lasted through most of dinner until he grew fussy and then was handed off to Margaret, who was waiting in the kitchen for just such an occurrence.

Early November was slow for news of the steel business. Mr. Carnegie was in Pittsburgh and raising hell with everyone in his office, but that wasn't anything new. He was in a wrangle with the Navy about the price and quality of the steel plating that had been ordered for the battleships that were patrolling the oceans from Cuba to Hawaii and all the way to the Philippines as a result of the Spanish-American War. He gave an interview with the papers and denounced the naval inspectors that haunted the plants with their meaningless testing. "They know nothing about producing steel and slow down our mills with their interference."

Carnegie also announced that he would be financing a new finishing mill in Erie. The Morgan-backed Federal Steel was buying up manufacturing plants around Chicago, and Carnegie wanted to make it very clear that it was not going to be easy for any other company to gain a toehold in what he considered to be his private domain. "We have more resources than even the great Morgan," he bragged to the press. "We will run our mills at full capacity and produce goods at a price that Federal will never match. Carnegie Steel will prevail."

I went into the paper and filed a story every few days on the Carnegie Company's struggles with the federal bureaucracy, as well as Mr. Carnegie's surprise visits to his steel towns, Duquesne, Braddock, and Homestead, promising more libraries and telling the sparse crowds that America should always seek peace, not war. This last declaration was brazen hypocrisy since Carnegie Steel was the federal government's largest supplier of war matériel. Right after Christmas, he returned to New York.

Mr. Frick was nowhere to be seen. Once the battle with Mr. Carnegie was resolved, he suffered from one of his nervous collapses and took a liner to Europe, along with his wife and A. W. Mellon, in search of more art treasures. Whatever happened to Carnegie Steel, his future wealth was assured with the revaluation of the book value closer to what the company was truly worth. He was not expected back in Pittsburgh until the spring.

With no deadline pressure, I stopped off at Amberson Avenue early one evening. As we stood in the front hall, I asked Father what more he knew about the University Club dinner.

"Only that it is to honor Charlie Schwab for his leadership in the steel industry," he said. "J. P. Morgan will be there, as will Mr. Carnegie. You know what those things are like: lots of heavy food and hot air. Charlie will be expected to make some amusing remarks. I've seen him in these situations before, and he can be very glib. I guarantee it won't be anything weighty. Charlie's a crowd-pleaser."

Just then mother walked by. She was still aglow from her new health regime and wrapped me in an embrace. Father gave a wink and said, "Eleanor, shouldn't you tell your son about your speech in New York that same night?"

Mother looked embarrassed. "What speech, Mother? Why haven't you said anything?"

"Darling, it's nothing."

"Don't be modest, Eleanor! It's an honor."

"Oh, all right. The Suffrage Association has asked me to speak at their national convention on the recruitment success we have had in Pittsburgh."

Father put his arm around her, and I said, "That's quite an honor! Would you like help with your speech?"

"Mrs. Anthony and Mrs. Cady would be very angry if they knew a man, even my son, had written my speech." Then she winked and said, "But I might ask you to look at it on the train to New York."

"It's the same night as Charlie's speech," Father said. "Maybe you can take your brother and sister to a play or a restaurant that night. Or are you angling for an invitation to the University Club dinner?"

"As much as I'd like to see Morgan lording it over the rest of you, I'll take a pass. I'm sure you'll let me know if I missed anything."

— • —

The second week of December, I was surprised when I got a telephone message at the *Sun*. All it said was "O'Reilly's six p.m."The person refused to leave their name, but I knew it was Charlie. I called Rita to let her know that I was meeting Schwab and might be late for dinner. I hadn't met him there in over a year, and she didn't seem to mind.

When I got to O'Reilly's, Charlie was already sitting in the back. Now that he was president of the Carnegie Company, I was surprised he had time for me. I supposed he liked my company. At thirty-eight he was only a few years older than me, and there was no one close to his age at the company with any responsibility.

"Jamie, good to see you. Sit down. I've something very important to discuss," he said. "You've heard about the speech I'm giving this week at the University Club?"

I nodded that I had.

"I want you to help me with it. They are expecting something entertaining from Good Old Charlie, but I have never had an opportunity like this. Morgan himself will be there! And Mr. C., of course. And E. H. Harriman, Auguste Belmont, Jacob Schiff, and H. H. Rogers from Standard Oil."

Was this something I wanted to do, write a speech for a man I covered for the paper? "Tell me what you're thinking," I said.

"I want to send a message to all these men that there is a smarter, more profitable way to do business and that's by cooperating, not competing. I have a general idea what I want to say, but I need your help with the tone of the speech. It should be casual but confident. I want Morgan to agree with me and make Mr. Carnegie an offer at the price he's looking for, whatever that might be. At this point in his life—he's sixty-five, you know—Andrew can stop worrying about the cost of coke and steel plates and concentrate on giving away his money. You've read his *Gospel of Wealth*? 'A man who dies rich dies disgraced.'" Then Schwab chuckled. "I can't believe he means that literally. I want to be as rich as I can, as long as I can."

Then he told me what he considered the most important ideas he wanted me to convey. Centralize distribution so plants could be organized to serve the closest markets. Consolidate rolling plants so there is no duplication of efforts. Compare costs across plants to find hidden efficiencies. Discover new technologies to improve productivity. Find new uses for steel.

"That's a lot to cover. How long a speech?"

Charlie laughed. "They expect it to be ten, fifteen minutes, but I don't care how long it is as long as they pay attention to what I'm saying. And I want a big finish. I'll promise them my plan means increased sales and higher profits. I want them standing and cheering at the end."

"I don't know. This is a pretty sober group."

"Don't worry. I've already thought of an opener. 'I guess I'll talk about steel since I don't know anything else.' A guaranteed laugh!"

I owed Charlie for all the information he had given me over the years, but I would have to talk to Cleve before I agreed to be Schwab's ghostwriter.

"Charlie, there has to be something in this for me, for the *Sun*."

"You have the exclusive on my speech! What more do you need?"

"What about afterwards?" If Morgan was swayed by the speech, we both knew what was at stake.

Schwab chewed hard on his cigar. "If anything comes of it, I'll let you know. But time's a-wasting. Will you do it or not?

"When do you need it?"

"First thing tomorrow! My private car is being hooked onto the Pennsy train that leaves at eight. I have a couple of days of meetings in New York. The dinner is on Thursday, and I'll be back in Pittsburgh the next day."

With the promised access, I was sure Cleve would let me write Schwab's speech. "I better get right to it." I smiled, then took my leave and returned to the *Sun*.

After some initial grumbling, Brooks assented. "But he better come through on his promise to give us the exclusive," he said. "You know he can't pay you, don't you?"

I laughed. "Not much chance of that. He already feels like he's doing me the favor."

Since Schwab had given me the outline of what he wanted, all I had to do was fill it out, add in some bon mots, and build momentum for the rousing finish. I was done in a couple of hours. After reading it over a few times at home that night, I delivered it to Charlie at the station the next morning. In the rush it hadn't occurred to me to tell him I would be in New York the night of his speech and staying at the Savoy Hotel, a few short blocks from the University Club. It didn't seem important at the time.

—◆—

The whole family was excited about the trip to New York. Rita and I looked forward to a few days off from our normal routine of motherly duties and daily deadlines. Mother was giving her speech at the suffrage convention, while Kat wanted to see the new Lord & Taylor store that had recently opened at 23rd and Broadway. Wills was attending cotillions with his friends from Pomfret. Father, despite his protestations, was thrilled about the prospect of mingling with the top men of industry and finance at the Schwab dinner. After that he would be joining the rest of us at the Savoy.

We boarded the early train that Thursday at the Shadyside station. The ride was uneventful, and there was not much to see other than the bare trees on the sides of the Alleghenies, but, no matter your age, the Horseshoe Curve always fascinated. From the last car, we could see the engine belching smoke and most of the rest of the train as it wound around the long, graceful curve. After that we occupied our time with lunch and rummy until we pulled into the Hoboken station at five o'clock for the short ferry ride into Manhattan. We were met at the 34th Street pier and whisked up to the Savoy Hotel on Fifth Avenue at 59th St. in two large broughams that Father had arranged through the Carnegie Company's New York office. With the agreement over the Iron-Clad resolved, Father and even Henry Phipps were back in the good graces of Mr. Carnegie, despite their previous affiliation with Mr. Frick. Mr. Carnegie was a very forgiving man, but Mr. Frick was still anathema to him.

Our Dalton group arrived at the hotel just after seven o'clock. The others paraded in ahead of me, while I oversaw the drivers delivering our trunks and valises to the Savoy's porters. With all the different events scheduled for the next three days, we were not traveling light. We had dinner at the hotel that night and went sightseeing all the next day: we took a carriage down to the spectacular Park Row Building, at thirty-one stories the tallest office building in the world; then a ride on the Staten Island Ferry past the Statue of Liberty, just fourteen years since its dedication; and last a stroll through Central Park, so much more detailed and finished than the wilds of Pittsburgh's Schenley Park and only steps away from our hotel.

After a quick stop at the Savoy, we headed to Madison Square Garden for Mother's speech to the suffrage convention. Although she had given speeches in other cities, she was very nervous. Everyone in the movement would be there, and she was scheduled to speak first. She needn't have worried. It was hard to hear at our seats far from the stage, but the spotlight made her look radiant. We could see her gain confidence as the crowd applauded and then stood as she finished. She was beaming when she found us, and we took a brougham back to the Savoy so Father could get to the dinner at the University Club.

As we walked into the hotel, one of the men at the front desk took me aside and said, "Mr. Dalton, a note for you. A young lady dropped it off an hour ago." I could see it was from Zofia and slipped the man a dollar for his discretion.

"It's probably from Sam. Lunch at the Yale Club," I told the group.

I opened the envelope like it was nothing important. "Meet me at the central kiosk in Grand Central Depot. Come as soon as possible. I can't wait long."

She sounded panicked. What was she afraid of? Perhaps she had discovered what Hasçek and Emma Goldman were planning?

I shook my head and said to Rita, "I'm so sorry. It's not from Sam; it's from Charlie Schwab. He is staying at the Grand Central Hotel and wants to go over the speech one last time. The dinner starts in an hour."

This time Rita wasn't so quick to give her blessing. "We are all having dinner in the Palm Court while your father is at the banquet. This was our time to forget about responsibilities. Must you? We will all be disappointed if you're not here."

"Darling, I promise to be back in a half an hour."

I gave her a quick hug and flew out the door. In the dim gaslight of the December evening, I tried to sprint through the crowds of people, but a light rain had fallen, and I slid through the slippery muck. I raced under the Vanderbilt Avenue portico, pushed through the glass-paned oak doors, and looked out over the vast interior. When I saw Zofia, she was headed toward the 42nd Street exit. I shouted her name over the din as I hurried after her, bumping and jostling train passengers and porters along the way. She finally turned to me. "Thank the Lord you have come. It's happening, and I'm sure it will be tonight."

"What is going to happen?"

"As we left her flat, Hasçek said to Goldman, 'Capitalism dies tonight. Everyone will know the name Miloš Hasçek tomorrow.' That's all I heard."

My mind raced. It could only be one thing. News of the dinner at the University Club had been in the New York papers, and Goldman and Hasçek knew where a mighty concentration of wealth and power would be that night. And my father would be there.

"Zofia, I must get back to the University Club. That's where Hasçek will attack, I am sure of it. You must get out of the city, or you may be swept up as Hasçek's accomplice. Don't even go back to your apartment."

"But I'm . . ."

"It doesn't matter. Now go. We will talk again after this is all over." I didn't know whether that would turn out to be true, but there was no time to waste. After a quick embrace, I ran back up the steps of the station onto Vanderbilt Avenue. I had to get to the University Club in time to stop Hasçek.

———✦———

As I ran into the club, I was surprised to see Mr. Carnegie leaving. At least he was safe. Not wanting to wait for the rattling elevator, I ran up the stairs to the seventh-floor dining room. In the minute it took to get there, it occurred to me that I wouldn't be allowed into the banquet. I wasn't on the guest list, and I wasn't properly dressed. That's when I saw Sam Lawrence in his white tie and tails. I gathered myself so he wouldn't see how agitated I was.

"Any chance you can get me inside?" I implored, trying to keep the panic out of my voice. "I want to hear Schwab deliver the speech that I wrote for him."

Sam laughed in a jolly fashion, and I suspected he'd had several cocktails before dinner. "Not exactly dressed for the occasion, are you, old boy?"

I held out my arms to show off my gray-flannel Brooks Brothers suit. "I don't look like a vagrant, and I'm not going to sit down to eat. I'll loiter in the back and leave as soon as Schwab finishes."

"There are a couple of Pinkertons here tonight. Blend in with them, I say," Sam guffawed.

I thought back to my other experience with the Pinkertons. Due to the public outcry after Homestead, Allen Pinkerton had decided that the future of his company did not lie in hiring shiftless thugs as strikebreakers. Now he chose his employees with care and trained them as private security.

Sam put on what was for him a serious voice and intoned to the man guarding the door, "Mr. Morgan's party." The man started to object, and Sam took on his most condescending tone. "Don't make me report you to Mr. Morgan himself." With that the man opened the door to the banquet hall.

No matter how many times I had been in that room it never failed to startle me with its magnificence. Running the whole length of the club, the half block from Fifth Avenue west toward Sixth, the room was three stories tall and thirty-five feet wide. The ceiling was divided by red-stained beams into bays that were painted blue and gold. The walls were a rich walnut and topped with crenellated moldings. Courtesy of Mr. Morgan, Thomas Edison had built a generator nearby, and the wall sconces and chandeliers sparkled with electric light.

The long dining table was covered in a bright-white damask cloth and festooned with shining silverware and gleaming crystal glasses, at least five for each place setting. Eighty men, resplendent and self-satisfied in formal attire, sat around a U-shaped table. There looked to be forty on each side, eighty in all. In the middle of the head table I saw Charlie Schwab, and next to him was the grim, beady-eyed visage of J. P. Morgan. Charlie was quaffing his wine, but Morgan sat bolt upright with his hands in his lap and was clearly enduring the dinner, not enjoying it. Scanning down the table I saw my father sitting at the very end seat on the same side of the room as me near the service entrance. A man I didn't recognize was introducing Schwab. " ... who at the age of thirty-five rose to be the president of the Carnegie Steel Company, the country's largest industrial concern and the worldwide leader in the production of steel. Gentleman, it is my honor to introduce to you Mr. Charles Schwab."

The diners rose as one and applauded with even the portly Morgan struggling to his feet. Schwab took a last pull on his glass and stood to address the assembled.

"I guess I'm going to talk about steel ... " he began, but the speech was the least of my concerns. From my inconspicuous position in the corner nearest the exit, I kept a vigilant eye over the whole room.

"Consolidation, not competition," I heard Charlie say as I scanned the hall. Other than the clipping and lighting of cigars, the only sound was Schwab's voice. As he hoped, the mighty and powerful were paying attention, particularly Morgan. He stared up, nodding his head in agreement with the various points Schwab was making, while he absentmindedly tapped his chunky gold lighter on the table. There was nothing amiss, as far as I could see.

True to his word, Schwab spoke longer than expected, but his audience was mesmerized by his vision of industrial combinations on an unheard-of scale. When Charlie reached the finale and extolled a future emblazoned with riches, even the mighty Morgan was back on his feet, clapping and cheering and slapping Charlie on the back. Charlie looked out over the crowd; then he saw me and smiled in appreciation. The speech was all he had hoped for.

As the men sat back down, waiters poured out of the kitchen with brandy snifters on trays. Nothing unusual there. Then the last waiter out of the service door, which was just behind where my father was sitting, caught my attention.

He was of medium height with short rust-colored hair and a trimmed mustache. Didn't look anything like what I remembered of Hasçek, who had long brown hair and a dark beard, but the man had a limp and looked unnaturally bulky around the middle. It had to be Hasçek, and I couldn't waste a second.

Father saw me running toward him, no doubt dumbfounded as to why I was there with such a panicked look on my face, but I could pay him no mind. I had to get to Hasçek before he could detonate whatever he had under his jacket.

He never saw me coming. I threw myself at his back, harder than I had ever made a tackle for the Yale eleven. Hasçek's breathe left him in a whoosh, but he had the presence of mind to twist out of my grasp while he fumbled for what I assumed was some kind of trigger. We were on the floor hidden behind the table, and the only noise up to this point had been the clattering of the dropped tray and the dozen glasses. One of the Pinkertons on that side of the room had seen all that transpired. Rather than join the struggle for the detonator, he pulled out a sap and struck Hasçek hard across the back of the head. The would-be assassin went limp.

We both were instantly aware that Hasçek's thwarted attack needed to be handled as discreetly as possible. Of course, the police would have to be called, but with Hasçek unconscious that could wait until later. The Pinkerton man introduced himself to me as Samuel Flynn and said, "We have to get him out of here, quick." We each grabbed one of his legs and pulled him through the service door and out into the corridor leading to the kitchen.

Flynn and the other Pinkerton managed to get Morgan and Schwab out of the room without alarming the other guests. My priority was to get

Father to safety. I darted back into the banquet hall. Father stared at the broken glass on the floor. As far as anyone else in the room knew, a waiter had merely tripped and dropped his tray. Flynn and I had kept as low as possible to avoid notice. Grabbing Father by the sleeve, I whispered, "You must come with me. Right now!"

Flynn's partner met us in the service corridor. "I got the big wigs out without suspicion. Just the normal after-dinner escort at the end of an evening. They are already in their carriages. Morgan home, Schwab to his hotel."

While Father and I struggled to regain our composure, we all looked at Hasçek lying on the floor with his waiter's coat flung open. Strapped to his chest were eight sticks of dynamite. There was also a wire from the explosives to a trigger that lay on the floor at his side.

The partner knelt next to Hasçek and began fiddling with the wire that led from the dynamite sticks to the trigger. "Jacobs here is an expert, used to work in the coal mines around Lancaster," Flynn said. "He'll have that wire disconnected in another few minutes. Nothing to worry about here."

I wasn't so sure. The one thing that I knew about dynamite was that it was unstable. I mouthed the word, "Mother," and Father ran down the nearby service staircase. Mother and Rita and Kat and Wills were still at the Savoy, and we both understood how important it was that they stay there for the time being. I was glad he was gone because the sweat running down Jacobs's face was doing nothing to reassure me that the situation was by any means under control.

We all held our breath for few minutes; then Jacobs exclaimed, "I got it!" Then he threw the now useless trigger to the side. Jacobs untied the dynamite sticks from Hasçek's chest and carefully cradled them as took them out to an armored van. Even the unflappable Flynn looked relieved.

"We have to get the city police involved," he said to one of the others. "Please find a copper on Fifth. He'll know what to do."

Hasçek had started to stir. It took a few moments for him to realize where he was and to comprehend his failure, but he remained defiant. "You have stopped me once, but I will never quit. If not me, then others will destroy the oppressors. The scum will die."

I got in one solid punch to his face before the two Pinkertons restrained me. They held my arms behind my back as I tried to wriggle free.

"He is the one who should die," I shouted. I got myself under control, and they let go. It was not me who would bring Hasçek to justice. Four burly New York City policemen in their long blue coats and their conical helmets entered the room. They handcuffed Hasçek and led him away. Hasçek was still shouting his tiresome slogans, but no one was paying any attention to him.

With my family out of danger, I resumed my reporter's role. I wired my piece on the speech back to Pittsburgh from the Western Union desk in the club's lobby but decided not to risk reporting on the assassination attempt since it could reveal my own involvement and possible prior knowledge.

I met Father in the lobby of the hotel, and we decided that we would say nothing to the family about the near bloodbath at the University Club. Rita could tell that I was disturbed but didn't quiz me that night. She waited until the next morning before we were even out of bed.

"Tell me what happened. I know it was something. Both you and Richard were pale and shaking when you got back to the hotel. Why were you at the University Club in the first place?"

She deserved to know what had happened, but I couldn't tell her how I knew about the possibility of an attack.

"After talking to Charlie at his hotel, I wanted to hear how the speech was received." Then I told her the rest of the story, trying to downplay my role in thwarting Hasçek.

"First off," she snapped, "you were a damn fool for trying to tackle him on your own. Wasn't that the Pinkertons' job? You have a wife and son to think about, not just yourself!"

"I'm sorry; I wasn't thinking. There was something suspicious about him, and with Father sitting right there, I just reacted. Once he was on the ground, the Pinkertons took over. Father was safe, and after the police finished their questions, I came right to the Palm Court."

She shook her head. "What made you suspect him?" I hesitated, then gave her an answer I hoped she would accept.

"I'm not sure. He limped, and that reminded me of someone I had seen during the Homestead Strike. Then there was the bulk of his jacket."

She looked skeptical at first, but then her expression changed to one of relief. She threw her arms around my neck and with tears in her eyes said, "You could have been killed, my darling. The important thing is that we are all safe. But promise me on our child's life that you will never do anything as reckless as that ever again."

"Believe me, my sweet, I am chastened. My vigilante days are over."

The rest of our New York holiday went as planned. We saw James O'Neill and young John Barrymore in *The Count of Monte Christo* on Broadway and ate at the famed Delmonico's in lower Manhattan. The ladies visited the fashionable shops that were popping up around Union Square, and the men explored Central Park up past the reservoir and were impressed by the outcroppings of Manhattan schist. On the last night we all went to see Evelyn Nesbit, known as the "Girl in the Velvet" swing, perform at Madison Square Garden. I was surprised to see a fellow from Pittsburgh that I knew, Harry K. Thaw, but he was so mesmerized by Miss Nesbit that he never noticed us. It was just as well. Thaw's unstable reputation was well-known in Pittsburgh and had preceded him to New York.

I'd been back in Pittsburgh a week, but there was no word from Charlie. I didn't want him, or anyone, to know how I stopped Hasçek, but he might have at least thanked me for how well the speech had gone over. And he had agreed to tell me Morgan's next move.

The next morning, I presented myself at the Carnegie Steel offices and asked for Mr. Schwab. I got the usual blank stare from the man at the front desk, but Charlie must have heard me because I heard his booming voice say, "C'mon in, Jamie."

"That speech was a fire-cracker!" he said from behind his desk as I settled into one of his deep lounge chairs. "Can't tell you all the compliments I've had. And I see your piece got picked up by all the wire services." Then he paused.

"Did you hear what almost happened? I saw you at the end of the speech, but the guard hustled me and Morgan down the front stairs and onto the street, and I didn't see you again. That damned radical could have blown us all to kingdom come!"

Should I tell him that I was the one who tackled Hasçek? Once again, it would raise too many questions. And I didn't want to use my role in thwarting the assassination plot to find out what was going on with Morgan.

"I saw the Pinkertons take the guy down, but my only concern was getting my father to safety."

"Very smart! Well, we all survived it."

I hoped Charlie would volunteer information from his conversation with Morgan at the dinner. Was he toying with me? "Do I have to remind you that you promised more than the story on the speech?"

Schwab gave me that grim, stern look, then said, "There is very little I can tell you."

I paced back and forth in front of his desk. "You have to do better than that! Can't you even tell me Morgan's reaction to the speech?" I was leaning toward him, grabbing the sides of his desk.

Charlie furrowed his brow and squinted, but then he grinned at me. "He liked it."

"Dammit, Charlie!"

"Easy, my friend, I have to make you work for it. A deal's a deal, but if you leak any bit of what I'm about to tell you, I'll deny it and you will look like a fool." Then he broke into a big smile. "How would you like to have an exclusive on the acquisition of the Carnegie Company by John Pierpont Morgan?"

Even with all the background I had, I was still shocked. "Are you serious?"

Schwab rocked back and forth on his heels, grinning with the satisfaction of his insider's knowledge. "I am the only one that knows this and now you." Then he laughed. "Not even Carnegie and Morgan."

He saw my confusion. "I'll explain," he said. He sat in the other chair in front of his desk and leaned toward me. "As I took my seat after delivering the banquet speech, Morgan whispered to me, 'We will discuss your ideas further.' At that moment I didn't realize how soon that would be.

"The Pinkertons brought us out to the street and told us what had happened. Before we stepped into our separate carriages, Morgan said to me in a low voice. 'Tell your man to stop at 52nd and Fifth and join me in my coach.'"

Charlie stopped abruptly. "But I can't tell you any more than that."

"There has to be more than a surreptitious carriage ride with J. P. Morgan. Will there be a sale or not?"

"Don't be so impatient!" Charlie laughed, being legendary for that same character fault himself. "There will be a sale, but I can't give you any of the details until the deal is signed and about to be announced."

"When will that be?" I asked.

"Not rightly sure," he answered, "but when I have the details, I will contact you. You will have the inside account before anyone else."

I was flabbergasted, thrilled, and wary at the same time. "Charlie, how can you guarantee this won't leak before the deal gets approved? Mr. Carnegie loves nothing more than to tease the press with his vast knowledge."

"The way I see it playing out, things will move fast after he has agreed to a price."

"What about Morgan's men? I have a friend who is very close to Morgan. He's been a valuable source, but he is indiscreet."

"Morgan won't want this bandied about. Who knows if the Rockefellers might not sweep in and take the deal away from him? As many transactions as Morgan has financed, nothing approaches the size of this one. It will be his legacy, and he won't say a word until it's complete.

"For now, Jamie, enjoy Christmas and New Year's with your lovely wife and baby boy. Leave the rest to me. Your present will come soon enough."

It was senseless to argue any further, and he was right. It was Rick's first Christmas, and both my parents and the Heinzes planned to make it as memorable as possible. There were new outfits from Joseph Horne's in Pittsburgh and Best & Co. in New York. Unbeknownst to me the whole family had ventured to FAO Schwartz while we were all in Manhattan and bought Rick enough toys to fill his tiny room in the house on Kentucky.

After the first of the year, I started getting anxious, but I didn't dare show my face in the Carnegie Company offices. No one there ever talked to me besides Charlie, and I didn't want anyone suspecting that he was my source. I hung around O'Reilly's, but no one had seen Schwab since before Christmas. "The other day he said he was going to New York," one of the bartenders told me.

I thought about following Schwab to New York, but I was sure he wouldn't want me hounding him. And there was Zofia. I told her I would be in touch, but that seemed like a bad idea. Our lives had gone on very different paths. I had Rita and Rick. Zofia was a strong woman and could start a new life.

Through the cold, snowy Pittsburgh winter, Rita noticed how restless I was. "What's wrong?" she finally asked.

I tried to laugh it off. "You don't like being cooped up any better than I do."

"We're not talking about me. I want to know why you seem so jumpy."

Charlie told me that I couldn't speak about the possible Morgan deal to anyone, but I shared everything with Rita. She had grown up in one of the country's leading industrial families, and she didn't need me to tell her to be discreet.

"I am sitting on the biggest story you can imagine, the kind of scoop reporters dream of. But Charlie Schwab is teasing me with bits of information, and I've promised not to put anything in the paper until he gives me the green light.

"Rita, J. P. Morgan is trying to buy Carnegie Steel! All the plants, Frick's coke operation, the whole thing! Pittsburgh will never be the same."

The normally unflappable Rita opened her eyes wide and shook her head in disbelief. Then she gathered herself. "Now I understand what's been bothering you. Can you trust Schwab? You know his reputation."

"This deal will be the making of Charlie Schwab. Morgan is sure to keep him on to run all of his steel interests. He wants the merger to go as smoothly as possible. And he believes what he said in the University Club speech. He's playing straight with me."

"I hope you're right," Rita said. "Now, for heaven's sake, go down to the PAA and lift some dumbbells or box or whatever you do there and get rid of some of your nervous energy. And I'll call Virginia Rea for doubles."

I heeded her advice and took out my frustrations at the gymnasium. At the paper I got a week of stories on the appointment of Philander Knox to Cleveland's cabinet as attorney general.

The long month of January lived up to its reputation, until on the morning of Tuesday, January 29, Schwab called me at the *Sun*. All he said was, "I've taken rooms at the Monongahela House. Meet me there at one."

When I entered the parlor of his suite at exactly one o'clock, he pointed to two plush easy chairs. "Let's get comfortable, my friend. I have a lot to tell you."

I knew I had the biggest story of the new century.

━━◆━━

Morgan to Acquire Carnegie Steel
U. S. Steel will be
Country's Largest Company
Scores of Pittsburghers
Become Millionaires
Exclusive to the Pittsburgh Sun, reported and written by James R. Dalton

Andrew Carnegie has accepted an offer of $480 million from the renowned financier J. P. Morgan for the assets of the Carnegie Company, composed of Carnegie Steel, H. C. Frick Coal and Coke, Keystone Bridge, and various other concerns. The new corporation will be known as U. S. Steel and have its headquarters in Chicago.

U. S. Steel will also incorporate non–Carnegie companies such as National Steel, owned by former Carnegie suitor William Moore, and Federal Steel, whose president, Judge Elbert H. Gary, will be U. S.

Steel's board chairman. Charles Schwab, who has served for five years as president of Carnegie Steel, will assume the same title at U. S. Steel. Mr. Morgan and three of his associates will be granted seats on the board of directors and are expected to maintain strict oversight.

Mr. Carnegie alone will receive $226 million in 5% gold bonds from the sale. Another $75 million in those bonds will be split between his cousin, George Lauder, and Mrs. Lucy Carnegie, widow of Mr. Carnegie's brother, Thomas. Henry Phipps and Henry Clay Frick will receive $72 million and $29 million, respectively. It is estimated that over sixty men of this city, some with as little as a one-quarter of one percent share of the Carnegie partnership, will now be millionaires.

Behind the Scenes

The Pittsburgh Sun has the exclusive background story on what led up to this momentous transaction. The following is a chronological explanation of those events.

Wednesday, December 12, 1900 At a dinner in his honor at New York City's University Club, Charles Schwab, president of Carnegie Steel, espoused cooperation, not competition, to achieve maximum profits. Later that night Mr. Morgan and Mr. Schwab conferred on potential consolidation in the steel industry.

Friday, January 11 Mr. Schwab arrived at the Blenheim Hotel in Atlantic City for a meeting with Mr. Morgan who was indisposed with a head cold. Mr. Schwab was discouraged, but in a brief telephone conversation found Mr. Morgan eager to discuss a possible merger. Mr. Morgan proposed another meeting in ten days at his home.

Monday, January 21 From the list of Federal and Carnegie companies Mr. Schwab and Mr. Morgan selected only companies that were not duplicative to be a part of the new enterprise. At that point Mr. Morgan told Mr. Schwab to "Ask Andy for a price."

Wednesday, January 23 After delivering a business update to Mr. Carnegie at his 51st street home, Mr. Schwab asked Louise Carnegie, the magnate's wife, the best way to approach Mr. Carnegie about a sale. Mrs. Carnegie was enthusiastic about her husband being relieved of his business worries and suggested Mr. Schwab introduce the subject following a round of golf when Mr. Carnegie always feels the most relaxed.

Friday, January 25, afternoon After Mr. Carnegie and Mr. Schwab played nine holes at the St. Andrews course in North Yonkers, Mr. Schwab raised the prospect of a sale. Mr. Carnegie was negative at first, but as he talked through the pros and cons with his protégé, he concluded that it was time to devote himself to his oft-stated goal of donating his fortune to charity. "What price should I tell Mr. Morgan?" Schwab asked. With a pencil stub that he had used to record his round, Carnegie wrote "$480 million" on the back of his scorecard.

Friday, January 25, evening Mr. Schwab handed the scorecard to Mr. Morgan who glanced at it and said, "Tell Mr. Carnegie I agree to his price."

Monday, January 28 Mr. Morgan suggested he and Mr. Carnegie meet at the offices of the Morgan Bank the next day. Mr. Carnegie demurred. "It is farther from Mr. Morgan's home to his office on Broad Street than it is from his home to mine on West 51st." The meeting was set for the following morning at Mr. Carnegie's residence.

Tuesday, January 29 Mr. Junius Pierpont Morgan and Mr. Andrew Carnegie met to sort out the final details. The Carnegie Board would approve the sale at its February 4th meeting. By the end of February Mr. Carnegie would deliver to Mr. Morgan a memorandum of understanding as to the details of the transaction. On March 3rd Mr. Morgan would announce the creation of the U. S. Steel Corporation.

At the close of their meeting Mr. Morgan stood and extended his hand.
When Mr. Carnegie grasped it, the financier smiled and said,
"Congratulations, sir, you are the richest man in the world."

⸺

But how rich was he? Or were Frick or Phipps or any of the other Pittsburgh Millionaires, my father included?

These and so many other questions had bubbled up in my head in the weeks after the Morgan buyout was announced.

What had the steel men's newfound wealth cost the working people of western Pennsylvania? The men in the steel mills and their families led impoverished lives in company housing. With their unions gone, did they have any hope?

Every public building in Pittsburgh was soiled black. Lung disease was the city's biggest killer. How could the mass of people who didn't escape to the Laurel Highlands on weekends and New England and Canada for the summer expect to survive?

More than two thousand died in the Conemaugh Valley. Was only God to blame, as the courts said?

Andrew Carnegie espoused noble intentions with his galling conceit that he was a friend of the working man. He preached peace while benefiting from war. He created noble institutions that his workers had neither the time nor the inclination to frequent. From his comfortable confines in New York and Scotland, he drove his lieutenants like Frick and Phipps to kill off any threat to his company, be it other steel firms or unions, and show no mercy. Would his libraries and museums ever expunge his hypocrisy?

Henry Frick was deemed ruthless and unbending, but he had lost two children, and his business career was punctuated by nervous collapses. While the men in his mills worked twelve-hour shifts, he recovered on ocean voyages and private railcars through Europe. Would his art and his board seats, so far removed from the thrill of being in command of an enormous enterprise like Carnegie Steel, be enough to sustain him?

The Pittsburgh Millionaires built new mansions in Pittsburgh and splashy summer homes but were deemed grubby arrivistes when they sought a place in East Coast society. They tried to show sophistication by patronizing European art houses that didn't hesitate to sell them forgeries and fakes. With all their profligacy, would their fortunes last more than another generation?

And I was the top reporter in Pittsburgh, covering the country's most essential industry. But in my drive to be the first to report on the grand dramas of our age, what had it cost me?

My dear friend from college was dead. Did I share the blame for his death since my ambition outstripped my loyalty to someone who had needed my help?

Had I crossed ethical lines by exploiting and doing the bidding of my father and Charlie Schwab to the professional and financial benefit of us all?

I loved Rita with all my heart, but my infatuation with Zofia scared me. Could something like that happen again, with her or someone else? I had stopped drinking, but I had to be vigilant. Could I stay on the water-wagon for good?

I was still stewing over all these the questions a month later when Father and I went for a Sunday drive in the family's first automobile, a runabout built in Detroit by a man named Ransom E. Olds. My father was proud of what Mother called his new toy, and we donned our leather dusters and goggles and headed up Wilkins Hill. We wound our way through Squirrel Hill, then stopped at the highest spot on Forbes Street, where we could look straight out over Schenley Park and Oakland toward downtown. To the left we could see the glow from the mills along the Monongahela.

"Son, you have such a happy life with Rita and Ricky, but you seem distracted. What's bothering you?"

Father's concern gave me leave to pour out all the things that I had been pondering, leaving out some of the more personal issues. When I ran out of steam, Father smiled and said, "That's quite a burden you've been carrying."

He could see my face flush; then he put his hand on my shoulder. "I'm not trivializing what you're feeling. You're questioning whether this newfound wealth has been worth all the lives lost, the poverty, the smoke and dirt? History will decide that, not James Dalton. And no one, not even Cleveland Brooks, will expect you to have the answers." I was calmed by his wise counsel and relaxed as best I could back into the hard wicker chair of the Oldsmobile.

"Jamie, Pittsburgh is a tough, brutal city. You know that better than I. But it's also a miracle. No place is more vital to the economy of the United States. Pittsburgh's steel will make us the greatest country in the world over the next century. I know many have sacrificed their lives for steel, but hundreds of thousands more have been given jobs and the possibility of a new life in a new country."

I thought about arguing, but what was the point? Father and I had never agreed on the proper balance between the needs of owners and workers, and doubtless never would. I didn't interrupt.

"Capitalism isn't perfect, never will be," Father continued. "Nothing should stop you from pointing out the system's failings and seeking the truth. But try to see beyond what you deem exploitation and recognize how this money can be used for good." He gestured toward the mills, then back across the park to Oakland and two massive, gleaming stone buildings. "Look at the library and museum that Mr. Carnegie has built. And east of that is the site of a new technical institute I've heard he's planning. Western University is moving to Oakland as well, and I hear it will be renamed the University of Pittsburgh. Those institutions will be here long after the mills are gone. Jamie, for all its excesses, we are lucky to have lived through such a dynamic era."

Father and I sat in silence for several minutes; then he turned to me and said, "But nothing that has happened in the last ten years is more important to me than being your father. I know it's been difficult at times, but I have so much respect for you and hope you have the same for me. Think of all we've learned from each other." Then with a catch in his voice, Father held his arms open to me, and as we embraced, he said, "I love you, Jamie."

Unused to this kind of intimacy, we broke off with embarrassed smiles. Then in mock exasperation I said, "But what will I do now? I will never have another exclusive like J. P. Morgan's purchase of Carnegie Steel."

My father laughed. "You could study law and join me in representing Mr. Frick. I'm sure your friend Charlie Schwab could find you a job. But trust me. Our Steel City has more stories to tell."

Epilogue

Purchase price of the Carnegie Company in today's dollars: In 1901 the $480 million price for the Carnegie Company represented 2 percent of the United States' GDP. Two percent of today's GDP would be over $400 billion, making the Carnegie transaction the largest corporate buy-out of all time.

Slabtown: Many of Pittsburgh's most successful industrialists, including Andrew Carnegie, Henry Phipps, George Lauder, Henry and George Oliver, and Robert Pitcairn, grew up in this impoverished immigrant neighborhood in Allegheny City. Slabtown was located between where PNC Park and Heinz Field stand today, near the former site of Three Rivers Stadium, which was demolished in 2001.

Willis F. McCook: Richard Dalton is loosely based on my great-grandfather, Willis F. McCook, who was Henry Frick's attorney. With the money from his share of the Carnegie sale, McCook and other beneficiaries created Pittsburgh Steel Company. My father's first cousin, Allison R. Maxwell Jr., was president of Pittsburgh Steel from 1956 to 1973. In 1968 he oversaw the company's merger with Wheeling Steel. After a series of reorganizations and bankruptcies, the Wheeling-Pittsburgh Steel name disappeared in 2008. Pittsburgh Steel's Monessen works are still operational and owned by ArcelorMittal, a Euro-Indian firm, headquartered in Luxembourg.

In 1907 Willis McCook built a mansion on the northeast corner of Fifth and Amberson Avenues, where his daughter and my grandmother, Katherine McCook, married Harry J. Miller in 1909. The house was seized in 1940 by the city of Pittsburgh for nonpayment of property taxes, and beginning in 1949 it was a boardinghouse for students at Carnegie-Mellon University. After a second-floor fire in 2004, it was purchased in 2010 by a couple who restored it as well as another home on the property that had originally been built for Mr. McCook's oldest daughter Elizabeth and her family. Today the two houses are known as the Mansions on Fifth, a small boutique hotel.

Mr. McCook also acquired a large home named Bagnell Hall in Coburg, Ontario, where my father spent his summers until World War II, when it was confiscated by the Canadian government to be used as an army hospital. My family visited the house when I was thirteen, and what I remember most about that visit was my father being overcome with emotion at seeing the shell of what had been such a happy part of his youth.

Andrew Carnegie (1835–1919): True to his word, Andrew Carnegie did spend the rest of his life giving away his enormous fortune, over $200 billion in today's dollars, to a variety of organizations. Besides the $41 million he donated to build nearly two thousand libraries, his major philanthropic enterprises, all of which still exist today, are:

- Carnegie Hall
- Carnegie Museums (Pittsburgh)
- Carnegie Institute of Technology, now Carnegie Mellon University
- Carnegie Institution for Science (Washington, D.C.)
- Carnegie Hero Fund Commission
- Carnegie Foundation for the Advancement of Teaching
- Carnegie Endowment for International Peace
- Carnegie Trust for the Universities of Scotland
- The Peace Palace (The Hague, the Netherlands)

In 1911–1912 Carnegie had tired of making philanthropic decisions and endowed the Carnegie Corporation with $125 million to make those choices for him. That bequest would be valued at over $100 billion today.

Never returning to live in Pittsburgh, Carnegie built a new home for himself and his wife, Louise, in 1902 at the corner of Fifth Avenue and 91st Street in Manhattan and lived there until his death in Lenox, Massachusetts, on August 11, 1919. The home was owned by the Carnegie Corporation, and Mrs. Carnegie remained there until she died in 1946. In 1972 the corporation donated the mansion to the Smithsonian, and in 1976 it was reopened as the Cooper-Hewitt, Smithsonian Design Museum. The area around the museum on the Upper East Side of Manhattan is now known as Carnegie Hill. From 2000 to 2022 I lived five blocks away from the former Carnegie home.

Henry Frick (1849–1919): Frick received $29 million (over $30 billion today) from the sale of the Carnegie Company. For the next fifteen years he remained on the board of directors of U.S. Steel and was a trusted advisor of Judge Elbert H. Gary, who became the company's president in 1903. It was said that Frick was the country's largest owner of railroad stocks in the first decade of the new century. He twice declined offers to be named senator from Pennsylvania and secretary of the treasury.

In the early twentieth century, Frick was the largest landowner in Pittsburgh, and his twenty-two-story Frick Building cast a shadow over the adjacent fourteen-story Carnegie Building. In 1905 he and his family moved to New York City and rented the Vanderbilt chateau at Fifth Avenue and 52nd Street. In 1912 he began construction on his magnificent sixty-room home at Fifth Avenue and 70th Street. At the time he said it would make the Carnegie house, a mile north on Fifth, look like a "miner's shack." With his vast wealth, knowledge of art, and discerning taste, Frick filled his home with the finest works of European artists such as Rubens, Raphael, Manet, Monet, Renoir, and Goya. His wife, Adelaide Childs Frick, died in 1931, and the Frick mansion was opened as the Frick Museum in 1935 with an endowment of $15 million.

Frick's daughter Helen lived at Clayton, on the corner of South Homewood and Penn Avenues until her death in 1984 at the age of ninety-six. I grew up in a house at the other end of the block, in much more modest circumstances. All the kids in the neighborhood disliked her for directing the Frick Park police to kick us off a vacant lot on her property that was perfect for football and baseball. Miss Frick was one of the personal connections that sparked my interest in Pittsburgh history.

The long-term impact of the philanthropy of the two "steel men": With all due respect to "the Frick," beloved by so many, Andrew Carnegie's philanthropic legacy has been more impactful.

Charles Schwab (1862–1939): Schwab was only 39 when he was appointed president of U.S. Steel and soon fell out of favor with his mentor Carnegie over his gambling and dissolute lifestyle. At U.S. Steel Schwab didn't have the same power to reinvest in the business as Carnegie always had and disagreed with the board of directors' decision to pay ever-increasing dividends. He resigned in 1903. Schwab later became the head of Bethlehem Steel and made it the second-largest steel company in the country.

His later years were not happy ones. In New York City he built what was then the city's largest home, the chateau known as Riverside at 72nd and Riverside Drive. It boasted ninety bedrooms, a sixty-foot pool, and its own power plant. Because of his extravagant lifestyle, by the late 1920s he had spent nearly all his $25 million fortune and the value of his remaining Bethlehem shares was wiped out in the stock market crash of 1929. In the 1930s he wasn't able to sell Riverside, and when he couldn't pay the property taxes, it was seized by creditors. The abandoned mansion was razed in 1940 after Fiorello LaGuardia decided it was too grandiose to be the residence of the mayor of New York City. Charles Schwab died in 1939, $300,000 in debt.

U.S. Steel: After the Homestead Steel Strike of 1892, Carnegie Steel and later U.S. Steel remained bitterly opposed to organized labor. It didn't officially negotiate with a union for another forty-five years.

At the time of the sale to J. P. Morgan, the company commanded 67 percent of domestic steel production and had a valuation of $1.1 billion, nearly a trillion dollars today, the size of Amazon or Apple. As substantial as the company's assets were in 1901, the gold bonds issued to Andrew Carnegie left U.S. Steel with a heavy debt load, and it became cautious about capital improvements and expansion.

Despite that, U.S. Steel, known on Wall Street as "the Corporation" with the ticker symbol "X" on the New York Stock Exchange, was number three on the Fortune 500 list as late as 1955. After a steady decline it now ranks 247. In 1991 U.S. Steel lost the place it had held since 1901 as a component of the Dow Jones Industrial Average. In 2014 it was removed from the S&P 500. U.S. Steel's market cap in 2021 is well under $10 billion. It has lost money for the last three years.

The U.S. Steel Building in Pittsburgh, the tallest office tower in the city, opened in 1984 and was topped with a twenty-foot "U.S. Steel" logo that loomed over the city. Today the building is no longer owned by the steel company, and the sign says "UPMC," the abbreviation for the University of Pittsburgh Medical Center, the building's main tenant and the region's largest employer.

Pittsburgh: In 1900 the city of Pittsburgh had a population of 322,000, the eleventh-largest in the country. It was still ranked twelfth with a population of 677,000 in 1960 when it began a steady decline. The population of Pittsburgh today is less than it was in 1900, and it's the sixty-fifth-largest city in the country. The Pittsburgh metropolitan region has fared better and at 2,325,000 in 2020 is ranked twenty-seventh.

With the decline of the steel industry beginning in the early 1960s, Pittsburgh fell on hard times. With few jobs in the area, many residents moved to other parts of the country to seek work. In the late twentieth century, it sometimes seemed the only bright spot for Pittsburgh was its professional sports teams: the Steelers won the Super Bowls after the 1974, 1975, 1978, 1979, 2005, and 2008 seasons; the Pirates won the World Series in 1960, 1971, and 1979; and the Penguins won the Stanley Cup in 1991, 1992, 2009, 2016, and 2017. Because of the exodus from Pittsburgh, you will always find a substantial number of black and gold jerseys in opponents' stadiums and arenas, and there are Steelers bars all over the country.

In recent years Pittsburgh has experienced a rebirth fostered by the entrepreneurial advances at Carnegie Mellon University and the University of Pittsburgh Medical Center. The Strip District, a rundown section of the city between the railroad tracks and the Allegheny River, has been reclaimed for trendy restaurants and clubs, and the city has become a "foodie" paradise.

In recognition of this twenty-first-century renaissance, in 2018 *The Economist* ranked Pittsburgh as the second most livable city in the United States, behind only Honolulu.

ACKNOWLEDGMENTS

My everlasting thanks to:

Jed Lyons who took a chance on a seventy-year-old unpublished author.

Estelle Laure, a skilled editor who taught me that historical fiction needs to be fiction first, history second. And Lauren DeStefano at kn literary arts, who put us together, and to Patricia Chadwick, who recommended kn.

My editor Gene Brissie, Melissa Baker, who created the maps, Alden Perkins in production, cover designer Sally Rinehart, the aptly named Alyssa Messenger in publicity, and and all the other kind and helpful professionals at Globe Pequot Press, who shepherded this book from manuscript to publication. You've helped me realize a lifelong dream.

My sister, Freddy Davis, the strongest woman I know and fellow English major at Trinity College. And my extraordinary nieces, Morgan Davis and Faith Davis Iselin, and Faith's husband, Alex.

My son-in-law, Graham Flanagan, and Sara Miller's partner, Rima Rabbath, for always caring.

Sam Allis, a great writer and friend and early reader, who told me I could do it.

The Steelers gang: Holly Childs, Christine and Jamie Hilliard, Connie Hilliard, Tim Hilliard, Franny and Charlie Stewart, Kim and Will Whetzel. Our deep friendship and shared heritage have been an inspiration throughout. And a special shout-out to Jamie, who led me to Jed Lyons and gave me invaluable leads on research and cover art.

The Greensboro kindergarten group: Becky and Matt Healy, Katie Houston, Susan and Hardie Mills, Nancy Moore, Mary Norris and Pat Oglesby, Judy and Len White, Lauren and David Worth. And the best neighbors in the world: Ann and Mason Banks. I so appreciated your enthusiasm.

Gary Bradley of the Cambria County Historical Society, who brought to life the Cresson Springs Hotel; Ron Baraff of Rivers of Steel Museum for his riveting account of the Battle of Homestead and the horrific Gauntlet; the fascinating Rivers of Steel tour of the Carrie Blast Furnaces—if you are ever in Pittsburgh and have a spare two and a half hours, don't miss this; James Wedell and his illuminating walking tour of Point Breeze—he told me more about the neighborhood where I grew up than I ever knew; and the docents of the Frick home, Clayton, for showing me the human side of "Clay" Frick.

And all those whose friendship and support buoyed me through the ups and downs of the years it took to research, write, and edit this book: Robyn and Greg Ahern, Tina Barney, Kitty and Charlie Berry, Joan Beth and Scott Brown, Jane Cannon, Sophie Cottrell Caminiti, Paul Dewey, Caroline Franklin, Olga and Lyman Goff, Margaret and David Gordon, Susan and Bill Gridley, Pam Heller, Nancy and Bill Hellmuth, Hillary Heminway, John Heminway, Helen and Ned Hetherington, Judy Hottenson, Bob Hottenson, Ann and David Johnson, Jane and Tom Kearns, Melissa and James Keyte, David Kirk, Jean and Brad Kopp, Susan Loney, Lee and David MacCallum, Jen and Bruce MacLear, Linda and Layng Martine, Alice Moore, Dee Moore, Liz and Chips Moore, Suzy and Sputty O'Reilly, Buff and Jim Penrose, Caroline and Rob Rodier, Deborah Royce, Vicky and Rob Saglio, Cynthia and Tom Sculco, Jean and Bob Severud, Anna Shields, Lea Simonds, Kate and John Townsend, Cee and Paul Verbinnen, Sophie and Tom Wynne, Mel and Brian Vogt, Jen and Will Vogt, Peter Wheelwright, Kathy and Laurence Whittemore, Sissy Zimmerman.

Bibliography

Achorn, Edward. *The Summer of Beer and Whiskey: How Brewers, Barkeeps, Rowdies, Immigrants, and a Wild Pennant Fight Made Baseball America's Game*. New York: Perseus Book Group, 2013.

Anderson, Kurt. *Heyday*. New York: Random House, 2007.

Baatz, Simon. *The Girl on the Velvet Swing: Sex, Murder and Madness at the Dawn of the Twentieth Century*. New York: Hachette Book Group, 2018.

Baker, Kevin. *Dreamland: A Novel*. New York: Harper Collins, 1999.

Baldwin, Leland D. *Pittsburgh: The Story of a City*. Pittsburgh, PA: University of Pittsburgh Press, 1937.

Baughman, Jon D. *The Bedford Springs Resort*. Privately published, 2009.

Belfer, Lauren. *City of Light*. New York: Dial Press, 1999.

Bell, Thomas. *Out of this Furnace*. Pittsburgh, PA: University of Pittsburgh Press, 1941.

Bellamy, Edward. *Looking Backward: 2000–1887*. Boston: Ticknor & Co., 1888.

Benedict, Marie. *Carnegie's Maid: A Novel*. Napierville, IL: Sourcebooks, 2018.

Bridge, James Howard. *The Inside History of the Carnegie Steel Company: A Romance of Millions*. New York: Aldine, 1903.

Cambor, Kathleen. *In Sunlight, in a Beautiful Garden*. New York: Harper Collins, 2016.

Cannadine, David. *Mellon: An American Life*. New York: Alfred A. Knopf, 2006.

Carnegie, Andrew. *The Autobiography of Andrew Carnegie*. Boston: Northeastern University Press edition, 1986.

Carr, Caleb. *The Alienist: A Novel*. New York: Random House, 1994.

Casson, Herbert N. *The Romance of Steel: The Story of a Thousand Millionaires*. New York: A.S. Barnes & Company, 1907.

Chabon, Michael. *The Mysteries of Pittsburgh*. New York: William Morrow and Company, 1988.

Cheever, Susan. *Drinking in America: Our Secret History*. New York: Hachette, 2015.

Chernow, Ron. *The House of Morgan: An American Banking Dynasty and the Rise of Modern Finance*. New York: Atlantic Monthly Press, 1990.

———. *Titan: The Life of John D. Rockefeller, Sr*. New York: Random House, 1998.

Coopey, Judith Redline. *Waterproof: A Novel of the Johnstown Flood*. Mesa, AZ: Fox Hollow Press, 2011.

———. *The Furnace*. Mesa, AZ: Fox Hollow Press, 2014.

Couvares, Francis G. *The Remaking of Pittsburgh: Class and Culture in an Industrializing City, 1977–1919*. Albany: State University of New York Press, 1984.

Davenport, Marcia. *The Valley of Decision*. Pittsburgh, PA: University of Pittsburgh Press, 1942.

Dickens, Charles. *A Tale of Two Cities*. London: Chapman & Hall, 1859.

Doctorow, E. L. *Ragtime*. New York: Random House, 1974.

Dreiser, Theodore. *Sister Carrie: A Novel.* New York: Doubleday, Page, 1900.

Gaffney, Elizabeth. *Metropolis: A Novel.* New York: Random House, 2005.

Gage, Tom. *American Prometheus: Captain Bill Jones.* Arcata, CA: Humboldt State Press, 2017.

Goodwin, Doris Kearns. *The Bully Pulpit: Theodore Roosevelt, William Howard Taft, and the Golden Age of Journalism.* New York: Simon & Schuster, 2013.

Gregory, Richard. *The Bosses Club: The Conspiracy That Caused the Johnstown Flood, Destroying the Iron and Steel Capital of America.* Self-published, 2011.

Harvey, George. *Henry Clay Frick: The Man.* New York: Frick Collection, 1936.

Hessen, Robert. *Steel Titan: The Life of Charles M. Schwab.* Pittsburgh, PA: University of Pittsburgh Press, 1975.

Hillstrom, Laurie Collier. *The Muckrakers and the Progressive Era.* Detroit, MI: Omni-graphics, 2010.

Hofstadter, Richard. *The Age of Reform: From Bryan to F. D. R.* New York: Random House, 1955.

Hogan, Mary. *The Woman in the Photo: A Novel.* New York: Harper Collins, 2016.

Horan, Nancy. *Loving Frank: A Novel.* New York: Ballantine Books, 2007.

James, Henry. *Portrait of a Lady.* Boston: Houghton Mifflin & Company, 1881.

Johnson, Owen. *Stover at Yale.* New York: Frederick A. Stokes, 1912.

Jonnes, Jill. *The Empire of Light: Edison, Tesla, Westinghouse and the Race to Electrify the World.* New York: Random House, 2003.

Josephson, Matthew. *The Robber Barons.* Boston: Houghton Mifflin Harcourt Publishing, 1934.

Kaplan, Justin. *Lincoln Steffens: Portrait of a Great American Journalist.* New York: Simon & Schuster, 1974.

Kazin, Michael. *A Godly Hero: The Life of William Jennings Bryan.* New York: Random House, 2006.

Kelley, Brooks Mather. *Yale: A History.* New Haven, CT: Yale University Press, 1974.

Kidney, Walter C. *Pittsburgh: Then and Now.* San Diego, CA: Thunder Bay Press, 2004.

Kobus, Kenneth J. *City of Steel: How Pittsburgh Became the World's Steelmaking Capital During the Carnegie Era.* Lanham, MD: Rowman & Littlefield, 2015.

Krause, Paul. *The Battle for Homestead 1880–1892: Politics, Culture and Steel.* Pittsburgh, PA: University of Pittsburgh Press, 1992.

Larson, Erik. *The Devil in the White City: Murder, Magic, and Madness at the Fair That Changed America.* New York: Random House, 2003.

Lorant, Stefan. *Pittsburgh: The Story of an American City.* New York: Doubleday, 2000.

Lowy, Jonathon E. *The Temple of Music: A Novel.* New York: Random House, 2004.

McCullough, David. *The Johnstown Flood: The Incredible Story Behind One of the Most Devastating Disasters America Has Ever Known.* New York: Simon & Schuster, 1968.

McCullough, Hax. *So Much To Remember: The Centennial History of the Pittsburgh Golf Club.* Pittsburgh, PA: Pittsburgh Golf Club, 1996.

McGerr, Michael. *A Fierce Discontent: The Rise and Fall of the Progressive Movement in America, 1870–1920.* New York: Simon & Schuster, 2003.

Mellon, William Larimer, and Boyden Sparkes. *Judge Mellon's Sons.* Privately published, 1948.

Moore, Graham. *The Last Days of Night.* New York: Random House, 2016.

Morris, Charles R. *The Tycoons: How Andrew Carnegie, John D. Rockefeller, Jay Gould and J. P. Morgan Invented the American Supereconomy.* New York: Henry Holt and Company, 1942.

Morris, James McGrath. *Pulitzer: A Life in Politics, Print and Power.* New York: Harper Collins, 2010.

Nasaw, David. *Andrew Carnegie.* New York: Penguin Books, 2006.

Okrent, Daniel. *Last Call: The Rise and Fall of Prohibition.* New York: Scribner, 2010.

Pendergrast, Mark. *For God, Country & Coca-Cola: The Definitive History of the Great American Soft Drink and the Company That Made It.* New York: Basic Books, 2013.

Perelman, Dale Richard. *Steel: The Story of Pittsburgh's Iron & Steel Industry 1852–1902.* Charleston, SC: History Press, 2014.

Phillips, David Graham. *The Great God Success: A Novel.* New York: Grosset & Dunlap, 1901.

Rayback, Joseph G. *A History of American Labor.* New York: Free Press, 1959.

Robinson, Roxana. *Dawson's Fall: A Novel.* New York: Farrar, Straus and Giroux, 2019.

Roker, Al. *Ruthless Tide: The Heroes and Villains of the Johnstown Flood, America's Astonishing Gilded Age Disaster.* New York: Murrow/Harper Collins, 2018.

Rosen, Renée. *What the Lady Wants: A Novel of Marshall Field and the Golden Age.* New York: New American Library, 2014.

Rugoff, Milton. *The Gilded Age.* New York: Henry Holt & Co., 1989.

Rutherfurd, Edward. *New York: The Novel.* New York: Doubleday, 2009.

Sanger, Martha Frick Symington. *Henry Clay Frick: An Intimate Portrait.* New York: Abbeville Press, 1998.

Schreiner, Samuel A., Jr. *Thine is the Glory.* Greenwich, CT: Fawcett Publications, 1975.

———. *Henry Clay Frick: The Gospel of Greed.* New York: St. Martin's Press, 1995.

Serrin, Judith and William. *Muckraking!: The Journalism that Changed America.* New York: New York Press, 2002.

Skrabec, Quentin R., Jr. *George Westinghouse: Gentle Genius.* New York: Algora Publishing, 2007.

———. *H. J. Heinz: A Biography.* Jefferson, NC: McFarland, 2009.

———. *Henry Clay Frick: The Life of the Perfect Capitalist.* Jefferson, NC: McFarland, 2010.

———. *The Carnegie Boys: The Lieutenants of Andrew Carnegie That Changed America.* Jefferson, NC: McFarland & Company, Inc., 2012.

Spencer, Ethel. *The Spencers of Amberson Avenue: A Turn-of-the-Century Memoir.* Pittsburgh, PA: University of Pittsburgh Press, 1983.

Standiford, Les. *Meet You in Hell: Andrew Carnegie, Henry Clay Frick and the Bitter Partnership that Transformed America.* New York: Random House, 2005.

Steffens, Lincoln. *The Shame of the Cities.* New York: McClure, Phillips & Co., 1904.

Stiles, T. J. *In Their Own Words: Robber Barons and Radicals: Reconstruction and the Origins of Civil Rights.* New York: The Berkley Publishing Group, 1997.

Stoddard, Brooke C. *Steel: From Mine to Mill the Metal That Made America*. Minneapolis, MN: Zenith Press, 2015.

Strouse, Jean. *Morgan: American Financier*. New York: Random House, 1999.

Styron, William. *The Confessions of Nat Turner: A Novel*. New York: Random House, 1967.

Tarkington, Booth. *The Magnificent Ambersons: A Novel*. Garden City, NY: Doubleday, Page, 1918.

Toker, Franklin. *Pittsburgh: A New Portrait*. Pittsburgh, PA: University of Pittsburgh Press, 1989.

Tolstoy, Leo. *War and Peace*. Moscow: The Russian Messenger, 1869.

———. *Anna Karenina*. Moscow: The Russian Messenger, 1878.

Twain, Mark. *Adventures of Huckleberry Finn: Tom Sawyer's Comrade*. New York: Charles L. Webster and Company, 1885.

Twain, Mark, and Charles Warner. *The Gilded Age*. Hartford: American Publishing, 1874.

Vanderbilt II, Arthur T. *Fortune's Children: The Fall of the House of Vanderbilt*. New York: William Morrow, 1989.

Vidal, Gore. *1876: A Novel*. New York: Random House, 1976.

———. *Lincoln: A Novel*. New York: Random House, 1984.

———. *Empire: A Novel*. New York: Random House, 1987.

Wall, Joseph Frazer. *Andrew Carnegie*. New York: Oxford University Press, 1970.

Warren, Kenneth. *Triumphant Capitalism: Henry Clay Frick and the Industrial Transformation of America*. Pittsburgh, PA: University of Pittsburgh Press, 1996.

———. *Big Steel: The First Century of the United States Steel Corporation, 1901–2001*. Pittsburgh, PA: University of Pittsburgh Press, 2001.

Warren, Robert Penn. *All the King's Men*. New York: Harcourt Brace & Co., 1946.

Wiebe, Robert H. *The Search for Order: 1877–1920*. New York: Hill and Wang, 1967.

Wharton, Edith. *The House of Mirth*. New York: Charles Scribner's Sons, 1905.

———. *The Age of Innocence*. New York: D. Appleton, 1920.

IMAGES OF AMERICA SERIES

Kidney, Walter C., in partnership with the Pittsburgh's History and Landmarks Foundation and the Carnegie Library of Pittsburgh. *Oakland*. Charleston, SC: Arcadia Publishing, 2005.

Squirrel Hill Historical Society. *Squirrel Hill*. Charleston, SC: Arcadia Publishing, 2005.

Boehmig, Stuart P. *Downtown Pittsburgh*. Charleston, SC: Arcadia Publishing, 2007.

Burns, Daniel J. *Homestead and the Steel Valley*. Charleston, SC: Arcadia Publishing, 2007.

Doherty, Donald. *Pittsburgh's Shadyside*. Charleston, SC: Arcadia Publishing, 2008.

Pittsburgh Post-Gazette and Carnegie Library of Pittsburgh. *Pittsburgh 1758–2008*. Charleston, SC: Arcadia Publishing, 2008.

Ross, Alison Reed. *The Bedford Springs Hotel*. Charleston, SC: Arcadia Publishing, 2012.

Gutowski, Melanie Linn. *Pittsburgh's Mansions*. Charleston, SC: Arcadia Publishing, 2013.

Dorsett, Robert S. *Lost Steel Plants of the Monongahela River Valley*. Charleston, SC: Arcadia Publishing, 2015.